IN SEARCH OF A TRIBE

THEE A. L. LANG

ISBN 978-1-09837-313-9 eBook 978-1-09837-314-6

ONE

It rivaled sniffing the aroma of bread baking in the oven, being fixated on her. One sense arousing another: smelling and then wanting to taste the bread, seeing and then wanting to touch the girl. The two pervs figured her to be the last virgin teen in their neighborhood, at least the oldest one. *How in the hell was that?* they wondered. Although uneducated on neighborhood ratings, the twenty-four-year-olds wouldn't have disagreed with the D-Plus score in their own community. So, their self-centered opinion of the girl's purity within it was as such: *That bitch is sadity.*

She was above their nothing-to-do lifestyle, and they knew it. What gave them the nerve to express their desire was that she wasn't beyond it. Here it was the middle of the day, and them and the girl were in the same vicinity, as it was when they went to their respective beds and rose from them.

"No matter how clean and pretty that bitch is, she ain't anything special." The smaller of the two pervs told the bigger one, further explaining, "She still one of us. We live here and so does she." Watching her cross Hough

1

Avenue toward one of the area's last remaining black-owned convenient stores, he pointed to himself and then to her. "Hough hood. Hough hoe."

The big perv gave a hard, short laugh. "Ha, man, you know that girl ain't no hoe. Even if she do live around here." Still, he got his partner's meaning and, as usual, agreed with it, that she wasn't too good to speak to them. When she left the store about ten minutes later, they both decided the time had come for her to know that.

Relieving his blunt, darkened, and swollen lips of a Black & Mild, the smaller one asked her, "What school do you go to?" He hadn't freaked the slim plastic-tipped cigar, replacing the tobacco with weed, thereby making it a blunt. So, he figured her sadityness wouldn't mind the smoke, especially since it was cherry scented, and as far as he knew, all girls liked sweet things. Besides, dragging on it made him feel cool and in charge of the moment. With his chest pushed out, standing two arm-lengths away from the pretty, he'd boldly thrown his rough voice directly at her big hoop-adorned ears.

For months, the pervs had lusted over getting close enough to smell her, to be able to orchestrate a fake accidental bump-into or rub-against her slender, yet curvy, body. Neither of which would happen today. She didn't stop. The pervs would continue to itch for her. *Damn to cop a feel. Man, she can't be using no cheap-ass soap or lotion. Can't be.* Her dark skin, to them, belonged in a beauty-in-a-bottle commercial, just like her speedy, sophisticated walk belonged in one for overpriced clothes for the busy yet stylish woman.

The girl was too busy for their liking. So the smaller one got bolder. Projecting his voice as if addressing a crowd without a mic, he again imposed. "What school do you go to?" Head high, the girl kept on her way.

This was their first time daring to speak to her. Being blatantly ignored lit a fire in the smaller one's chest. "Young ass bitch!" he mumbled, having decided the girl wasn't old enough to have an opinion on men, even the kind he knew them to be—broke and busted. *What in the hell can she know outside of her school books and pompoms? She can't know one dick from another. Bitch ain't even seen her first one. I ain't never seen her with no dude.*

 The big perv dug a large hairy hand into a family-size bag of barbeque chips. "Damn, she is so, so, so sadity. Uppity as hell. She acts as if she made of gold."

 She wouldn't even make eye contact with them. Unable to accept the rejection, from that day on, the two pervs began to follow the girl whenever they saw her. Wanting their presence to appear somewhat coincidental, they always stayed back about twenty feet. Barely pacified by the stalking, many times had they thought to close the distance between them and her. They tried to think of something to say that would make her acknowledge them, though everything about the way she moved translated to them as, *No! You stink! You're dirty! A bum! A broke ass funny looking bum, who could never touch me. A piece of a shit!* Words they'd each heard many times from at least a dozen women. This girl, they decided in their frustration, would be the one to reap the hell sowed from those insults for two reasons. She thought herself too good to speak, even to insult them. *She acts as if she made of gold.* Secondly and mostly, *no matter how clean and pretty that bitch is, she ain't anything special.* She was a nobody.

 Gent, Isaac, and Janet were somebodies, as were Cherry and Merv. Those were some of the names heard often as the pervs passed the girl's home. The two-story had foot traffic five to ten times heavier than any other on the street. "House of a thousand kids," they'd overheard it being called mockingly by some of its neighbors. While difficult for the pervs to discern the visitors from the residents within the "house of a thousand kids," their resemblance to one another confirmed that most of them were related. Concerning was the muscular, streetwise-looking male contingent. Though it was soon apparent whoever the girl was to them—sister, cousin, daughter, niece—she wasn't in the care of their strength. She didn't go or come with them. Cars came and went, and one belonged to the home for sure, but no one gave the girl a ride. No one even ever walked her to or met her at the bus stop. Occasionally, one of the other neighborhood girls strolled with her to a store. Other than that, she was vulnerable—even to amateurs. The smaller perv, holding the biggest grudge against her, was the impetus for the abduction plan. The bigger perv went along for the ride.

"We could take her and have fun teaching that ass some damn manners. Fucking ignoring me!"

"Hell, yeah!"

"Someone's going to turn that ass out, anyway . . . eventually."

"For damn sure!"

"She's too good to speak to us, huh! But bouncing and switching around here in those short-ass cheerleader dresses. One way or another, that coochie gonna get got by somebody. I mean what else is a coochie for?"

"Well, you know, shit happens."

"Hell yeah, shit happens! Why not some good shit like that happening for us?"

"Gotta make it happen."

"Yeah, we'll take her. We'll get that ass!"

"Man, shit, my balls are tingling! Let's do this!"

Ball-tingling anticipation of their first full-blown abduction—still they were nervous. Eagerness didn't blind them to the loose ends. For starters, this was not a fifty-pound second-grader they were robbing of her lunch money. This girl, they could tell, weighed about a hundred pounds. Since neither captor owned nor had legal access to a vehicle, they'd be transporting her by foot. In addition, there were no working utilities in their preferred hostage prison, a condemned and abandoned home. Two others concerns were how long to keep her and what to do with her at the end of that time.

Addressing loose ends didn't make it onto the agenda. The pervs instead maintained a three-bullet-point checklist. Point one: snatch. Point two: subdue. Point three: screw. It was all about how to get her so they could have her when they wanted, as often as they wanted. In their self-groping excitement, the hollow plan was determined to be good enough. Her hundred pounds definitely seemed a manageable load for two grown men. Improvising, their daily method in surviving their infinite poverty, they believed would also solidify the abduction's success. Loose ends would be tightened as they unraveled. For one, if she fought harder than expected (although neither wished to ugly the prize), they'd beat her. They'd figure out how to control her. They'd figure out how to move her if they needed to switch locations. They'd figure out how to keep her from escaping if they should need to leave her unattended. They'd figure out how to muffle her screams, without the cover of a loud television or stereo. *No electricity.* And that aforementioned question of what to do with her at the end would also be figured out—when the end presented itself. Right now was about the beginning, getting ready and staying ready, to be able to take advantage of the right opportunity. So much mental work for two short bus-riding junior high dropouts. They felt all their planning was worth more than a hard-on. They were done fantasizing and masturbating about this girl. The theft of duct tape, padlocks, flashlights, condoms, and baby wipes put them on the path to do more than watch. They were said to be cheesing, smiling big as if expecting a big lottery check. It was a pity for the girl that none knew the true reason for their cheesing.

TWO

Standing on the corner of East 66th and Quimby, BETY |Betty| Junior faced Lexington Avenue watching a Number 4 bus head east. The twenty-three-year-old wasn't waiting for anyone who would be on a bus; it just caught his attention as it traveled into view, though when he saw the girl exit the back door, warm acknowledgement softened the stern set of his face. Red and white pompoms bouncing, the girl quickly began walking toward where he stood on Quimby. He'd noticed that she was always about getting to where she was going. Today was no different. The girl's graceful stride was, as usual, energetic and focused. BETY Junior guessed her to be enjoying an unspoiled youth, beyond the cracked sidewalks of her neighborhood. Most of the neighborhood was fairly healthy, but there was no vintage grandeur in these turn-of-the-century structures. Hough and all its side streets, including Lexington and Quimby, began its dissolution about three decades before this pompom girl arrived in the world. Hough, like many other areas, nearly failed its racial turnover, becoming no longer predominantly white. It suffered an economic turndown that lasted decades. Money, however, wasn't all that was lost. Violent hate crimes hit the area, the worst being the Hough Riots of 1966 that turned the neighborhood into a hell that burned for a week. It claimed four lives, all colored, the politically correct term of the time. The city's first colored or *black*—as was coming into use at the time—mayor was elected that following year. Though he did little to return this Cleveland neighborhood to prominence. Twenty-three years later, as this brown child walked its streets, there was the second, as we now say, *African-American* mayor in office. Hough, with few renovations, was still rough. Although not a gang-banging ghetto, it wasn't exactly friendly, and it definitely was not prosperous. Another community of African Americans that didn't belong to the African Americans inhabiting it. Mostly Arabs and Asians, with their stores and restaurants, were profiting here. What was plentiful for the residents were creeps, poor hustlers, and hoodlums. Yank and Milky, socially impotent and deviant, were creeps. BETY Junior knew what was up with them: nothing. Losers. He deemed them lower than most of the wino bums sleeping on their elderly mama's couches and the crackheads beating up their own fathers, stealing their family's televisions and VCRs. He didn't worry over them, but kept them on his hood radar in the section of the grid labeled "Lowlife Dumbasses." When visiting the area, BETY Junior always saw them wasting away, either throwing their tired game at uninterested females or being posted up against a pole or building waiting to get something for nothing. Today, BETY Junior noticed the two dumbasses with idiot grins were obviously chasing the arrival of a highly anticipated something. They were circling the block repeatedly.

What are these nothings up to?

The pompom girl, coming from Lexington Avenue, had nearly reached Quimby when BETY Junior turned in the opposite direction toward Hough Avenue. He saw his ride turning into Mr. Dan's grocery store's parking lot. *Corned beef sandwiches*, he thought, turning back in time to see the girl crossing the street. Instead of crossing at the corner, she'd walked diagonally over the grassy curb, most likely to avoid going too near him. The girl wasn't known to mingle with strangers, especially men. Neither did she make eye contact with them. BETY Junior deemed her aloofness appropriate, because he was a stranger and a man, and she, a girl. A horn blew, so BETY Junior turned toward it. While it came from the right direction, it wasn't for him. It had been too fast for the corned beef sandwiches to have been prepared and cashed out. He continued looking at Hough Avenue for a few minutes, just watching traffic. Running his long fingers through his beard, he turned back, expecting to see the pompom girl further up Quimby Avenue. She was on East 69th Place, though all BETY Junior could see of her were her white tennis shoes kicking in the air. BETY Junior went still. "What's this shit?" Soon he was running. "Fuck just happened?" It took him less than a minute to the clear the distance between 66th and 69th. Getting there, he turned in circles looking for a sign of the girl. 69th Place, a short narrow street cramped with three houses on either side, was a dead end—and was nearly dead itself. Only two of the six houses were occupied. Two abandoned, one waiting for a renter or buyer, and one condemned. The girl and whomever had taken her were out of sight. BETY Junior figured she most likely was carried into one of the three houses to his right, because they were closest to where she was snatched. He could tell the first home was lived in because of the music he heard coming from it. He was going toward it to knock or kick on the door when he heard a bang like a screen door hitting against the side of a house. The sound had come from the very next home, an abandoned eyesore with boarded windows. BETY Junior raced toward its driveway. When he got there, he removed his jacket, newsboy cap, and platinum chain; from his lips ripped the words, "Motherfuckers! Lowlife . . . Gri-my motherfuckers!"

THREE

The girl's pompoms were still attached to her wrists, shaking as she kicked within the confinement of Milky's large arms. He held her with her back against his chest, her arms trapped against her sides. Yank, trying to grab her legs so Milky could turn her into the house, caught several hard kicks to the face. *I'm doing this bitch first*, he decided, which went against the original plan. Milky was scheduled for the first bang, out of respect for the fact that it was his strength that was their means of capture and transport. A topic they began discussing again as they hurried with her.

"Remember, man. I'm the muscle. So, I'm first."

"Yeah, yeah, yeah. Okay. I know."

Yank, getting the worst of her resistance, wanted compensation. Admittedly the bigger loser with females, he was sure Milky wouldn't object to the last-minute switch.

Milky was a gorilla of a guy. By age ten, he had a voice that, if not for his juvenile conversations, could fool anyone on the phone into thinking he was an adult. By fifteen, he had a full beard and was only two extra-large pizzas away from three hundred pounds. Being knock-kneed and imma-ture, he stood awkwardly at six-foot-three. Having always looked too old and strange for girls his own age, he'd welcomed the exploitation of his size by older women. Everyone in the hood knew he was an old hag's rag. He'd lost his virginity at fourteen to his mother's drinking buddy. Sex in these last ten years had been about being around the wrong women at the right time. They only wanted what he had to give: his indiscriminating dick and his youthful stamina. Without being popular, likeable, monied, or smart, Milky's drab life still included regularly "getting some." Yet, although his libido wasn't starving, he was not without longing. He desired something other than the withered rose type. This girl was to be his rose bud.

Yank, a rabid spider monkey to Milky's gorilla, was most often dismissed by the opposite gender, both fresh and withered. Yank's opportunist demeanor and the shrewd way his small green eyes stared at females suggested he'd molest even if the sex was consensual. Typically, he provoked feelings of offense and anxiety. If they didn't run from him, they fought him. He'd had lustful anticipation slapped out of him on at least three of Hough Avenue's corners. Yank was a sexual scavenger, raping the incoherent females who drank or smoked too much or the naïve and scared ones. For Yank, sex was mostly a solo act. Either way, out of fear of being caught, it was usually quick pumps or hasty masturbation. He figured all that was in the past, now that they had this pretty, fresh thing. Since she'd be staying a while, he had looked forward to taking his time. Now, however, she'd made him angry. "This bitch is kicking the shit of my face! Me first with her ass, man! I'm gonna be Mr. Fuck Machine and knock the bottom out of her!"

After positioning himself behind Milky to avoid her wild kicks, Yank began to repeatedly slap her face. Jumping from side to side behind Milky, he alternated hitting her first on the right, and then on the left. "We've been waiting too long for your ass!" *Slap.* "Too long!" *Slap, slap, slap.* "Yeah, you was fucken ignoring me! Can't do that now, bitch, can you!" *Slap.* "It's our time now, and you ain't so fucking special!" *Slap.* "Just another pretty bitch, who ain't too good to get fucked!" *Slap.* "Hear me, bitch? You can get fucked! What else is a bitch for?" *Slap.* "Been jacking off thinking about you, but not today! Today, I'm fucking you!" *Slap, slap, slap, slap.* "It's happening, bitch, so stop fighting, bitch, and give us our time." *Slap.* "Bitch, fucken bitch, bitch." *Slap, slap, slap.* "Sadity, uppity bitch gonna learn a lesson today!" Yet, her reaction was the exact opposite of what he intended, and her struggling only intensified. Yank jumped in front of her. "Bitch, you ain't nobody! You ain't nobody and ain't got no man! And ain't nobody looking for you!"

FOUR

Two gunshots reminded residents of absent loved ones, those expected soon and those already past due. At 1728 East 70th and Hough Avenue, the youngest girl—a granddaughter—had been expected soon. Ten minutes or so after the shots were heard, the home's fifty-six-year-old matriarch Coddy Lee exited the front door. Down the stone steps she went toward the direction from whence the gun shots had come. Her neighbors hadn't ever seen her walking any further than to her car, which was operational and parked in the driveway. Her familial entourage was also missing—at least one younger adult or adolescent was always with her. That was true even when she sat on the porch. So, afoot and alone, Coddy Lee was a spectacle. She walked, and her neighbors watched. She wasn't known for chit-chat, so no one felt comfortable questioning her. Just as well, none were sure they wanted any involvement. Gunshots had rung out, and they wanted no part of their cause—or effect. Curiosity, nonetheless, followed behind Coddy Lee's determined march toward Quimby Avenue. Unknowingly, she began to lead a growing crowd of young adults and teenagers. Entertaining themselves with the dramatics of "We're going to see what went down," they no less stayed back at a distance. Others, older and more cautious, remained perched on porches and rooted in yards. *We're going to stay put and let what went down come to us when it cools down.* Still, they shared ideas on her destination. Willy, her common-law husband, had the idea she was going to hell with a very iffy chance of returning. Willy, if able, would have gone in her place. No longer her muscle, now he could only worry as he lay in the bed in his home hospice room. Having slept through the gunshots, he was, ironically, awakened by the telephone ringing, and then kept awake by the subtle sounds of Coddy Lee's rushed movements upon the carpeted floorboards in her room. From his room across the hall, Willy waited for her to come into view. He became quite disturbed soon after she did. She'd changed out of her long floral polyester house dress into an outfit of the same material but thicker—a dark pink paisley-printed senior misses top and blue pants. Afterwards she'd slipped on a cream zip-up knit sweater. She'd then sat on the edge of her bed working around her pudgy middle to put on her favorite shoes, those designed for comfortable walking for women of a certain age. When she reached for the chain around her neck, Willy knew for sure something had got her goose, his farm-raised way of saying she was riled up. The stainless-steel necklace held her diabetic identification disc and a small key that opened the top drawer of her night stand. Opening the drawer after hastily getting dressed meant bad business. Coddy Lee was going into battle. Willy, having lost his vocal cords to cancer, cackled before popping his lips, pleading for her to forgo her mission, whatever it was. Coddy Lee, however, was deaf by preoccupation. Drawer open, Coddy Lee, still sitting on her bed, had leaned back and removed her .22 from under her pillow. Calmly, with the bullets she'd retrieved from the drawer, she loaded the clip. Then after securing the pistol in its holster, the left cup of her bra, she stood and headed downstairs.

Soon after hearing her landing upon the first floor, Willy had heard the opening of the front and then the screen door. Listening with desperate hope, he waited for the sounds of a retreat, if not Coddy Lee's own reconsideration, then a returning household member or visitor convincing her not to go. Willy, meticulously tucked in with care and immobilized by the painkiller fentanyl, waited for a voice: "Granny!" "Mama!" "Ms. Lofton!" "Where you going?" "Oh no, now wait a minute!" To Willie's dismay, there was no voice, and the soft snap of the screen door came only about five seconds after the quick, heavy, secure sound of the front door closing. Coddy Lee had gone. Too late Willy remembered his other voice, the hand bell next to his bed.

FIVE

Sirens announcing the approach of more medics and cops, as well as the chanting coming from Quimby, increased the curiosity and anxiousness of the crew behind Coddy Lee. For her, it was all a whispery buzz of soft static. Her determination kept her even, her mind focused, and her steps moving steadily forward. What slowed her pace was the tightening in her chest at the sight of familiar pompoms shaking in strange hands. Coddy Lee had cleared the distance of the five houses between her home and Quimby. As she rounded the corner, there came two young boys running toward her, one on either side of the street. Happily, as if they had won a prize, each child paraded one red and white pompom.

A husky female voice shot from behind Coddy Lee, "Hey, badasses! Where y'all get those from?" Both boys replied with a shout of laughter and by running faster.

Coddy Lee felt the depression of her thoughts, of how the young boys may have come to have those pompoms. Coddy Lee had gotten a call that her youngest granddaughter was surrounded by hoods. *Rogues*, as she would say. That after the gunshots, her granddaughter fell to the ground. Although she was seen in a sitting position, her condition was unknown. Maybe she'd just tripped or fallen out of fear. Maybe she'd been shot. Coddy Lee, not wanting hopelessness to end her mission, put her mind back on

15

the task in front of her. Still, she'd lost a bit of momentum and her chest remained tight. *Should've rubbed on a heart patch.* She regretted, briefly thinking back on the box of nitroglycerin in her purse, which she'd left on her dresser.

Making it to the scene was like walking under a rain cloud from the side that didn't contain enough water to the side that had too much. Coddy Lee had walked the warpath under the threat of a heart attack and stroke, to arrive in an even more threatening war zone. Stepping on to 69th Place, she immediately felt a charge drizzle over her body, a fiery energy from the crowd of civilians. Not quite an angry mob, yet they weren't merely onlookers. Their purpose had created its own weather system that Coddy Lee felt even while several feet away. The air was thicker, warmer, and more humid. And that sharp charge felt like a warning. *Keep forward, old woman, at your own risk. Here is where you can die.* Coddy Lee, as if she'd sprinted instead of walked, unknowingly began panting to keep herself cool.

Whatever the crowd had been chanting about in chorus had now devolved into individual shouts, something about injustice or lack of police protection. Coddy Lee couldn't tell and couldn't be bothered to find out. She hadn't come to listen but to see—then to do. She was looking to first find her heartbreak—then her target.

Coddy Lee checked if anyone sat in the back seat of any of the many police cars. She wouldn't hesitate to shoot through the glass. *Hoogie-ran police can't be trusted to do anything right about anything black,* she'd decided some time ago.

Born a thousand miles south in the middle of the Jim Crow era, unjust violence had burned away nearly all of Coddy Lee's confidence in the law, into ashes amongst the flames of a twelve-foot cross set afire in her front yard. Coddy Lee was alone with her two youngest, Connie and Cherry. "Mama, is that the devil?" five-year-old Connie had cried out seeing the shadows of flames against her bedroom walls as Coddy Lee lifted her into the crook of her left arm and her four-year-old sister Cherry into her right. The gentle yet persistent wind, infused with the smell of wood and kerosene, could have been the devil's breath Coddy Lee thought and so was tempted to reply, "Yes, it's the damn devil. The white devil." She wanted to provide assurance to her children, whom she'd startled out of a deep sleep, so instead, braver than she felt, answered, "God is with us. He woke me up to save y'all."

Coddy Lee prayed for their safety. Even so, the loneliness she felt, as the children cried and clung to her, made her bitter. It was all on her to get them through the white hell. So, in between her persistent prayers were curses. About the girl's come-and-go father, she mumbled, "Your shit ain't even worth fertilizer." About all the other men she'd dealt with, "All y'all want to do is piss and poke then leave the woman alone to fight by her gotdamn self." In retrospect, Coddy Lee was relieved her home had been empty of men, as one with her estranged husband's burly presence might have ignited a worse crime to their family. Now over two decades later, that fiery night, while filed away to its time, was still deeply ingrained in her psyche, existing more as an awareness than a memory. It gave her a resilience that matched how she loved: peculiar. A great-grandmother now, Coddy Lee again chose calm over panic, telling herself God was with her. He was marching her aged and swollen legs on uneven pavement against the pangs of a weakened heart. Though it was unclear if she was a deployed saint of war or a vengeful sinner. Though God may have been pushing her body, the flames that had danced across Connie and Cherry's bedroom walls were in her mind. Consequently, although she wasn't cursing this time, neither was Coddy Lee praying. Her roused spirit was most focused on channeling itself through her trigger finger. Coddy Lee hadn't ever been afraid to shoot, from hunting to defending herself against would-be date rapists in her heyday. Thus, as it had been, it still was now; advancing age and declining health hadn't done anything to unnerve her.

Coddy Lee decided to first confirm her fears before taking inventory of the squad cars. Keeping toward the ambulances, she noticed a hostile interrogation of a young man in cuffs. Coddy Lee gently rubbed at her left breast for reassurance. Feeling the pistol was in its place, she made a mental note of the cuffed man: *Rogue*. She then refocused her attention on the ambulances; she had to know who was in them, especially since they weren't moving.

SIX

Martin Luther King Jr. High School, on East 71st Street, was just around the corner from Novella's home. The curriculum was designed for students focused on medicine and law. Not showing any interest in those subjects, Novella was bused to West Technical High School on West 93rd Street.

Busy with many extra-curriculars, including prom committee, student news anchor, and high-stepper, Novella left by school bus in the morning and returned home by city bus. West Technical was only about eight miles away, but the trip took two city buses. The RTA, which stood for Rapid Transit Authority and had been nicknamed the "RiTA" by the city's urban population, was Novella's main method of transportation. Leaving school, she normally took the 22 Eastbound from West 93rd and Lorain to 3rd and Superior downtown at Public Square. From there, she crossed over to 4th Street to transfer to the 38, which she took her to East 70th and Hough. Today, she would dare a detour because of a craving for French fries and a frozen yogurt cone. Exiting the 22, Novella saw that the Number 38 was already at the bus stop. It was on layover. Looking down at her watch, Novella confirmed it would not depart for ten minutes, giving her just enough of time to satisfy her craving and still catch the bus. In blue jeans, a sweatshirt hoodie, and tennis shoes, she felt dressed comfortably enough for a quick run. So, in perky schoolgirl spirit and with pompoms bouncing, the sixteen-year-old dashed off to McDonald's. It was just around the corner on 3rd and Euclid. Rushing inside as if it were five minutes to closing, she found the line was short. Then also getting lucky with fast service, she was quickly on her way back. Novella took the liberty of window-shopping at two of her favorites: Petries Women's Wear and The Wild Pair shoe store. She felt to be browsing quickly. However, the clock was ticking faster than she dipped fries into her frozen yogurt. Her sweet and salty gratification ended up costing her more than the $2.12 she paid for it. She got brain freeze and missed her bus by seconds. The 38 RiTA was pulling away from the corner just as Novella reached the crosswalk across the street. The walk signal was red, and didn't turn green until a few seconds after the rear of the 38 had passed her. Disappointed, she crossed the street and took a seat in the nearly empty bus shelter. She had an idea of how long she'd be waiting, yet still she reached in her purse and pulled out the bus schedule. She had just begun unfolding it when Number 4 rolled around the corner. That RiTA would also get her home, but didn't provide the ideal route. The next 38, however, wasn't due for fifty-eight minutes. The number 4, after a fifteen-minute layover, would have her on way. So, in the time she'd have to wait for the 38, she'd be home.

Humph, Novella pondered, watching passengers unload from the RiTA. Minutes later, Novella, hearing its gears shift down, was reminded of a large animal being sedated. The engine, a reluctant beast, hissed against the driver's manipulated decompression until being rendered idle by it. Novella had nothing against wild beasts being wild. Still, she'd always liked these sounds: a few hisses before a long whining like a dying siren, and then *ca-ssssh!* Until finally, *sssssssh!* The driver was the last to exit the unit. He ventured out onto Public Square.

Novella leaned against the back of the bus shelter bench and contemplated which RiTA to take home. She hadn't quite made up her mind when the driver returned about ten minutes later. With a bottle of grape soda tucked under one arm, he was munching on salt and vinegar potato chips. Pointing toward the bus, he spoke to Novella as if he knew her, "Come on, baby girl. Let's get from down here." His friendly tone feeding into her eagerness to get home overruled her instinct to wait for the 38. It would have dropped her on Hough, just three houses from her home. Having decided to take the 4, her stop would be on the next main road west of Hough: Lexington Avenue. Novella's walk home would be nearly a quarter of a mile, an easy stroll for her athletic legs. Her hesitation had been because she viewed it as an unsavory route home. Some years ago, five buildings on Lexington Avenue had been demolished. The lots were still empty. Novella found the openness eerie, because it encompassed three of the four corners that she was to pass. Sometimes taking this path was uneventful; other times the riff-raff got after you. There was a basketball court, and some of the fellows, instead of watching the game, would be hunting females, heckling and whistling, even daring to follow pretties like Novella. "Hey slim, slow down!" Then there were the old men just hanging around, years drowned in Wild Irish Rose, Thunderbird, Mad Dog, and Colt 45, throwing game on every female except their wasted equals. "Ain't nothing like a pretty young girl. I bet ain't nobody even had you yet. Hmm, you look too fresh." As far as their wasted equals, they were worse: bitter, used-up women harassing the potential they saw in a young girl. "These young bitches out here these days think they're so fucking fine and smart! But ain't nothing new under the sun!" One had even chased Novella for a few minutes. "Hey, come here, little girl! I said come yo ass here! Let me ask you something!" The saddest in the area were the children, self-liberated from inattention, abuse, and empty kitchens. They wandered lost in their own neighborhood, finding or making trouble. The area on Lexington where Novella would get off was wide open like a desert. Novella would see any of these dangers coming, but if they couldn't be outrun, there was no place to hide.

Novella, nearing her stop on Lexington, pulled the line above her head to signal the driver to stop. Getting to her feet, she noticed a guy standing a block away at the corner of Quimby. Thankful there was no one else hanging about, she hoped this solo homeboy would leave her alone. After pulling the lever to open the door, the driver nodded goodbye to Novella. She nodded back at him. Exiting the RiTA, she started on her way toward home.

Novella passed the solo homeboy without having to endure any heckling or staring from him. He'd kept up his way of keeping to himself. Relieved, she relaxed her shoulders but maintained her rushed pace. The fries and frozen yogurt had done the little that they could do for an active teen. She was hungry again. Nearly home, she began to imagine dinner. But before she could add imaginary sides to the desired baked pork chops, she was grabbed. Her left foot had just followed her right foot off the sidewalk and onto to East 69th Place when fire entered both shoulders. She didn't see who had grabbed her; she just felt pain as she was lifted from the ground. A small fist to her stomach quickly followed, draining her of the air she needed to scream. Though it was hardly necessary, since right afterwards, tape was slapped over her mouth. The large hands released their excruciating hold on her shoulders only to grab her waist. She was tossed upward, and then immediately caught by rock-hard arms that trapped her in a bear hug. Then began her abduction. Being carried like a bag of groceries, she saw a small guy jogging just ahead of them. She figured the sucker punch to her belly had come from him.

The big body carrying her wasn't moving very fast, but it was moving and her kicking backwards at it did not nothing to free her. The dilapidated houses they passed suggested that, if anyone was witnessing the abduction, they were unlikely to care. She guessed herself to be in a "mind-your-business-and-be-happy-it-isn't-you" zone. Just one block up, her predicament would at the least be worth some shout-outs: "Hey now, whatcha doin to

that young girl?" "Y'all two, leave her alone!" Then, even if done anony-
mously, there would be a call to the police.

From behind the sticky muzzle, Novella raged, "Put me down! Put
me down . . . right now . . . Put me down! No! No! I said put me down! I
said put me down!" Her words, however, were translated by the duct tape
into squeaks.

Novella struggled, trying to twist into a position from which she
could climb out of the long, hard arms or be dropped. She couldn't move
around enough to make either happen. So, after exhaling as deeply as she
could from her squeezed diagram, she began to scream. An unintelligible
and muffled scream for help would still relay urgency, Novella figured. She
prayed someone in this "mind-your-business-and-be-happy-it-isn't-you"
zone would pity her. Enough to call the police, if not to intervene themselves. Novella screamed and screamed. The duct tape, remaining in place
across her mouth, kept her screams in close range. If anyone beyond her
abductors were to hear it, they'd have to already be on 69th Place.

Novella's head bobbed from side to side wildly, as her eyes scanned
her surroundings. Seeing that there was no one around, it came to her that
not escaping the abduction was a strong possibility. That she'd get locked
away from the world. *How will they find me?* she wondered, remembering
that she wasn't on her usual route. *How will anyone know that I was almost
home?* She felt her purse still fashioned across her body, so she knew there
was no chance of it falling to the ground. Zipped close, as always, it had
no chance of spilling a trail of clues. She presumed her pompoms would
disappear along with her. Their stretchy loop handles were secured behind
a watch on her left wrist and a hard leather bracelet on her right wrist.

SEVEN

They tried and tried to get her through the side door of the abandoned home, but Novella wouldn't stop fighting. It had been easy enough for Milky to carry the struggling girl down the street, but now he faced the low ceiling of the basement's entrance and the steepness of its steps. The narrow, closely-set wooden planks that led to a concrete floor had complained under his weight when they had scoped out and prepared the home. Milky was nervous of taking a life-changing fall that would most likely also break something on their pretty brown captive. The risk of his health and their prize going to waste, in a nasty tumble down the steps, gave him pause.

"This is taking too long," Milky breathed out heavily. It was an instant later when he thought to turn her over his shoulder that he saw a clearly angry dude rush into the driveway. Yank, also seeing him and feeling caught, immediately backed away from Novella. Scared, Yank's body jerked a few times as he fought the impulse to run inside the abandoned house. Both Milky and Yank recognized BETY Junior. A year ago, Yank had tried to get work from him. BETY Junior had promptly dissed them, "Don't fuck with me!" Now Yank wanted to tell him, "Don't fuck with us!" though he didn't dare. Despite BETY Junior's polished appearance, Yank also thought he looked capable of delivering a bloody beatdown. "He's here to fuck us up!" Yank whispered to himself, also asking, "But for what? We don't have no beef with this dude." Yank had heard the guy call them low-life motherfuckers as he'd run up the driveway. Then, obviously getting into fight mode, BETY Junior had dropped some expensive-looking jewelry on the ground. Yank would have definitely already tried to run off if for not trying to salvage their kidnapping. He also believed Milky had a chance at beating the dude.

Yank looked to Milky to step up. Milky returned the look with one that read, *Uh, duh, I'm holding the girl.*

Yank shook his head to say he'd handle it. With words, of course. He'd try to handle it.

EIGHT

BETY Junior, advancing up the weedy pavement, was met by the nervously smiling Yank, who, attempting to mirror professionalism on the hood level, casually said, "Man, we handling business right now." Then, after sucking his teeth, he added, "We gotta set this girl straight real quick, so will have to get with you later."

BETY Junior, catching him by the throat, lifted him up and tossed him to the ground. He had no patience for the dirty little dumbass. BETY Junior knew the true fight for the girl was with the bigger, more hygienic dumbass. "Let her go!"

Milky's reply painfully squeezed Novella, before it barked at BETY Junior, "This ain't yo shit! And this ain't yo hood! So walk away, man!"

Yank was quick to jump back onto his feet, but didn't attempt to retaliate. Massaging his aching neck, he instead gave Milky a desperate yet contemptuous look.

BETY Junior was also looking at Milky as he had no intention of walking away without the girl. "Bullshit!" he barked back. "Bullshit!"

Milky, nodding his understanding, released Novella to Yank. "Hold the bitch." Milky, stretching away the tension accrued from holding her, then raised and rolled his shoulders and arms. Coincidently, the quick movements appeared to be efforts of intimidation. He had a few inches in height and about fifty pounds in solid weight on BETY Junior. Neither discouraged his latest contender. He and BETY Junior quickly connected in a thunder-clapping of cuffs.

Seconds before the start of their heavy-fisted brawl, a featherweight fight had commenced. Kicking had been everything for Novella. Muted by duct tape, she'd made the loudest noise she could by desperately drumming her feet against that rickety screen door. Metal banging against the wooden house was her best attempt for help. And help had arrived. The way she saw it, the odds were now even. Adrenaline helped her rip the duct tape from her mouth right before throwing her toward the smaller of the two kidnappers.

Yank wasn't much bigger than Novella, who at 5'4" weighed 112 pounds. On button pushed, she was still no "rowdy rah-rah street-fighting hood-rat," as her generation would have put it. Also, to her disadvantage, for all the street-running males in her family, none of them, nor anyone else, had taught her any self-defense tactics, the kind a father, big brother, or an uncle would teach a young woman to fend off a too-hands-on boyfriend—or these pervs. Still, an amped-up Novella was more afraid of rape and death than of a beating. Screaming like a warrior charging into battle, she went after Yank. He had been reaching for Novella when Milky shoved her toward him, and had meant to catch a scared schoolgirl. Instead, he caught a wild cat. Novella's arms swung now like her legs had kicked his face earlier. Her small fists, although not hurting him much, did frustrate him. Her pompoms, still looped on her wrists, crashing against his face were even more frustrating. Even with her screaming, Yank could hear their shredded-paper-being-shook-in-a-box sound. *Chh. Chh. Chh. Chh.* Novella began clawing her long natural fingernails through her pompoms. She went at Yank as if she meant to expose his skeleton. She also went at him another way. Trying to reach through the flying red and white blurs,

Yank soon saw more red than white. "My balls! My balls! My balls!" The high-kicking high-stepper Novella had decided to give him her best routine. She kicked and kneed him where she'd make the best impact. No music needed, she performed the show of a lifetime in Yank's groin, and had the show on repeat until he was able to back away. His bright green eyes, surrounded by acne and an overgrown fade, stretched wide as he coughed, "Bitch . . . just wait . . . I'm gonna fucken choke you! You ain't getting away!"

Then Novella heard, "What are you doing, girl? Run! Run! Run, right now! Go!" In between jabs with the big kidnapper, her rescuer was telling her to go. Novella, surprised, hesitated as she'd presumed she was supposed to help fight for her survival. It was two against two and a proportionally matched fight. When again urged, "Get your ass home, girl! Go!" Novella obeyed, and so made sure her way was clear. She executed a few jump kicks at Yank yelling, "Get the hell away from me!" Her first kick hit his right forearm, forcing him backwards at an angle nearer to the next house. "Get the hell back!" Her second kick hit his chest and finished the job. He was knocked against that house. Novella was surprised she'd actually made contact. *I'm kicking this yuck-face pervert! Kicking him down!* With no time to further relish in her *wow* moment, she ran.

NINE

Out the driveway, and then up 69th Place, Novella didn't even turn to see if the little one was in pursuit. She was half a block away from her home on 70th when guilt stopped her. *The guy.* Leaving him to fight against her two kidnappers alone made her feel ungrateful. She hadn't even looked to see if he was winning. Quickly, Novella thought about what would happen after she made it home. *It would good for her, but not for the guy.* If any of the men in her family were at her home, neither were likely come to his rescue. Then, Novella thought about the police. *They were sure to arrive too late.* Novella was running backing down 69th before she consciously knew she'd decided to turn around. She was surprised by the sight of her pompoms in the street, not remembering sliding them off just seconds ago. She made a mental note to retrieve them. *I paid twenty dollars for those.*

She had just entered the front yard of the abandoned home that was meant to be her prison when she was met by Yank. The rock he carried as he ran from the driveway told Novella he was a lefty. He swung the rock, just missing Novella's head as she tripped awkwardly over some sort of plastic block. BETY Junior, having darted from the driveway, grabbed Yank in a choke hold with one hand, bending his arm backwards with his other, forcing him to drop the rock.

BETY Junior, changing the chokehold into a sleeper hold reminded Novella, "Told you to run!"

Novella, as awkwardly as she'd fallen, got to her feet. "Was trying to help you." The yard was littered with small bits of debris, and Novella, with eyes on her abductor and rescuer, wasn't watching where she stepped.

BETY Junior, shaking his head disapprovingly, took his first close look of her face. *So innocent.* "Little girl, I didn't need you. You needed me. And coming back almost messed up your chance to get away and not get hurt."

"And what if you couldn't get away and got hurt?" she countered.

"Girl . . ." BETY Junior let out a light laugh. "These asshole lowlifes are grown-ass men, and so am I. You're . . . a baby out here. When shit goes down . . . and your little, young self is told to run . . . that's what you do. Run . . . and don't stop running."

Novella started to reply when she noticed the waning Yank. The sleeper hold was actually working. Her days of watching the World Wrestling Federation and the Gorgeous Ladies of Wrestling were about five-and-a-half years behind her, as were the juvenile wrestling matches in her room with her bed serving as the ring. Many times had she pinned an opponent, winning as her partner dramatically did the countdown before yelling her victory. *Smackdown!* Novella had been the Queen of Smackdown in her bedroom. Her older cousin Isaac had been one of the losing contenders until his pride had backed him out of the matches. She went on wrestling without him, but had never attempted a sleeper hold. She doubted it was real, and besides, none of her wrestling companions wanted their head squeezed.

Now watching the consciousness dim from Yank's eyes, she thought, *It's really happening . . .* Yank didn't make any attempts to fight, only to keep awake. More than once he held a hand up high as if to ask permission to ask a question. Mostly, he reached out, making a "T" with both arms fully extended. Balance or surrender, Novella didn't know.

Quiet had fallen between Novella and BETY Junior, while Yank was neutralized. BETY Junior calmly held him and applied pressure. Novella imagined being wrestled to sleep was no fun, but it didn't look painful.

In the last stages, Yank began a sequence of attempts to hold onto BETY Junior, no doubt for support, as his feet were slipping. When his arms fell for the fourth and last time, his toes lifted, causing him to fall back on his heels.

Novella gasped, "Oh my god! Oh . . . my . . . god! You put him out cold!"

BETY Junior nodded. "Yep, neutralized." Then he asked her, "You okay? You don't have to tell me anything personal, but do you need an ambulance?"

"I'm okay." She looked up from Yank who'd resembled a child in BETY Junior's arms. A dirty child.

"Good," BETY Junior replied. Then nodding toward the ground, he told her, "I dropped that. Grab it for me."

Novella looked down at the white plastic brick that had tripped her. She picked it up and, turning it over, realized it was a portable phone. She'd never held one before and had only seen them on television and in the hands of crack dealers.

"Call the police," BETY Junior told her. "It's better that you call them." Noticing uncertainty on her face, he instructed, "You see that last button on the left?"

"Yes." She placed a finger on it.

"Press it hard and hold it," he told her. "That'll turn it on."

Doing as she was told, Novella watched the dial pad light up.

31

"Turn it toward me," BETY Junior told her.

She did it in a way that looked as if she was handing it to him.

"Good, it's on," he said. "Now, you see the red button on the right? Press it. You'll then hear the dial tone."

She again did as told. Novella, hearing the dial tone, felt a wrench in her gut. Her adrenaline, although still high, wasn't the rocket fuel that had blasted her into battle. It was now a creepy crawl across her skin and a fearful thudding in her chest. She could hear in her mind what she wanted to say to the police: *They snatched me and beat me. They were going to drag me in that house and do whatever they wanted. Rape me . . . kill me.* Her mouth was dry, and she could feel tomorrow's hoarseness rising in her throat.

"Baby girl, it's ok," BETY Junior assured, seeing the reality of the situation come down on her. "This shit is over." Opening his long arms, he allowed the unconscious Yank to drop gently to the ground. "Motherfucker's down . . . It's over. Done and done. You're about to go home and be with your people."

Novella, shaking her head in acceptance, nonetheless fell into a thoughtful stare at Yank, who was now twitching. So many times she had passed him pretending as if she didn't hear or see him. Today marked the last day of that. He'd slapped her into full acknowledgment of him. Slapped her and slapped her. Novella touched her face as the burn from his rough hands increased and her adrenaline continued to drop.

"Little sister!" BETY Junior called to her.

"Huh?" Novella looked at him.

"Call the police," he gently urged. "The call should come from you because I'm going to be a suspect."

"911, what's the emergency?" came a nasal impatient female voice.

Novella's own voice, now tight, was hard to push around the newly formed lump in her throat. She placed the phone to her ear, but then brought it down in front of her mouth. Holding it like a slice of pizza, she then stared at it.

"Is anyone there?" the nasal voice asked louder.

"Umm . . . yes," Novella answered, timidly. "I'm sorry." She suddenly didn't want to talk, and knowing she had to made her want to cry.

"What's your name?" the operator asked.

"Novella."

"Novella, what's your last name?"

"Lofton."

Having her full name, the operator was no warmer and went on as if taking inventory on canned tomatoes instead of gathering details to dispatch assistance. "What's the emergency?"

"Two guys tried to kidnap me. They're still here, but . . ." Novella placed a hand to her chest, suddenly realizing the big kidnapper was missing. "Oh my god! Did he get away?" she asked BETY Junior. "The big one? Where is he?" Not knowing where he was sent a chill of panic up her spine. "Jesus . . ." Novella whispered, wanting to know where he was, needing to know. A sneak attack could put BETY Junior and her at a disadvantage. Novella quickly did a 360° scan of the street. Straining her neck as she raised herself up on her toes, she then squatted down on her thighs, and ducked her head to peer at the houses around them, thinking he could be watching and waiting to pounce.

Realizing she'd become too distracted by her panic to talk, BETY reached for his phone, "Let me have it."

Extending her arm to pass him the phone, she was startled out of her second 360° scan. BETY Junior's large hand grabbed her forearm. In shock, she sucked in her breath hard, as he slung her behind him. His strength forced her to leap slightly in order to keep herself upright. Quickly settling herself as much as possible, she turned to face him and was met by his broad back. "Wha—" she started before hearing the humming of an engine. Staying behind BETY Junior, she crooked her neck to peep around him. Creeping their way was a black Chevy Blazer. "Who is that?" she whispered. The SUV's license plate read "BLCKGOD." From the front passenger window hung a hand gaudy with gold nugget rings gripping a gun. Above the weapon was a grimacing face with gold teeth beneath a pair of wide-rimmed gold-plated sunglasses. "Help us!" Novella spoke into the phone. "Oh my god, send help right now!"

TEN

Desperately trying to think of something to say or do to help her out of her predicament caused Novella's mouth to hang slightly open. She shook herself, and then took a deep breath. *Check yourself, Novella, and sort it out.* She, however, could only think of being shot dead. She shuddered imagining the pain of her skin being blown open—and then not feeling anything ever again. She wanted to run. A voice in her head told her, *Stay calm. God is with you girl, so don't get ahead of him.* Whether the advice was truly from an angel or a manifestation of her anxiety, Novella wasn't comforted and still wanted to run. Staying put, waiting for whatever this would turn out to be, felt like surrender.

From what she could make of their approaching company, they were hoods, clean and polished. Possibly too hood-rich to be associated with her poor abductors. Oversized gleaming wheels and deeply tinted windows suggested tiny plastic bags filled with illegal content were stashed throughout the interior of the Blazer. It was no overstatement in Ebonics to say the ride looked literally "dope."

What could they want? Novella anxiously wondered. *And why the gun? I don't know them, and they don't know me.*

Guns had been around Novella for as long she could remember, but not gun violence. She knew the locations, in her home, of a BB gun, a shotgun, a .22, and a .48, though she hadn't ever held any of them—or any gun. No one had offered, and she hadn't been curious. The closest she had been to a point-and-shoot lifestyle was being within earshot of bloody gossip and watching the local news. She wasn't aware of knowing any shooters or any victims. Today, it seemed that her education on gun handling was going to come from the harmful intent of a stranger.

The Blazer, creeping slowly but steadily, abruptly came to a stop within about twenty feet of her and BETY Junior. Novella's love of action movies now worked against her, as she imagined the different ways she could die: a bullet tearing into her chest, hot lead piercing her forehead. A chest shot, presumably killing her slower, would be the worst; she'd consciously live through her last moments in pain and fear. Novella also imagined being forced down to her knees for an execution-style death. Unknowingly she shook her head no to experiencing the gut-wrenching anticipation of hearing the click of no tomorrow. *No, I won't do it!* Her thoughts shook her head slightly from side to side. She wouldn't cooperate. *They'll have to kill me to kill me!* Novella was mind-tripping and she knew it, but she couldn't stop. *This is not my life!* She continued to trip. *Why is this happening to me? This shouldn't be happening to me! I shouldn't be here! I didn't do anything to cause this to happen!*

There was no fighting and getting shot on the today's agenda. Her afterschool to-do list had baking pork chops and boiling rice and green beans on it. And then taking a bubble bath, changing her nail polish, and reading while it dried. Now, for the first time, she admitted to herself what she had been teased about her entire life: *I'm a good girl. A very good girl.* So, she inwardly asked herself, *How could I not make it home? How could I die here? How could this all be happening? I was just walking home from school, minding my own business, and then . . .* That was it; her mind didn't need to trip any further. *Stupid girl!* she chastised herself. *These thugs could shoot you, Novella. That's how you could not make it home. That's how you could die on this no-good street. Yeah, I was just walking home and got snatched like the kids on milk cartons!* "Have you seen me?" could be me. Novella was back and focused on the thugs and her surroundings. *How am I to live through this?* Her mind searched for ideas.

ELEVEN

Novella heard BETY Junior exhale deeply as he remained still as a statue in front of her. She presumed he was just blowing out some steam to maintain the cool he'd projected through the entire ordeal.

In all Novella's thinking of dying this way and that way, there was also remorse for the grave possibility her rescuer might die as well. "I'm sorry. And thanks for trying to save me." She wasn't sure if he'd heard her, because he didn't respond. He didn't move. If he was ignoring her, she didn't blame him. He could be thinking up a life-saving plan for them both—or just himself. Besides, what was there for him to say? *It's okay that I'm going to die for trying to help you.* He didn't even know her, and she had ignored him as much she had Yank and Milky. So she'd understand if he was thinking only of his own safety.

Novella's instinct for self-preservation was telling her to run. *Why wait to die?*

Suddenly, the sound of two gunshots caused her to shake so hard she lost her balance. Trying to catch herself, she'd reached a hand for BETY Junior. Having only caught the tail of his thick polo, she went down. After losing her grip, she hit the hazardous yard bottom first. Her right cheek met a wooden plank, her left the edge of a brick. A terrified and painful yelp escaped her. Despite the pain, she quickly, inwardly, shut herself up. *Novella! No dumb broad screaming! Shut up! Shut up! Shut up!*

"You okay?" BETY Junior asked without turning around. His eyes were fixed on the shooter, who still sat in the Blazer.

Easing her bottom on the ground while trying to regain her calm, she didn't answer him.

"Baby girl," he sang with urgency. "You alright?"

Novella didn't answer him, but she did speak. "Black God," she said into the phone. The operator, had of course, held the line. "It's a Blazer. The license plate says Black God. B L C . . ."

"Who fuck you talking to?" the shooter exited the Blazer.

Novella, a bit thrown off by him addressing her directly, stopped talking. The shooter, now walking toward BETY Junior and Novella, dropped his shoulders low and swung them side to side. He looked ready to start performing a rap song. Instead, he asked again, "Bitch, I said who the fuck you talking to?"

Novella looked down at the phone in her hand. *Thank God!* she thought at how blessed she was to have use of a mobile phone. So, she kept using it, "B L C K G O D, that's on the license plate. Two guys in a black Chevy Blazer." Novella didn't know exactly what street she was on. "We're between Lexington and Hough near 70th. A raggedy side street. It's a dead end."

The hood, having stopped about ten feet from Novella, wasn't close enough to hear what she was saying into the phone. Though it was obvious he was beginning to realize that his gun hand may not have the tightest of grip on this situation. His was voice was less cocky as he again asked, "Who the fuck you talking to?"

Novella didn't want to talk to him, but thought it might buy BETY Junior and her time. "I'm talking to the police. To the police, and I just gave them your license plate and told them where we are. So, go away! Go away!"

The shooter, as if shocked by it all, gawked, "What?"

Novella gawked back, "What yourself!" Then dared to further engage him. "What's your name, thug . . . motherfucker? I can give that to them, too."

"Calm down. Sweetie?" The emergency operator had finally changed from a data-processing robot to human. "We need time to get to you. I know you're scared."

Novella was indeed very scared. "Motherfucker!" she again called him, and then told the operator, "The motherfucker has gun on us . . . for no reason!" Yeah, she was finally saying it. *Motherfucker*. It was a long time coming. Many had tried to coerce her. The first was a new girl at her elementary school. "Novella, say it. Say motherfucker. No one's going to tell on you. Say motherfucker. Just say it. Mo-ther-fuc-ker." Novella, a little shy, hadn't ever been a fan of cussing, so it was too much for her. "Motherfucker" had felt like the cherry popper of profanity. *If one was comfortable saying motherfucker, one would say anything.* Novella was a chatterbox, but not a foul-mouthed one. Besides she thought it a perversion, compounding the words "mother" and "fucker." Nonetheless, she felt saying it was *real* cussing, part of the vocabulary of bitches and thugs. She wanted this killer, or wannabe killer, to understand she was fighting for her life. That, if need be, she could be a bitch, bad enough to have called the police and be telling them every *mo-ther-fuc-ken* thing.

"Stupid motherfucker!" she yelled, still seated on the ground. "Go away! We haven't done anything to you!"

"Bitch, that's my cousin!" The thug pointed to Yank who, still unconscious, was sprawled out not far from where Novella sat.

She fired back, "I got your bitch! Yeah, your bitch is coming with cuffs and more guns than you got! You're about to find out what a bitch is! And your yuck-face cousin is a kidnapping rapist!"

BETY Junior slowly lowered himself to the ground next to Novella. He had to shift around a bit to find a safe spot to rest. After finding one, he spoke causally to the thug. "Come on, man. Fuck this day. This little girl didn't do anything for it turn on her like this."

"Little girl?" the thug snarled. "I see bitches and hoes like her out all time of night. And who the fuck is you?"

BETY Junior shrugged. "Maybe she's older or younger than some you know, but, man, she *is* a little girl. And this isn't the middle of the night; we're out here in broad daylight. And those are her pompoms there in the street. C'mon, man. She was on her way home from school." Nodding toward Yank, he said, "Let the police deal with your cousin, and let this girl get home to do homework, watch cartoons, or do whatever she was about to do before he snatched her. And, man, I'm nobody. I'm just here."

Finally came the sound of sirens.

The Blazer's driver leaned out the window. In contrast to his gun-wielding passenger, he didn't appear to have any gold teeth or any other gaudy accessories. "Let's make haste, my dude! Leave this shit as is!"

The gaudy gunman yelled back, "It's my ride, bitch! Get your punk ass out and run if you want!"

So he's Black God, Novella thought. *The guy driving is his hood-boy chauffer or something. Punks!*" Novella then told the operator, "The guy with the gun is called Black God. His street name, I guess."

A reluctant defeat sank into Black God's stance. While the sound of sirens signaled the end of his ego trip, BETY Junior and Novella knew they weren't truly safe until he was actually gone. The police, judging by the increasing volume of the sirens, would be turning down Quimby in a few minutes, but it would only take a few seconds for both BETY Junior and Novella to be shot dead. If killing was the thug's intent, it was possible he'd chance it before fleeing.

"I can't stand riding with squeamish-ass motherfuckers!" he yelled back at the driver, who had revved the engine a few times to emphasize his urgency to leave. Black God gave BETY Junior and Novella his gold-embellished scowl one last time, and then turned and ran back to his ride. He jumped in and the driver, gassing it, did a U-turn even before Black God had completely closed his door. Within seconds, they were off down Quimby and out of sight.

After a few moments, BETY Junior rose to his feet. Then, with his eyes still focused on Quimby, he extended a hand down to Novella. She took it, using more his strength than her own to get off the ground. Her body felt like it had been planted on the ground for years and her butt had been hammered flat. When up and steady, her eyes followed BETY Junior's gaze. She then turned to him. BETY Junior turned his head and looked down at her. Still holding hands, he gave hers a little squeeze. "Baby girl, we're both going to sleep very hard tonight . . . or not a damn wink."

TWELVE

Getting through the crowd was harder than Coddy Lee expected. Her arrival was one of many, and she wasn't the only person arriving with followers. She was just one of many moving ahead for a better look. Younger, more agile bodies were quickly adding more depth and width to the crowd. Coddy Lee had just achieved a shallow infiltration into the crush when she hit a wall of closely gathered onlookers. *Dear God, what to do?*

"My granddaughter!" she croaked. Coddy Lee was unaccustomed to projecting her voice further than the girth of her modest two-story home, but she tried, "I'm looking for my granddaughter!"

From behind her came a fiery female voice, "We'll get you through, Ms. Lofton. Hey y'all, this nice old lady is looking for her granddaughter. Probably the girl caught up in this mess. Any of y'all know where she's at?"

The voice was familiar, but Coddy Lee, afraid of losing her balance, didn't dare turn to look. At the present, Coddy Lee didn't think it mattered how she knew her. The woman sounded about twenty-something and like she had lived hard, not the type to be in her granddaughter's circle of friends. Besides, the woman obviously didn't know her granddaughter's name or whereabouts.

"Hey, Ms. Lofton," came a man's voice. The baritone she guessed belonged to a friend of one of her grandsons. "We'll help you find her. Hey, y'all, the grandmamma is here! Let her through! This the grandmamma! This . . ." His voice was drowned out by an abrupt explosion of angry shouting that quickly melded into chanting. "Police brutality! Police brutality! Police brutality! Police brutality!"

Coddy Lee, afraid of being knocked down, reached for an anchor in one of the young people. The baritone, being male, her preferred choice in protector, had come from behind on her left, so her hand went in that direction. Unfortunately, it found only the front jeans pocket of someone who was too focused on protesting to help her; Coddy Lee's hold on their pocket went unnoticed. The crowd was so tight, Coddy Lee couldn't tell to whom it belonged. Worried of being pulled down if whoever it was rushed forward, she let go. She knew she'd be finished off by the crowd if she fell. She'd be stepped on a dozen times before her body would register in their outraged minds as flesh. Then a dozen more times before some would actually stop to check on her. She stretched her neck as high as she could, but couldn't see anything other than fists being pumped in the air. Coddy Lee's chest felt full of sparking wires, and she worried how long she'd last. Feeling eyes on her, she turned to see her daughter Canella Lynn. Nearly twenty years dead, translucent, she was in the crowd but not a part of it. She smiled. Coddy Lee quickly turned away. She wasn't ready to receive a death message about her granddaughter—or herself. She knew she didn't get to dictate the way of these things, so she wasn't surprised that, over the shouting voices, Canella's message slipped into her hear, "Not your time. You'll be okay, mama." Great, no death message, but Coddy Lee didn't feel any better. She widened her stance to relieve some of the pressure from her hips and back. She felt a wave of exhaustion sweep over her, and her chest pains persisted. Fortunately, before leaving, Canella had brushed against the baritone. Coddy Lee saw him turn around to face her, giving her a blank but intense stare. Coddy Lee knew he'd been inspirited. One of his long arms wrapped around her waist and took a strong hold of her. Coddy Lee's gratitude came out in a grunt, "Thank you."

The baritone then slowly and very cautiously began working them through the crowd. Gently tapping on shoulders, and then nodding toward the weary Coddy Lee, the baritone was able to coax protestors aside. Each one they encountered helped in further parting the crowd. When they at last had the protestors behind them, Coddy Lee saw the reason for their anger: a young man in cuffs. Blood dripped from his busted lip. Coddy Lee, not knowing what role he had played in her granddaughter's situation, had no sympathy for him. *Damn rogue, probably getting what he deserves.* The crowd, however, felt the opposite. "Police brutality! Police brutality!" they chanted.

The police were focused on crowd control. Though, to the discredit of Cleveland's so-called finest, Coddy Lee and the baritone were able to make it over to one the ambulances. Out of the crush, the two could now hear one another speak.

"Let me see if she's in there." Coddy Lee nodded her head toward the ambulance's rear door.

The baritone hesitated. "Ma'am, I can't afford to go to jail. And the way those cops are beating that brotha over there . . ." The baritone however didn't let her go. His dark pupils flickered, as if he had an intense debate going on inside his head. It didn't last long. He was soon telling her, "Well . . . you're the grandmamma. You got a right to know." He then moved Coddy Lee closer to the door of the ambulance. After she placed her hand on the handle, he placed his own just above hers to help her swing open the door. Inside the ambulance there were no medics, only a big body lying still on a stretcher. The sight of it gave them both pause.

An officer broke their stare as he yelled, "Hey!" He gave Coddy Lee and the baritone a curious look over. "Who are you people?"

Coddy Lee, still focused on her mission, turned toward the second ambulance. "Is somebody dead in that other one too?"

"Who are you looking for, ma'am?"

"Officer, she's the grandmama. And she's feeling kind of weak. She really wanna find her grandbaby."

"Oh my god!" Coddy Lee looked past the officer.

"Granny!" Novella leapt out of a nearby squad car. "Granny!"

The officer standing next to Coddy Lee nodded. "Okay. This is your girl. You're Coddy Lee Lofton. You live around the corner."

Coddy Lee wasn't paying him any attention. Her eyes were on her slimmer, younger twin.

Novella, after rushing over, wrapped her slim arms around her twin, "Granny!"

Coddy Lee, wincing from the pain in her chest, huffed, "Noey . . . what are you doing on this street? You don't have . . . no business . . . on this street. None . . . at all!"

Novella, seeing her granny's distress, didn't bother answering her. Novella knew she needed to be taken to the hospital, and that it would mean an exam. Novella was well-learned on how her grandmother handled bad business. From her purse, which was still draped from her shoulder to her hip, she retrieved her treasured Strawberry Shortcake handkerchief. Although carried in her purses, it was treated like fancy towels hung in bathrooms. She'd never used the item to wipe anything. Today, however, Novella used it to dab Coddy Lee's face, and then Coddy Lee's chest. Then, slipping the soft pink hanky down into Coddy Lee's left bra cup, she made eye contact and said, "Granny, let me take your wallet. You need to let the medics check you." Careful not to drop the piece or pull its trigger, Novella transferred it to her purse. She then turned to the officer, "Can you please have them check her? She has a heart condition." Two of the medics had already come over. One gave Novella a nod, a signal for her to step back. After she did, both medics relieved the baritone of Coddy Lee and went to work on her. After a few moments, the medic who'd nodded turned to the baritone, "She needs to go in—now!" The baritone looked to Novella, "Y'all okay from here? I can push off? I'm gonna go!"

Novella shook her assent to the stranger. His presence was exchanged for that of another. Right after his quick departure, a social worker appeared. The wide-hipped woman looked ready to arrest her. "Novella Renae Lofton!" The woman's shape reminded Novella of the hand bell next to Willie's bed.

"I'm your caseworker Ms. Brenda Marble," the woman told Novella.

"I'm going with my granny!"

"I'll permit it, but you're riding with me."

"I don't know you." Novella folded her arms.

"I just told you who I am," the caseworker snapped.

"Right! You just told me, so I just met you. I . . . don't . . . know . . . you!"

The caseworker cocked her head. "How do you think you're getting to the hospital? The cops aren't going to take you anywhere but downtown to my department! You don't think . . . that you're riding in that ambulance, do you?"

Novella stared at her.

The caseworker went on, "The ambulance is no place for a child, and the medics need to work on your grandmother. You know, to save her life!"

One of the officers intervened, "It's okay, Novella Renae. We called Ms. Marble. She's a verified social worker. You are to go with her. Only other option is to leave with a female officer who'd escort you to Child Welfare Services. You've been involved in a crime, and your grandmother isn't in position to assume custody of you right now. And you don't have any other family here. Do you understand?"

Novella, rolling her eyes, dropped her arms and shrugged that she understood. The case worker then flipped a hand at her. "Let's go. We'll follow behind the ambulance."

Novella reluctantly turned to follow her, but stopped when she heard her granny's voice. Coddy Lee was complaining, "No! Not Mount Sinai! I don't like Mount Sinai! . . . I don't care! I don't care that it's right up the road! Too many people I love have died there! Take me to Saint Alexis; it's not that far."

Novella went and leaned into the ambulance, "Granny, please! You gotta get somewhere soon! Maybe they can move you afterwards."

The caseworker came up behind Novella. "Please don't ignore me, young lady. It's a bad show on your part, and it will not help your grandmother."

Novella turned to the woman, thinking, *This woman has a problem! A serious problem!* The two females faced off briefly before Novella's mind wandered off to thoughts about BETY Junior..

"Oh my god!" Novella rushed back to the lieutenant. "He didn't do anything wrong!" she began pleading. "Now I don't know him, like I already said, but I'm sure he's a good guy. I'd probably be raped and dead, and no one would know where I was, if he hadn't saved me. That's a good guy over there!" She then turned and screamed in vain to the officers surrounding BETY Junior, "He didn't do anything wrong!" Novella had witnessed the thundering of batons and leather-gloved fists upon her rescuer. She'd never witnessed someone being hit so hard. The sight and sounds shattered her heart. She'd tried to intervene but was carried away like a child having a temper tantrum. She was then locked in a squad car. "Why? Why? He's not one of them! Listen! Listen . . . to . . . me! I made the call to 911. I'm the victim and I am telling y'all. I called with his phone. He is the good guy!"

Inside the squad car, where she could no longer see him, she prayed, *Oh, God, don't let them kill him! Please, God, hear me! Don't let them . . . don't let them kill him.*

"This is so crazy," she sniffed. "These cops . . ."

"Yes. Cops. Let them handle it," drawled the caseworker.

Novella screamed at her, "They're beating him for no reason!"

The caseworker started to reply, but Novella cut her off to ask, "How come most of you social workers don't like people? Don't like really helping them when y'all's job is to look after the welfare of people? Why did you become a social worker, if you don't care about people?"

The caseworker pointed toward the emergency vehicle, "Ambulance is leaving. Grandma or boyfriend? Who's more important?"

Novella thought back to being slapped by Yank. *Now, this is someone to slap over and over!* "Being in charge, or being helpful?" she spat back. "What's more important to you?"

The tilt in the caseworker's head implied the desire to slap was mutual.

The lieutenant intervened, "Ladies. Go on and head out to the hospital." He then whispered to the caseworker loud enough for Novella to hear every word. "Tag, you're it, honey. You're now responsible for this girl. So, get control of her, and get her off my crime scene. We got enough problems here with her boyfriend."

"He's not my boyfriend!" Novella snapped at them both. "Okay? He's not my boyfriend. He didn't do anything wrong. I'm a stranger that was in trouble . . . and then he jumped in the nick of time and saved my life! Please tell those cops to stop. Let them go find the thugs with the gun—Black God!"

She got nothing from the lieutenant. So, Novella accepted that she couldn't help BETY Junior, not here anyway. So she turned to the case-worker, "I'm ready."

THIRTEEN

BETY Junior as an amateur boxer and martial arts student was a technical fighter. He, however, could still give and take a street beating. He'd been jumped six times as a teenager. So, he'd learned to add a feral quality to his technical skills. *Be a well-trained savage when fighting in the streets.* The last time he was jumped was four years ago, when he was nineteen. That jump was similar to the five before it. He was alone, and had to be ruthless to win, meaning survive with no serious injury.

Bariah Elijah Tomas Young Junior aka BETY Junior, wasn't a "hood boy." His initials, being his nickname, wasn't from the streets, but was bestowed on him by his Air Force lieutenant father. His father was proud of his full name, but didn't always have room to write it out in full. So began the habit of signing with his initials. Other airmen began to call him BETY, and he'd pass that nickname on to his first and only child, a son who wouldn't experience drug addicts and dealers roaming their neighborhood—or any type of poverty. Hough, as Milky had barked, was not his hood. BETY Junior had grown up and still lived in Shaker Heights, an upper-middle-class suburb. Unlike many of his peers, he wasn't given an allowance as a kid. Instead, he was encouraged to earn his pocket money, which he was supposed to bank more than pocket. He went at it, selling bootleg cassette tapes, mowing lawns, and cutting hair. He could afford to go on dates, hang with the fellas, and build a decent savings account. Hustling took him all over the Cleveland area. Mostly, he made friends. Always, he found lovers. BETY Junior had always played as hard as he worked. He hadn't long left the bed of his latest when it all went down with the pompom girl.

He was from an entrepreneurial family, so, after completing his senior year of high school, the idea of paying tens of thousands of dollars to attain a bachelor's degree hadn't appealed to him. He was inspired to get certification as a personal trainer, become a licensed realtor, and an independent multi-line insurance writer. The last was indeed one of those pyramid businesses, but not a scam. BETY Junior didn't have to recruit people to earn money. He did well enough selling policies to the people he sold homes to.

Being a personal trainer brought in the least amount of money, yet it was his favorite business. It was also part of the reason he'd been jumped. His physique, was said by many, jokingly but in earnest, to look like it belonged to someone who regularly beat the hell out of people. Had so since he was twelve. Two of the three times he was jumped had been tests to initiate him into gangs. The first recruit had said, "Need you on our team, man. You could be out here crushing dudes." The other had said, "Shit, you was rocking with all of us, and we ain't soft. Kick it with us, man." Both fist-delivered invitations were turned down.

BETY Junior had a clean rep, no underground business: a pencil-pushing hustler, and one of the coolest dudes to know. The man. Nevertheless, mingling on both sides of the socio-economic scale got him the attention of several green-eyed monsters.

That last jump, BETY Junior had been pounced on by a group of guys all about three years older than him. BETY Junior was leaving a gym called Boneheads. He trained many of his East-side clients for sporting events there, as well as sculpting them for modeling and acting gigs. That day, he had been sparring and spotting inside the gym, but he carried those jabs through outside it: breaking noses, ribs, an arm, and giving a concussion. The thugs had landed enough blows to deeply bruise BETY Junior's light brown skin as well as split his bottom lip. With nothing broken, he'd done well for himself. Five against his one for the entire eight-minute altercation. It had been an amazing show for Bonehead's gym members and anyone passing by. No one had called the cops. Bittersweet. No drama with the law, but no justice either. After peeling themselves off the ground, the roughnecks who'd jumped BETY Junior had fled as fast they could manage, packing themselves back in the Buick Regal they had left running. Had they been called, the police would've only found skid marks and blood spots.

Aside from being true, this day for BETY Junior went on as a fairy tale. His morning, starting later than usual, began with him wrestling the prior night's demons. To banish them, he drank a spinach leaf potion. It energized his whiskey-hung-over body well enough for his ten-mile run. Afterwards, he drank a beet-root potion to restore what the concrete had taken from him. Later, a long-legged goddess, who moved as fluidly as the black oil she seemed to be made of, entranced him with her four natural wonders: curves, thick lashes, silky skin, and, in BETY Junior's own words, "an ass that could bless and curse a man at the same time." BETY Junior, having his own magic, compounded her spell by casting the two of them into another dimension, where their labored breathing drained nearly all the air from that world. Not long after, he bravely rescued a young princess being assaulted by vermin. It was that turn in today's trek through life that had brought him to his current situation of being beaten by pigs.

"Citizen's arrest?" a pudgy face smirked at him. "The ghetto version? That's what you were doing, homeboy?" BETY Junior hadn't expected a medal, but was nonetheless getting plenty of steel and brass.

BETY Junior's hands and feet were shackled. Each time his restricted body moved, the police whacked him, even though it was their rough handling that moved it. Rolling back his shoulders to ease the strain in his arms got him a baton in the stomach. Steadying himself as they pushed against him got him a round of what can only be called "sucka shots."

"You killed some random guy to save a girl you don't know?" said a tall one whose breath suggested there was skunk in his DNA. BETY Junior, watching him strut, squaring wide but round shoulders, presumed the cop was fooling himself that his shoulders and height were dwarfing the sizable belly fat hanging over his gun belt. BETY Junior thought, but didn't say, *Sorry as cops . . . on some egotistical bullshit! All these motherfuckers probably got their asses beat in school, and pissed in the bed until they were twelve!*

Having done what he could for the princess, BETY Junior knew he now needed to focus on his own well-being. The safety of Hough's community, however, was a concern. BETY Junior had been forcibly turned away from the street, so he heard more than saw that a good portion of the community had come to the scene. He'd also heard the voice of his cousin, the ride he'd been waiting on. He'd come and gone, having yelled. "Hey cuz, I called Uncle Pop. We'll meet you down there!"

Until then, BETY Junior was here in the violent hands of crooked cops and in the riot-filled hearts of the people. To BETY Junior they were yelling, "We're here . . . young blood . . . we're here! We see you!"

"We'll be in court to say what we're seeing right now!"

"Believe that!"

"This police brutality bullshit will stop!"

"Believe that!"

"I got my camcorder! And I'm rolling! I'm rolling! Recording this . . . all of it!"

BETY Junior appreciated that what started as a neighborhood figuratively trying to devour one its own, had turned into a we-stand-together demonstration. "Police brutality! Police brutality!"

BETY Junior also heard bullhorn-projected warnings to cease and desist. He was sure it wasn't so much directed at the people chanting, as it was at those throwing bottles and rocks. The makeshift missiles were crashing all around him. The magic that created social change was in the air—as was the danger that came with it. He didn't want the crowd to be tear gassed, or to escalate into mob violence. There was already too much hell in this fairytale.

BETY Junior had thought at each passing moment that the next the moment would bring the end of the beating. So he'd kept quiet, having figured that talking would only make the attack worse and last longer. He now understood that *he* was the timekeeper, not the police. If he was to sleep in his own bed tonight, and prevent a riot, *he* had to move things along.

BETY Junior called out to the fat cop who was parading around like he was the legendary Shaka Zulu, "Officer Shitty Breath!"

Taking the bait, the cop closed in tight on BETY Junior, close enough to kiss him, though that was not likely under the circumstances. BETY Junior told him, "I don't know if that's your ass I'm smelling, since it's so high up on your shoulders, or if it really is your mouth and you need to see a doctor. But besides that, since neither you nor your fellow pigs care that one of our little sistas was almost fucked to death by lowlifes, then almost shot to death by two more lowlifes, I got nothing to say except I want my lawyer!"

Batons whacked his back. The assault only lasted a few moments.

After BETY Junior caught his breath, he continued, "And stop fooling yourself, big bird, you're not husky. Your ass is fat. I want my lawyer!"

More baton action caused his feet to slide as if he was standing on ice. To stay afoot, he had to hunker down nearly to waist level. When the assault stopped, the foul-breathed cop told him, "Keep talking, homeboy."

And BETY Junior did, as if it was a sincere request and not a warning. "And just because Peter Pan's is twenty-four-seven, doesn't mean midnight needs to find your fat ass posted at the counter. I want my lawyer, pig!"

A blur of silver sticks rained down on him in a much longer session. BETY Junior nearly fell to his knees, but resiliently remained standing. He knew the pigs, high off the blood dripping from his mouth, were now after his strength and would kick it out of him if he fell beneath their feet.

The Peter Pan remarks were presumptuous digs, BETY Junior not knowing anything about the fat cop besides him obviously being crooked. It was the gut and breath that caused BETY Junior to conclude he was a regular at somebody's after-hours grease pit. BETY Junior had himself visited Peter Pan's on occasion. Located in the small city of East Cleveland, it was a twenty-four-hours-a-day, seven-days-a-week artery clogger. Coffee, donuts, ribs, fried wings, and shrimp. Sauced fries and coleslaw atop fat pork and beef sausages, respectfully called a po boy and po girl. Damn good food! Especially after a night of music, liquor, and women—as BETY Junior usually enjoyed it.

BETY Junior braced himself, but no blows came. Instead, more words, again from Officer Shitty Breath, "You like talking shit, don't you, boy?"

BETY Junior, spraying blood as he spoke, replied, "If your own brotha won't keep it real with you, who will, brotha?" He over-enunciated the word "brotha" each time he spoke it. To avoid the droplets of blood, the officers, including Shitty Breath, had backed off a few steps. BETY Junior used the extra space to get a better look at them. Daring to raise himself to his full height of six-foot-two, he scanned the racially mixed mob of officers. He spoke to the black ones, "You Black Bucks have done your massa well today!" He was immediately thanked for his cynical praise with two brass-knuckled fists: one branding his right shoulder blade, the other his left pec. They landed with enough force for the pain to heighten to a sensation that suggested he might burn to death where he stood. Right at the moment BETY Junior thought he'd collapse into ash, his body was relieved of the knuckles. Then he was shoved into a squad car. After the beating he had taken, he needed a gurney, not a backseat. As it was, he was leaving the scene, being one step closer to the end of this hellish tale.

FOURTEEN

Two Days Later
Sunday, April 21, 1991

"So, Noey, why did you take the 4?" asked Coddy Lee's daughter Cherry. "Why take a longer walk home? Don't make no sense to me." Much like the social worker, Cherry challenged Novella's predisposition to respect all adults.

"I missed the 38 and didn't want to wait a whole hour for the next one."

Cherry crossed her arms. "You must have been taking your time, after getting off that 22. That's the bus you take from West Tech, right? The 22?"

The interrogation was on. Novella had been spared it for a few days, but only because of Coddy Lee's hospitalization. Her granny, having been released a few hours ago, was now home. As was everyone else, and two regular visitors: Connie and the aforementioned Cherry, who'd assumed the lead in Novella's interrogation. Cherry had phoned Novella before heading out to the hospital, "I'm on my way to go get mama. We're picking up her medicine and then coming straight there. So go on downstairs and be ready to talk." After arriving with Coddy Lee, Cherry promptly seated herself at the dining table across from Novella. Novella had been playing solitaire and hadn't bothered to look up or stop her game until Coddy Lee said, "Put those cards away, Noey. We gotta sort this out."

Novella couldn't believe Cherry was not only front and center, but was apparently being given a stage to ridicule her from. *Not this one,* Novella thought. *Not miserable conceited Cherry in my face.*

Novella, staring into her aunt's eager eyes, inwardly coached herself, *Don't give her what she wants. Don't let her run you.* Novella, doing her best to mask her intent to mentally trip up her aunt, asked her to clarify what she meant, "Taking my time? What does that mean?"

Cherry gave her a look. "It means instead getting your tail home, you was lollygagging."

Novella raised one of her thick eyebrows. "Lollygagging on what time schedule? Do you know what time I usually walk in the door? My afterschool activities, my job? What time schedule do you have me on to say I was lollygagging?"

Coddy Lee warned from the receiving room, "Noey, don't be smart!"

Cherry tapped her cracked and chipped pink fingernails on the glass round of the dining table. "Don't know what your deal is, Noey girl. I'm trying to talk to you; might save you from punishment."

Novella knew her aunt wasn't trying to save her from anything. "Punishment for what? Cherry, whatever you were doing to get pregnant when you were a teenager is not how I am living my life."

Cherry's face grew tight. It was no secret that they weren't the other's favorite person. Yet Novella outwardly expressing it was new and unexpected.

Coddy Lee's voice again came from the receiving room, "Alright, Noey! But since you being smart anyway, tell us then! How are you living your life, with that grown man? We are all trying to understand."

Novella, feeling betrayed by her granny, turned from her aunt's contemptuous stare toward the receiving room that was adjacent to the dining room. Aside from Coddy Lee, sitting in it was her daughter Connie and three of Novella's cousins.

Looking at her granny, Novella reflected on how she had risked health and jail time to march to war on the streets for her. Novella's heart had leapt with her legs when she suddenly saw Coddy Lee on the scene. Right now, Novella's heart was breaking because of her granny's apparent disregard for her feelings. *Why can't this be a private conversation?* Novella wondered. *Why is she doing this to me? I do everything she asks, and don't ask her for anything.*

"We waiting!" Coddy Lee urged.

Novella's lips parted, although she didn't know what would come out of her mouth. She felt herself getting emotional. Novella wanted to stay in control of herself, because she knew that her only power was her self-control. She knew telling it all without crying would be hard enough, because she wouldn't be able to get the story out uninterrupted. That she'd only say a few sentences before one or two of her family members would add their two cents. Her family wanted drama, and as sensitive as this situation was, she could not expect any sympathy from them. Novella felt as mentally tripped up as she'd meant for her aunt to be, as well as stuck.

Fortunately, Novella's twenty-four-year-old cousin Gent exited the kitchen and said, "Now wait! This a delicate and personal situation, and she's just a girl. You might as well be asking her to talk about her period in front of everybody."

Novella's other cousin, eighteen-year-old Janet, waved from the love seat. "We're family! We can't know?"

Cherry, finally able to relax her face, agreed with her niece. "Right. We can't know what went down? I bet it's all out in the streets."

Gent shrugged. "Okay, yeah, the family should know. But not every-thing. Not everything that happened should be discussed in the open. Some of it should be a closed-door, all-female conversation." What he said next was directed at Janet. "And if you're not helping the girl, it ain't your business even if you are a female. This stuff is sensitive."

Coddy Lee, now opening a bottle of pills she'd retrieved from her purse, was called to give the final decision. "Mama?" Gent asked his granny. "This girl ain't gotta answer in front everybody right?"

"Well, we need to talk about it." Coddy Lee shook out her prescribed dose. "That's not her route home and I'm still trying to understand why she was back there. And how she knows someone that much older than her."

Anger compounded Novella's feeling of betrayal and she thought, *What is she talking about, my route home? I get here how I get here. She doesn't even buy my bus pass. I get myself around.*

Her aunt Connie began tapping out a Newport. "Noey, is he your boyfriend?"

Coddy Lee, before tossing the pills into her mouth warned, "Damn rogue better not be!" She washed down the blood pressure meds with cola, which she also counterproductively used to flush down glucose inhibitors for her diabetes. Coddy Lee, having avoided recreational drugs and alcohol her entire life, was no less a junkie. She had five vices: canned oysters and saltines, fried catfish, lemon pound cake, banana popsicles, and cola. Her worst habit being the cola, which she drank about forty-eight ounces of daily.

Novella's voice had a defeated tone in it when she again had to repeat what she'd already told the police, the social worker, and Coddy Lee multi-ple times, "I don't know him."

"He knows you!" yelled her seventeen-year-old cousin Isaac. "Got to, cause ain't no dude gonna throw down two against one for a broad he ain't feeling! That he ain't *dealing* with!"

Isaac and Novella's love-hate ratio was always fluctuating. Today it sat at about 20 percent love to 80 percent hate. Novella, expecting his dirty two cents, was ready to cash him out, "We all know your chicken butt would have run, even if it had been only the little one. You're not for helping anybody!"

Cherry, being his mother, quickly defended him. "Don't call my son no names! And he wouldn't have been wrong! The two who snatched you could have had knives or guns. And the one who saved you is obviously some type of dangerous rogue his self, being able to put one to sleep and kill the other, all with his bare hands."

Gent, intrigued, repeated, "His bare hands." That was the part he most wanted to know more about. "How he do it, Noey? You had to see something, girl. And it had to be woohoo, really something else."

Before she could answer, Isaac threw in a late response. "And if you could run your legs like you run your mouth, they wouldn't have got you!"

Janet followed with her own dig. "Couldn't leave her boyfriend." She pursed her lips in her usual know-it-all smile. Novella wanted to palm Janet's face and squeeze the smugness out of it and then wipe the loveseat's backrest with the back of her head, doing so until the band slipped from her ponytail and her hair resembled a shaken mop head. Novella, however, kept her palm to herself. Novella, after giving her aunt a fearless stare down, rolled her eyes. She then turned to Gent. "Not really. He told me to run home, and I did."

"No, you didn't," Coddy Lee said evenly. "You went back to him."

Cherry, still a bit offended by Novella's crack at her son, felt a little redemption in her mother's scolding of Novella. "You see, when the gangsta got there with the gun, Noey, you could have had your tail home already. But you ran your tail back to help this dude. But you sitting here telling us that you don't know him."

Isaac added to his mother's point, "He didn't need any help. And she had to know that, watching him beat down two dudes." He waved a finger to elaborate his point. "There's more to this story."

Gent had always been able to check Isaac without reprimand, and he did so now. "Shut up, boy!"

Janet threw up her hands. "Of course, always Noey's public defender!" She then gave their oldest cousin a get-your-head-out-of-the-clouds look before saying, "Gent, the goody, goody, good girl is lying! She's lying!"

Challenging her integrity was one of the surest ways to get a quick rise out of Novella. She pushed away from the table so far and hard that it slid forward against Cherry's middle. "Noey, girl . . . watch it! Watch what you doing. You all in my stomach."

Novella, jumping up from her seat, didn't notice her aunt's hurt or even hear her words. "You're a liar! And talking about boyfriends, Janet, how many have *you* messed around with?" Novella rushed over to the threshold shared by the dining and receiving room. Placing a hand on the wall, she leaned into the receiving room. "That's why you're probably on your second baby, because you lie about where you are, and you lie about who you're with. You even lie to yourself! So, mind your business and take your birth control pills! I'm not a freaking liar. You're the liar and we can all see that! He's right there . . . His name is Victor. And he doesn't have a daddy!"

Cherry hissed. "Noey, please! You not the one to be talking about who ain't got no daddy!"

Janet's eighteen-month-old son was next to her on the loveseat. He'd been looking out of the window. Excited by the yelling and hearing his name, he'd turned around and was now yelling back at Novella in baby jargon, all the while holding up his chubby arms for her to pick him up.

Janet threw back at Novella, "Granny had a baby at sixteen, so—" but was promptly shut down by Gent.

"So . . . so what? Girl, you shut your mouth. That's disrespectful. Your granny ain't your excuse for messing around!"

Janet, hurt, said, "Noey thinks she's better than all of us."

"Yes, she does," Cherry exclaimed as she snapped her fingers.

Her sister Connie, now with an unlit Newport between two fingers, shook her head. "She does not. Y'all tripping way too hard."

Novella was still furious. "I'm not lying." A bit winded and shaky from her flare-up, she returned to her seat and dropped down with a long exhale. "I don't know who you think you're fronting on, Janet, but you're just being cynical because you're a—" She stopped, knowing better than to finish the thought in front of Coddy Lee and Little Victor. So, instead, she finished it in her head, *a hoe.* With the exception of Little Victor, it was a thought heard by everyone. Entertained and shocked, they were barely able to repress their smiles, but there was an unspoken consensus not to stray from Novella's situation. Still, it was obvious everyone wanted to laugh except Coddy Lee, and Janet.

Cherry, however, still went at her. "I hope you can afford that ten-dollar word, smart girl." Cherry was referring to *cynical.*

Novella's calm, yet edgy, reply figuratively slapped a crisp ten spot in front of Cherry. "I know to how spell it, and know what it means. So, yeah, I can. I've been dotting my i's and crossing my t's for a long time now. Reading and writing *are* fundamental."

Cherry, who hadn't finished high school, got her meaning. "Yeah, okay, Noey girl. You real smart. But not smart enough. Not a few days ago, anyway."

Novella wanted to call her a dropout and a dummy and tell her what not being "smart enough" really meant—not getting pregnant as a teenager, not being a boo-boo weed head. That being smart enough meant having a job and stuff to do besides sitting around drinking and talking snot about everyone. She didn't, however. She was smart enough to know it would be going too far. Cherry was her aunt, her elder, and one of her granny's favorites. Novella did, however, give Cherry a very hard look.

For Novella, anger under continued stress always led to tears. She'd always been sensitive, and so learned to not so easily lose herself in emotion. She wanted to scream, "*Why is this family so messed up and stupid? Is everyone in here, except Gent, so dumb? Stop coming at me like this!*" Although starting to cry, she was maintaining some emotional control. She instead screamed, "*Doesn't anyone care that I was almost killed? They punched me. Slapped me, called me the B word! He slapped so many times and so hard! They were beating me up! Then that guy . . . He saved my life! But y'all acting like he did something wrong! Did y'all want me to die?*"

FIFTEEN

After a few nights in Mount Sinai Hospital, Coddy Lee had come to want her own bed and to be able to check on Willie more than she wanted answers. For the moment, Novella's tears had quieted everyone's curiosity. They knew Novella was still going through it hard, and today obviously wasn't a good day to push for details.

Coddy Lee had arranged, before her discharge, for a family meeting. She'd facilitated one every month to keep order in her home of contentious teenagers. For this meeting, she'd invited her daughters Connie and Cherry although they were grown and gone from her house. Coddy Lee thought, for this unusual situation, the more people involved, the faster the issue would be resolved. Now she realized she should have only invited her daughters, that her grans were a distraction. Specifically, Isaac and Janet. Coddy Lee respected Gent as peacekeeper, but thought him too soft on the girls. His empathy, she felt, changed the interrogation into a pity party. Answers meant more to Coddy Lee than Novella's feelings. Coddy Lee knew no other way of ensuring Novella wouldn't be the umpteenth teen mother in the family.

In spite of suspecting Novella of being inappropriately involved with a grown man, Coddy Lee believed her to be an obedient child. So, her getting a bit sassy and withdrawn when emotionally charged always got her a temporary pass. Actually, she felt Novella had a better attitude than most of the family and was easier to manage. Adjourning the meeting for the day, Coddy Lee pushed up from her throne. Trimmed in faux wood, the upholstered chair fitted with a gray corduroy fabric was her seat of choice when not in her bedroom. She had to be upstairs or out of the house for anyone else to dare sit in it.

"Heading up, Mama?" Connie stood up with her cigarette back between her fingers and a lighter in her opposite hand.

"Wore out," Coddy Lee replied. Everyone understood she'd soon be sound asleep.

A scattered chorus of goodnights from her children and grandchildren rang out. From her tiny great-grand came, "Night night."

The stairway was behind Coddy Lee. As she turned away from everyone and toward it, Gent began to follow her. "You want anything else?"

"Uh-uh," she told him.

As she ascended the stairs, Gent began his status report, "Willie's bathed and on clean sheets."

Coddy Lee thanked him. "Good, I'm glad you could still do it."

Gent continued, "Nurse stopped in on him yesterday and this morning. And the landlord came by. Told me to tell you he'll replace that back fence in a few weeks."

Gent placed a hand on her back to support her climb, which was a challenge given her general achiness and the tightness in her hips, buttocks, thighs, and calves. The push Coddy Lee got out of them a few days ago, for sake of Novella, would not be soon forgotten. Knowingly, Gent coaxed her, "And, Mama, you good to go on ahead and lay it down. There's nothing you need to do right now. Call it a night, baby."

Coddy Lee exhaled deeply. "I do mean to."

As they rounded the staircase toward the second landing, he assured her, "I'll keep the kids quiet." Included in that promise were his aunts, who he knew were good for a few beers before they themselves would call it a night. "No one has been in your room except Noey." He ushered Coddy Lee up the last step. "She kept herself locked in there, so it's probably cleaner than how you left it." Novella had assumed the duty of cleaning Coddy Lee's room when she'd come to live with her a few years ago. For years, Connie had assumed the responsibility for Coddy Lee's laundry, and Cherry had run errands for her. Gent took care of the heavy lifting, repairs, and the things the others felt themselves incapable, above, or unable to stomach— such as assisting with Willie. After he assured Coddy Lee that Willie knew she was back home, Gent would tuck her in.

As she sat on her bed stripped down to her cone cup brassiere and knee-length bloomers, Gent handed her one of the many floral gowns from her top dresser drawer. Gent helped fit and power on the oxygen mask for her sleep apnea, and then stayed with his granny until just a few moments before she closed her eyes. Leaving her to sleep, he adjusted her door so that, when her eyes reopened, they would have a clear view of Willie across the hall.

SIXTEEN

Downstairs, Connie stepped out on the porch to finally light her Newport, followed by Cherry. The sisters would talk, the subject matter depending on who joined them and who was likely to overhear their conversation. Eleven months apart, they were close enough for love and loyalty to prevent any consideration of whether or not they actually liked one another. Connie's own opinions were often in opposition to Cherry's. The two, nonetheless, were able to disagree and argue while remaining best friends and confidants.

Janet, handing her son to Novella, who happily took him, followed them in the hope of hearing some uncensored and unchecked trash talk about Novella.

Connie's Newport finally lit, she was taking her third drag when Janet came out and stood beside her. "Let me get a hit, Auntie."

Connie handed her the cigarette. "You really think Noey go with that dude?"

Although doubting it was true, the idea made Janet jealous. "Her pubic hair probably ain't as thick as his mustache."

Cherry, who stood on the other side of Connie, shrugged. "Getting some grown dick will grow a bush on it. She might be cutting school to spread her legs for him. Hell, we all did it."

Connie had doubts. "Not Noey. She too deep in her books."

"She's only merit roll, As and Bs," Janet reminded them. "Now me, I was honor roll. Straight As, baby. And let me tell you both something: smart people get laid like everyone else in the world."

Connie took back her cigarette. "You just jealous."

Janet hissed, "Please! Jealous of what? Noey's a skinny, stuck-up prude. If she is as smart as everyone thinks she is, then she *is* giving BETY Junior some. His sexy ass. He's a good catch. His family owns a lot of businesses."

Connie was not convinced. "Well, I don't think Noey thinks like that."

"But she might be grateful," Cherry told her sister. "So, if he wasn't already getting it, she's probably gonna let his ass have it now. Probably feels like she owe him. And when you think about it, what a dude gotta do to earn some coochie? He saved her life, right? That's the story we all running with, right? So, what chic wouldn't want to do it with the good-looking dude who will to throw down for her? Kill for her."

Janet smiled. "I'll pay him back for her. I just might hunt that fine dick down."

"Girl, you too grown!" Connie laughed at Janet while looking at her sister Cherry. Their niece had long exalted herself their equal in sexual maturity but could still surprise them.

"Don't you mean slutty?" Cherry laughed. "Slow yourself down, niece. You got plenty of time."

Janet felt no shame. "I'm not doing anything y'all didn't do at my age."

Isaac eased out on the porch. "Y'all talking 'bout Noey?" Before they could answer, he positioned himself between them. "She got a bad attitude, right?"

Connie shrugged at her nephew. "Runs in the family."

He agreed, "Yeah, okay." But countered, "She was real funky in the family meeting. Extra funky!"

Connie, after exhaling a long smoke ring, said, "Probably just tired." She then added, "I think Gent may have been right, though. She shouldn't have been asked in front of everybody."

Janet disagreed, "Well, if she didn't have anything to hide, what's the big deal?"

Isaac looked to Janet. "She got in your behind deep, didn't she? Straight fronted on you."

Janet, not liking the reminder, didn't reply. Her irritation wasn't lost on any of them, including Isaac, who now decided to rephrase his point. "It wasn't right how she dissed you like that in front of everybody. Yelling at you in front of your baby."

Janet accepted the roundabout apology. "I don't care what anybody thinks about what I do, but Noey does need to check her snooty attitude."

Connie's second cigarette was shared by all four of them as they stood in a circle. Puff to puff, they continued to feed off each other's opinions. They had been on the porch for a few hours when Coddy Lee's oldest son, Merv, rounded the corner. Parallel parking with a lead foot, he swerved more than necessary. He backed the 1986 Ford Taurus in between two cars across the street. His sisters, niece and nephew gave each other knowing looks. *He was a show-off.* As he exited the car, the brilliant shine of his loafers was cause for another shared look.

"Poetic," Isaac sang to his mother, who agreed.

"Always. Big bro always clean."

Connie and Janet were not as impressed but unable to deny that Merv was meticulous. Bad hygiene, wrinkles, scuffs, and all things unkempt were blasphemies to Merv Lofton Junior. Making his way over to the porch, his white teeth gave an illuminating accent to his smooth dark skin. He smiled, "Hey, hey! What's happening, fam?" Merv hadn't been invited to the family meeting, yet he had heard about the reason for it. He was there to find his role in the drama.

SEVENTEEN

Novella heard her uncle's voice out on the porch. She knew her aunts had stayed on to gossip about her business, and Novella now figured their piss would be richer for it. Uncle Merv, being the show-off he was, never arrived empty-handed. His generosity, uncapped as soon as Coddy Lee was out of sight, usually poured from one of two bottles: the long neck calabash of E & J Brandy, or the embroidered flask of Seagram's Gin. At least half a bottle of whichever of the two he was favoring at the moment was brought for sharing, usually tucked under his left arm. He prided himself in treating his sisters up from their usual Colt 45 and Miller. Occasionally, he enthralled them with the last swallows of his velvet-bagged Crown Royal or his Jack Daniels Black Label. Whiskey wasn't their forte, but Merv knew they wouldn't turn down a drink they otherwise couldn't afford. Grey Goose and Bacardi Rum, more to their liking, were brought untapped as birthday or Christmas gifts. Merv, considering himself a sort of connoisseur, criticized the cheaper liquor their boyfriends brought to the table as rock gut. "Fools might as well be drinking lighter fluid." He advised his baby sisters to aim higher. "Men that poor who still wanna drink are petty and will always be poor." Merv also enjoyed sharing his reefer joints, but often being laced with cocaine, they weren't always accepted.

"Where's my pretty niece?" he said as he paraded through the door into the receiving room. "Noey, they told me some rogues got after you."

Rocking little Victor to sleep, Novella was to his left in the living room. She sat on the end of the couch furthest from the threshold. "Yep," she answered flatly.

"You alright?" He strutted over with more effort than needed for the five or so steps it took to reach her.

"Yep, I made it. I'm okay." Novella squeezed Little Victor a bit tighter, hoping to be left to her baby rocking. She feared being put on trial again, being further scrutinized. She hoped the brown paper bag her uncle carried wouldn't allow him to get too comfortable talking to her. Merv, obviously in no hurry to get his little party on, plopped down beside her. Novella's heart sank with the couch pillows. As usual, her uncle's cologne was refreshing—unlike him. Amusing himself, he told her, "Well, your uncle can't blame them for trying, but I'd still shoot them." Amusing himself further, he laughed, "I get it from my mama." He then looked around. "And where is that pistol-packing woman? Granny on Patrol. My gangsta mama."

"She went to bed, Unc," Isaac said as he came in from the porch, followed by the others.

"Good for her," Merv replied before refocusing his attention on Novella. "Well, niece, if you want your first drink tonight, it's on your Unc. Ain't nobody gonna blame you. Or tell Mama on you." Stretching his neck, he beckoned the family for confirmation. "Right? Ain't no one gonna tell Mama?"

A jumble of "I ain't got nothing to do with it," "That's her business," "Whatever" came back to him.

Merv then offered, "I can run and get a pack of wine coolers, if you want something softer than this E & J."

Novella didn't take long to answer. "No thank you, Uncle Merv."

"Prude." She heard Janet whisper. Because of the mixed company, she replied only in her head, *Hoe*.

Her uncle stayed at her side for a little while, babbling about the nature of men being lustful yet also misunderstood, how women created sin and thus are always subjected to it even when they're not being intentionally provocative, as the very nature of a woman is provocative. Novella had just leaned forward to stand up and escape whatever nonsense she felt him trying to convince her of when Cherry called him into the dining room. "Bro, come on with the drank. Noey's had enough attention for today. And, as a matter of fact, her attitude earlier said she was done talking."

Merv stood. "Here I come, Sis." Before leaving the room, he gave Novella a wink, "We'll talk later."

No, we won't, she replied in her head, though she knew they would.

Now free of her uncle, she kissed Little Victor's tiny nose in relief before turning her attention back to the television. She saw that a rerun of Sanford and Son, one of her family's favorite shows, had come on. Novella tried to get lost in the episode, but before long, her eyes were staring blankly at the screen. In her daze, she heard Gent say something to her she couldn't process as anything other than an encouraging chuckle. Then she heard the welcoming chatter of him joining Uncle Merv and crew at the dining table. A bit later, as she emerged from the daze, she heard the kitchen door whining. Familiarity with her family's habits put the smell of reefer in her nose, and the image of Gent and Merv standing in the backyard in her mind.

Novella's eyelids had grown as heavy as Little Victor's resting body, which was wearing out the crook of her arm. Both her and the baby needed lying down, but Novella had no intention of heading upstairs.

Her granny was home now, so now Novella had to go back to her own room. Sleeping in Coddy Lee's bed made Novella feel as loved as she had when Coddy Lee had come for her, as loved as she had felt when hearing Cherry brag, "Yeah, damn rogues need to recognize that we come for ours! Always! We don't need the po po!" Novella, for the first time, had felt part of a tribe. Contrary to what her family thought, Novella didn't want to be away from them—only their contempt. Novella wanted them to be better about the situation, loving. She laid her second cousin down on couch, and then placed pillows in front of it just in case he rolled onto the floor. She stood up and looked down at him, contemplating where to go in the house and what to do when she got there. Novella wanted to fill her friends in on what had happened, but knew she was still too much the point of interest. She barely had the emotional energy to tell them the story, so definitely not enough for an encrypted phone conversation. Nosiness must have been an inherited trait, Novella figured, because no one in the family had any shame when it came to eavesdropping. No one except her.

She decided to take company in the quiet comings and goings of her neighbors and went out onto the porch. She sat in the chair that gave the widest view of her street, 70th, and Hough Avenue, which was to her right. She felt a presence on the porch to her left. It didn't bother her; she knew those particular neighbors wouldn't disturb her. The elderly couple were always friendly and didn't ever impose.

EIGHTEEN

Novella stayed outside long enough to grow uncomfortable in the plastic chair. Her head was now resting on her arms, which were folded atop the banister. The heaviness of sleep weighing heavily on her body, she stood wearily before walking slowly toward the door. She only went as far as the middle of the porch before wrapping an arm around the porch column and looking up at sky with a soft smile. The moon was a golden globe, and so big and clear it looked as if climbing on a rooftop or up a hill would enable her to reach it. Her eyes were still admiring it when her uncle Merv creeped out from the house. Novella didn't hear him until he was beside her. "Not as pretty as you," he whispered, startling her. Novella's gasp made him chuckle, but didn't distract him. "You like older men?"

Even though she couldn't see much of him in the darkness, his intentions were still clear, the question within the question. Anxiety replaced her fatigue. *Is this really happening?*

"That's what your aunties and cousins are saying," Merv went on. "That you don't mess with boys. That you might even mess someone my age."

Novella turned backed to the moon. "They say a lot of things."

Her uncle stepped in closer. "I'm curious."

Walking off the porch into the night was a thought in Novella's mind, as were the words, *Yes, this is happening! He's trying to get with me.* Novella would have never imagined that a man so fine and desired would have in him the kind of wickedness she associated with sickness and desperation—incest. Novella knew her uncle to be the type of man who always had a woman, a backup, and one on standby. With her own eyes, she had witnessed him slyly slipping his hands into women's blouses and between their legs. Beautiful, shapely, grown women who also took liberties with their own hands, inspecting and being impressed. Novella had overheard the results of these raunchy exchanges, and, per the gossip, Merv was a great lover. He didn't have to chase women. He wasn't desperate. Novella had also witnessed teen girls gushing over him, but never imagined he took them seriously. *So, what if he did?* She now figured. *I've never tried to entice him.*

As if reading her mind, Merv grabbed her arm just as she was about to turn toward the door. He then pushed her hard enough to walk her, against her will, back into the corner she'd come from. "You ain't gotta be ashamed with me. Women in this family don't usually hold their virginity no longer than fourteen, fifteen. And I see you as one of our women. You ain't in diapers no more." He took both her hands and brought them so close to his face she feared he might kiss them. Instead, he inspected her nails. "They say you almost scratched the life out of the little one. Had his skin and blood under these long things of yours." He chuckled. "First thing I'd do, girl . . . is cut these nails. Or maybe, I'll bite them off." He cocked his head backwards. "But you wouldn't hurt your uncle Merv, would ya?" When she didn't answer, his hands tightened around hers. "Would ya?" She tried pulling away, but he held her tight. After a moment he asked, "Tell the truth: you still a virgin?" Again, she pulled, but still he held her. "Most girls your age have already had sex. All your aunties and cousins were messing around at your age—and younger. Your own mama. And I know you know about your granny. She got married when I was already in her belly. Pssst, girl, don't act like you think I'm lying." Merv swung her hands as if they were enjoying a playful exchange. "Have you at least given it some thought?'

Novella, refusing to become a pawn in his word game, kept her lips tight. It was all she could think to do. Screaming for help seemed premature. Besides, today's family meeting confirmed the burden of proof would be on her.

Merv's thick hands, locked around Novella's, did not caress. Still, their warmth melted the chill that had set into her body from the night air. An invasion—Novella felt Merv was all over her, his cologne molesting her sense of smell. Novella didn't realize she was squirming until Merv finally released her hands. With a gasp, Novella fell back with clumsy steps. Rushing into the house, she was met by Isaac. He was en route to the porch to remind their uncle of his year-old promise to teach him and the others how to play gin rummy. Novella's panicked appearance quickly drained his enthusiasm. He gave a quick look behind her, seeing their uncle just as the screen door closed. Isaac's lanky frame shifted from side to side a few times, his love-hate ratio with Novella fluctuating with his movement, going from 20 percent to 80 percent on the love side of the scale. Isaac placed a hand on her shoulder to inquire after her, but his own fear shamed them both out of acknowledgment of their uncle's inappropriateness. He was just a year older than Novella was and had no more of an idea what to do about incest than she did. She was running and, in a way, so was he. Kind words were all Isaac had the courage for. "You not tired, cuz? Girl, you gotta be. Better go on upstairs and get some rest."

Novella related to the feeling of inadequacy exuding from her cousin, so she absolved his cowardly avoidance with a soft reply. Using their granny's lingo she said, "I do mean to."

NINETEEN

Merv, alone on the porch, started to light a cigarette when the smoke from another one hit his nostrils. He turned quickly to his left, finding a woman on the next porch. Even in the darkness, he could tell she was stamping out her cigarette in an ashtray. He wondered how he had missed the smell. Thinking about his advances, which he had presumed hidden by the night, he grew uneasy. He awaited the outcome of her unknown presence. Wordlessly, it began as she stood up from her low chair. He was surprised to see her rise to a height that nearly matched his own of five-foot-nine. Her narrow face, outlined by the streetlight, was a shadow behind wide-rimmed glasses. It was fixed on Merv. He could feel her contempt for him, and he imagined hard eyes full of judgement. Her weighted silence was broken with words laden with disgust, as if regurgitated from a spoiled stomach, "Good evening and good night, you dirty-ass dog!" She then turned and opened her screen door. Reaching inside her house, she flicked on her porch light and then turned back to face Merv, boldly giving a full account of who had called him out.

Merv's fist balled, breaking his cigarette, the lit portion burning out on the porch in front his shoes. The fire in the ash flickered for about five seconds before he stamped it out. He wanted to do the same to the old woman. Being of the mind that all females need it from time to time, Merv had a troubled past with women that wasn't far enough behind him. He had warrants in Florida, Alabama, and Mississippi. As things were, all he could do was stare back at the audacious woman. If she were one of his drinking buddies, or lovers, he'd already be standing over, beating an apology out of her. Finally, to his relief, she flicked off her porch light and returned defiantly into her home. Merv was shaking and didn't want to enter the house so upset. As this wasn't an encounter he could openly discuss, he went for another cigarette to find calm. After about four drags, he had a bit of it, but still held enough hostility to murmur, "Old bitch."

TWENTY

The Next Day
Monday, April 22, 1991

"Pop!" BETY Junior yelled for the fifth time. "Damn, do I need a bell? Pop!"

His grandpop entered the room just seconds later. "Are you for real with all this noise? Shut the hell up!"

BETY Junior gave a playfully serious look. "Whoa, bedside manner! Is this how you provide care to the injured?"

His grandpop sat next to him on the bed. "How about I injure your smart mouth with my cane?"

BETY Junior, in spite of his bruised ribs, laughed. "You mean that fancy stick you pretend to need, but is actually a conversation starter? The only thing that expensive floorboard is holding up, Mr. Silver-and-Suave, is your ego."

His grandpop stared at him. "Who in the hell do you think you're talking to?"

BETY Junior stared back. "A pimp!"

They both then laughed until BETY Junior bellowed in pain.

Immediately, his grandpop reached for the ibuprofen. "What you get for having such a smart mouth."

"Pop, I feel like I'm burning on the inside," BETY Junior moaned.

His grandpop, crushing the 800-mg tablet, empathized with him. "It's a shame none of the good cops I know were there to stop that nonsense. I'm sorry, son. I'm so sorry, but not sorry you helped a little lady in big trouble. More people need to do the right thing. She'd be dead if it wasn't for you. The way you said she fought, she wasn't going to make it easy on them. And cowards don't like that, so they would've had their way with her and killed her fast."

In the fold of a square scrap of aluminum foil, he handed the pill powder to BETY Junior. After loading it on his tongue, BETY Junior accepted the water Pop had brought in with him.

Medicine down, Pop asked, "Dinner?"

BETY Junior handed him the now-empty glass. "Hopefully not eating by myself again."

"I'm in the entire tonight," Pop replied, and then waited. When he didn't get an answer, he growled. "What son? What do you want to eat?"

BETY Junior stroked his goatee. "Oxtails and rice . . . and cornbread with green bean and tomato stew."

"Tails will go better with biscuits or loaf bread," Pop suggested.

He was immediately countered by his sarcastic patient who told him, "Well, sir, when you ask versus tell someone what they want, you have to accept their answer. Cornbread, sir. I would like cornbread . . . and thank you."

They briefly shared a look before Pop warned, "You know there's no one here to save you from me. And I doubt you could make it out of this house, even to a phone, before I broke your narrow behind . . . with my fancy stick."

"Floorboard," BETY Junior reminded him. "Your fancy floorboard. It's a carved and painted two by four."

Pop warned him again, "Keep it at, boy."

BETY Junior picked up and waved his new mobile phone. "I'll call 976-KIDS on you."

"Nobody's coming to save your grown ass from me," Pop told him.

"As my nurse, you have a duty to provide care." BETY Junior lay back, trying to get comfortable amongst his pillows and covers. "So, just do the right thing here. The ethical thing. Instead of making threats, fluff my pillows."

Pop waved a fist in the air.

"Thou shall do no harm," BETY Junior laughed. "You know what, let's just hire out. Get a fine sista in here to fluff and all that. A fine, thick woman with a very good and very warm bedside manner. I'd heal so much faster, and you could back go doing whatever old, cranky people do."

Pop gave up and headed out of the room to go start dinner. It was early in the day, but oxtails took time.

Just as he reached the door, BETY Junior changed his mind on the cornbread, "Biscuits, please."

"Yep," Pop replied not missing a step, "I had no intention of making cornbread."

BETY Junior smiled. "Thanks. And I love you, Pop!"

"You're welcome . . . and of course you do." His grandpop disappeared to the kitchen.

When BETY Junior was finally able to rest without pain, he drifted off to sleep to one of the best aromas in his world: rosemary, garlic, onions, and other earthy ingredients making love to rounds of beef. He awoke aching for his dinner and another dose of ibuprofen, but first needed to relieve his bladder. His grandpop at his side was ready to assist.

The bathroom trip was taxing even with Pop's help, but he was rewarded with more pill powder, which quieted his pain. The food, however, made him louder.

"Yes, Lord!" he said as he bit into the juicy meat. "Let the church say, 'Amen!' Amen!"

Pop, spooning rice and oxtail bits with a biscuit, could only shake his head and smile at his grandson's satisfaction.

About three hours later, BETY Junior was asleep. The need to release the last fluids he'd consumed before nodding off awoke him around ten. He heard his grandpop moving around the house and didn't like it. Pop was usually in REM sleep by now, rejuvenating his good-as-gold spirit. BETY Junior worried he was a burden. His Pop-Pop was strong, but still an old guy.

BETY Junior, deciding he was able enough for a go to the toilet on his own, began carefully inching from his bed. Feet on the floor, by the light of a nightlight, he got one foot moving after the other. He was getting along fine in the near darkness until he reached for the support of a dresser that he didn't know had been moved to give Pop more room to be his nurse and human crutch. BETY Junior extended an arm, leaning his aching body toward where his muscle memory told him the five-drawer-tall oak dresser was. Finding nothing there, he lost his balance and dropped to the floor, making three bangs against the wall. "Gotdamn it!"

He was still on the floor groaning when Pop appeared at the doorway, "Aw, son, don't be a jackass. Why bother when I'm right here? Right here, boy."

"Just trying to make it to the bathroom. You need to rest, Pop."

Kneeling down beside him, Pop told him, "Well, I won't be able to rest if I'm stuck repairing the wall and scrubbing your piss out of the carpet."

BETY Junior, defeated by pain and reason, didn't argue.

"Get up, son," Pop offered his support. "Come on. You won't be hurting for much longer. Until then, lean on me."

TWENTY-ONE

BETY Junior, in spite of still feeling fire throughout his upper torso, was up on his own within a week.

By the doctor's orders, there was to be no boxing, running, or any other strenuous exercise. Just as well, BETY Junior broke a sweat doing simple things. Good hygiene was a labor of love. He was weaning himself off the ibuprofen, but alcohol was still off the menu. As were women since there was no main woman. He had women to take the edge off and kick it with, but none to earnestly comfort him.

In the middle of week three, he was back to jogging lightly and training clients who didn't need him to spot them on heavy lifts.

When completely healed, at least physically, he was due in the criminal division of the Cuyahoga County Municipal Court. He came with the hope of seeing the little pompom girl. A few times, BETY Junior had nightmares in which they were both killed by the police. He knew that seeing her at the court would be healing. He'd found out that Novella Renae Lofton was her name. A minor, as he had figured, she was seven years younger than him.

Wednesday, September 25, 1991

BETY Junior, hearing the squeaking of the courtroom doors, turned around from the defense table. Eager, with an unabashed show of interest, he would do this several times. Though he had been a champion athlete, her rescue was the only challenge where his winning truly meant every-thing. No referees, no safeguards, no backup. The only reward he wanted was to see the life he saved prosper. His anticipation spread throughout the courtroom. Others, watching him watching the door, began to watch the door themselves.

BETY Junior nearly missed Novella's entrance, as it was preceded by a stocky, wide-hipped woman. Novella's slim frame, hidden by her girth, was exposed by a black purse. BETY Junior saw her fuchsia-painted fin-gernails in one of the quick dips of the stocky woman's hips. Novella was dressed like a junior professional in a long-sleeved, button-down blouse tucked into a knee-length pencil skirt. She came into full view after advanc-ing past the first two rows. Nervousness appearing to be her only ailment, she glowed like the unmarred princess BETY Junior remembered her to be. She was guided toward the front where he sat. Ready to exchange the pleasantries of those meeting again after surviving a feat, he stood up. He sat back down realizing he was being dogged by the hippy woman. An identification card hung from a dog chain around her thick neck. Brenda Marble, Cuyahoga County Department of Children Services, was printed under the picture of a face that looked a lot friendlier than the one she was giving BETY Junior. The words, "No, no, no, and no," emanated from a scowl, creased by too many layers of makeup. BETY Junior realized the princess wasn't just being led, she was being guarded. Following her was an older woman whom she greatly resembled. BETY Junior guessed Novella to be that woman's last child, likely born when the woman was around the age of forty. The maternal figure relayed her own subliminal message to

BETY Junior: *Stay back from her, rogue.* A third woman, who appeared to be entertained by it all, walked in behind the maternal figure.

Novella was sat in the first row, right behind BETY Junior. The low wooden banister that separated the bench seats from the courtroom floor would have easily allowed for a gracious handshake or a hug. BETY Junior, however, knew it was best to obey the implied restraining order. The age difference between him and Novella was small enough for genuine mutual attraction, romantic or platonic. It was, however, still large enough to make him a criminal should he act on it. Bariah Elijah Tomas Young Junior knew he already had enough to contend with on the day's docket.

TWENTY-TWO

The cause of death for Michael "Milky" White was asthma exacerbation. BETY Junior had dropped him by beating his torso like a drum before delivering two incredibly hard blows to his stomach. The pain and lack of oxygen lowered Milky into a standing fetal position, from which he fell onto his left side. BETY Junior had heard his wheezing, but Novella had remained his priority. Damon "Yank" Taylor had run out of the driveway, and BETY Junior knew he was after her.

Catching and subduing Yank didn't take long, nor was it strenuous. BETY Junior didn't remember Milky until seeing him being carried away in a body bag. By that time, he was hoping not to share the same fate. As far as what happened to Milky, BETY Junior had no regrets. A choice between a lowlife and an innocent is an easy one.

When court was over, BETY Junior hugged Pop. While shaking his lawyer's hand, he couldn't help but scan the room for Novella. She was being quickly ushered out of the courtroom. BETY Junior noticed her sly attempt, in spite of being rushed out, to make eye contact with him. She was not sly enough as she tripped at the end of the row on a hump where the carpet ended and the tile of the main aisle began. Her two female escorts mildly scolded her to pay better attention.

TWENTY-THREE

The following morning, Pop and BETY Junior sat in the breakfast nook, their favorite place to eat and talk.

Pop asked, "Still thinking about her?"

BETY Junior, cutting into a stack of waffles, paused, resting his wrists against the tabletop edge. "Yeah, sure."

Pop poured himself a cup of tea. "She's very pretty."

BETY Junior, taking a bite of his waffles, agreed, "And young."

"So are you." Pop spooned honey into his tea.

BETY Junior shook his head at his grandpop's implication. "Mr. Matchmaker. I'm an adult, and that's how I'll be charged if I mess with her. And I just beat a wrap. Are you trying to get me brought up on more charges?"

Pop sat back in his chair. "I'm trying to have a conversation with you."

BETY Junior sat up taller in his own. "Alright, Pop-Pop. Yes, I'm still thinking about her, but not like that."

"Oh, no? Why not?"

"You're serious?"

Pop explained, "In about a year or so, she'll be eighteen. No longer too young for you, just younger than you. And there most likely won't be much difference in the way she looks then from how she looks now. So, yes, Bariah, I am serious. I saw her grandmama in court with her. The girl takes after that weathered fox, so I know she's sure to fill out her curves nicely."

BETY Junior waited for him to make his point.

Pop gave it, "Listen here, son . . . Hear me when I speak. Our laws can change and change, but they're just ideas. Many don't even represent the ideas of the majority, so the majority of us will always progress slower than the latest idea of how we're supposed to act. Passing a law doesn't automatically change our nature, just the consequences for it. And in my day, which wasn't so long ago, a fella your age marrying a girl her age was commonplace. Yeah, I want to know if you're interested. Be surprised if you're not. The girl's a looker."

BETY Junior told him, "Well, Pop-Pop, don't fall out your chair, because I'm not interested. I didn't help her because I wanted her for myself."

Pop smiled. "That I know, son. You're a good person through and through, and I am proud of you. Every day, I am."

BETY Junior smiled. "Thanks."

Pop nodded a welcome, and then continued, "Bariah, son, what I'm asking is if during or after it all, did something click between you two? Girl in trouble; boy saves girl. Boy and girl fall . . . Well, you know the rest."

BETY Junior conceded, "Well, if she was taller, thicker, wasn't carrying pompoms, and was *older*, then, yeah, she could've gotten the business. But she didn't fit the profile. So, no click, no tap, no knock-knock. Just me helping her out."

Pop nodded. "Alright, Bariah."

Pop stared out of the picture window that had a view of the large magnolia tree that stood between the east side of Pop's house and his neighbor's garage. Pop studied the magnolia's leaves, which had turned from deep green to amber. Pop was relieved his grandson wasn't romanced by the emotional charge of rescuing a pretty girl. However, he felt the air was still moist with his grandson's sweat and the girl's tears—from their shared struggle. It was something that had just happened. There was still time, Pop figured, for feelings to develop, especially now that his Bariah had healed, physically, from the police beating. It would be natural for him to want to seek out the *not-so-young* girl. Waiting months and months for a nearly grown female's age to catch up with her mature body could prove too long and too hard for any man, even in situations where there was no shared traumatic experience.

Clearing his throat, BETY Junior turned Pop's attention away from the tree. BETY Junior, after downing a swallow of orange juice, said, "Now, baby girl is as cute as most pompom girls, but I don't do cute. And, Pop, you should know that from the brick houses you've seen me with. You know how I do."

Pop huffed. "Well, you're such a slut I can barely get a good look at any one of them before you're off humping a different one."

BETY Junior forked up some waffle and a piece of sausage. "My, my, my, you're so vulgar. We're a church-going, God-fearing family. Yes, sir, we are. So, I don't know what's the problem with your mouth. I hope you're not spewing that sinful language when you're teaching in Bible study, *Deacon Young.*"

Pop, grabbing a sausage link from his plate, said easily, "Bariah, sometimes I regret not kicking your ass more when I was bringing you up."

BETY Junior told him, "No worries, Pop-Pop. No, sir, you raised a fine, wholesome boy." Then, to further vex his grandpop, he winked, "I'd make any deacon proud, so be encouraged. Yes, indeed. Let the church say 'Amen' on that. Amen, amen, and amen. I'm such a nice guy."

TWENTY-FOUR

Saturday, September 28, 1991

"Young men aren't nice; they're horny" was Coddy Lee's summation. At Novella's age, she wasn't shaking pompoms and mall-shopping with friends. She never had pompoms, and she didn't have any friends. She had a husband and Merv Junior, the first of nine in her womb.

Coddy Lee, a child of the Depression, grew up quickly to be the little woman of the house while her widowed mother labored long hours as a house maid. Nevertheless, Coddy Lee developed into a hormonal teenager. As spying neighbors could attest, she'd tried to outsmart her pubescent urges with kissing, heavy petting, and dry humping. She hadn't realized Mother Nature was smarter, an ancient genius.

Coddy Lee soon went from feeding her younger brother at her mother's table to feeding him alongside her own child at a table provided by her husband. Her schoolbooks, left behind in a modest room shared with her brother, along with other belongings such as her sticker collection and jacks game set, aged into the vintage whatnots of a forsaken youth. Coddy Lee's education ended the second semester of her sophomore year. There was a reformatory for pregnant teens, but Coddy Lee didn't go there, because Merv had married her. She wasn't the county's welfare case; she was Merv's responsibility. With both her mother and husband working, Coddy Lee, raised a domestic, would remain one. Her youth surrendered to babies and to men, she became fairly jaded on the specific correlation between the two: the science of one springing from the other. Relieved of birthing babies since 1962, Coddy Lee now peered out of her bedroom window and into the afternoon activities of her neighbors. Reflecting more than spying, she shook her head from side to side in disbelief of the chasteness of BETY Junior's intent. *Young men aren't nice; they're horny.*

In her bedroom, Coddy Lee sat in the chair nearest the window, diagonal from Novella, who sat in a chair near the door. Cherry, on the edge of Coddy Lee's bed, was between them. Voicing her mother's skepticism, Cherry was questioning Novella.

"I haven't did it with anyone," Novella blushed defensively. Aside from self-exploration, she'd had no sex life. No one but her had touched her, and she had no immediate intention to change that.

"He's tried, though?" Cherry assumed. "Nature of a man. You old enough to know that."

Novella was as tired of the accusations as she was of hearing herself say, "I don't know him. He's had no chance. I don't spend time with him. It's not like that."

Cherry looked to Coddy Lee, who turned from the window, showing her doubtful face. She then went back to gazing through the parted curtains. Cherry, recognizing her mother's cue to continue, refocused her attention on Novella.

Cherry hoped to frustrate her niece into a confession, thinking the worst truths come out when people get mad. Hot-headedness was a family trait. Coddy Lee's grandmother, Dottie, said it was caused by an inherited quart or so of the devil's blood. Dottie said having it inside them was no different than having the genes for diabetes, and so called it an honest demon.

Novella had more than once screamed at Isaac loud and long enough to still the house into an awkward silence. "Noey can really get beside herself sometimes." It was often said of her, followed by, "Yeah, but you know she got it honest." This was surprising to Novella, who didn't think that way of herself. She'd heard how Connie and Cherry used to have tantrums as children, especially when fighting one another. Novella hadn't fought anyone in her family. Coddy Lee, however, would remind her that liquid wasn't the only components of Novella's blood; a demon was in there as well—and could never be bled out.

Novella had come home upset from school one day because her least favorite teacher had told her, "You have a bad attitude, Novella Renae Lofton." She'd rushed straight into Coddy Lee's room to complain.

After hearing her out, Coddy Lee turned back to her soap opera. "You should have told her you got it honest. Bad attitudes run in the family. And if you're doing your work, then that teacher of yours need to shut her damn mouth."

Cherry, deciding now was the right time to bring out Novella's bad attitude, her honest demon, told her, "Don't forget, *I* was there in court with you and Mama, and I saw how the dude's eyes were all over you. And the police said y'all were holding hands when they arrived. Probably the reason they beat his ass. They knew by looking at him he was too old to be touching you."

The words "they beat his ass," as well as the inflection with which they were flung, incited a rapid flashback of heartbreaking moments. Novella's chocolate skin took on a red undertone.

Excited by the show of color, Cherry stoked the fire, "They were right to *beat* his grown ass. Hell, as if there ain't plenty of grown women out there for him to screw around with. He's just playing with you anyway. You're too young for anything else."

Cherry's manner with Novella didn't come from a place of hate. She was their Noey girl; she belonged to them. So, her good had to serve them, even more than it served her. While Novella didn't have to be just like them, neither could she be any better. Novella could tell Cherry was itching to say her usual, "We all were hot in the ass at your age, and you ain't no betta," though Novella also knew Cherry wouldn't dare. The statement would also implicate her own mama, Coddy Lee, who married to legitimatize the result of being, as she called it, "hot in the ass."

Cherry, barely out of a training bra when she had Isaac, had left him with Coddy Lee, "not feeling ready to parent, to do a good job." Now seventeen years and two more children later, her parenting skills were still no less juvenile. Novella was more mature and more clever than Cherry. Even pulling rank as auntie, Cherry usually couldn't win with her. Always too eager, she spoke before she thought. Novella always proved her wrong. Today, Coddy Lee had given Cherry an advantage: she could cross-examine her niece, with no consequences, as Novella was already presumed guilty. This time there wasn't to be any interference. The house was full, yet all residents aside from Coddy Lee, Novella, and Willie were downstairs. Gent and Isaac both were entertaining company. Janet and Lil Victor were on the front porch waiting on a ride. Still, as an added measure, Cherry had closed Coddy Lee's bedroom door. She was determined to get a confession from Novella.

TWENTY-FIVE

Novella had been ambushed after returning home from work. She hadn't long removed her McDonald's uniform, bathed, and slipped on jeans and a sweater, when she was once again put on trial in the Lofton family court. She had planned to meet her best friends Yadara and Ardellya, aka Dell, downtown. They were going to eat hot subs at Mr. Hero's, and then head to the Tower City's cinema to watch Child's Play 3. At seventeen, they weren't old enough to get into the R-rated movie. Dell's older brother, a cashier at the cinema, had promised to sell them the tickets and get them in. Novella was digging in her caboodle for the glitter nail polish she was to loan to Yadara when Coddy Lee called her across the hall.

Novella tried to stay calm as she was being cross-examined by her aunt. She couldn't, of course. The abduction attempt was still giving her nightmares, as well as daymares. "I don't want to die." She'd occasionally whisper to herself. Her family's reaction to the abduction attempt was giving her grief. Inside, Novella was a rolling boil. Novella's Honest Demon had burned most of what could've resulted in tears in the months since the attack. So, Novella wasn't so much prone to pitiful crying fits as she was to angry outbursts.

Eye to eye with her aunt, Novella's Honest Demon was trying to take over and do the talking. Radiating like a pair of twin treetops in a brush fire, Novella's pupils had narrowed under her thick eyebrows. She wanted to respect Cherry as her aunt; however, Novella's Honest Demon wouldn't let her forget what type of aunt she had and, so, wanted to char every acidic ounce of Cherry's callousness. The internal conflict caused Novella's voice to shake, "We were almost killed. I . . . was . . . still . . . scared. I didn't know that I was holding his hand."

Cherry persisted, "You can't be that naïve to think we grown women don't know betta. Now tell the truth. Has he ever tried to talk to you before that day?"

Novella shot up from the chair. "I'm not a liar!"

Cherry, though having wanted Novella upset, was still a bit put off by her temper. "Alright, alright! Now, girl, just answer the question."

"I already did!" Novella yelled, her voice no longer shaking. "So, make up whatever answer you want . . . and go yell it from a mountain! There are plenty liars in this family . . ." She paused to emphasize the words, "young and grown. But I'm not one of them! Been, what, five months now? See my belly? Am I pregnant? Am I? Wanna count my maxi pads?"

Cherry leaned back. "Whoa now, Noey girl! For real? Mama, Mama, you hear her?"

"You called me a liar! I don't lie, and I'm not messing around!" Then, lowering her voice, she said, "I'm not like you were at my age. Don't got a baby, not trying to make one."

Cherry cocked her head. "Now listen, niece. We all know you a *good girl—*"

Novella, yelling again, cut her off, "That's right . . . I'm me and you're you. Stop getting us confused!"

Cherry stood up. "Listen, Noey girl, now you listen! The man sure acted as if he knew you. As if you were important enough to him for him to fight and kill for you."

Novella shrugged. "So you're not used to good men. Well, too bad! I got saved by one, so obviously they do exist. Try and find one for yourself. Try to make your son one of them!"

Cherry stared from Coddy Lee to Novella, before replying, "Yeah, you smelling yourself. You doing something, with somebody."

Novella waved a hand. "I'm just tired. So tired. This is all so dumb. Think what you think, Cherry! There's nothing I can do about what you think, you know."

Coddy Lee turned from the window. The judge in this courtroom, she finally engaged herself in the proceedings. "I can do something. And I do mean to."

Coddy Lee had waited five months for the baby bump that Novella had pointed out didn't exist. Coddy Lee had also awaited the official details she felt Novella wouldn't admit to. Going to court, however, hadn't given her any additional information. Just that Novella and BETY Junior were giving the same account. *Got their stories straight*, Coddy Lee figured. She'd felt the vibe between Novella and this so-called "good guy" and "hero." It had warmed the stony atmosphere of the criminal courtroom. It roused Coddy Lee's Honest Demon. She couldn't sense anything beyond the platonic, yet it was very strong, resistant to her disapproval and cynicism, as well as her authority over Novella. Inside that courtroom, Coddy Lee felt Novella belonged with BETY Junior and his grandfather, that Novella was more like them than her. She kept envisioning Novella standing up, walking over to first to the grandfather, and kissing his cheek. Then she saw Novella walk over to BETY Junior and take his hand in her own, and then leaving the courtroom with them. Coddy Lee had been a seer of the ghostly as long as she could remember, being visited and being told of future things. Her pride, however, wouldn't allow her to accept this foretelling. Although having experienced the supernatural, she was of the opinion that, "There's no such thing as magical moments. Shit just happens. Shit we do, and shit that's done to us." So, she'd decided that, for Novella and BETY Junior, *This isn't real friendship or love. It isn't anything special. Just horny young people who almost got themselves killed.* She wanted to take a switch to Novella and a backhand to BETY Junior. Coddy Lee, instead, used her eyes as blades to cut down any thought of a reunion. Novella would later tell Yadara and Dell, "Granny looked like she wanted to turn me in. Like she'd brought me to court to send me to jail."

Coddy Lee didn't imprison Novella then and there. Though, here and now, she charged and sentenced her: "House arrest with work privileges."

TWENTY-SIX

Coddy Lee had requested Novella be excused from school until finals. Principal Lewis at West Tech gladly granted her request. From metal workshop to trigonometry, Novella's abduction was a disturbance. Anticipation of her return was high. Even dropout Isaac had been asked when his cousin could be expected back at school. Neither he nor Novella knew the answer.

Missing school, initially, hadn't bothered her. The reclusiveness helped her decompress as much as she could considering her home situation. Coddy Lee, however, surprised her when telling her that she'd miss another week. So, Novella had made a secret call to the director of her college prep program, Upward Bound. The director then called Coddy Lee. She was told that a grad student interning in Upward Bound was available to tutor Novella free of charge. If Coddy Lee didn't like her, there would be no problem replacing her. Coddy Lee allowed the tutoring. Preferring Novella stayed home, she requested it be extended for the remainder of the school year. Novella enjoyed being an only student because of the positive attention. She worked extra hard to show much she appreciated it.

Novella wasn't allowed to go any further than the front porch, so Coddy Lee started inviting her to ride with her on errands. Novella initially only said yes when it would be just the two of them. She couldn't deal with her granny's usual co-pilots Cherry and Connie. Most times it was one or the other. Connie wasn't as abrasive as her sister, but Novella knew they were in cahoots, always trying to get in her personal business. It was no secret that no secret was safe with Cherry or Connie. Still, Novella eventually began to ride with her granny no matter which aunt accompanied her. She feared a worse intruder: Merv.

He started dropping in during the day, in the quiet hours when there was no Connie and no Cherry, no Gent and no Janet, only Isaac sleeping in or lazing around and Coddy Lee watching her soaps. Novella would normally have been at school, but now she was not. First Merv chased her tutor, but soon gave up. "I can tell that young broad is one of those smart ones who think they too good for a regular cat. She sure is sadity. Can't give a brotha a few words. Not even about his own niece."

Getting Novella's homeschool schedule from Isaac, Merv began visiting on the tutor's off days. He'd go straight to Coddy Lee's room to chat as if his visit was for her. Before long, he'd make his way downstairs, talk to Isaac or watch television, and he'd wait for Novella. She knew he was waiting on her. As soon as she came downstairs, he'd immediately invite her to join the conversation or watch a show. "Have a seat, niece. Relax with your Unc-Unc."

I don't need you to tell me to sit down! Novella wanted to say. *I live here. I know where to sit when I want to sit. Go to hell*, her Honest Demon wanted to tell Merv. Instead, it raged at Isaac, "You shut up!" because he always urged her to oblige their uncle, "Noey, you don't have anything else to do. Can't go anywhere."

"You don't know what I'm doing," she'd tell him. "You don't know! I didn't come down here to talk. I came to get something, then go back up to my room."

Most times, she'd thought Merv had already gone. Stepping down into the receiving room, she'd be surprised to find herself facing him. Novella would cringe; Merv would laugh.

"Oh, my God!"

"Hello, to you, too."

Unchecked, he continued his odd visits. One day, he'd coaxed Isaac, the only able-bodied person in the house aside from Novella, out of the house. The dying Willie was of course no threat.

Novella, not having to leave out for school, had started to stay up late and sleep in until ten on her tutor's days off. Sometimes, Coddy Lee would already be out and about. One day, when Merv popped over, the house was empty except for Isaac, the bedridden Willie, and a sleeping Novella.

After emptying her bladder, Novella went downstairs for water. Drinking it, she strolled around the downstairs. She stopped when she saw Merv standing on the porch. His back was to the door. He was watching Isaac walk away from the house.

Novella darted upstairs, and was dressing and stuffing her purse before she knew it. *Granny is going to have to be mad. I'm getting out of here.*

She then crept back downstairs and around the staircase to the side door. She waited for a passing car or any other noise loud enough to cover the sounds of her unlocking, opening, and then closing the door. She soon realized being heard was better than being caught. *Just leave, Novella,* she was telling herself just as Merv called her name. "Noey, gotta ask you something!" Having entered the house, he was closing the front door. "You wanna come down here, or do I come up there to you? Can I come up?"

Novella ran, deciding to keep running until she saw a 38. From her home on 70th, she'd made it to the Hough Clinic on 83rd Street before finally hearing a RiTA hissing behind her. She then turned and ran back toward the bus stop she'd just passed and waited in line to board. After taking a seat, she retrieved her Strawberry Shortcake handkerchief. It had been a coveted treasure, a collector's item, until she'd used it to hide Coddy Lee's pistol. Now, Novella used it for a practical purpose once again, dabbing away her sweat as well as the short burst of tears that caused an old man across the aisle from her to give her a sympathetic look.

Novella had no idea where to go. It was a school day and during school hours. All her friends were in school. Catching a movie would be a good way to pass the time, but she was heading the wrong way. Tower City was downtown, and she was heading uptown. She'd decided where to go when a group of people began exiting at East 105th Street in front of Mount Sinai Hospital. Novella decided the hospital's cafeteria and courtyard would suit her fine until she could go home to the safety of a full house.

Novella had visited a number of people at Mount Sinai Hospital, and had always been impressed with the cheapness and decency of the cafeteria food. After eating, she went to the gift shop. She'd always liked the idea of buying things to lift a sick person's spirit. She enjoyed reading the "Get well soon" cards and seeing all the cheerful merchandise.

She'd just hugged a large teddy bear and was returning it to its shelf, when she heard her name. It was a classmate of hers. She couldn't decide how to feel about seeing her there, although she was glad it wasn't a family member. She surely didn't want to be asked whom was she visiting. It would be embarrassing to say no one. Her classmate, however, she soon discovered, was the more embarrassed of the two of them. "Don't tell anyone that you saw me here," the girl, whose name was Gia, said. She wore loose-fitting purple pajamas that were designed to look like a day outfit. Novella also saw that Gia was in Cabbage Patch house shoes. Gia hadn't been seen in school, or anywhere else, since last year. Rumor was that she'd moved out of town to live with her aunt. "Has everybody been asking about me?" she asked Novella.

"Yeah."

"What are they saying?"

"That you're out of town."

Gia laughed. "Nope, but that's good because that's what I want them to think."

Novella was sorry to stare; she wanted to look away but couldn't. She hadn't ever seen a dying young person. She and Gia were the same age. Gia had run with the "it" crowd, though she wasn't as mean-spirited as most of her crew. It hurt Novella to see her so frail. Gia's high cheekbones, full lips, and round hips had lost most of their landscape and filling. Novella didn't want to seem insensitive, so she did not ask what was wrong with her. Gia made it so that she didn't have to.

"Have you heard of sickle cell?"

Novella shook her head. "No. Well, maybe."

"That's what I have."

"How bad is it?"

"There's no cure," Gia told her plainly. "I'll have it forever."

"But there's medicine?" Novella asked.

Gia's face got tight and serious, as if she might reprimand Novella, and then she laughed. "Girl, you've really never heard of it." Before Novella could respond, Gia grabbed her hand. "Come on, keep me company. I get so bored here. I can get you free snacks. Anything healthy, like nuts and fruits."

Novella roamed the hospital with Gia for a few hours. Novella had no idea they were being watched, but a nurse trailed them and approached when Gia turned and waved to her.

"Stay right here," the woman told her, before leaving to return with a wheelchair.

"Come see my room, so you'll know where I'm at. I know you can keep a secret, and I want you to come back and visit me."

Novella said she would and then stayed until Gia fell asleep in a room decorated to be as homey as possible.

Before leaving the hospital, Novella called home to make sure Coddy Lee had made it back. She was so relieved when Coddy Lee answered the phone that she had to catch her breath before she could speak, "Hi, Granny. Hi. You were gone when I woke up. Everyone was gone. I didn't want to be alone. I'm on my way back now." She was even more relieved that her granny didn't question or reprimand her, even though she, like everyone else in the family, knew Novella enjoyed being home alone.

"Okay, alright," was all that Coddy Lee said.

Novella would find out later that Merv had still been in the house when Coddy Lee returned. So Coddy Lee knew Novella was lying.

TWENTY-SEVEN

Novella returned home and was allowed to settle in without any questions. She knew Isaac's departure had been bought by the way he avoided her eyes. *Weed*, she figured. *Merv probably gave his chicken butt some joints. Sold me out to get high.*

Novella didn't want to think about Coddy Lee. It was too much to worry about whether Granny would be as determined to protect or avenge her if her own son was the perpetrator. *This is it, until I move out on my own*, Novella told herself. *It could be worse.*

The next day, Coddy Lee did say something to her about her having left the house. "Don't get used to just leaving when you feel like it."

"I won't," Novella replied quietly.

House arrest with work privileges. She was still allowed the city bus commute that took her to and from her job at McDonald's. She'd been permitted to return to work about two weeks after the abduction. "Of course!" Yadara, who was no fan of Coddy Lee, had cracked. "If she doesn't let you work, she gotta come off that fifty dollars she stole from you."

Aside from cashiering, Novella dropped fries and apple pies to pay for things like pompoms and school field trips. Her McDonald's checks also paid for her clothing, shoes, and toiletries. After she'd started picking up paychecks, Coddy Lee saw no reason to continue Novella's fifty dollars per month allowance. Novella didn't think it was fair because working had been her idea. She never complained to Coddy Lee, but neither did she forgive her. *She feeds and keeps a roof over my head.* She'd tried to see the reason behind the decision. *And I do have my own room.* But Novella felt it was unfair that she had to buy everything for herself.

Yadara, rolling her eyes, said, "She doesn't really care about you. Not really."

During the school year, Novella worked every Saturday and Sunday. She walked out of her sleeping home at 5:00 a.m. Alone in the dark, she crossed Hough and Carnegie Avenue to reach Euclid to catch the number 6 RiTA. Coddy Lee's only confirmation that Novella never skipped work was that she never asked her for money. Coddy Lee's only assurance Novella hadn't been hurt in the commute was that she returned home in the afternoon. Yadara had pointed out that her family made more fuss about Novella's opportunities as a pretty young girl than they did about her vulnerability as one.

Frustrated by Yadara's constant negative thoughts about Coddy Lee, Novella was tempted to ask, "And what if my granny doesn't care? What am I supposed to do about it? Where I am supposed to go?"

Novella did know that not everyone was subject to Coddy Lee's justice.

Seventeen-year-old Isaac, who hadn't been virtuous even when he was a virgin, was a relentless girl chaser. However, he, like Gent and all the other men in the family, didn't ever get in trouble about sex. "If any girl let them, well, shame on her, right?" Novella heard said by Coddy Lee, Cherry, and Connie. Neither Isaac nor Gent got in trouble for dropping out of school. Isaac, having always denied the need for remedial coursework, couldn't even name all fifty states.

Neither Gent nor Isaac had gotten in trouble for underage drinking. Sure, neither had slurred their words or raised a bottle in front of Coddy Lee. Still, she, like everyone else in the family, knew they weren't holed up in their respective rooms from drinking soda and Kool-Aid. "Under the bed," Willie called it. Nearly every Monday morning, Isaac and Gent slept in until about two in the afternoon.

Janet had turned eighteen this year, and she had celebrated as if freed from prison. Their entire family considered her the smartest grandchild, though she'd been a "hot in the ass" opportunist as early as fourteen. Two years later, her Little Victor was born. Ironically, his birth liberated her. It was as if Coddy Lee had said, "The hell with it. She's ruined." Maybe she was. With all her potential, she was now working on baby number two, with baby daddy number two.

Novella always checked in, was hardly ever late, and never went MIA. So, Coddy Lee met her granddaughter halfway in terms of her modest interest in the opposite sex. Novella was allowed a boyfriend, but she could not go on dates. No males other than Isaac, Gent, or Merv could take her anywhere—not that those three ever did. Novella couldn't meet a boy any place other than a school dance that took place during school hours. Her boyfriends were welcome to visit the family home in any open room on the first floor. Coddy Lee and Gent saw to it that the teenagers, sitting in clear view of the family, were left to themselves. Hand-holding, pecks on the lips, and whispering were allowed. Now because of the good deeds of the twenty-three-year-old BETY Junior, Novella was no longer trusted. All her privileges were revoked, including the educational Upward Bound.

When he heard about that, Gent pled to their granny on his baby cousin's behalf. "Mama, that's her school program, to help with her homework and stuff."

Coddy Lee, whose mind was already made up, did not take her eyes off *All My Children*, one of her favorite soaps. "Hmm, well, she's smart enough already."

Upward Bound was more than a study group for Novella. It gave her inspiration and guidance from productive and positive adults. It also introduced her to like-minded teens. If not for Upward Bound, Novella would have never met her two best friends, Yadara and Dell, girls who were bookish and grounded like her. The trio bonded over being more committed to movies, music, and shopping than to boys. Novella's weekday FaceTime with them was through Upward Bound, because neither attended West Tech nor lived on or near Hough.

TWENTY-EIGHT

Novella being on house arrest riled everyone's Honest Demon. If Novella wasn't threatening to scratch out Isaac's eyes or pointedly ignoring Cherry, she was throwing pillows at Janet. Novella couldn't imagine causing harm to any of them, but her Honest Demon had a different idea. Novella's Honest Demon had created what in about twenty-five years would be called a meme. It was a short video clip of Isaac, Cherry, and Janet standing shoulder to shoulder and side by side. Novella, in front of them, leans way back, and then serves up a hard slap that falls across each of their faces, causing them to fall like dominoes to the floor.

Novella let the Honest Demon run, but didn't let it lead. When she felt like slapping, she ranted under her breath instead, "I hate this house! I hate this house! I hate this house!" Novella, only being allowed to leave home for work, at times wanted to climb atop the roof to get away from her family.

Janet, Isaac, and Cherry hadn't ever smiled at her so much. All in spite. Her being home so much they had more chances than ever to try to bring her down to their lazy level.

"So, you're just going to just read books, play solitaire, and do word puzzles?" Janet asked.

"You'd rather do all that than talk to us?" asked Isaac. "You really do think you're better than us. Just like my mom said."

Novella laughed. "You know, Isaac, I see your mouth moving, but all I hear is clucking."

"Noey, you betta shut up."

"Or what, chicken boy?"

"My mom told you to stop calling me names. When she comes back over here, I'm going to tell her that you're still at it."

"You and yo mama can go lay an egg."

"Granny!" Isaac told on her. "Noey saying yo mama jokes."

"Sort yourself out," Coddy Lee said to Novella. "Nobody got you on punishment but yourself."

"You need some weed and some you-know-what, to make you chill out on all that sadityness," Janet suggested. "Noey, you're just not normal. You don't have a life. You don't know how to have fun." She'd go as far as to invite Novella out. "If I go somewhere, you want to go with me? I know someone who'd like you. I can sneak you out."

Novella wanted only to shut her up for good. "No thanks, I like not being a hoe." She didn't trust Janet and wouldn't dare go on a blind date she'd arranged.

"I know you didn't call me hoe. I will tell Granny."

"I said that I like not being a hoe. You are whatever you are, Janet. So, no thank you and leave me alone. I don't want to get high or run the streets with you."

Novella knew if she did and got caught, she'd get the worst of Coddy Lee's reprimand. Janet was a legal eagle, so could fly as high as she wanted, as long as their granny wasn't inconvenienced. Novella was still "Noey girl," the young baby chick. Although she did a lot of fending for herself, she was still being told what not to do and where not to go. *You knew better*, she could hear Granny scolding her, while Janet would be watching silently. Not even Gent would defend her. Novella appreciated when he stepped up to help her, but knew he didn't believe in her. He believed what he could see of her, studying, working, and making curfew. If she were caught sneaking out, drinking alcohol, smoking weed, or having sex, she'd lose his support. To Gent, Novella was an angel. And doing anything worldly, aside from saying an occasional curse word, would taint this view of her. Novella heard and saw his condemnation of her when she laughed at something naughty. "Oh Noey, you think that's funny? Humph." When she was obviously speaking in code to one of her friends on the phone, he assumed she was speaking to a boy. "Oh, don't tell me you've started, Noey." What had hurt her was when he saw a bruise on her shoulder blade and mistook it for a hickey. "So, you've already started letting dudes suck on you?"

No matter how much Novella repressed her feelings about Coddy Lee's behavior toward her, she knew her place. Novella was the last of four grandchildren who came to reside with Coddy Lee. Isaac was left with her when Cherry moved out with the first of her string of live-in boyfriends. Gent, who lost his mother Canella Lynn to a brain aneurysm at ten, came second. Janet followed a few years later, when her mother Cadee Leah and her father died in a car crash.

Although both Novella and Isaac had living parents, only Novella was ostracized. She was as the least amongst her cousins as had been her mother amongst her siblings. Coddy Lee's first six children were Merv Junior, Memphis, Marshall, Charlee Lu'a, Cannella Lynn, and Cadee Leah. Novella's mother, Cara Louise, was number seven and was not Merv Senior's child. Cara's existence was judged as Coddy Lee's worst sin against her marriage. Back then going by her nickname, Cotton, she'd left Merv before Cara's conception. Still, her name was burning everywhere from the juke joints to the church pews. "Y'all heard Merv's wife, Cotton, left him.

Right? Well, now the woman has went and had a baby by another man. I tell y'all, that Cotton is something else."

Coddy Lee's eighth and ninth children, Cherry Latoya and Connie La'Shell, were also conceived outside of her marriage. Unlike Cara, their father claimed them. Cara Louise, rumored to be sired by a married man, had been given Merv Senior's surname. In the thirty-five years since Coddy Lee left him, including the twenty since they'd seen one another, neither had filed for divorce.

Cara did not resemble her siblings, so it was easy to see why she had been deemed a bastard. Coddy Lee never attempted to shield her from the gossip, nor had she offered any explanation on why Cara's father hadn't been around. Seventeen-year-old Cara was pregnant with Novella when Coddy Lee opened one of her photo albums and said, "This is Dale, your daddy. He gave me money for you. Anyway, he's dead now." When Novella came to live with Coddy Lee, she'd introduced him the same way. "Your mother's father. Been dead a while now." Novella was intrigued, but also a little offended. To Novella, Coddy Lee's neutrality suggested that it was Cara's own fault to have a different father. Novella had stared at her plain-face granny thinking, *That's all you're gonna say about my grandfather.*

Cara had given her daughter Novella exactly what Coddy Lee had given her, an absentee father.

"Ain't none of us ever seen your daddy," Cherry had said to Novella on Father's Day years ago. "Have you ever met him?" Novella had not. After that painful, unprovoked dig, Novella had decided to purge her want and need for him. Finding out he was in prison was still embarrassing for her. He wrote Novella not long after he was sent up. That was last year. Novella would have written back, if he hadn't confused her Honest Demon by addressing the letter to Novella McCloud. Trying to find a respectful yet pointed way of saying "How dare you try to claim me, after fifteen years, just because you're locked up and lonely?" was too much for her. So she took a very deep breath, and then blew out her blues in a long exhale, to be carried by the wind to the birds.

"Blo out yo blues, babe

And let da birds sang bout dem

Dey betta da whole world's music

Than one person's whole world"

Those therapeutic lyrics were from Willie, who'd passed them down from his grandfather, who he said was a guitar player and blues singer.

Tino McCloud continued to write, each letter at least five pages long. His persistence didn't impress Novella, her thought being, *He doesn't have anything but time.* Novella never seemed excited to get his letters, so Coddy Lee decided to read one before giving it her. "Tino had sent impressive artwork drawn on a large handkerchief and was begging for a reply," Coddy Lee told both Cherry and Connie, who told everyone else. They, including Gent, agreed Novella was wrong and being cruel. "Really, Noey? You're really something else," Cherry had said to her. "Cara's your mama. What did you expect? She's as common as any weed growing between the cracks in a sidewalk. What, you thought somehow your daddy was one those dudes in *Jet*? As if one of those types would even deal with someone like crazy-ass Cara. No matter whatever you're dressing yourself up to be, with those five-dollar earrings and putting dimes in your penny loafers, you are what you are. No better than your mama and daddy, and no better than any of us. We proud to be real and regular people, and you need to learn to be grateful."

Crazy Cara was a secret nickname that wasn't really a secret. Cara, whenever she got intensely bothered, had a way of looking downward to her left, as if getting guidance from her Honest Demon. Looking back up would be the face of Crazy Cara, who then went off. Cherry always blamed her behavior on her zodiac sign. "Gotdamn Gemini, split personality ass.

These fucken Geminis . . ." No matter what Crazy Cara's siblings thought or said behind her back, when in their company, she was respected.

Cara also had another problem that ironically proved her more similar than not to some of her siblings: she was addicted to crack cocaine they had all tried at various parties. Cara's addiction was as unintentional as Cherry becoming a social smoker. It was common knowledge that Cara wasn't the only child of Coddy Lee's to have dabbled in some hard drugs. But she was the one to get strung out, which only served to further ostracize her.

Janet, in a dig at Novella, had explained, "It used to be a medicine, but it was outlawed because of people like your mama. Not knowing when to quit. People who are predisposed to addiction. Maybe she's a crackhead because of whoever her daddy was. Cause we all know it wasn't Merv Lofton."

Cherry had praised Janet for being so smart for knowing the drug's history before Janet had continued, "My mama was Granny's best girl. She never drank or smoked anything." Something Janet must have been told, because she was too young to remember much about Cadee.

As it was, Novella was treated as if her mother was the worst of her granny's children. Sometimes Novella believed it, as she sometimes believed she was lesser of the grandchildren—the most in need, the least loved.

TWENTY-NINE

Being the grandchild forbidden to leave the house to socialize, Novella had many times found herself alone with her second cousin Lil Victor. Janet one day led him to Novella's room, and then quietly left the house. Another day, Janet asked Novella to take over feeding him, giving the reason that she needed her hands free to make lemonade. She snuck out of the back door. She was gone for fifteen minutes before Novella realized she'd heard no sounds coming from the kitchen. A few days after that, Janet took the telephone out onto the front porch, as if to make a call. But it was a front. She left the telephone next to the door before making her escape.

Today, the house was full. Lil Victor, having gone in on his own, was in Novella's room, where he had fallen asleep on her bed. Novella, sitting on her bedroom floor with her nail polish caboodle in front of her, suddenly realized how convenient it would be for Janet to make another stealth escape. Novella quickly closed her caboodle and placed it on her armoire out of Lil Victor's reach. After softly padding downstairs, she found Janet in the kitchen having a hushed telephone conversation. Twirling the curly phone cord, Janet's suggestive smile grew as the conversation came to an end. Turning around after returning the receiver to the base, Janet's smile dropped as she caught sight of Novella. Caught, and mad about it, Janet opened her mouth to dig into Novella. But she didn't recover fast enough to speak before Novella did.

"Just because I'm on punishment, doesn't mean I'm here to watch your baby."

Janet tried to dismiss her. "Girl, get out of my face."

Novella was fixed on setting her straight. "Get off your back, at least on my time."

Janet stepped in closer to Novella. "You better shut the hell up."

"I'm not scared of you." Novella brought them even closer by stepping forward. "Take care of your own baby."

Janet gave her a dogged look. "What do you want girl? Some damn money? Oh, but you can't go anywhere to spend it. So, shut the hell up. You're just mad you don't have man."

Novella finally released the words she'd been holding in. "You're a hoe."

Janet gave a short laugh. "Having sex doesn't make me a hoe, Little Miss Prissy Prude."

"With a whole of bunch of guys, yeah it does. Having babies by this one and that one. Lil Victor's father doesn't even talk to you. And what are you doing? Leaving Lil Victor to go make another baby. And everyone calls *you* the smart one."

Janet let out a roll of sarcastic laughter. "Girl . . . girl, girl, girl. You're so damn jealous. Well, I . . . am . . . the smart one. You wish you could be like me. And if I run into your hero BETY Junior, I'll prove it to you."

Novella shook her head at what she considered a weak dig. "Any hood rat can get a dude to bone her, try getting one to stick around. Where is Lil Vic's daddy? Yeah, okay, you shut the hell up. Hoe!"

Soon the two were rolling necks, flipping hands, snapping fingers, and marching, from the kitchen through the dining area to the receiving room: Novella in plush Cabbage Patch Kids house shoes, an apple-sized baby head above the toe area of each one, and Janet in suede Nikes. Staying ahead of Novella, Janet's steps were meant to carry her out of the house, again without her baby. When she got near the already open front door, Novella jumped in front of her. Janet was amused by Novella's boldness. Rolling her eyes, Janet sized up her merit-roll-pompom-girl little cousin. Janet, the former honor student and star basketball player, was pretty sure Novella was being too bold for her own good. Although a few inches shorter, Janet outweighed her cousin by at least twenty pounds.

Isaac, who was in the living room watching a movie, hadn't realized his cousins were into it until they got louder than the television. He'd turned to yell for them to quiet down when he noticed their rolling necks and flipping hands. "Hey, what's wrong with y'all?" He stood from the couch and walked over to them, only to be ignored.

Janet snapped her fingers at Novella. "You're not anybody to be in my face!"

"I'm not your freaking babysitter!" Novella snapped back. "That's who and what I'm not."

Janet pointed hard in Novella's face. "You're not anything."

Novella pointed just as hard. "I'm not a hoe. And . . . I am not your freaking babysitter!"

"You're just a stupid girl," Janet told her, "who thinks she's better than everyone!"

"I don't think, Janet. I *know* I'm a not hoe!"

Isaac told them both, "Look . . . y'all two . . . need to squash whatever this is."

Again, they ignored him.

"Get out of my face and out of my way!" Janet warned Novella.

"You are not leaving me to watch Lil Vic. He's your baby!"

"Alright, Noey!" Janet stood up taller. "Alright, I'm really trying to make you understand. Trying to tell you, girl. Get . . . out . . . of . . . my . . . face. And out of my way!"

Isaac knew a countdown to a throwdown when he heard one. He went to the staircase and shouted, "Somebody needs to come down here! Like asap. These girls . . . They into it, and it's getting serious. Really serious!"

Janet didn't want anyone to come downstairs, not before she got out the front door and around the corner. "Get of out my way!" She got more aggressive, trying to get around Novella, who wouldn't let her.

Janet's Honest Demon was bolder and meaner than Novella's and wasn't above hurting Novella. She'd always been the first to take the opportunity to get at Novella. Janet had always been mean to Novella, even when they were much younger.

Eleven summers ago, Novella sat at a picnic table with Janet and Isaac. Dipping a nugget in the small barbeque sauce cup, the happy Novella looked up to see the seven-year-old Janet smirking at her.

"What?" Novella smiled.

Janet, having the attention she wanted, took a bite of her bacon cheeseburger and answered as she chewed, "You know . . . those are . . . fried chicken titties? You know that, right? Right?"

Six-year-old Isaac didn't catch on that it was a joke on Novella at first. "What? What are you talking about, Janet?"

To get him in on the joke, Janet gawked at him. "Isaac . . . you know what I'm talking about. Don't be stupid! Tell Noey they're chicken titties."

Novella's eyes, big and worried, were focused on her box of nuggets, so she didn't see Janet's bug-eyed cajoling of Isaac to join her in the joke.

Novella, the youngest of the three cousins, still believed nearly everything they said.

"Oh yeah!" Isaac got in on the joke. "Noey, yeah . . . they . . . are . . . chicken titties. That's why I don't eat them anymore. Yeah, I stopped when I found out."

Janet giggled. "Nasty little Noey loves those chicken titties."

Isaac, spitting out some of his soda, laughed. "Tittie eater!"

That did it. Novella was done with her dinner.

Janet didn't stop. "Make sure you brush your teeth after all those chicken titties."

Isaac, laughing uncontrollably, nearly fell off the bench. He added, "Noey's eating all those titties. She's going to start clucking like a baby chicken soon."

Janet and Isaac, enjoying their Happy Meals and their success at fooling Novella yet again, didn't care that their young cousin was in tears, that she would go to bed hungry and get in trouble for wasting food and money. Fast food had been a luxury for their family.

Hurting Novella physically had also been a game. Janet used to spank her. "I can whoop you because I'm your big cousin. You have to do as I say, and if you don't, I can tear your tail up."

Janet hit Novella for three years until Gent caught on. "So, it's okay for me to beat you then?" He'd snatched the belt she was using to intimidate Novella. "I'm older than you, so now it's my turn to whoop you. Right?" The then ten-year-old Janet ran out of the room.

Today, Janet would again get physical with Novella. She attempted to bum-rush her. With squared shoulders and raised forearms, she tried to push Novella out of her way, knock her down if that's what it took to get by her and out the door. Novella, taking advantage of Janet's raised arms, hugged her tightly, and then dropped into a squat. Bouncing up, she lifted

Janet, despite her swinging arms and her kicking feet, right off the floor. Isaac turned from the staircase just in time to see Novella body slam Janet. "Oh shit, Noey!" he exclaimed. "You in real trouble now."

A teary and sore Janet agreed, "You betta get the fuck off me, Noey!" Being picked up and slammed had frightened her. Now trying to shift gears from fear to causing her cousin fear, she yelled with a shaky voice, "I said, get the fuck off me! Fuck off me now!"

THIRTY

Upstairs in Coddy Lee's room, Cherry heard the thud of the slam and yelled, "What the hell . . . was *that*? What are you kids *doing*?"

Isaac rushed over to the stairwell. "Noey's beating Janet! I'm not joking! It's really wild down here! Really wild! Noey's out of control!"

The sound of Cherry's footsteps on the stairs said she was on her way down. "You lying to me! I just know this girl is not . . ."

Janet remained pinned under Novella. "You better run when I get up!"

Novella was hardly scared, and neither was her Honest Demon. "Shut up. Just shut up!"

Janet would not, so Novella palmed Janet's face with her hand, mugging her. "Always talking mess . . . just always talking. So, shut up . . . for once . . . shut up!"

Cherry, having made it down to the first floor, came over and stood over her nieces. "Noey, get the hell off her!" Cherry bent over and grabbed Novella's shoulders, but feeling her flex, she immediately let go and backed up. "Whoa! Whoa!" Cherry stared. "This girl . . ." She took a few more steps away from the rumble, and then began to clap her hands authoritatively.

"Novella . . . Renae . . . Lofton!" She got a bit louder. "Damn, girl . . . you need to be sorted the hell out!"

Isaac joined in with his mother. "Noey! Noey, get up. Get off her! You know Granny is gonna get after you hard."

Cherry's hands clapped on. "Seriously, this is damn ridiculous, Noey! Novella! Novella! Noey! Girl, gotdamn, that's your own cousin, your own damn cousin you've jumped on! No . . . vella! You hear me? Girl, I know you hear me!"

Novella's Honest Demon looked up at Cherry. "You need to shut up, too! Just like Janet . . . and your chicken-heart son . . . you talk too much. Don't even have anything worth saying . . . but just talk and talk. Shut up. You're not even a real auntie!"

Cherry bent her thick frame down toward Novella. "Girl . . ."

Connie stepped down from the staircase and looked at Novella sideways. "Have you lost your mind, girl? Get off Janet."

Holding a cigarette and a lighter, Connie had obviously been on her way outside for a smoke before Isaac called for help. She placed her unlit Newport in her mouth, only to immediately remove it to sing up the stairway, "Ma-ma, let Noey out of here! Let . . . her . . . out . . . of . . . here! She got Janet down here on the floor! And she is not moving!"

Isaac added, "Yeah, she going crazy!" He then yelled at Novella, "You got a problem, girl—a serious problem! Go on back to your nerdy committees, if that's what this is all about. You straight wildin out in here. Just out of control, girl!"

Connie gave a diagnosis. "For real! She stir-crazy . . . with that log cabin fever or whatever they call it. She just needs to get out of the house. Since when does this girl get fighting mad?"

Gent appeared at the screen door. "Fighting! Who? Who in this house is fighting?" He tried the knob, but it didn't turn. "One of y'all hurry and open this door."

Isaac rushed over and unlocked it.

Gent had barely passed the threshold when Cherry told him, "Go ahead and defend her. Noey, that's right. Look at her! She got Janet pinned down on the damn floor! She's the one in here hell-raising!"

Connie, with hand on her hip, asked her sister, "So why are you the one shouting? Gent can hear you, Cherry; he's standing right there."

Gent, assessing the situation, accused everyone of being responsible for the mess. "Y'all just standing around, letting them beat each other up?"

Cherry answered defensively, "Like we wanted to get pushed around by these young-ass girls."

Gent looked to Isaac. "And what stopped you?"

Connie immediately answered for him, "Short of them hurting Mama, he better not put his hands on either those girls."

Cherry agreed, "And we all know if he would have accidentally hurt one of them, you'd be beating my son's ass right now."

Gent was known as "everybody's daddy." At twenty-four, he was the oldest grandchild in the house. His aunts Connie and Cherry had only seven and eight years on him, respectively. He had coach and counselor potential, but "everybody's daddy" had his vices and his pint of devil's blood. Many times had his Honest Demon gotten loose and ahead of him. Sometimes he drank too much, and started fights. More than once he'd slept with a close friend's girlfriend and, when confronted, fought the friend. He'd lost two jobs for threatening his bosses. Yet, more times than not, Gent stepped up in family matters and regulated for the greater good. Years ago, he had to check Isaac. "Fuck around and find out," he'd dared him. Isaac had threatened to slap Novella for making his friends wait outside until he returned. When the five boys arrived, Novella was home alone and didn't feel comfortable letting them in. Isaac, raging at Novella, was silenced when Gent entered the house, "Boy, see what'll happen to you if you touch her . . . or any female in this family." Connie and Cherry were correct—Isaac was still upright because he hadn't tried to intervene in Janet and Novella's fight.

"Mama!" Connie called for Coddy Lee who was upstairs. "Can you come down?"

Janet, wrestling harder to gain her freedom, was getting frustrated, mouth draped open, bottom lip hanging, breathing heavy, eyes running tears, whining instead of huffing. "I'm . . . fucking . . . you up, Noey! Get off me! Get off me!"

"Bum-rush me, like you tried to," Novella dared her. "Get me off you!"

Their exchange soon became little more than unintelligible screeches.

"Enough!" Gent began pulling them apart. "And I mean it . . . enough! Either one of y'all try to hit the other . . . Janet, you know I know you . . . so don't even! Let go, Noey! Let go now, girl. Now! It's done; it's done!"

As soon as she was up off the floor, Janet lunged at Novella, though she quickly fell back. No one saw Novella's leg swing upward until her foot was a hair away from Janet's face. "Noey!" everyone except Janet yelled. She'd screamed and covered her face.

"Stay back, Janet!" Gent warned, and then he turned to talk to Novella. Before he could get a word out, Novella's Honest Demon rushed toward Janet, smashed into her, and pushed her down onto the sofa. Janet began swinging her arms, but Novella had already retreated. She was too far away for Janet's blows to reach her. Gent grabbed Novella. "Girl, I know you fed up, but this shit is done now. So, relax and go sort yourself over there next to Connie."

Novella took a few steps forward.

Gent warned, "Girl, I said it's done!"

Novella pointed toward the floor. "My Cabbage Patch babies." Her house shoes had come off during the fight, and her babies, as she called them, were on their sides. Rescuing them, Novella slipped them back onto her feet. She then took a seat next to her aunt Connie.

Cherry then told Gent, "Listen, nephew, bump feeling sorry for her. Noey been real funky around here since Mama put her on punishment. She just needs to deal with it."

Gent turned to his aunt. "How are you gonna say for her to deal with it, being punished for almost getting raped? The girl got dragged down the street on her way home from school."

Cherry snapped her fingers. "And we all sorry for her, but she need to sort herself out, because ain't nobody in here get after her coochie."

Just then, Merv stepped in the front door. "Fam, fam, fam, what's with all the fussing?"

Isaac's eyes, which had been dogging Novella, quickly dropped to the floor. Isaac knew there was something inappropriate about their uncle's interest in Novella.

Merv assessed the room. "Don't y'all look mad in here."

Cherry pointed from Novella to Janet. "Noey's mean ass. She just jumped on Janet. Gent had to pull her off. Bro, if you'd walked in here not ten seconds ago, you'd have seen Noey holding her down."

Janet began pouting. Huffing, as if shocked and overwhelmed by it all. Of course, it was all an act for sympathy.

Novella noticed the change in her disposition. "Get real, Janet. Don't even act you didn't start this! You tried to bum-rush me! Tried to knock me down, so that you could run out of the house and leave me stuck watching your baby. I was defending myself. You don't push me around!" Janet shook her head as if Novella was making it all up.

"Okay, Noey, stop yelling," Gent said. "We're turning the temperature down in here. Mellow, mellow now, girl."

"What is anyone going say to her?" Novella pointed at Janet. "It doesn't matter! I don't care! Don't even care!" She turned and headed to her room. Just as she reached the stairs, Merv caught up with her, and grabbed her arm, "Niece?"

She pulled away hard, causing her to trip over the second step and hit both of her shins. She yelled out twice. Once in pain, and then again in panic as she felt her uncle's large, hot hands around her waist.

"Hey, hey now." Merv pulled her up straight. "What's got you riled up, Noey? Tell your unc-unc what's going on."

Novella's Honest Demon wanted to pistol-whip Merv. Having no pistol, a lamp, broom, or mop would do. Novella was still angry enough to allow her Honest Demon to wild out on him, as Isaac would say. Though, even her Honest Demon knew better than to try it. Merv outranked her in the family.

Cherry yelled, "Y'all see that heifer? She ain't so goody-goody when she not getting her way. Look at her being disrespectful when Merv helped buy her school clothes last year." He'd done no such thing, and if Novella hadn't been so distracted by his hands on her, she would have said so. Cherry went on, "Go on, girl, tell your uncle what your damn problem is."

Connie came to Novella's defense. "Cherry, let her be. She got it honest. We're all a little evil. And right now, you're the worst demon in here! Leave the girl alone. Noey can have a little attitude, and she can go to her room if she wants to. Mama will sort this out later."

Gent agreed, "Let her pass, Unc."

Merv let go. "Fine. I'll get her to tell me later." Turning back toward the others, he found Connie staring, gazing more in him than at him. His baby sister wasn't the first in the family to give him that I-see-you look.

Merv had been exactly who and what she saw and more for too long for him to be worried. Connie was just another "female" to him, and he'd had plenty of females. Many just like her, and like Novella, with family issues. Merv met Connie's eyes. His Honest Demon smiled at her. Merv's entire being knew and relished where he was: in a hush-don't-tell family, especially since his old mama was sick and her old man was more than sick. Merv was confident Connie wasn't going to bother Coddy Lee with something that would be simple enough for him to deny. Merv was sure that Connie suspected their mama already knew about him. Merv was also sure that Connie was aware that he knew their mama better than she would ever want to know her. Merv was the only one of the first six of her children to even consider living anywhere near Coddy Lee—the elephant in the room. There was no doubt that Connie knew their mama to have had, or to still have, the wickedest Honest Demon of them all.

Connie did exactly what Merv expected: she said nothing and turned away. Merv strolled past her to place his liquor-bottle-filled brown paper bag above the fake fireplace. Afterwards, he helped Isaac straighten up the things that had been knocked around by Janet and Novella. "What went down in here, nephew?"

THIRTY-ONE

Opening her bedroom door, Novella found her bed empty, so she instinctively turned toward Coddy Lee's room. As usual, when she was home, her door was wide open. There in the largest of her two accent chairs sat Lil Victor shredding a *TV Guide*. The handsome toddler shot Novella the sweetest dimpled smile before throwing a tiny fist full of paper bits in the air. Just as Novella began to wonder where Coddy Lee was, she heard her voice from inside Willie's room. Thankful that she hadn't come upstairs to a lecture, Novella quickly entered her room. Inside she grabbed Bright Heart Racoon, her Care Bear Cousin she'd had since the eighth grade. Then, nestling amongst the other stuffed animals on her loveseat, she rested her head on last year's Mama and Papa Christmas Bears. Johnny, her Pound Puppy, appeared neglected, most likely because he'd been her friend a year longer than Bright Heart Racoon. Novella picked up the Pound Puppy, placing him on her stomach alongside the Care Bear Cousin. Amicably, the two rested together against her legs, which were draped over an arm of her love seat. Novella stared up at her stucco ceiling, the only one in the house, while gently squeezing the two animals. She then smiled the biggest smile she'd had in months. She felt good. Almost great. Surprisingly, she realized the fight with Janet had been therapeutic. For the first time, she'd let her cousin know she was not the one to be pushed around. To hold on to the thrill, Novella punched her small fists in the air and whispered, "Boom, boom, boom, boom, boom!" House arrest had suppressed too much of her youthful energy. Her body missed high kicks, shaking pompoms, and dancing at pep rallies and games. It was football season. The teen had the urge to sprint around the block and then do cartwheels in the backyard. She also had the urge to scream. She missed making school announcements, attending prom committee meetings, going to Upward Bound study sessions, giving and getting the 411 with her friends. All the activities that allowed the chatterbox she was meaningful and fun conversations. Now, Novella had to settle for talking to herself about the fight with Janet. "What she thought?" Novella whispered. "She could just push me around. Let her try that again. Always trying to front on somebody . . . try to bum-rush me." A knock at her door interrupted her conversation with herself.

"Sort yourself out, Noey," Coddy Lee warned. "You hear me? Sort yourself out, girl."

Of course, she couldn't be on my side, Novella thought. Keeping her voice neutral, she rolled her eyes and said, "Yes, Granny."

"I'm not gonna put up with cursing and roughhousing from you." Coddy Lee slowly pushed open Novella's door, just enough to stick her head in the room. "And I know you better than all that anyway. Am I right?"

Novella met her eyes. "Yes, Granny."

"Alright then. And since when do you have a problem looking after Victor? You're always holding him anyway."

"But, Granny, I shouldn't have to watch her baby. Not without her asking me. And if say no, then it's no."

Coddy Lee exhaled, and started to reply when Novella heard Connie, who'd just come from downstairs, whisper something to her. Afterwards Coddy Lee ended the conversation with, "Well, still no reason for roughhousing. Just come to my room in the morning. I'll sort it out then."

"Yes, ma'am."

Novella hated being in trouble, especially with Coddy Lee. She'd saved her. The Cuyahoga County Family Court had ruled that Cara Louise Lofton was unfit to be a parent. To regain custody, she was required to attend rehab and parenting classes. She'd done neither. "Couldn't be bothered, I guess," Novella had overheard Coddy Lee say, summing up Cara's disregard for the court order. If not for Coddy Lee, Novella quite possibly would be living with a stranger, one maybe fostering her only for the stipend. Novella had met kids in that predicament. The hell they went through . . .

Novella would leave her room for a peanut butter and jelly sandwich, and then tuck herself in for the night. She wanted a long hot soak with a cupful of Coddy Lee's Epsom salts, but never bathed when the house was busy. There was only one bathroom, and it was small with a claw-foot tub with no shower. Novella, using an extendable metal rod, had installed a shower curtain. She hated that during her baths Connie and Cherry expected her to let them in to pee. Cherry was always the worst. "Noey, get fa real! Are you hiding a pregnancy? Because we got the same things, except I got more." That was true, in that Cherry's parts were bigger and hairier. Novella had accidentally seen for herself. The sight of them, and Cherry's brazen response, didn't make Novella any less committed to keeping her privates private. As it was, her aunts weren't the only reason for the shower curtain. Novella felt Isaac's movements were suspect when she or Janet were bathing. The bathroom sat next to the staircase, between the second and third floor. Back and forth, up and down, Isaac went, moving the slowest when neither Coddy Lee nor Gent were home. Built in 1900, their house still had doors with keyholes, those that were perfect for peeping. The feeling of being watched put the childhood melody "Ain't Your Mama Pretty" in Novella's head. Though, there was a slight edit to the dirty lyrics, fitting them to an I-spy game for Isaac, "Ain't Your Mama Pretty" becoming "Ain't My Cousin Pretty."

"Ain't my cousin pretty

She got meatballs on her titties

She got bacon and eggs between her legs

Ain't my cousin pretty."

Novella's other reason for skipping the bath tonight was Merv. Novella felt her uncle's chance at doing whatever he wanted to do to her was always there, no matter who else was around. So much could be lost in the seconds of turned or bowed heads, with the distraction of phone or side conversations, during family get-togethers drowned in alcohol or hazy from weed, someone's run upstairs or down to the basement for laundry. The worst opportunity being a run to a store. Merv's hands, as well as any-thing else he could position, would go as far as time allowed. No way would she risk being naked while he was in the vicinity. Novella hadn't told any-one, not even Coddy Lee, about the encounter on the porch. Didn't know how, and she was too embarrassed and afraid. *Where will I go if Granny doesn't believe me? Where will I go if she does? Merv is her son. Her firstborn.* Yet, Novella was fairly sure that, if she did tell Coddy Lee of any moles-tation, Coddy Lee would fight for her. Even still, her brave heart wasn't comforted, because telling of the violation wouldn't erase it from her body. Novella was conservative with how she dressed and carried her curves. She was selective of her boyfriends, and selective of which of them had been allowed to touch her. Falling in love and being intimate were things she was looking forward to—when *she* was ready, with whom *she wanted*. Right now, the seventeen-year-old was in love with the idea of being in love: with lacey underwear, romance novels, movies, and poetry, being caught up in her celebrity crushes, patiently growing into herself. Novella didn't want to be *ruined*. She didn't want what was to become of her sex life to begin with rape. *Who would?* Other females, both her age and older, had confessed to her of crimes against them. Novella wondered how they stood so strong from such a dirty experience. Aside from being murdered, being raped was the worst thing Novella could imagine happening to her.

THIRTY-TWO

An episode of *The Fresh Prince of Bel-Air* took Novella's mind off the bath and the reasons she wasn't taking one. She fell asleep easily. When shaken awake, she couldn't tell if she'd been asleep for an hour or for the entire night, but she felt it hadn't been long enough. Her bedroom door had been pushed halfway open, allowing the light from the bathroom to stream into her room. Too bright for the small bathroom, the glare of the sixty-watt bulb was blinding in the middle of night. Novella usually slept bundled up with her head under the covers. If not for being shaken, she would have continued to sleep in spite of the light. Too sleepy to be startled, she emerged from under the covers grumbling, "What . . . What's wrong?" Whoever stood over her was as cold as they were silent. The chill Novella felt coming off them implied they'd just come in from being outside a long time. The oddity of the situation wasn't enough to coax Novella far from her cozy abyss. She hadn't yet opened her eyes; she wasn't ready to subject them to the light. She waited for a familiar voice to tell her who the person was and what they wanted. No voice came in the ten or so seconds she waited. So, reluctantly, Novella opened her eyes. Squinting up at the figure, she pushed her voice around the sleep frog in her throat, "Who are you?" Even louder she urged, "And what is it? Is something wrong?" The light from the bathroom, stinging her eyes, only outlined the figure without illuminating any revealing features. *Who is that?* Novella wondered. Broad shoulders told her it was a man, but she needed to see him better to name him. Nevertheless, she decided it was probably Isaac, because who else would try to scare her like this? That's what she figured; he was trying to scare her by not speaking and hiding in the dark. "No." She whined and swatted. "Leave me alone." There was some doubt in her mind that it was him, because Isaac hadn't ever disturbed her sleep, nor had he ever opened her door without permission. Neither had Gent, but of course, it wasn't him. Gent, everybody's daddy, didn't play games. Gent, after turning on her bedroom light, and then shaking her awake, would've immediately got to the business of why he had awakened her. In less than a minute with Gent, she'd know what the hell was going on. Novella was sure her uncle Merv wouldn't be over so late. Though, if it was him, she figured he'd be more inclined to keep her quiet.

The person left her room only to stand in front of her doorway. They gestured for Novella to get up, but her cozy abyss was too comfortable to abandon. "No, and I said leave me alone, Isaac!" She sat up to close her door, which, in order to do, she had to crawl partially out of her bed. She did, slamming the door.

Novella quickly shuffled back under the covers and closed her eyes. A rainbow of hues sparkled behind her lids, as her pupils recovered from the blast of harsh light. Her heart rate was slightly elevated from the disturbance, so it took a few minutes for the abyss of sleep to begin its reclaim of her.

Novella was nearly enveloped by the abyss when she sensed that the person was still lingering in the hall. She couldn't rest. Just as she pulled the covers from over her head, her bedroom door opened, with enough force for it to smack the door stop. Novella sat up to scream Isaac into another dimension, but felt like she had entered one herself. Darkness in front of her, Novella stretched her neck high to see the face of the man in her doorway. She looked hard. Her mind spinning, unsure of whether or not she had seen the bathroom light being switched off.

"Whoever you are, you better stop playing," she warned, and then asked herself, *How is it that I can't see?*

It was so dark she wondered if her door was now closed. Sensing open space beyond her feet, she knew it had to still be wide open. She wondered, *How can a normal size person cover an entire door?*

Straining, she began looking for the tiny rays of light from the bathroom that always filtered through the gaps between her bedroom door and its threshold. There was only darkness. She didn't have a lamp, and the light switch next to her door was too far away. She turned toward her window to make a lantern of the moonlight, but her curtains were closed. After turning back toward where she knew her door to be, she stared.

After a few moments, Novella dared to slap a hand into the darkness. "Who in the hell are you?"

Her hand met nothing, and she received no answer. So, she swung both arms. "Why are you bothering me? Get out of my room! Get out! You better leave me alone!"

She'd felt nothing. She was about get up to charge at whoever was playing with her, when the darkness grabbed both her wrists. The shock of the unseen rough hands produced a long, guttural shrill from her, "Aaaaaaaaaaaaargh!"

She was on the floor before she could muster the words, "Let go of me! Let me go!" Struggling in vain against whoever it was, she then told them, "I'm not playing. It's not funny!" "Noooo!" She continued her unsuccessful resistance against the mysterious shadow person. "Noooo!" Their grip, although not painful, was tight and was paralyzing her arms.

Dragged out of the bed, across the carpeted floor, out into the hall, Novella now knew for sure whoever it was they weren't playing with her.

"Somebody help! Something's happening to me! Everybody wake up! I'm being taken! I'm being taken!" She indeed was being taken, across the landing, past the bathroom and the staircase, past the closed door to the third floor where her cousins were sleeping. She was released in a heap by the threshold of Coddy Lee's open door.

"Granny!" Novella crawled inside the dark room. "Granny! Someone's in the house! Someone's in here!" Novella looked back to see the shadow person. Still, in spite of the light, they were only outlined and not defined. Novella, although unable to see its eyes, knew the shadow watched her. She did see something moving in the middle of its black face. Novella, keeping her eyes on the shadow, got to her feet. She took a few steps toward Coddy Lee's bed, "Granny! Granny wake up. Wake up!" Then Novella saw it, the thing in middle of the shadow's face—a crescent moon of teeth. Whatever or whoever it was, it was smiling.

"Oh, my God! Oh my God! Oh my God!" Novella covered her mouth with her hands.

With a long dark arm, the shadow gestured for her to turn around toward Coddy Lee. Novella didn't want to turn her back to the shadow. Being grabbed from behind, she knew, might make her hysterical. Novella stepped backwards, stopping only when the back of her thighs hit the edge of Coddy Lee's bed. Novella, trying to rouse her granny, purposely dropped her butt down hard upon the mattress. Extending a hand backwards, Novella shook Coddy Lee. The shadow person gestured again for Novella to turn around. Novella risked it this time. "Wake up, Granny! Wake up!" While she was facing her grandmother, the shadow pushed her down toward Coddy Lee, it's penetrating hands grabbing her. Hysteria overtook her. Novella shrieked, "Eeeeeeeeeeeeek! Eeek! Eeek! Eeeeeeek!" as her body shook uncontrollably as if being electrocuted. Then, as if possessed, she hollered, "Granny, Granny, Granny, Granny, Granny!" The fit lasted for about ten seconds, before she was able to calm herself, having decided it was time to fight. She didn't know why no one had woken up or who this harassing being was, but she'd do whatever she had to do to save herself. After counting to three, Novella turned around wild and hard and threw her body toward the shadow. It was releasing her just as she made her move, so, having nothing to land on, she almost fell face first onto the floor. To stay upright, she had to grab Coddy Lee's nightstand. It shifted, and the items atop it shook. Regaining her balance, Novella saw the shadow person moving back out into the hall. Crossing the landing, it entered Willie's room. Novella's jaw dropped. "Oh no! Willie!" She then wrapped her arms around her slender torso and squeezed. A slow drawl poured forth from her, making her sound decades older than she was, "Oh my God, Willie's dead . . . and he's haunting me! Loooord, why is he haunting me? Why me? I've never done anything to him. I was always respectful to him. I never got smart with him."

Novella wanted to crawl into Coddy Lee's bed and beg her to tell her dead man to leave her alone. Novella continued to hug herself in the dark, worrying and wondering. "Help me, Lord, I can't live in a haunted house. Lord, why would he bother me? Why wouldn't he come in here to Granny? She's his woman." Suddenly, she understood and exchanged one fear for another. "Granny!"

Novella didn't hear the wheezing until after flicking on the light. Coddy Lee's oxygen mask for her sleep apnea had slipped off, and she was reaching for it. Though still asleep and deprived of oxygen, she was too weak to resecure it to her face. Novella wanted to help her, but didn't trust herself. She had never touched the mask before. After doing her best to refit it, she shook Coddy Lee. "Granny. Granny, wake up! Let me know that you're getting air! Wake up, Granny!" Fear that she may have done something wrong or worsened the situation caused her voice to hollow, as if she were disappearing. "Please, Granny! Granny, please . . . can you hear me?" Novella knew better than to keep at it alone, and so reached over and dialed 911. After begging for an ambulance to be sent right away, she asked the operator to hold while she ran to get her oldest cousin. She placed receiver on the end table. Knowing the call could be traced to their address, she didn't want to waste time that could be used to get more help. She darted out of the room. Opening the door to the third floor, she went up yelling, "Gent! Granny can't breathe! Granny's mask . . . Her mask came off! Gent!" Novella pushed hard against his door, expecting to hear the back of it hit the wall. Since it was locked, it only squeaked under the pressure of her weight. So, with the side of her fist, Novella pounded on it. She was determined to raise her cousin out of whatever abyss had him— hard labor or hard drinking. "Gent! Gent! Wake up, Granny's mask came off!" Then she began pounding with both fists. She called his name one last time. "Gennnnt!" Hopelessness laid her against his door, but only briefly. Pushing up, she turned to enlist the help of the other cousins who roomed on the third floor: Janet and Isaac. Though when she turned around, they were already two blurs thundering down the stairs to the second floor. "Granny!" Isaac announced. "We coming!" Novella's spirits were lifted. She rushed back to Coddy Lee's room right behind them, the third soldier in their cavalry.

"What we need to do, cuz?" Isaac looked to Novella. She looked to Janet, who returned her look with, "Noey?"

Novella, although surprised the older ones would turn to her, awkwardly yet quickly took charge of the situation. Grabbing Janet's arm, she urged her to follow her lead as she climbed atop Coddy Lee. Janet complied, getting in the bed on the far side of Coddy Lee.

"Raise her head," Novella instructed. "We need to wake her up to make sure she is getting air." Novella then looked to Isaac and spoke to him with more calm than she ever thought possible, "I think Willie died."

Janet, pushing a second pillow under Coddy Lee's head, sighed sharply but didn't look up.

Isaac, his eyes having immediately widened, asked, "What make you say that?"

Novella knew better than to tell him that Willie's ghost had dragged her out of bed. She instead replied, "Just go check on him." Isaac's nervousness, compounded by the fear of the task he had been assigned, caused him to complain, "Noey, why didn't you dial 911? I'm not a doctor. What am I supposed to do?"

Novella told him, "911 is on the phone. Now, Isaac, you're going to have to sort it out yourself, and do your part. I can't keep talking to you and help Granny."

Isaac didn't move. Since the cancer had immobilized Willie, Isaac had only occasionally ventured into his room. If a chicken is the symbol of cowards, then it was also Isaac's spirit animal. Big-mouthed Isaac talked, but didn't do much else. Stories of him running, leaving a girlfriend or a buddy behind, were many. On separate occasions, he'd left both Janet and Gent. Isaac was even afraid of their house, not liking to be in it alone. "It's haunted in here," he often said. When the two-story was full of people, Isaac appreciated the space within its eighteen hundred square feet. When alone in it, a basement, first, second, and third floor were too many levels— all with four corners for ghostly activity to manifest in and come at him. To Isaac, Willie's impending death was one of the many things haunting the house. Isaac only visited Willie's room when someone accompanied him, never at night, and he didn't ever go any further into the room than the doorway. They'd had an easy relationship, as most did with Willie. He'd never tried to be a parental figure to the grandkids. He was Coddy Lee's man and their older friend. Isaac and Willie had bonded on a fraternal level when Isaac contracted his first venereal disease. Willie had overheard the noisy bathroom visits. Isaac sounded to be on the losing end of a beating, each time urine passed through his infected penis. He'd tried to hide the disease, but his painful bathroom sessions were easily overheard by the man who was attuned to every squeak in the house. "Open the door, Birdman," Willie had sympathetically commanded. "It's gonna be alright." Birdman was a family nickname for Isaac, a slender boy with long arms and long legs. For almost ten years, the family had regularly called him Birdman or Bird until he complained about the nickname embarrassing him in front of girls. Ironically, messing with the wrong girl had embarrassed him into trying to hide an STD.

"I'm alright!" he'd replied in a cry to Willie, the only person in the house he was fine with still calling him by the nickname. "I just ate something bad. It's my stomach."

Willie knew better. "Bird, that volcano in your dick won't go away on its own. Now I'm gonna help you, son, and it'll stay between us men."

Isaac's STD did stay between them by way of Willie keeping his word. It got out, however, in two ways. The first was Janet and Gent seeing Coddy Lee bleaching the toilet and tub—she didn't usually do housework. Willie had to go to her for Isaac's health card, his first time doing so. Coddy Lee knew her grandson's reputation for sleeping with any willing girl. The other way, word got it, was the entire household witnessing another first— Willie and Isaac leaving the house together. *Isaac had an STD.*

Two years ago, cans of Ensure preceded Willie's return home after the removal of his vocal cords. Coddy Lee had explained to the curious Isaac that Ensure was made for cancer patients who had difficulty eating regular food. Isaac was even permitted to try one, and had chosen the strawberry flavor. The fifteen-hundred-calorie drink had looked and smelled like a milkshake, but assaulted his palette like sweet liquid chalk. "He gotta drink this stuff every day?" Isaac asked as flatly as he could, trying to mask the sadness brought on by sampling the drink. Special food that didn't taste anywhere near as good as the meals Willie had cooked made it clear to Isaac that Willie was seriously sick and would be a different man than he had been. Although, having entered the house on his own two feet, with no voice he coughed and knocked on tables and walls. He wasn't as strong as he had been before surgery, so while he occasionally repaired things and cooked food, he was never again the domestic king who provided the comfort most of them had taken for granted. After his last extended hospital stay, he came home on a stretcher, and Isaac understood he was beyond sick. Willie had returned so much smaller. Each time Isaac stole a glance at him, he appeared to be almost gone. Willie's eyes no longer had a spark, but could still open and stare intensely. His skin had become dull and waxen. To Isaac, Willie resembled a possessed mannequin, and he was not going to check on him. Isaac's loyalty and sympathy, which wavered at the best of times, completely dissipated in awkward situations. Over the course of Willie's decline, the now eighteen-year-old had become completely creeped out by him. Isaac wasn't about to let it be his job to confirm if the man's condition was still only almost dead or if it had changed to completely dead. Isaac was so agitated that even watching Novella's successful efforts with their granny left him unimpressed. She'd given him what he felt was the worst thing to do. *Who does Noey think she is?* He inwardly fumed. *I can't do shit for a dead or dying man! And I ain't about to do shit!* Outside in the quiet night, a car door slammed. Shortly afterwards, there was the sound of keys and their front door opening.

Isaac yelled in relief, "Gent?"

THIRTY-THREE

June 4, 1992

Masonic Temple and Performing Arts Center, Euclid Avenue

If not for the gold earrings accenting her face, Novella Renae Lofton would have blended in with the other red-robed graduates. The large metal spirals on either side of her chocolate face, revealing her position in the queue, indicated to her guests her name would be around the hundredth or so to be called.

On this day, 276 diplomas were to be awarded, thirty-nine of them to teenage mothers. Their attendance at the school had nearly divided the educational staff. In Novella's sophomore year, three large classrooms on the first floor of West Tech were combined to house a daycare. Accomplished students interested in careers such as in health and human development were permitted to intern, alongside certified childcare providers. Notification letters to parents, when the initiative was only a proposal, made it obvious that a daycare inside a high school was not welcome by all. "Our staff is doing their best to consider the impact of this, proposed, controversial initiative without bias." Coddy Lee thought it was a great idea, and wished such a thing had existed when she'd gotten pregnant. As for Janet, Coddy Lee didn't want her dropping out, but didn't appreciate her taking her time getting back home from school. So, the daycare kept Janet honest, because she didn't like taking the busybody Lil Vic on hook-ups. Each day after her last class, Janet picked up Lil Vic, and then went straight home.

While the daycare relieved Coddy Lee, other parents as well as many teachers thought it rewarded bad behavior and sent the wrong message to good girls.

"Real easy to end up that way," said a teacher to Novella when she'd patted a pregnant classmate's belly. Chemistry class had ended, and the two girls were the last students to leave the room. The pregnant girl, after hearing the teacher's comment, moved a bit faster, leaving the room in a huff.

With just the teacher and Novella in the room, he told her while wiping the chalkboard, "That damn daycare shouldn't even be in here."

Novella responded without thinking, "Well, then almost all of the girls would have to drop out." When the teacher turned his hazel eyes on her, she almost didn't finish. After a deep breath, she went on, "The boys don't—aren't responsible for the kids. So, only the girls wouldn't graduate, when the boys are just as guilty."

The teacher folded his arms. "What are you saying, Novella? That it's okay, and you want to get pregnant, too?"

"No. I don't want to get pregnant. I'm saying everyone deserves an education. Having a baby young is bad, but not getting an education is worse." When she turned to leave, she bumped into her biology teacher who had entered the room without her noticing. Novella, surprised, gasped, "Oh my God, Mrs. Butler, I'm so sorry."

With pride in her eyes, the teacher assured, "You're okay, Novella. And keep being smart—and fair."

An honorary diploma was being presented posthumously to the parents of one of the four valedictorians who had been the unintended victim of a drive-by shooting. Now where he was supposed to be seated, a 12 × 13 reproduction of his senior picture had been propped up.

Those in attendance for Novella were split between two rows. Yadara, Dell, and Connie were in the seventh row. Behind them were Janet and Charlee Lu'a, Coddy Lee's oldest daughter who just happened to be visiting. Janet hadn't forgiven Novella for the body-slam, but felt pressured to attend. There weren't many graduates in their family, and Janet considered Novella and herself part of the accomplished and upper class of their blood line. They were both smart, nice dressers, pretty—and both had diplomas. Also among the upper class of the family, according to Janet, was her mom, the only one of Coddy Lee's children with a diploma. Janet had also gone to the graduation because it was an opportunity to dress up. Coddy Lee, for unspecified reasons, had opted not to attend. "Couldn't be bothered," Janet had whispered to Novella, adding, "She didn't come to mine neither. So it's like that. You know Connie and Cherry, dropout asses, are her favorites."

Novella had no doubt of that, but still gave Coddy Lee a pass. She'd put her Willie away, handled his remains without ceremony. He hadn't died that night his ghost had pulled Novella from the bed. Coddy Lee had lost him two-and-half months later. Willie had become unresponsive around nine in the morning and was gone by noon. Within a day, his room had been cleared. Three weeks later, his ashes were in a plain black urn on the mantel above the fireplace. There had been no funeral. Coddy Lee's daughters Canella Lynn and Cadee Leah had funerals when they died. Copies of their obituaries were in the photo album and in Coddy Lee's Bible. Novella decided her granny's age and poor health had kept her from attending formal events. So, while Coddy Lee continued to read the Bible and listened to gospel music, she no longer attended church. She ate restaurant food as long as it was ordered to-go.

Yadara and Dell had a different opinion about the woman who never showed up to any school event to support their friend, and who never gave her a ride anywhere: she was a bad grandmother.

Janet, Connie, and Charlee Lu'a would leave Novella and her friends to celebrate the graduation on their own. It was during this time that Yadara told Novella, "I know this may hurt your feelings, Noey. But I'm just gonna say it. Your grandmother is not right. That march she did to go find you was out of possessiveness, not love. Love would have brought her today, and many other times."

Dell had chimed in, "She's not too sick to climb the steps to go play Bingo. So, yeah girl, it's foul for her not to have come."

Novella had no words, because while not wanting to, a part of her believed them.

THIRTY-FOUR

March 13, 1998

BETY Junior eased off gas the pedal, watching a Honda Civic slide into the lane ahead of him. The mounds of snow all over the Greater Cleveland area were in a slow melt. This week's average was a crisp forty-one degrees. It was getting warmer, and the overnight freezing temperatures caused only a pause in the thaw. One of the effects of this seasonal transition was the asphalt cocktail of ice, snow, and slush that made driving a dangerous proposition.

The Honda Civic fishtailed, and BETY Junior shook his head. "Need new tires or something. We're not even going that fast." The show didn't last long, but in those few moments, BETY Junior's shoulders stiffened. If the Civic spun out, his Blazer was more than likely to get smacked. The tailgating Buick Regal behind him was likely to slam its engine to BETY Junior's trailer hitch should things go wrong. Luckily, the Honda Civic's driver regained control. BETY Junior took the opportunity to increase the distance between his rear bumper and the Regal's front bumper. He then continued his conversation.

"Listen," he explained to his second cousin, who was riding shotgun, "this is a card party. Fried fish and liquor, and it's done. We do this the

149

Saturday after next. And we do it unceremoniously, baby. Meaning let's just make calls, make moves, and make it happen."

"Okay," agreed Purcell. "First move?"

BETY Junior would make it himself. "I'm calling Ms. Pudding," he said. "I don't want no one else's fish. Well, maybe Sister Raffie's, you know, on Superior, but her place doesn't cater."

"DJ?" Purcell asked.

BETY Junior laughed. "You notice how every year the DJ is the biggest problem?"

"Hell, yeah," Purcell remembered, and then added, "But I know someone."

"Oh yeah?" BETY Junior replied. "What's up with him?"

"Her," Purcell said plainly, waiting on his cousin's reaction. When BETY Junior gave him a quick look from the steering wheel, Purcell couldn't help but laugh. "Yeah, cuz, a female DJ."

"Never had one of those." BETY Junior shrugged.

"Aren't you an equal-opportunity employer?" Purcell laughed, raising his cap only to quickly lower it back down, his signature habit.

"Female DJ, huh?" BETY Junior thought out loud, and then asked, "What she after, canines or felines? She want them to bark or purr? And is she fine?"

"What's it to you, Mr. Don't-Mix-Business-with-Pleasure?" Purcell reminded him. "You know your so-called ethical code. The one you abide by at your dick's discretion."

BETY Junior, after giving a short, robust laugh, barked, "Answer the questions, cuz!"

"Man, whatever!" Purcell dismissed the order. "All that don't matter. If she has the skills to make the party jump, she's hired. It's on me. I'm paying. Happy birthday!"

Born March 29, BETY Junior partied the entire cycle of the Aries zodiac, from March 21 to April 19. BETY Junior and Purcell were planning as they headed to the chosen spot for this year's party. Having arrived, they were now leaving the warmth of BETY Junior's Chevy Blazer.

"Damn, spring in C-Town is bitter!" Purcell growled, stepping into the weather. "The beginning of spring here is like the middle of winter everywhere else. It was thirty degrees when I came for Christmas in December, and it's thirty damn degrees today and it's almost spring." He tightened his scarf around his neck "Damn cold is baptizing me, but I ain't no better for it. Shit."

BETY Junior shrugged. "Well, stop crying. This liquor will knock the chill off your southern ass." BETY Junior had never hosted a dry party, but for crowd control had told people the party would be BYOB. BETY Junior's mission statement was the same every year, "The end game is to have them feeling good, not fucked up. Pissy drunk is for the hole in the wall bars, where the barflies look like buzzards. My jam is for the grown and the sexy."

He and Purcell were setting up in one of BETY Junior's vacant rental properties, which he was still unsure about making available for Section Eight tenants. The upside of the low-income program was that 70 percent of the rent was guaranteed to be paid timely by the county. The remainder carried potential risk that outweighed the benefits of the guaranteed rent. Existing homeowners, potential buyers, and non-subsidized renters usually didn't want Section Eight neighbors. Property values were known to drop, increasing the potential for negative equity on mortgages, and less return on investments. Section Eight brought lower-income people into a neighborhood in which they could otherwise not afford to reside.

There were very negative opinions about the voucher recipients, and being everyone else's tax burden was the nicest of them. The stigma attached to Section Eight tenants was as much based on false, derogatory stereotypes as it was on facts. BETY Junior could luck up with one of the dynamic families, whose success over adversity would later become America's feel-good movie of the year. He could also strike out with one with violent domestic issues and destructive kids. If BETY Junior registered the home, his would be the first in the area that was a mix of middle-class renters and homeowners. He could potentially start the depression in the neighborhood. It was a dilemma, and in order to come to a resolution, BETY Junior would chew on it with Pop during their next meal. Right now, the vacant rental property was to be the Ram's den, the Aries birthday kickoff party center. Three tables for playing cards, and a fourth for dominos, were to be positioned in each corner of the home's great room. BETY Junior and Purcell had even hauled in a pool table that was set up in the dining room. Even with the all the tables, the players would have elbow room; those mingling and dancing would have leg room, until the latest of arrivals pushed in around midnight or later, making it nearly impossible to move about without bumping into someone. No matter how thick the crowd, BETY Junior would keep the party restricted to the main floor. Using empty liquor bottles from prior events, he had closed off the upstairs. Decoratively yet strategically, he had placed them on each step so there would be no way to bypass them. He did so both as a damage control measure for his investment property, and so that the cleaning crew would not have to clean up discarded condoms, panties, drug paraphernalia, and other personal items left by guests.

The Party

"Let's get away from these fools for a little while." The guy nodded toward the steps.

"It's blocked off," the woman looked around the room at the other partiers.

"I'm not talking about upstairs." The guy nodded for her to look further. "The basement."

Unimpressed by the idea, her answer was flat, "I wanna play spades."

After an eye roll and lip smack, he challenged her, "How are you going to get a seat at one of the tables? You don't even know these people, and they don't know you."

"They don't know you either," she reminded him, "but you're on your third cup of their liquor. Anyway, I know how to mingle."

A little offended, he asked, "Mingle for what? You're with somebody—me. I invited you here."

"Yeah, but who do you know? Like, whose house are we in?"

"The dude is my cousin's friend."

The dude he spoke of, BETY Junior, inching past them to return to a card table, stopped and welcomed them. "Hey, how y'all doing?"

The woman, a link to BETY Junior's past, was the first to answer, "Good." Smiling eagerly up at him, she introduced herself, "I'm Ardellya. Everyone calls me Dell."

"Nice to meet you, Dell. I'm BETY Junior." He smiled back at her.

There was no click between BETY Junior and his link, no connection to their common interest. There was, however, knocking: Dell's female desire against his male appeal. BETY Junior offered a hand to her date to show that he wasn't pushing up on her. Dell reached in front of her date. Taking BETY Junior's hand, she stepped a half foot closer to him. "Nice to meet *you*." Dell had never been so enthralled by a man's hand. To her, BETY Junior's felt capable of punching a hole through concrete. Dell had no doubt that gently wrapped around her palm were the digits of an iron fist. *This guy is built.* She gave his figure a quick scan. She held his hand long enough for him to respond with a tender squeeze. Messaged delivered—now it would be his move and she hoped he'd soon make it. Slowly she let go.

BETY Junior again extended his hand to her date. "Bro, how you?"

The guy took it, shaking it weakly. "I'm cool." He matched BETY Junior in height, yet was completely overshadowed by him. BETY Junior, although never flashy, was well-groomed and confident. Dell's date and BETY Junior didn't run in the same circles.

"Thanks for coming," BETY Junior said, earnestly welcoming both Dell and her date.

"Is it your birthday?" Dell asked in a puckered smile.

"Yes, it is, sweetie." BETY Junior rocked back in forth in a quick dance.

"Alright then." Dell returned his dance with a wiggle of her hips. "Happy birthday!"

Her date looked away.

"Thanks. And thank y'all both for coming." BETY Junior was about to continue on his way when he noticed the guy was looking toward one of the card tables. He asked, "You play?"

The guy immediately moved his gaze from the table to the people socializing near it and shook his head disinterestedly. "Nah." It was a lie. A more truthful answer would have been, "Not for money."

"I play," Dell invited herself to be invited to the table.

BETY Junior, although feeling the distance between them, was certain they had come together as a couple. Yet the woman clearly had an agenda that would leave the dude stag. BETY Junior, not one to stoke the fire in relationship issues or fight over women, pointed toward the domino table. "Well, introduce yourself to the guy sitting over there. He's organizing all the games. Signing people up, making sure everyone who wants to play gets to play." As BETY Junior leaned back to point out the pool table in the corner, a woman with a hive of burgundy dreadlocks piled high atop her head caught his eye. She'd eased out from the crush of partiers, as if escaping the flame they'd gathered around for warmth. She looked like she might smell of vanilla or cinnamon, or both.

BETY Junior smiled as he stood taller, preparing to greet the obviously very welcome guest. He titled his chin upwards at her, a gesture to say both hello and come on over here. Watching her stunning approach, his patience ended; he could no longer wait to touch her. So, when she stepped within his impressive eighty-inch reach, arms that drove powerful jabs and hooks helped close the distance between them. He pulled her against his side, resting an arm atop her round hips, which were outlined by an ankle-length cheetah print dress. She was five-foot-seven, with long, full curves. The majority of the freckles on her face made their home under her chestnut upturned eyes. Her smooth, radiant, and unblemished complexion was the color of butterscotch. The only makeup she wore was mascara and lip gloss.

Dell and the dreadlocked vixen were close in height and weight, and just as her date was overshadowed by BETY Junior, so was Dell by this woman.

Dell, also an attractive woman, wore a denim knee-length dress. The bodycon accentuated her hourglass figure, but hadn't stunned BETY Junior like the one in the cheetah print had. Dell, also a minimalist when it came to makeup, had only done her lips and eyes with her favorite red matte and black mascara. Her golden yellow complexion with only a few small pimples was otherwise clear and bright. Dell drank plenty of water and ate her vegetables. Obviously, so did the woman pressed against BETY Junior's side.

IN SEARCH OF A TRIBE

Give me a break. Dell's ego huffed. Hmm. *He's into those hard ropes on her head, and spots on her face? Whatever. Well, he can have Ms. Animal Kingdom, if he's into that. I was raised to comb my hair.*

Dell's date dismissed the woman like a man with used Ford hatchback money at a Porsche dealership.

The woman, comfortable in her skin, didn't seem to notice Dell or her date. Through sultry eyes, she stared up at their host. "Hey, Bariah."

His lips brushing against her ear, BETY Junior asked, "Aren't you gonna wish me happy birthday?"

Playfully she rolled her eyes. "Bariah, your birthday isn't until tomorrow. Can't you wait?"

He told her, "Not for everything, and I waited long enough for you to get here."

BETY Junior had forgotten he had been talking to Dell and her date until he started to lead his gift of a guest away for privacy. Turning back, he told them. "Oh, yeah, y'all take it easy. Be encouraged. Eat, drink, and play. Enjoy yourselves, alright." He then left Dell and her date as he found them, romantically out of place with one another.

Dell had actually dumped the guy a week ago. The way she saw it, she was his new hang out and potential screw buddy, not his girlfriend. The two hadn't been to the movies, a restaurant, any place that charged an entry fee, or offered anything that required them to spend money. Their first outing had been to a house party, as had the two that followed. So, three low balls in a row on the dating field struck him out with Dell. She wanted to be courted. She began ignoring his calls. But then came a call from Novella, her best and only real friend. She'd asked for wardrobe advice for her date with a very handsome man they'd secretly nicknamed Dr. Night Time due both to him being a doctor and his smooth blue-black skin. He was willing to pay for nice dinners. Tonight, he and Novella were at The Island, a

Jamaican seafood restaurant. It had a rating of two-dollar signs above that of Red Lobster that was Novella and Dell's usual nice dinner or lunch spot for celebrations. Dell's green lady growled under her fake enthusiasm as Novella went on about which dress to wear. So, the "Low Budget Busta of the Year," the secret nickname for Dell's date, got another play on the field. Dell had just hung up with Novella when he called. Seeing his number in the caller ID initially only soured the bitter feelings she hid helping Novella decide on her outfit. So, she let the phone ring four times before her pride took a step back to allow her to answer. When invited to go to a card party she accepted, reasoning it was better than a solo Blockbuster video night. Dell, however, was not a passive settler. She'd look to score a better prospect while enjoying the advantages of not going alone. She'd have someone to chat with and a guaranteed dance partner, but not being his girlfriend, she could swap phone numbers with any man she fancied. They'd arrived together, would leave together, but weren't really together. Dell didn't need a meal at The Island to feel properly courted. She'd gladly dine on an Ultimate Feast and strawberry daiquiri at Red Lobster rather than have buffalo wings off a paper plate and gin and juice out of a Styrofoam cup in a stranger's living room. Hell, she'd be fine with Cracker Barrel, or Hometown Buffet, as long as they also did something along the lines of catching a movie.

Now that BETY Junior had left, his name echoed in Dell's mind. Seemed like she'd heard it before, like maybe she knew someone who knew him. Trying to make the connection she felt was giving her a headache, so she turned to her date to try to salvage the evening, at least until she came across another prospect. Ms. Animal Kingdom's landslide win with BETY Junior had challenged Dell's inner huntress. Claws extended, she'd now be more audacious than cautious. She'd driven them to the party, so she felt to be in a position of power. *It's on!* proclaimed her ego. If her date pulled her card, fronting on her about flirting, it would be to his disadvantage. *He can catch the bus home, if he gets an attitude*, she thought. *He's not my man.*

Her date, still nearby, had stepped back and copped a spot against the paisley wallpapered wall. Dell, turning to see him relaxing, decided to do the same. Scoping out the potentials, she figured, would be easier.

The wall was about three arm lengths away, or so she thought. Surprisingly, just taking a few small steps, she crashed right into it. She stumbled backwards into a few guests, who offered her a helping hand only to get her off them. Free of her, they left her mostly upright, dizzy and confused. She had enough clarity to be grateful that she was wearing flats. She also understood quickly that she needed to hold on to something. She turned and reached out toward the wall. Hallucination blurring her limited vision, she saw it inching away from her in short smooth waves of pulsating technicolor. "Dayum!" Dell, feeling ever desperate for an anchor, kept trying to reach the wall. Seconds felt like minutes. When her left hand finally met the wall, her relief created vibrations in it. Her date and the other wall flowers looked up from their drinks and conversations. Dell's hand had slapped the wall hard, before her body fell against it. "Shit!" Her head spinning, she could still tell she was being given that "she-can't-handle-her-liquor" look from about twenty guests. Her date took her drink that she had somehow managed not to spill. "It's okay, baby. I'm here," he told her. "Let's get you home."

Her last memory of being at the party was hearing someone yell, "No basement business. Get it on elsewhere!"

THIRTY-FIVE

"Girl, you're lying!" Novella exclaimed in between spoonfuls of cereal.

"No," Dell continued, "I'm not. When I woke up, we were in my car, but in the back seat."

"Shut up!" Novella reached for the box of cereal. While balancing the phone between her head and shoulder, she refilled her bowl. "So, the low-budget buster is a damn rapist."

"Yep," Dell sighed. "Guess, his broke ass thought my ass was free too. I open my eyes to see his nothing having ass putting a condom on his giant python penis. I was like—"

Novella interrupted, "Girl, wait a minute. How big?"

"Bigger than big," Dell answered impatiently. "I said giant and I meant giant."

"I need clarification," Novella said plainly.

"Damn, Noey!" Dell huffed. "I trying to exhale here. I need to get this off my chest."

"When you tell a story, you gotta be clear," Novella insisted. Collating data was their way, always getting every last detail. They were still at the age of over-confiding in one another, not yet having the finesse to give a juicy yet shallow account. As Novella saw it, the assault was over and Dell was alive, so she had to tell it. All of it.

Dell, knowing she would be just as persistent if it had happened to Novella, conceded, "Girl," she said calmly yet intensely, "a sista gotta be more than Duncan Hines moist to be on the receiving end of that. Like it belonged to a horse. I'm serious. Maybe the length of my forearm. He could have done some damage."

"What?" Novella dropped her spoon on the kitchen counter. "Girl, that is the gin and the drugs he slipped you talking. No way it was that big!"

"I know what I saw!"

"You were tipsy. And drugged. Tipsy and drugged!"

"Were you there? Noey, were you there?"

Novella countered, "Were *you* there? 'Alice in Wonderland', porno version! Tipsy and drugged, were you there? Not all there, for sure! There are no horse dick men in the world, Ardellya. Just like there are no mermaids, all tittie-licious and waiting to be discovered and screwed by a human man. And, girl, remember you said that after we watched that mermaid movie? Now girl, seriously, trauma and drugs girl, you were messed up!"

"You got a problem," Dell said dismissively. "But we're talking about me right now. We'll have to fix your crazy ass later."

"All I'm saying," Novella explained, "is you were floating on a dark cloud. You know it was a dark and stormy night, and your ass couldn't tell the difference between an arm and a dick." Novella let out a loud roll of laughter.

"Noey, dayum! Are you serious with these gotdamn jokes?"

"Oh so, you can laugh at me but . . . okay, okay I'll chill. But, but, but . . ." Novella gently pressed, "you were under the influence of alcohol and drugs to the point that you blacked out." Then pointedly, as if enlightening Dell, she added, "You were high." Novella said with an air of finality,

"Something was going down or trying to down with the Low Budget Busta of the Year, but everything wasn't as it seemed. Sure, his dick was out, but you obviously misjudged the size. Humans don't have horse penises."

Dell, quite annoyed by Novella's explanation, asked, "Did I dial the Anatomy 101 hotline by mistake? Because I didn't call for a lecture on the biology of dicks. I'm trying to exhale to my best friend about my night from hell. Can I do that?"

"Carry on, my friend," Novella sang. "Carry on. I am your girl. I am here for you."

Sarcastically, Dell said, "Thank you, friend." Then she picked up her story in a tone that dared Novella to challenge her. "And I wake up to him strapping up his giant . . . python . . . penis."

Novella's challenge was indirect and spoken in a patronizing voice, "It would have been like childbirth in reverse. How did Mr. Python think you were going to sleep through being plugged by something so big?"

"Girl, how in the hell should I know?" Dell nearly screamed. "But you know what, Ms. Queen of It-Ain't-Going-Down-Unless-I-Say-So wasn't having it! I tried to plug his ass with my hammer!"

"Hammer?" Novella began crunching on the flakes she'd just spooned into her mouth.

Dell exhaled for sanity. "Whew! Girl, remember the hammer I bought last month, but then I couldn't find it? I couldn't remember if had actually left the store with it, or if I had lost it somewhere in the house."

"Yeah."

"Well, it turns out, I left the store with it, but I never took it out of the car. Somehow it ended up on the floorboard, and I saw it there when I woke up. When I saw what he was doing, I started looking around for a way to save myself. And bam, there it was, right in arm's reach."

"Thank God!" Novella placed a hand on her chest. "Thank God!

"Yeah." Dell rolled her eyes. "Thank Handy Hank's Hardware, is more like it."

"Did you bust him up bad?"

"No," Dell said with real disappointment in her voice. "He got to backing up and covering that python when he saw me reaching for the hammer."

"I bet," Novella imagined the scene.

"I swung anyway because I wanted him out of my damn car!" Dell said angrily. "And I kept swinging until his bare ass was sitting on that cold concrete, holding his dick and begging me not to hit him." Dell's anger grew as she continued, her voice rising and falling, shaking as if reliving the ordeal, "It was only because he was so tall that I didn't get him like I wanted to. And he got the door open so fast. Girl, you know what I'm like: I was screaming m'fer this and m'fer that, I'll kill your ass, you can't mess with me, I'll f you up, I'm gonna beat your pecker to a stump and bash your m f'ing brains in! Girl, I was going crazy. Swinging that hammer and cussing up a storm."

"Wait a minute," Novella said. "Pecker? Where did you learn that? How you long been moonlighting on the west side? Sista-Girl, you're from East 105th. There aren't any peckers there, just dicks."

In spite of it all, Dell laughed. "Shut up."

"Well, this lowlife needs to be outed," Novella told her. "Sistas need to be aware. What's his full name? Let's put a shout-out in the network."

"What network, Noey?" Dell asked.

"The network of Sistas Gotta Look Out For Each Other," Novella declared. "This week's update: I know a rapist. Now what's Low Budget's full name? You know what, all of them. His Christian name, government name, family nickname, and his street name. Let's out his rapist ass."

"Antwan Smith," Dell told her. "Maybe some folks call him Twan."

"Middle name?"

"Um, I don't know."

"Where does his work?"

"He does temp jobs for Manpower downtown. He doesn't have a regular job right now."

"What kind of car does he drive?"

"His mama's."

They shared a laugh, and then Dell said, "The RiTA mostly. He has a monthly bus pass. He buses it when he can't borrow his mama's ride. She has a green Ford Taurus; it's kind of new."

"I guess it's kind of good he doesn't have a car. His date-raping ass would have too much access. Anyway, if someone mentions an Antwan, you blast him on high." Novella gave her an example. "Who? What Antwan? I know not Antwan Smith who temps for Manpower! That no good did such and such and blah, blah, blah."

They laughed again as Dell agreed, "Yeah, girl."

"Yeah is right," Novella insisted. "Run it down to them on full blast. Full blast! That's how we're gonna do this. Freaking creep! He's a criminal!"

Dell agreed, but when she tried to say the word "right" it came out like a dry heave. Novella, still standing at her kitchen counter, spat out the cereal she'd just started to chew when she heard the sounds coming from her friend's mouth. She moved the phone away from her ear to keep the corn flakes in her belly from re-entering the world. Sounds can give insight and create visuals; in this case, unpleasant ones. After taking a few deep breaths, she brought the phone back to her ear, "Is that the drug, girl? . . . You need me to come over?"

Dell dry-heaved again. She sounded miserable. Novella didn't want to clean up her friend's vomit, but she could drive her to the hospital. Novella waited for Dell to return to the phone.

When she finally came back on the line, Novella was surprised that Dell told her not to come.

"That's ok, girl." Dell's breathing was labored, and Novella wondered what the situation was like over there. What did it look like? Were there pools of vomit on the floor? Was there one in her bed, since she was pretty sure Dell was still in it when she called.

"Dell?" Novella questioned.

"It's okay," Dell assured her. "Right before I came back to the phone, I let Cornelia in. She's on her way to church. She stopped by to raid my kitchen for coffee and something to eat."

"Oh, good."

"Uh-huh," Dell grunted knowingly.

"I would've come," Novella smiled.

"Yeah," Dell cleared her throat. "And threw up next to me."

Novella couldn't argue. The two hung up so Dell could explain the evening to Cornelia.

"You got slipped a roofie?" Novella heard Cornelia say right before returning her cordless to its base.

She had just showered and dressed to head to grocery store when Dell called again.

"Hey, girl, whatcha doing?

"On my way to Finast," Novella told her as she checked her purse for her debit card.

"I need you to take me to urgent care."

"What happened to Cornelia?"

"She went to her new church."

"Um," Novella muttered as she thought but didn't say, *You leave your sick sister to go pray and sing with strangers?*

"You know Cornelia," Dell replied to her friend's unspoken question. "We both know some Bible-thumping church mama didn't get her to go there. There's probably some Cadillac driving deacon she's trying to get with. You know, she forever trying to land Mr. Perfect."

Novella asked, "Isn't she still married to Fred, or Frank, or whatever his name is?"

"You know Cornelia."

"On my way."

What little Novella knew of date rape drugs came from the television, but what she did know was that while the first twenty-four to forty-eight hours could feel like a really bad hangover, Dell was going to be fine. She'd awakened clear-headed enough to recognize she was in danger, even if the python-sized penis was a hallucination. She had also had the strength to fight off her attacker and drive home. The downside was that, if Dell had any intention of pressing charges, she had probably already expelled the drug from her system, which was eventually confirmed during their visit to urgent care. Dell decided going to the police would be more trouble for her than it would be for the Low Budget Busta. Dell wasn't raped, bruised, and had no proof she had been drugged. She figured her best shot at justice involved hunting him down and going off on him. She called him on the phone and threatened to "fuck him up on sight!" She also called his mother and told her, "Your lazy son is a rapist. He's gonna get busted up out here trying to screw women against their will. He got a real problem! Maybe you do too."

Novella stared at Dell after she'd hung up. "You should have been nicer and more respectful to his mama. This could be her first time hearing something like this about him."

Dell stared back at her. "Huh, well, now she knows. And I don't owe the mama of a rapist anything."

THIRTY-SIX

April 11, 1998

A Piece of Africa

On E 55th and Superior Avenue sat A Piece of Africa, a novelty store. It was near the beginning of the city's downtown business district, in a bland area where the city transitioned from houses and apartments to office buildings. A bit of distance from Novella's home on the upper east side, the area offered nothing of interest to her other than A Piece of Africa. The books, supplies, vibes, and ample parking justified the commute to get there. There was also the owner, who was called Mr. Africa. The Cleveland native, with mocha-colored skin, was everything. Well-read, traveled, resourceful, and funny, he was the good kind of bad boy. He was always claiming many of the African beauty products he sold to be aphrodisiacs. Soaps, oils and butters, shampoos, even incense and candles were, Mr. Africa guaranteed, to help customers get their freak on. Bodacious, the married proprietor wasn't lewd or flirtatious.

Novella was to meet up with Yadara at A Piece of Africa. Afterwards, they were to go for food. Yadara, the first to arrive, stepped inside and immediately acquired an admirer. Sitting in the store's often overlooked small lounge, BETY Junior watched her, all two-hundred-voluptuous pounds on her five-foot-eight-and-a-half-inch frame. A beaded curtain in the lounge's doorway hid him from view. The streams of sunlight cascading through the partially open curtains of the main lobby illuminated her. She was another unknown link to his past. If BETY Junior had not been minutes away from an appointment to discuss a real estate deal, he would have introduced himself. *Can't get to them all*, he thought. Admiring her big curves in motion from afar would have to do. *Solid*, he imagined, as the only jiggle in her confident stride had been slight. The store sat below street level, and her size Fs had bounced with each step as she descended the stairs onto the sales floor. From her sophisticated and composed demeanor, he guessed her smooth gingerbread skin was more likely to be splashed with one of the store's more sultry smelling oils like Black Coconut. When Novella, BETY Junior's past, entered the store a short while later, he'd had already shifted his attention from women to business. He'd moved deeper into the lounge and started his meeting. When it adjourned, both the link and the past she clicked into would be gone.

THIRTY-SEVEN

Novella and Yadara headed back to the upper east side after their visit to A Piece of Africa, stopping at a beauty supply store for nail polish on the way. They were now settled at Novella's dining table sampling their buys. The cheese and crackers they were munching were not nourishing or filling enough after four hours of shopping. Novella was about to ask Yadara if she was ready to head out to dinner when her cordless phone rang.

"Whaddup, girl!" Dell yelled after Novella said hello.

"'Bout to get something to eat," Novella told her, knowing Yadara would hate it if Dell joined them. Novella received the subliminal message of *Tell her no! She can't come!* even before she looked up from the lavender polish she had just applied to her left pinky nail. Novella refused to choose between her two best friends. So, blowing Dell off or lying to her just because she'd hooked up with Yadara first was, in Yadara's words, "hell to the nah-nah."

"Oh yeah?" Dell had replied. "Where?"

"Yadara and I were in the mood for Red Lobster," Novella replied easily.

"Damn, big spenders."

Novella laughed. "Well, we want seafood."

"Ok then. I can eat some scampi."

"You can choke on them too," Yadara fumed in a low voice, keeping her eyes fixed on Novella.

Novella, shaking her head at Yadara's ugliest comment yet about Dell, said, "Ok, girl, we getting ready to head out."

After she hung up, Novella screamed in laughter. "Girl, that was a terrible thing to say. Dayum, you used to like her. Do you hate her now?"

"No." Yadara applied a coat of gold on her thumbnail. "But I really don't like her. I *really* don't like her."

Novella shrugged. "Well, I love you both. So, can we go?"

Admiring her polish, Yadara said, "Bitch invited herself; bitch can wait."

"Ya-da-ra!" Novella stood from the table.

Yadara didn't rise, but instead turned her hand around for Novella to admire.

Novella refused to comment. "Girl, let's go."

Yadara threw a handful of cotton balls at her. "Damn your nice ass, Noey! You punk, you make me sick!"

Dinner ended up being a blast from the past. Glasses were clinked, and tears were shed from laughter at jokes none of them would be able to recount. The trio received mixed looks from the other patrons for their antics. Their daiquiris, they later discovered, were spoiled virgins; they each had alcohol. Novella didn't drink at all, Yadara only on occasion, and Dell had already had a Long Island iced tea before meeting up. Their differences dissolved in rum, they got along like the tight-knit trio they had been in high school, though the rum wasn't strong enough to carry Yadara beyond dinner. Although they were still laughing out in the parking lot, Yadara said no to joining them for a night of clubbing.

THIRTY-EIGHT

The Mirage on the Water night club was located downtown in The Flats, a warehouse district of factories, mills, clubs, and restaurants right on the coast of Lake Erie. Paradise Dance Club in the uptown University Circle neighborhood was much closer to where Dell and Novella lived. The Mirage, however, was a step up. It charged a higher cover and imposed age requirements of twenty-five for men and twenty-three for women. Novella and Dell were finally old enough to enter and ready to upgrade their mingling status. The Mirage was a small club with limited free parking, so the two were prepared for a short walk. Given their modest economic status, neither regarded night clubs highly enough to pay for valet parking. With the evening temperatures finally rising from freezing to just cold, The Flats, like most of the city's entertainment areas, was packed. Even the valet lot for The Mirage was full. The nearest parking was three blocks away and had a five-dollar fee. The nearest free parking was four blocks away.

"Hell, no." Novella refused to walk from the other lot. "Hell, no."

Her enthusiasm for dancing until the last call for alcohol or the white lights were turned on in the club were gone. Her head was stuffy from the rum, and she'd lost her buzz. "I'm not huffing a country mile just to go in there," she told Dell, who circled out of the free parking lot in agreement.

In respect to their efforts of changing clothes after Red Lobster, Novella suggested, "The Coupe One?" It would be a longer drive than either wanted at the moment, though when their night ended, they would be closer to home.

Dell moaned, "Noey, we went there last time."

"Well, damn. I don't know," Novella moaned back. "Paradise is out. I'm not in the mood for flying chairs. And even if it's chill tonight, the police are still going to be stomping around and bringing down our party mood."

"I know," Dell agreed. "Girl, you know cops go there to beat ass."

"Oh, wait a minute," Novella remembered. "The Blue Note. We've been talking about going there."

Dell rolled her eyes. "You and Yadara."

Novella returned the eye roll. "So, that means that *we* can't go?"

"Don't get an attitude with me." Dell threw up a hand. "I was just saying," she said, before changing direction and heading uptown to The Blue Note.

The lounge lived up to its name. Everything from the tiles, carpet, and curtains, to the vases, chairs, and tables had been done up in various hues of blue. Even the walls were blue. A microphone sheathed in cobalt-colored velvet was set on a small stage above the small dance floor. Neo-soul, jazz, and R&B were the only genres to be heard; some spoken word was allowed at the club, but never rap. The Blue Note was a place for the grown and sexy, and the patrons were a mix of silver foxes and yuppies. Novella liked the vibe. She felt dancing all night was fun, but chilling to smooth, soulful sounds was also a nice way to spend an evening.

"Wanna order wings?" Novella glanced up at Dell from the small menu.

"You wanna stay here?" Dell looked around unimpressed. "Thought you wanted to dance."

"I did," Novella admitted, "but this place is a change of pace. Let's give it a shot."

"And you're hungry again?"

"Girl, that shrimp and lobster is gone." Novella patted her flat belly. "I just need a little snack."

Dell picked up her menu, and while she looked it over, Novella scanned the room. Just as she was turning back to Dell, a face near the bar set off an alarm in her head. A square-jawed man was laughing and talking robustly with a much taller, round-faced man. Their animated conversation suggested to Novella that they were having an unexpected reunion. Broad shoulders raised and fell during a hearty handshake that preceded a hug that lifted the square-jawed fellow up off the floor. Novella was staring so hard that Dell was compelled to look in the same direction. Not able to pinpoint what was occupying her friend's attention, Dell waved a hand in front of Novella's face. "Earth to Noey."

The spell of nostalgia broken, Novella abruptly stood up. Looking down at Dell, it seemed she might offer an explanation for her behavior. Instead, she reached down and grabbed her soda. One sip to lubricate her speaking mechanics, another for a sugary boost of confidence, and then she was off to introduce herself.

The two men, still caught up in the shock and joy of seeing one another, continued talking loudly near the crowded bar. Novella saw that the round-faced man, a mountain in a thicket of trees, had big, bright, gray eyes. He asked, "How's Pop?"

"The best!" she heard the squared-jaw man reply. He's good, real good!"

Novella stopped at a distance, waiting for an opportunity that would make greeting him in these circumstances less awkward. She couldn't imagine that he wouldn't remember her. What concerned her was that he wouldn't to be bothered by her. Eight years was more than enough time to regret endangering yourself for a random girl, especially one whose family treated you like a pedophile.

Novella's increasing heart rate made her fear that her voice would shake, revealing her deep, heartfelt emotion. She didn't want that, because if he blew her off, the embarrassment and disappointment would be impossible for her to mask. It would also do more emotional damage than just ruining her night. What he'd done for her had helped sustain her faith in people. Before this unexpected yet long-awaited reunion she needed to make an adjustment, before she was embarrassed in a different way. Standing directly behind another patron who was seated at a table, she realized the man need only turn around to get a face full of her rear. And if he were to scoot back from his table, he would most likely knock her down. Carefully, Novella went about repositioning herself, sliding herself between occupied chairs and standing guests. After making her way past the crowd, she found herself just a few steps away the from the square-jawed fellow. He now stood alone, and he was looking directly at her. Novella had been prepared to give the surprise, not to be surprised.

BETY Junior rubbed a thumb against the side of his jaw, allowing his mind to dust off the effects of time to process and identify the woman standing before him. Another effect of the time that had passed was the additional fifty pounds on the woman's small frame, which filled her out nicely, just as Pop had assured him it would. Though, it seemed neither age nor weight had matured the pompom girl's face. Time had done nothing to dull her look of innocence. Still cute. BETY Junior laughed at how wildly good it felt to see her again. Stepping forward, he extended a hand. "Since when did they start letting kids in here?"

A swell of relief overtook Novella. She smiled bigger than she wanted to, and inwardly chided herself to keep her cool. Bursting into a cloud of confetti at this moment felt very possible. She replied with good-natured sass, "Not a kid anymore."

Accepting his hand, she allowed him to bring her into the fold of his long arms. She lost her fear of looking goofy. If not for his humility and courage, she could be a resident of Lake View Cemetery, or in an urn like Willie, or left to rot in that abandoned house. The hug was a long, tight one, and she allowed her gratitude to fill it.

"It's so good to see you looking good and well, little sister."

Novella, relieved yet taken aback by his sincerity, had to force a reply, "You too."

When the hug ended, BETY Junior looked around her. "You check your pompoms at the door?"

Novella rolled her wet eyes, "No."

"Are they outside in your trunk?"

"No more pompoms," she playfully replied.

A moment of silence fell between them as they stared at one another in delight.

Novella, dabbing tears from her eyes, was the first to speak, "Well, my name is—"

He interrupted, "I know your name."

A moment of silence followed, which he broke by asking, "How's your life, Novella?"

She let him know that she knew his name as well. "I'm still figuring it out, BETY Junior."

"Aaagh, you know my street name?" He laughed, and then told her, "It's that or Bariah."

"Do you want me to call you Bariah?"

"Call me whatever you want, princess."

He laughed at the goodness of running into her, and then he said, "This our night! Reunion time, baby girl! Unceremoniously, let's get about it right now…right here. Let's celebrate!"

THIRTY-NINE

Mildly irritated to be left alone in a club she didn't really want to be in, Dell spat, "What, did you see a cute honey you couldn't pass up?" She knew Novella didn't chase men, but her irritability demanded she lash out.

Although in earshot, the smiling Novella hadn't quite made it all the way back to the table. A few moments passed before Dell noticed BETY Junior trailing behind her, that he was *with* Novella. Dell's irritation increased, though she was unsure on which of them to direct it. With eyes locked on BETY Junior, she asked, "How do you know him?"

Novella giggled. "You ready for this?"

No, she wasn't ready. Dell remembered BETY Junior from the party, remembered how much she was digging him. But how much he was digging Ms. Animal Kingdom. The green lady in Dell wasn't ready to hear that he'd now chosen Novella, that he was possibly some new boo Novella hadn't gotten around to mentioning.

"*This* is BETY Junior." Novella nodded her head backwards, as BETY Junior stepped up for the introduction. "The guy who saved my life."

"Of course." Dell thought back to the party. "That's why his name had sounded so familiar. *BETY Junior.* Noey's hero from way back when. Damn!" Dell, giving a plastic smile, offered an eager hand. "You remember me?"

BETY Junior, accepting both her hand and smile, did not. "Where from, love?"

Novella was also wondering.

Dell, in a tone that suggested she'd been personally invited, explained to BETY Junior, "I was a guest at your party."

"Nice." He gently squeezed her hand. *Iron fists.* She remembered his hands. She warmed inside, and stayed so even after he said, "I'm sorry, Dell, but I don't remember you." His hand, which she was convinced could punch through concrete, holding her own made up for her not being memorable. Besides, Dell figured men like him ran through women.

BETY Junior continued. "Thank you for coming, though. It's my annual thing. Hope you enjoyed yourself."

"Sure, it was a nice setup." Dell held on to his hand, as she turned to Novella. "You told him my name?"

Novella's Honest Demon flexed. "Well, if he said he doesn't remember you, Ardellya, how else would he know your name? Girl, I told him at the bar when he asked who I was here with."

Dell laughed. "Well, excuse me. It was just a question." She then smiled back up at BETY Junior. "Anyway, nice to meet you again."

"Likewise." He gently detached his hand from hers.

Novella exhaled. "So, exactly when was this?" She looked to them both. "That you two met. What party?"

BETY Junior didn't want to dwell on it. "Just a few weeks ago. But listen, princess, let's get this here party started." Winking at Novella, he reminded her, "It's our reunion! We need to swap stories, catch up and all that."

Novella smiled. "Yes!"

BETY Junior then spoke to both Novella and Dell, "What are you lovelies drinking? This party is on me."

"Sprite," said Novella. "For me anyway."

BETY Junior stroked his shiny goatee. "Rum and coke, gin and juice, what the hell does sprite go with? Sprite is a punk."

"I don't drink," she told him.

BETY Junior gave her a doubtful smile. "You don't drink? What is that about? You don't drink, what, on Saturdays, when it's cold outside? You don't drink when? Elaborate on that."

"Ever?" She giggled. "No alcohol."

"Doctor's orders?" he asked.

"Novella Lofton's orders," she said.

"Is this a health or a religion thing?"

"It's a Novella thing."

Dell interjected, "And my thing is Long Island iced tea."

BETY Junior raised his chin to her, "And I got you, love." He then looked back at Novella. "Little Sis?"

"Sprite, bro," she told him. "I'll take a Sprite."

He gave in. "I guess your nickname should be DD, for designated driver. I need your business card." He then left to go get their drinks.

Novella, sitting down, looked at Dell, who went back to browsing the menu.

"Well," Novella urged, "tell me."

"No big deal," Dell continued to browse the menu. "Of course I didn't know he was *that* BETY Junior when I met him."

Novella popped a finger on the menu. "Of course it's a big deal. Me running into him being the bigger deal, but still, you meeting him first. You know . . . that's something."

Dell, not taking her eyes from the menu, gave a nonchalant smirk. "Yeah . . . something."

Novella gave the menu a second pop. "And how could you not remember? How many BETY Juniors has anyone ever heard of?" With another finger pop she added, "I'd expect to run into another Ardellya before another BETY Junior."

"Okay, damn, Noey," Dell finally looked up. "At the time, his name sound familiar, but I couldn't remember where I'd heard it. It was a long time ago when all that happened to you. And then you know how the night of his party ended. I was drugged and almost raped."

Novella accepted this answer, but still had more questions for her friend. "Yeah, but you weren't raped, and you nearly killed the Low Budget Busta. Soooooo, is there something I should know, girl? You look kind of funny. You even acting funny. Getting another drink? I know he's buying, but another Long Island ice tea after the daquiri . . ."

"I'm grown," Dell said, dropping the menu onto the table.

"Grown enough to know you'll get sick," Novella reminded her. "Like always."

Dell, in earnest effort to put an end to all her questions, asked Novella, "Are you interested in him?"

Novella answered quickly, "I don't have damsel-in-distress syndrome, Dell."

"He's fine." Dell nodded toward the bar, where BETY Junior stood balancing two conversations, one with a waitress and another with the mountain of a man he'd been speaking with earlier. "Girl, damn he's fine. And he looks like he's holding and knows how to put it down. You get what the hell I mean. Every woman needs that, even if it only ends up being just that. A grind fest to get all the kinks out. Relax every bone in a sista's body. You know a friend-with-benefits deal. Platinum benefits. And girl, if you won't, I will."

Novella didn't have any proprietary feelings about BETY Junior. Still, Dell's threat to pursue him felt aggressive and unfriendly. Especially, for her to be staging her pursuit on the same night of his and Novella's reunion. Novella believed that them not fighting over men was one of the things that set them apart from other women, another jewel in the crown of their friendship. They were queens; no hood rat, rah-rah chic drama for them. In Novella's experience, the so-called games that women played had always been played by women who didn't value true love amongst friends. Yadara and Dell were the most trusted people in her life, and tonight she had been reunited with the man who saved her life. She wanted Dell to rejoice with her, but it was obvious Dell was at play—foul play. That she was operating outside their norm was strange and concerning for Novella. She wanted to pull her to the side and ask her what her damn problem was. Yet, checking Dell would have to wait, as it was not as important to Novella as having a great time reuniting with BETY Junior. So, she tried to keep the conversation neutral. "Well, girl, if you want him . . ."

Dell rolled her eyes. "Like you don't."

Novella defensively responded, "Well, I just met him, so to speak."

"How long does it take?" Dell cocked her head. "I mean, Noey, really how long does it take for you to feel a dude? You kill me always acting so prude and proper. Like you don't like boning."

Novella, again, felt her Honest Demon flex. Something that didn't usually happen with her friends, especially twice on one occasion. Novella knew if that pint of the devil's blood was allowed to boil over, her reunion with BETY Junior would go up in flames. Fighting Dell was unlikely, but a nasty argument could still go down. When Novella got upset, it took a good while for her to calm down, so the reunion would be cancelled. In order to keep a cool head and find another way to deal, Novella sat back in her chair and studied her friend. Dell, a willing subject of her gaze, dramatically folded her arms and sat back in her chair.

She was still waiting on Novella's answer when BETY Junior returned to the table a minute later. He took a seat in front of them, but nearer Novella, "Alright, lovelies, Simone will bring over the booze and eats, and the *Sprite*."

Dell gave Novella a meaningful look, one that Novella read too late to be able to plug Dell's mouth with "a girl you better not say anything crazy" warning.

Dell asked BETY Junior, "Simone, huh? You know a lot of women, don't you? You know her family," she was referring to Novella, "thinks you took her virginity." Not waiting for a reply, she pointed to a stunned Novella. "Late bloomer."

Novella was outdone. "Are you for real?"

Dell, laughing, was growing louder and more dramatic. "Girl, everybody grown here. We can chop it up about sex, no big deal."

Novella reminded her, "That's not what this is about, though."

Dell, feeling herself, leaned back. "You're not my mama or daddy, my boss or my god. I can say what I want."

Novella was used to Dell inviting herself and making herself the center of attention. As Novella's friend, she had always been welcome, and once in, she knew how to *join* a party. Though, instead of *joining* this unexpected reunion, Dell was trying to cockblock her. She was engaging with BETY Junior as if Novella was her side kick, and she was the person of interest, that he should dismiss any possible attraction he had for Novella and hook up with her instead. It was wishful thinking on Dell's part. Novella knew Dell was aware that BETY Junior's attentiveness to her was no more than good manners, that he wasn't genuinely interested her. There were enough awkward moments, such as, when she'd leaned too far over the table and across Novella to touch him.

"Dell," Novella had shrugged her back for the last time, "you're making me sweat."

Dell, retreating to her side of the table, whispered, "Girl, can't you see what's happening here? You're in the way."

Novella raised an eyebrow. "In the way of what, Dell? Girl, what? You want me to switch seats with you, so that you can sit in his lap, for him to push you off? You need to relax, girl, and sort yourself out. You're way out of control here."

For a moment Dell sobered, so Novella slightly nodded toward BETY Junior. Novella wanted Dell to see and acknowledge that he was a man in control of his sex. There was no seducing him.

BETY Junior sat sipping the same glass of Merlot he'd started with, looking neither bored nor entertained. He wore the mask of a faithful husband accompanying his wife to an event that he wasn't interested in. Yet, since it was important to her, he was on his best behavior, smiling on cue and keeping her glass filled. BETY Junior was chill.

Novella saw the sting Dell felt as it finally sunk in that she wasn't winning. Novella almost felt sorry for her as she knew how much Dell wanted a serious relationship, a man to truly date and romance her. Though, before her pity could flower, she would see Dell dismiss BETY Junior's lack of interest. *This girl*, Novella thought.

Dell mellowed out for about an hour. Then after a trip to the ladies' room, she was back on the hunt.

"Y'all make sure to exchange numbers, so we can all keep in touch," she told Novella and BETY Junior. It was then that BETY Junior had finally remembered her. It wasn't triggered by her face or voice, but by her behavior: her abandonment of whom she'd come with and her overbearing forwardness.

Continuing to push, Dell told BETY Junior, "Noey's dating this African dude. Like regular negroes aren't good enough for her." She let out a shallow roll of laughter, and then said, "She always gotta be the one trying to be all different. I keep trying to tell her: around the way sistas need around the way brothas. You know, brothas from around our way."

Dell talked and talked, ate and ate, drank and drank. *A hot-ass mess*, Novella decided, correcting her judgment to *a hot-in-the-ass mess*. Indeed, Dell was most certainly a mess by last call. "Give me a hug, boy!" Dell threw her arms around BETY Junior's neck after he'd walked them to her car. Designated Driver Novella had quickly gotten inside the Ford Escort to start it up and get the heat going. *Let her freeze her horny ass off, if she's that hard up*, Novella thought trying to shake off the chill from their five-minute walk to the car. In order to get her off of him, BETY Junior had to physically tuck Dell inside the car. Afterwards, he jogged to the driver's side where Novella sat behind the steering wheel. "I'll probably call you later on today," he let her know after she'd rolled down the window. Then raising his chin toward a now sleeping Dell, he said, "But, not to be funny as I know that's your girl and all, but let's not have anyone at our after-party, running interference."

Novella nodded in agreement. "Yeah . . . don't worry."

She offered no explanation, no saving face for Dell. *Sometimes a sista has to think of only herself. If I won't look out for me, who will?* Novella decided. She wasn't angry, but she felt Dell should have handled herself better. Cleveland wasn't that big; still it felt like something of a miracle running into BETY Junior. *Shame on Dell for putting her hormones before my heart. And all of her damn ridiculousness made me forget to invite him over for dinner. The feast my family should have given him.* Novella was too tired, and it was too cold outside to start the conversation. As happy as she was to have reconnected with him, she was minutes past ready to roll up her window and get going.

BETY Junior clapped his gloved hands to keep away the chill. "You got far to drive?"

Novella shook her head. "Naw, about ten minutes."

"Cool. Now be careful on the roads. They are slick."

"Will do. And you too."

Saying goodnight, he raised his chin. "I will. Alright now, take care . . . Be encouraged."

The following evening, Novella was thinking about calling BETY Junior when he called her. Novella was planning to have them set a date when'd come over for that long-ago, well-earned feast, but immediately after they'd exchanged pleasantries, BETY Junior invited her to dinner. "I want you to meet Pop."

FORTY

Novella had no concerns about going to a house of men without any backup. BETY Junior and his Pop, she was sure, were good people. So she kept the invite to herself and went alone. *Sometimes a sista has to think only of herself.* The decision to do so had come fast, but not without guilt.

Yadara and Dell had given her the only real comfort she'd gotten after the attempted abduction. Novella had filled them in on what had happened to her at the downtown Cleveland Public Library, on the stairs between the fourth and fifth floors. Novella could still remember the unyielding cold hardness of the cement step beneath her. How her two besties had hung on to her every word. The echoing of their voices in the hollowness of the concrete stairwell. "Girl, Lord have mercy. Get some mace and a pocketknife," Dell had urged.

Yadara had given Novella a high-five, "Yessss! You fought for your life!" only to add, "But there was no need to do that 'cause bro man told your little self to run home. And that is what you should have done. Let a man do what a man does. But you ran back, trying to be his back-up and almost got a brick to the head." That was Yadara, always the mama of the three. Novella appreciated her for it, though Dell found her to be bossy and self-righteous. Dell did, however, agree with her on that occasion.

Novella was sitting on the bottom step, Yadara above her, and Dell above Yadara. Leaning over Yadara, Dell had said, "That was crazy! Why? Why didn't you run home? You were saved, girl!"

Novella answered with a question for them both, "You would leave the person who stepped in to save you to fight all by himself? To possibly die, all because he helped you."

Dell and Yadara shared a look of agreement. "No," they answered in unison.

Dell then said, "Girl, I'm so glad you didn't die."

"Me too," Yadara concurred.

Dell and Yadara's hugs were the only hugs of sympathy Novella had received since the incident.

So, guilt rode shotgun with Novella on the six-mile drive from her place on Noble Road in Cleveland Heights to BETY Junior's church home on Quincy Avenue in Cleveland. Inside Union Grove Baptist, as she sat on the second pew, her guilt was sandwiched between her and a stranger who was on her right, while BETY Junior and Pop sat to her left. After the service, her guilt again rode shotgun as she followed Pop's BMW to Shaker Heights. However, once she crossed the threshold of the beautiful brick house, her guilt became nothing more than an outside noise, decreasing after the door closed, and mostly ignored while she was engaged indoors.

The French-style home at 17723 Winslow Road was a find in Shaker Heights: a side-by-side duplex constructed in 1932. Though, Shaker wasn't a duplex community; all the other houses were single family homes. However, Pop and BETY Junior's thirty-five-hundred-square-foot home, while a duplex, wasn't meant for strangers. Positioned far back from the street, the fact that it was a duplex wasn't noticeable, until after one crossed the threshold of their covered front porch. The entrance to Pop's side of the house was to the left; BETY Junior's on the right. Once inside, the two could visit each other by way of the door that connected their kitchens or the sliding door in their dens.

Novella felt like she was finally in a place that had been waiting for her, a place she needed and one that needed her. As she laughed with BETY Junior and Pop, she felt like she was home, that she deserved this experience, without being concerned about anyone else.

FORTY-ONE

Thanksgiving Day, 1998

Novella was one of the last people she knew to get a pager. She was so late to the party that the affordability of cell phones had nearly made them redundant. Finally in the "page me" network, Novella was less than impressed with it. Her Motorola Advisor, even with eight lines of text, was just another thing to have. Besides, she found having it only made her more accountable than her answering machine. Returning a page had a higher priority than returning a voice message. Novella didn't like that. Neither did she like the way it allowed people to map her location, as she called it. "Where you at?" No matter whose page she answered, they expected her to say where she was. "I'm where I'm at," she'd reply with a smile in her voice, hiding her annoyance. Nevertheless, the little rectangle was more appreciated than not. It had been a gift from Yadara after she'd failed at convincing Novella to buy one for herself. That was two years ago, when her only nickname was Noey. Today, urging her to upgrade to the next level of wireless communication was BETY Junior. Both Pop and him affectionately called her Ella, and they wanted her to enter the new millennium with a cell phone.

"Really, Ella? You don't see the need for a cell phone?"

"I'm not in the streets like that." She shrugged. "Any and everybody can just catch me at the house. I don't need to be on the phone all day and night. And I don't want to be having personal conversations all over town."

"You are in the streets like that," BETY Junior countered. "You know what's up, Ella La Bella. All of us yuppies are out more than in, and we don't just kick it on the weekends. For true, we start our weekends on Thursdays. Even on hump day we're down for happy hour."

Novella laughed. "Yuppie?"

BETY Junior smiled at her. "Yeah, Sis. We're yuppies. Young urban professionals, doing what we do."

Novella accepted that about herself, but it was funny to hear BETY Junior refer to himself in that way. He was clean and professional, with dark intelligent eyes, but his muscular body hardly looked like it would be comfortable seated at a desk in front of a computer all day. In Novella's mind, yuppies were well-suited young adults who got addicted to coffee while clicking a mouse. BETY Junior didn't fit that image, and his deep voice calling himself a yuppie made her giggle.

"Yeah, ok, brother yuppie, but it's not that serious," she told him. "If I'm out, I'm out, and with who I'm with."

BETY Junior assured her, "But it will be that serious when you need to make call. Pay phones are going to start disappearing. Maybe a few will remain for emergency purposes, but how many us of are actually going to have the pocket change to put in them? Debit cards and credit cards are becoming more common even for young people. Instant gratification, baby girl, that's at the push of a button or the swipe of a card is the future. Believe that."

Novella looked at the cell phone between them on Pop's food-filled and well-plated table. "Okay, I hear you, Mr. Man of The Future, but—"

"If the mobile stresses the budget, cut the house phone," BETY Junior advised. "Cut the cable."

She giggled. "I see you're passionate about this."

BETY Junior continued, "Cut the unnecessary. Cut it all. Be encouraged, baby girl. Staying connected is more important than being entertained. And with a mobile you don't need a house phone at all. Just be smart with your minutes and keep your mobile charged."

Biting into a sugar cookie, Novella considered his points.

BETY Junior continued to make his point, "Listen, Ella, you're right. Mostly everybody can wait to make a call until they're home from work, the store, their friend's house, etc. But it's not about them reaching you; it's about you being able to reach whom you need to reach, when you need to reach them. Car break down and you need a tow? Get lost and need to call for directions? Check it, Ella, right now you're waiting on call back about a new job."

Novella's thoughtful smile told BETY Junior she was sold, so he presented her with her first mobile phone.

She beamed, but she didn't take it. After swallowing the last bites of her cookie, she told him, "Bro, I can get one myself." She knew she'd be splurging, but like he said, cutting the house phone would help offset the cost.

BETY Junior refused her refusal. "Be blessed, Ella. You don't need to since I'm putting one in your hand right now. Anyway, when you realize you can't live without it—and you will come to realize you can't live without it—step it up and get whatever you want. Now take it. Be encouraged to get with the times, baby girl."

So Novella accepted the Motorola StarTAC from BETY Junior. The flip phone was black and sleek. Admiring it, she giggled. "Thanks! Now, that I actually have it, I'm kind of excited!"

FORTY-TWO

Lawrenceville, Georgia
Saturday, March 27, 2013

The strawberry cake was decorated with an image of a fire-orange Hayabusa GSXR. Written in white icing on the front side panel on the bike behind the wheel was his name: "Chrystan." He was only eight years old and was riding dirt bikes, but had already decided that crotch rockets were his future. The one on his cake was his mother's favorite. Busa Baby was what she called it, and loving it so because she had first learned to ride on a Hayabusa. She had eventually bought her own, and she had never wanted any other bike. Busas were all she rode. Chrystan's first love was the Kawasaki Ninja. At three, he'd been given a kiddie electric motorcycle built to look like a Kawasaki Ninja. He'd fallen in love. His mother credited his crush to his youth and gender: a little boy enthralled with the idea of owning and mastering something called a "ninja." She was trying to get him to appreciate the Busas, which she felt were superior. Chrystan, regardless of his motorcycle preference, loved the cake.

This was his most elaborate birthday party, and he was suspicious of it. His last big party was for his fifth birthday, and according to his mother, his next major milestone was to be when he turned ten. In two days, he'd be nine, so in his mother's words, "he was feeling some kind way." His mother wasn't the worst, but Chrystan felt her shortcomings were "long-goings"; the issues they caused went on and on. And even after they finally ended, sometimes the drama came back. He'd told her so as she opened a bottle of juice for him. It was after she'd argued with a woman who had once been her friend in a beauty supply store. The woman had apparently been looking for her. The argument was loud and bad.

His mother had laughed at his comment. "Chrystan, what's it to you? What do you have to worry about?"

Chrystan wasn't yet able to articulate that he felt like an accessory, like a tiny dog carried in a purse. Even in the trendy clothes and shoes his mother dressed him in, and the tight fades she always made sure he had, he did worry. Chrystan hadn't seen much drama, but he had a fairly sound understanding of the mechanics behind his easy life. His mother's friends described them as ratchet. Grown-ups, for too long, had spoken around him as if he were an unaware baby, and nowadays spoke in code as if he couldn't catch on. He didn't talk much, which made some kids uncomfortable—and some adults too comfortable.

Chrystan was more proficient with his mother's iPhone than she was, and knew her password, as well as her bank card PIN. With her permission, he shopped online; ordered food; bought games, gadgets, movie and event tickets; and requested UBER rides. A kid of his times. Chrystan, soon to be nine, was already a doer. He was also a people-watcher and an apt listener. He had a penchant for filing things away until he could process them.

"Too smart for your own good," his mother warned him. "Just be a kid. When your feet start busting out of your kicks and you're hungry, then you can worry. Until then, stay out of grown folks' business. Now here, drink this expensive OJ."

The thing was, she hadn't paid for the expensive juice, or anything else for that matter. She was a gold digger, another tidbit he'd overheard. What his young mind understood was that his mother danced nearly naked in rap videos before he was born. He knew she was pretty by the way men and women looked at her.

He was worried now because he'd overheard that his father wasn't his daddy, also that his father had suspected as much. That was what he meant when he said that stuff always came back, because it had been two years ago when he'd first overheard the whispers about him only maybe being his dad's son. *Here we go again,* he'd thought, overhearing an argument just last week about that same stuff between his mother and the guy he used to think was his daddy. Since then, Chrystan had noticed that guy now only spoke to him to give him orders. "Go tell your mama to come here." He no longer asked, "You want to ride to the store with me?" or "What do you want from Burger King?" Neither was that guy, who they still lived with, at his birthday party. Thus far, this was the worst stuff that had come back from his mom's past. *I don't have a daddy anymore,* was a hurtful realization he kept to himself. With family stuff as it was, this whole birthday celebration—the catered food, the karaoke DJ, the custom photo backdrop—felt like a going-away party.

Chrystan had moved with his mother from an apartment on a street called Van Aken in Shaker Heights, Ohio, to Lawrenceville, Georgia. The apartment in Georgia was newer, fancier, and part of a complex with attractive swimming pools, one in which he'd learned to swim with a number of other young residents. Lately, he'd seen signs about a youth soccer team being formed by the complex. He wanted to join, but his suspicion that he would fly back to Cleveland with his slightly mentally challenged second cousin when school let out became a truth. His second cousin Denise was nice, so Chrystan hated to think of her by the ugly name that the guy who used to be his daddy called her: "Dumbnise."

"Your nana misses you," his mother lied, unaware that her mother's funeral arrangements were being organized at that moment. "She's going to be so happy and surprised to see you." In truth, she'd be buried a month before he arrived.

"You'll get to sleep in my old room." His mother had gone on about the house she had hated because it was in a poor neighborhood. The house was now locked and partially boarded up.

"Auntie Cousin Denise will help you get there, and help Nana take care of you." Though Denise was his second cousin, in terms of the traditional familial roles of aunt and cousin, she was more of an aunt. Chrystan's mom always referred to her as his "auntie" when giving her full authority over him.

FORTY-THREE

Cleveland, Ohio
October 5, 2001

"Ella!" BETY Junior extended a hand to pull her through the crush of people. They were at the Magic Johnson Theatre at Randall Park Mall in North Randall, one of the smallest eastern suburbs. *Training Day* starring Denzel Washington was premiering. BETY Junior and Novella were both into the buzz of opening nights, and this opening being on a Friday only added to their excitement.

Three of the theater's twelve screens were showing *Training Day*. Judging by the sea of black faces in the lobby, all three theaters would be packed.

"The lines for food are bullshit," BETY Junior told her.

"We can eat afterwards," she suggested.

BETY Junior stared at her.

She stared back. "Then we stand in line, bro." She took his arm and let him lead her to the concession area. They were both early for everything, so even after a fifteen-minute wait in line, they made it to their seats before the start of the preview.

When the ending credits began to roll, BETY Junior presented Novella with his fist for a bump. "Money well spent. Yeah, Ella Bella?"

"Yes." She bumped her fist to his.

A few hours later, they were at The Blue Note trying not to be spoilers as they talked about the movie to the club's patrons. As usual, chatterboxes Novella and BETY Junior were leaning in and out of multiple conversations. Even with movie talk, and the usual hype of a Friday night, the tragedy of 9/11 was the main topic of conversation at the club.

Pop had been the one to call Novella and tell her what had happened. "Princess, did you hear about it? You see the news?"

On September 11, 2001, terrorists crashed two airplanes into the World Trade Center. Another into the Pentagon. A fourth airplane, presumably heading to Washington, D.C., crashed in a field in Pennsylvania.

Novella, at home with menstrual cramps at the time, hadn't heard. She'd been in and out of bed, eating leftovers and drinking tea. Soon after Pop's call, she was curled up on his sofa. For the remainder of the day and night, she, BETY Junior, and Pop watched the news coverage. Being with the two of them for important things, including holidays, had become a way of life for her. In the past, she had spent the holidays with Yadara and Dell. Yadara still lived at home, and Dell was always looking for the cheapest seat at a holiday table, where she could go to eat the most and bring the least. Novella didn't hold any grudges against either of them, yet her heart needed a home. She fit easily with BETY Junior and Pop, and Yadara nor Dell didn't seem to miss her on the holidays unless theirs went badly.

"What did you do yesterday, girl?"

"Was with Pop and bro."

"Oh well, you could have joined me and my family."

Novella's Honest Demon responded, "Oh well, Pop and bro let me know before the holiday passed."

Dell was good for, "Well, I'm sure you preferred being with your so-called bro."

She did.

FORTY-FOUR

A Few Weeks Later

Baby Sister and sex are a clash in the psyche of most men, just as imagining their father banging the headboard against the wall while atop their dear mother. The thing is, most men forget that the women they lust for are dear to someone. And just as they lust after other people's dear ones, someone is lusting after theirs.

BETY Junior stepped into Novella's apartment to the sight of a guy stepping out of her bedroom. Not missing a step, he continued in, stopping about three feet short of the guy, who was only wearing boxers. BETY Junior, looking him over, decided he was a simple ass. How else could he smile so smugly without showing any concern as to who in the hell BETY Junior was to Novella?

"Hey, man." The simple ass offered a hand, which BETY Junior considered breaking.

"You're serious?" BETY Junior removed his jacket. "Stepping out my sister's bedroom and offering to meet me like that. In your damn drawers?"

Smirking, the guy began, "I'm her—"

"You're not shit," BETY Junior shut him down. "Not standing here in front of me like that."

Simple Ass lost his smirk as he began to size up BETY Junior. Simple Ass, a ripped marathoner, was a few inches taller than BETY Junior. Still, he was outgunned, and it didn't take him long to realize it.

Training for a charity boxing match, BETY Junior had the body of a bone crusher. His arms were loaded AKs, his chest an iron shield. BETY Junior, according to his gym mates and clients, was *swoll*. Slang for swollen, meaning he had big-ass muscles. Prepping as if it was a paid fight, he was his most swoll ever.

"Is this how you want it?" BETY Junior asked.

The guy was confused. "Man, I don't know what—"

BETY Junior gave him another chance. "You're not going to get dressed?" Just as BETY Junior opened his mouth to call for Novella, she stepped out of the bathroom. How she looked caused BETY Junior's skin to flush, "This bullshit today—"

Novella with wild sex hair was dressed for more *seduction*. The body dress she wore was little more than lingerie. It was so short, if she bent over, the scene would be X-rated. The thin dress, stressed by her curves, exposed the plaid bra cups pushing her breast above the collar line. BETY Junior could also make out the bra's matching plaid thong.

"Hey . . ." Novella, surprised and embarrassed, lightly touched her hands to her hair and body. "BETY Junior . . . I didn't know you were com- ing today. Good morning."

Simple Ass, looking to Novella for back-up, said, "Man, you walked in on us. So—"

BETY Junior had the keys to Novella's apartment. Novella hadn't been answering her cell phone, nor had she returned his texts. She had long since disconnected her landline, and BETY Junior couldn't remember the exact name of the new daycare she worked for, or its location. She'd been MIA for six days, so he'd rescheduled clients and skipped a day of his own training to find her.

Novella passed him to reach her nearly naked lover. "Please, could you . . ."

Trying to appear more relaxed and in charge than he was, he slapped his six pack. "Sure, baby." He then turned and disappeared into her bedroom.

BETY Junior turned to Novella. "Are we family?"

She threw up her arms. "Uh, yeah, but . . ."

BETY Junior, mocking her, threw up his arms. "Then what the hell, Ella? And where in the hell?"

"What?" Novella raised an eyebrow. "What are you talking about?"

BETY Junior stared at her before earnestly requesting, "Can you please send Simple Ass on his way so we can have it out?"

Novella didn't understand why she should. She was grown, and this being her place, she was the lady of the house and called the shots. Who was he to come in and say who was to be put out? She and BETY Junior studied one another for a few moments before Simple Ass returned from her bedroom, "Man, I get that you're her brother, but it's not like I was the first—"

"Are you serious?" Novella yelled. "What's the point in saying that?"

BETY Junior could feel the boxer inside him launching across the room to split Simple Ass's face. Reserving his aggression for his fight, he held his position, but said, "Put this motherfucker out!"

Novella and this guy had been hot for each other for some time. His perfect abs were complemented by a perfect smile, a smile that he'd flashed each time they passed one another during their respective runs. One day, after passing him on the trail for a few weeks, she found him stretching his long, lean, and ripped body near her car. About two months after that sparked meeting, came last night. A very long night of everything. Now with that same beautiful smile that he'd introduced himself, he'd created his exit out of her life.

"We're through." She motioned for him to leave, as he grinned. "You don't talk about me like I'm some a hoochie who slept with you on the first date."

It looked like he was about to say something to Novella, but the scowl on BETY Junior's face warned him anymore disrespect was likely to cost him his ass. Barely maintaining his smug smile, he slipped on his shoes, made the peace sign, and then left.

Novella was still looking at the door, angry and disappointed, when BETY Junior reclaimed her attention, "Ella!" He went and took a seat at the dining table. He gestured for Novella to join him.

She remembered how she was dressed and said, "Give me a minute." She rushed to her bedroom and changed into yoga pants and a t-shirt. Going to join BETY Junior at the dining table, she began, "Okay, Roger turned out to be a jackass, but you did walk in on us. I mean not while we were doing anything, but you let yourself in. Which is cool, but you got more than you bargained for, and that's not my fault."

BETY Junior shook his head. "No, that's not what I'm tripping about, but trust and believe we will talk about that. Right now, my question to you is: where's your phone?"

"Oh!" Novella eyes stretched as she sat down across from him. "My phone is broken! They've tried to deliver a new one twice, but I was at work and the rental office refused to sign for it."

BETY Junior was no less pissed. "How did that piece of shit get in touch with you?"

"We run at the same time."

"Does he have a phone? No phone at your job? You didn't think to hit me up? Or Pop?"

"BETY Junior, I didn't—"

"Don't bullshit me, Ella. Don't bullshit me. Have I ever used the key?"

"No."

"Okay, then. So, you were off the grid for days and days, nearly a damn week. And people dying out here, and not on their own. They're being made dead. What was I supposed to think?"

Novella jumped up. "Oh my God! That long? I thought it was only like three days." In her head she began counting how long she'd been without a phone. "Oh my God! I didn't even realize . . ."

BETY Junior, glad she finally understood, crossed his chiseled arms and watched the severity of her absence sink in.

"I am so sorry, bro. I really and truly am."

"Ella, you gotta do better than this shit."

"I'm so sorry," she pleaded. "Time got away from me." She then raised her fist for a bump. "Forgiven?"

"Do better, sis. For damn real. I mean, I didn't know if I'd find you dead and done, or maybe not find you at all."

Novella knew she was going to get served. She lowered her fist and leaned backwards, prepared to take her medicine. "I didn't realize how many days had passed."

"Really? Well, you got a new boyfriend. Guess he was occupying a lot of your time, distracting you from your friends and fam. So, you didn't want me to meet that simple ass that you let stay over?"

Novella blushed. Her sheets were still warm from their multiple cardio sessions. Cool Water cologne and Victoria Secret's Pear Glace were still getting it on: an erotically blended fragrance scenting Novella's bedroom. "Of course I wanted you to meet him."

BETY Junior suggested, "Maybe things were moving too fast for a proper introduction. Or maybe you knew he was the jackass he proved to be, and that I would've checked his simple ass on arrival."

Novella rolled her eyes. "Whatever."

"Really?" BETY Junior leaned back. "Whatever?"

"Didn't mean it like that," she huffed. "I'm glad you came to check on me."

"Always and forever, boo. I will always come for you. But, damn, this could have been avoided. Your young mingling ass, making peeps worry for no damn reason. Pop was like, go find my granddaughter."

"Pop?" Novella got doe-eyed.

"Uh-huh." BETY Junior pointed at her. "Yep, Pop-Pop was worried about you. How does that make you feel?"

Novella now felt worse. With a hand over her chest, she moaned, "Nooo, not Pop-Pop." Making him worry, she felt, was wrong on so many levels. He was an elder, and a sweet one, genuine and bighearted.

BETY Junior, seeing the deep remorse in her, stood up. "Glad I was able to set your ass straight. Now bring it in." He opened his long arms and Novella filled them.

"Oh my God!" She drew back. "Shaka Zulu is ready for war!" She then pushed him as if testing his strength. "It's like you're made of stone." She then laughed. "Poor Roger. You would have broken him in two."

BETY Junior shrugged. "That grinning idiot you just put out? Shit, then it would have been for a good cause." He removed his phone from his hip holster. "Let's call Pop." Before he dialed, he gave her a look. "We can omit how I found you."

She shoved him on one of his boulder shoulders. "You can't shame me. You think you're incognito, but I know what's up with your big-boo-ty-chasing ass. You're always trying to bone some broad."

"Watch your mouth, little girl." He held back a laugh. "I'm about to call Pop. Manners!"

Novella slapped the phone out of his hand.

"Damn, Ella!" He went to retrieve it from her carpeted floor. "Girl, you got a problem."

"Big booty chaser!" She giggled as she went into the kitchen. "What the hell?" she said after returning with a cup with a spoonful of honey on the bottom of it. Her water was still boiling in the kettle.

"I'm dialing him now," BETY Junior shrugged.

"What were you doing while I was in the kitchen?"

"Whatever," he told her. "I'm about to dial him now."

"Booty business," she joked. "You just might be the hoe of hoes, while you're trying to judge me. Hoe . . . of . . . hoes."

BETY Junior, who was in fact sending a text to a female he'd recently met, looked up from his phone. "Girl, you need to go to church or something. You got a serious problem."

She cocked her head at him. "How come we're not talking to Pop yet?"

"Why are you rushing me?" he laughed. "I just solved a missing person case full of sordid, X-rated details."

"Call Pop!" Novella ordered.

BETY Junior, reclaiming his seat at her dining table, shook his head. "I don't know who you think you're yelling at girl."

Novella enjoyed how her cussing always shocked and entertained him. "Call him, gotdamnit!"

"Girl, really!" He finished his text. "Seriously, your mouth is out of control. Are you baptized? Can't be."

She laughed. "Yeah, you know I am baptized."

BETY Junior shook his head in disbelief. "Well, you need to be dipped again. Where was it done the first time, in a pool at the YMCA? Somebody's backyard jacuzzi?"

"Get for real."

He laid the phone on the table, and then pushed the speaker button. "Well, something came back up with you."

Novella joined him at the table. "You're one to talk."

Pop's phone began to ring.

BETY Junior nodded toward her tea. "You're not the only person at this table. I'll take a cup, a large one, and breakfast. I've been in the streets searching for your young ass. Give me my damn propers. Get some food on this table, girl."

Novella huffed. "You can let yourself in, but you can't serve yourself."

BETY Junior smiled. "Handle it, sis. It's my cheat day. Whatever you cook make sure I get three eggs, five sausage links, and cheese grits. Buttered biscuits with strawberry preserves. You know I'm not picky, but get everything right."

Novella was about to give a him a cuss-laden reply when Pop's voice put a broad smile on her face and sweet ache in her heart. BETY Junior announced to Pop that he was on speaker, and then asked that he guess who he was with. Pop sung, "Ella La Bella."

FORTY-FIVE

Cleveland, Ohio
May 23, 2002

"Need you, sis," BETY Junior said thickly through the phone

Novella, at Soul Vegetarian soul food restaurant, stepped out of the line. "What's wrong?"

"Come through, alright." His voice cracked. "I'm at the house."

"On my way," she assured him. Closing her flip phone, she wondered if she should take food to him and Pop. People always need food during stressful times. Though she was definitely at the wrong spot for them as both Pop and BETY Junior had declined her invitation to explore veganism with her.

"You're attacking my god of muscle," BETY Junior had accused her. "The Bible says the Lord hath given us cattle to sustain us."

Novella, rolling her eyes, had told him, "You're always the one being ridiculous."

Pop had agreed with her, "You can count on him being ridiculous." Then he said, "But I must also say no. Princess, I love oxtails and I'm not ready to live a life without them."

Novella started to worry. *Pop! Oh my God! Please, don't let anything have happened to Pop.*

She occasionally looked at her phone while driving. Not knowing what was wrong, she wanted to call and ask if she should bring something, if she should do something. Eventually, she reminded herself, *Bro said come through, so just get there, Novella.*

Answering her prayer that he was well, Pop called when she was a few minutes away. "Ella Bella, how are you?"

"I'm good, Pop."

"Bariah call you?"

"Yes, sir, and I'll be turning the corner of your block soon."

"Alright, princess, see you in a minute."

Novella wiped a lone tear that had escaped down her cheek.

The long driveway was lined with cars, and she was irritated that *she* had to park on the street. She found herself on display as she walked toward the house. Boldly, she met the rudely curious eyes of the colorful people gathered around the house. She returned their ogling with her own curious stare. *Who are y'all to have Pop's place turned up like this?* They stared at her as if they were regulars and she was the stranger. In the mix of young adults, and those acting as if they were still in their twenties, Novella noticed one person who looked familiar; though, she couldn't place her.

Novella, entering the house, found Pop surrounded by three flashy women. *Who are these hoes?* Novella only felt little bad for being so judgmental and harsh.

Pop rose from his recliner. "Hey, Ella girl."

The anxiety and tension Novella had experienced on the ride over was still high and expanding. Questions were popping in her mind.

Hi Pop-Pop, um, who in the hell are these broads? Why are they all over you, as if you're their sugar daddy? Or are they charging you by the hour? Who in the hell are all those people out on your pretty green lawn?

Novella decided it was best to go with the flow, and went over and gave him a hug. "How are you, Pop?"

"I'm good." He squeezed her, and then nodded down the hall. "Go check on him."

Irritated by the curious gawking of the flashy women, Novella refrained from asking for details. "Okay."

Novella entered the kitchen and pulled on the door that led into BETY Junior's side of the house. She was surprised, yet happy, that it was locked. *Good*, she figured, thinking most likely no weirdo types like those outside would be in with him. Using her key, she quickly entered and relocked the door.

BETY Junior, hearing the click of the lock, presumed it was Novella. Laid out on the chaise in the small nook between his dining room and living room, he waited to speak until he saw her. "Sis," he muttered softly when she came into view.

He looked so sad. Novella's whole heart went out to him. "Bro, what is it? What's wrong with my dear sweet brother?"

"I'm fucked up." Tears rolled down his cheeks, which she began to wipe as soon as she sat down. He continued, "My mother's dead, and I don't know if I'm sad about it, or sad because I don't feel any loss that she's gone."

They shared an intense look in a moment of charged silence that Novella wasn't sure how to break. Offering condolence wasn't the first order here. The usual emotional response to the death of a parent seemed inappropriate here because of the nature of the relationship BETY Junior had had with his mother. In polite language Novella would have said, "His mother had a lot of issues that prevented her from being there for him." In real talk she'd say, "That woman never did shit for him." So, his mother just died, but . . . what should she say?

Novella walked a manicured finger of one of her soft hands across the fingertips of one of his bruisers. "Those are her people out there?" It now hit her why the young woman on the porch looked familiar. She was BETY Junior's aunt, his mother's youngest sister. She was around the same age as Novella. She greatly resembled his mother, whose pampered features reminded Novella of a doll. Propped up in one of Pop's contemporary accent chairs, she hadn't offered a hand nor hug when meeting Novella last Christmas. "Yes, that's right," she'd said as she raised her chin. "I'm the mama." She glowed as if direct from the spa or blissfully unaffected by life's ups and downs. Novella guessed the latter.

"Yeah." BETY Junior took a drink of Jack and Coke from a fat goblet he picked up from a small table beside the chaise. "They don't usually bother, and neither do I. So, I'm not about to join the fucking circus just because Minnie's dead." Saying her name brought back a memory. "Mama starts with M too," he said out loud. His mother had reprimanded him often, but to no avail. Often meaning constantly during her short, infrequent visits. She called him "Little Bariah," and he called her "Minnie." She never phoned, just showed up. There was no mother-son bond. "Minnie" was a model, a magazine cut-out, a beautiful woman. She hadn't liked to be bothered with anything that disturbed that beauty—like raising a kid.

Pop's wife Purdy had fallen in baby love and doted on BETY Junior since the day she met him. Neither she nor Pop was surprised when Minnie asked that they keep him during their son Bariah Senior's deployment. Although Minnie went with her husband, she said it was too hard to raise a child without extended family. After Bariah Senior was killed in a helicopter crash, no amount of help would have been sufficient for her to take on the role of a single mother. Pop and Purdy gladly kept BETY Junior, though by the time BETY Junior was eight, it was just him and Pop. Two years after Bariah Senior's helicopter crash, Purdy was killed in a car accident.

BETY Junior returned his now empty goblet to the table. "Minnie didn't earn any Mother's Day gifts, but I owe her something. Right? It would be pretty fucked up of me not to give a shit? She did give birth to me."

Novella exhaled softly and looked around the room.

"Don't do that." BETY Junior urged her to stay focused on him. "Keep it one hundred with me. All the way. I'd be something of an asshole not to give a shit that my mother died. Right?"

Novella had turned away searching for the right words, but he'd let her know her thoughts needed no editing. "No, she was the asshole," she said earnestly. "You don't care because she never gave you reason to care. She just wasn't there. When you leave people, if they're lucky, they'll find something else to do. They'll find someplace else to put their love. Someone else to give it to and get it from. Pop. He was there. Still is. Because of him, you got enough hugs and love." She grabbed one of his big hands. "Speaking from experience, sometimes it's a blessing to not care. What I mean is . . . to not be crushed. Knowing how we're supposed to feel when stuff isn't right is enough to crush us. If we're lucky, even if we can't sort it out, we can move on. And not get stuck on that stuff we can't do anything about. And that's what you did. So, you're not a little boy waiting on his mama to come and love him anymore. Now she's died, and you'll feel something, but . . . you've been without her for so long. Her death is bad news, but it won't change your day-to-day. You're not an asshole . . . you're just someone who moved on a long time ago."

BETY Junior leaned forward and kissed her forehead. "Don't ever leave me, Ella. Don't ever stop being my family."

Not wanting to get swept away in her emotions, Novella suppressed the swell of joy that ballooned inside her. She delivered her guarantee softly, "Always and forever, bro."

He still tapped the sap in her, and now it was his turn to give her his whole heart. "You're always at home with me, Ella. I love you, and I got you. You can always count on me. Always." A fist bump came next, and then a hug. When they released each other, BETY Junior finished his Jack and Coke. Then he stood up from the chaise. "I think I'm lit enough to act up. Come on with me, Ella La Bella, while I'll kick these damn clowns out of Pop's house! This ain't the fuckin' repass, and we won't be hosting it. Minnie was their family, not ours." Novella followed him as he marched toward the door leading to Pop's side of the house. "Count down with me, Ella. I'm going live in ten, nine, eight, seven . . ."

Pop's living room had filled to capacity. BETY Junior promptly went about shutting down the circus. Although Pop and Novella felt the same way about clearing the so-called mourners from the house, they went about it getting the people out in different ways. It was if Pop wasn't actually in the living room but watching it happen from behind a two-way mirror. He sat quietly in his recliner, as a spectator. Just as plain-faced and closed-mouthed as Pop, Novella followed behind BETY Junior, like his entourage. After BETY Junior had turned from locking the door after the last clown, Pop and Novella exhaled.

Novella said, "Well, you ain't gotta go home, but you gotta get the humph out of here."

Then Pop asked, "Now that that is done, you hungry, Bariah? Ella?"

FORTY-SIX

"When you leave people, if they're lucky, they'll find something else to do. They'll find someplace else to put their love. Someone else to give it to and get it from." Novella had done just that. Filling in the blanks that were really answers that had been erased. Just as BETY Junior had moved on from his mother, Novella had also moved on—from a number of situations, one being her half-brother. She hadn't stopped wanting love from him, but had stopped waiting on it.

Nolan was born when Novella was six. Another thing causing discord between her and Cara was that she wanted Novella to act as a second mother to Nolan. It was an easy pass for Novella, who didn't recall receiving any of the motherly care she saw Cara give to Nolan. Novella didn't dislike him, nor was she jealous; she just didn't want to take care of *Cara's* baby. Not that she dared call her mother by her name, though to Novella she was more of Cara than Mommy. A friend of Cara's who'd witnessed one of their heated interactions had laughed, "I think you two were sisters in a past life. And you fought like hell." Cara was amused by the thought, but had her own explanation, "Well, no. The truth is she's my *mother*. And she was so damn mean to me when I was a little girl that I had a witch reverse us and make her the child and me the mama so I could beat her ass, like

213

she beat mine." Novella, although feeling both jokes were at her expense, laughed.

Despite everything, there was something that drew Novella to Nolan, a bond that formed between them when they were outside their home. Novella also felt a duty to protect Nolan as "he was her little brother." But just when Novella felt Nolan was close to sincerely becoming a part of her and her life—that he might reciprocate her love—Cara's drug addiction separated them. Novella had only recently turned thirteen when, returning from school one day, she found Nolan gone and a social worker waiting for her. She missed him. More accurately, since he could often be difficult, she missed his potential to be someone with whom she could share unconditional love. *Everyone else in Coddy Lee's tribe had a tribe member who stuck by them*, Novella thought. Even if she had to share him with her mother, Nolan could still be her tribe companion. Novella held on to that hope even when she was placed with Coddy Lee while he was sent to live with his father's sister in Solon, a city twenty miles south of Cleveland.

After years of only seeing one another on holidays, Novella sought him out on her own. He was fifteen at the time, and she was twenty-one. She tried to build a relationship; he tried her patience. "Big Sis, can you spot me? Sis, your bro needs new kicks." He worked every angle. "Sis, I need a deposit to cover the candy my school wants me to sell to pay my way on our end of the year field trip." "Big Sis, I need cash for a bus pass to get back and forth to my new job." "Big Sis, I'm saving for a bike so I don't have to ride the bus so much." Novella loved being a "Big Sis," but she learned being Nolan's "Big Sis" cost too much—financially and emotionally. Eventually, she changed her phone number. It was easier than telling her only brother not to call her anymore. She also downsized to a one-bedroom apartment. Initially, she'd had a roommate, but the girl, an acquaintance from high school, became pregnant six months into the lease. Moving in with the baby's father, she left Novella to cover the rent on her own. She did, keeping the two bedrooms, in hopes of finding another roommate. She hoped that Nolan would move in with her after he turned eighteen. *The hope of family.* She thought they could help one another make it in the world. Heartbroken and a bit embarrassed when he didn't, Novella pushed him away completely. When he caught up with her at a holiday dinner organized by Connie, Nolan was surprised how nonchalant Novella was about seeing him.

"So, Sis, it's like that? You don't fuck with me no more? I'm one of *those* types to you."

"Nolan, you're to me what I am to you."

"Oh! Well, Mama say you don't have any family loyalty anyway."

"Whatever." Novella knew it wasn't true and that she shouldn't care, but the accusation still hurt her.

Nolan pressed, "Oh, so she's right?"

Novella remained nonchalant. "That's between you and your mammy. I don't have anything to do with what y'all think, and I don't have room or time in my life to care."

"So, she's right?"

"Go ask your mammy."

"I'm asking you if you—"

"Ask your mammy."

Novella hadn't yet reconnected with BETY Junior at this point in her life, but she'd moved on from expecting love from Nolan. It was a relief in some ways, especially as she was now able to give herself a bit of that love, money, and time Nolan had been draining from her. And Nolan could tell she was much doing better without him.

FORTY-SEVEN

Once, when Novella was running between her bed and toilet from food poisoning, Nolan had stolen her first car, a 1988 Chrysler New Yorker bought with money she'd saved working double shifts and living off of Ramen noodles and tuna fish sandwiches. Nolan had taken the keys knowing Novella wouldn't call the police. He used up a full tank of gas in two days of joyriding. When confronted, he'd downplayed the severity of his crime and the value of Novella's property. "That piece of shit," he'd said. A year later, Novella had upgraded to a 1992 Dodge Intrepid. *Sis, whoa, you moving up in the world.*

Nolan had also stolen her Lerner's New York credit card, which he used to amass inventory to sell on the street. Novella blamed herself for not immediately opening the bills when they arrived in the mail. She hadn't been shopping, so she presumed they were zero balance statements. Nolan, over the course of three months, had bought a few thousand dollars of women's clothing. Novella couldn't bring herself to press charges. Putting her young brother in jail was a scary thought. *What if someone hurts him in there? Or worse. He's not a real thug, just a little punk needing an ass-whoopin.* So, to pay down the debt he had run up, she again denied herself her favorite indulgences, like salmon steaks and turkey chops.

July 19, 2002

At Cherry's engagement party, a backyard barbeque, Novella looked as if she hadn't been through all the stress Nolan had put her through. In a simple yet elegant yellow sundress, Novella looked as if the party should have been for her. "You must be getting promotions and raises like what, Sis."

In addition to Nolan, Novella also had to deal with her host. Cherry, aware Novella was no longer eating meat, was so excited to be able put on such a feast she still begged her to attend. Cherry assured Novella that she would have fun, which Novella discovered didn't include being fed. Shortly after she arrived, Cherry, biting down into a hotdog, said, "Don't know what you're gonna eat, niece?" Posing in her Family Dollar cheap sundress, she stood the between the legs of her old new man who was sitting not too far from the grill. Cherry continued, "I guess you can eat corn on the cob, and you can take the bacon out of the baked beans. Right?"

Novella wasn't in the mood for the fake united family thing, especially if her uncle Merv the Perv was going to show up, so she had only planned on making a cameo appearance. Cherry's lack of consideration was her early ticket out. "I'll be alright. I'm actually overbooked today, so I won't be staying long enough to get hungry. I just came to show my face and say hey." Novella figured chit-chatting and hugging babies would take about thirty minutes.

Janet, buzzing off some orange marijuana, was weeded out higher than Cherry's front yard. She leaned out from the spades game she was causing Connie and her to lose. "What's the point of not eating meat? She ain't no smaller than she was the last time we saw her." She then laughed so hard she had to grab the table to not tip over and fall to the ground. Novella ignored her, and soon was saying her goodbyes.

"Why are you so funky towards me, Sis?" Nolan said as he chased Novella toward the exit to Cherry's backyard. "Hey, we're family. No and

No. Remember, when Mama spoke to both of us, at the same time? She'd say No-No, let's go. No-No, come eat. No-No, what are y'all watching. No-No," he laughed. "That was pretty tight. Come on, Sis, slow down."

"What is it, No?" Novella reluctantly stopped.

"You tell me, No." He shrugged. "Everybody's telling me that I've been replaced by the dude who saved your life years ago."

"He hasn't replaced you. I'm pretty sure stealing from me is not in him."

Nolan exhaled hard. "Ha!" He pointed his middle finger aggressively at her. "You still on that old shit? That don't even matter anymore. When are you going stop being a bitch, No? You really think you're better than everybody."

Novella was nobody's bitch. Not during friendly or catty girl talk— and for damn sure not to her thieving, bloodsucking brother. "Bitch?" She raised her brow. "And your finger in my face? Yeah, ok. We're done."

"Sis, according to you, we never started."

"Yeah, No," she agreed, "you are the worst brother I never had."

She went to leave, but he blocked her way.

"Whatever you want Nolan, the answer's no. Forever. Hell, no." She waved a hand between them, gesturing from her to him. "No-No don't live here no more."

Spreading his stance, he planted himself in her path. "I asked you why you're so funky towards me?"

Novella again tried to leave, again he stopped her.

"You owe me," he told her.

"The devil says the same thing, and we know he's a liar. Get out of my way, boy."

Nolan folded his arms. "Auntie Cherry said you threw it away. And you know what *it* I'm talking about."

The insult of being called a bitch was still stinging. "I don't care what you're talking about. You need to move. Move. Out of my way, boy. Move!"

"Lay's potato chips," he said matter-of-factly.

"What?"

"Lay's potato chips."

"You want me to buy you a bag of Lay's potato chips?"

"Hell, no," he laughed dryly.

"Just move, Nolan," she warned.

He again pointed his middle finger at her. "You threw my shit away. You owe me."

Novella decided to bum-rush her way out. With her shoulders jutting forward, she headed for the gate, pushing against Nolan. He grabbed her by the neck and pushed her back. Novella's eyes twitched in shock. He'd never done anything like that to her before. She relented, and he released his grip. Massaging her neck, she stared at Nolan. He laughed and spat on the ground. Feeling victorious, he was caught off guard when she again went forward. He thought to go for her neck again, but she was expecting it. She quickly seized his wrist and his opposite shoulder. He was bent over facing the ground before he knew it. She drove her knee hard into his side. "He's your bitch!" She served him four times. Just when she had decided to let him up, he threatened to bust up her face and her car. She brought him upright, but it was just a setup for her next move. Fixing a hand under his chin, she shoved his unimpressive goatee toward the sky. He bit his tongue.

She warned him, "Now back the fuck off, Nolan! Leave me alone, and let me leave!"

After a few painful moments for him, she released his chin. She stepped away from her stunned brother, unknowingly clearing the path for Gent to continue in her defense, "Gotdamnit, boy, who in the hell do you think you are?"

Gent and Nolan quickly began fighting. The way they were going at it, it was more like wrestling than fighting. Nolan was grunting something about Novella being his sister and his business. Gent didn't care and showed as much by slamming Nolan onto the ground. Gent wasn't fazed by Nolan calling him a crackhead. It was true, but it didn't make Gent any less "Everybody's Daddy."

Cherry rushed over as fast as the additional eighty plus pounds she'd gained in the last decade allowed. "This damn girl! Noey, sadity ass, always got motherfuckers fighting over her like she the pussy queen of the world."

Janet's current boyfriend, who as DJ had killed the music, also rushed over. He told Cherry, "Auntie, he choked her when she tried to leave."

Janet laughed. "Damn!"

Cherry dismissed the explanation. "Shawn, this is family business and you don't know about this girl. She is really something else. Some years back she jumped on your girl Janet. Noey got a serious problem."

It was obvious he didn't agree with her, but said no more. Everyone, except some of the young kids, was now near the gate.

Connie stepped in and pulled down Novella's dress. Her altercation with Nolan had twisted and raised it, leaving her rear barely covered. Connie's voice was full of barely suppressed excitement. "Girl, you looked like you were gonna push your brother's head off into the clouds. Where did you learn to fight like that?"

Before Novella could answer, she heard Nolan say to Gent, "Yeah, okay, cuz. Keep defending her. Your crackhead ass would want what No threw away. A whole bag of weed. Hybrid, millennium shit." Nolan was slumped against the fence. "Had it in a Lay's potato chip bag for easy transport. Left it in No's car by mistake, and she threw that good shit away. Six hundred damn dollars' worth."

Cherry assured everyone Nolan spoke the truth, "That's what she told me. He left a bag of weed in her car and she threw it away."

Novella shook her head. "Cherry, I didn't tell you that. I didn't tell *you* anything." Novella then looked to Connie who admitted, "I told her, and she must have told Nolan."

It was the truth. Nolan had left a Lay's potato chip bag packed with weed in Novella's car. Two days after she'd reluctantly given him a ride home, she found it. "This boy has *tried* me too hard now. Too hard," she'd said to Connie over the phone. Novella was in the parking lot of Finast grocery store, where she'd just shopped, so she tossed Nolan's weed into a trash can near the doors. Connie had begged her not to do it, but Novella was mad. And since she'd had her share of speeding tickets, there was no way she was risking getting stopped by the police with weed in her car. "Go dig it out of the trash can, if you want it," Novella had told Connie. That was months ago.

Cherry's fiancé stepped into the circle. "Come on y'all, let's get past this." He gently tapped Gent's shoulder. "Let him up, my man." Gent backed down and looked to Novella as Nolan was offered a hand up by the old man.

Cherry positioned herself in front of Gent. "I want to talk to you, nephew. I need to talk to you, right now."

Nolan, after pushing himself up against the fence, had begun walking to a table, his shoulders slumped.

Gent told Novella, "Hang out until you relax, baby girl. No one is putting you out, but damn that was a lot of weed to throw out. Gotdamn."

Cherry sang out in a high pitch, "Let her go if she wanna go! She's damn near ruined the party my man threw me. Beating her own brother's ass! Surely, you don't think she's the victim here!"

Connie grabbed Novella's hand. "Come on, Noey. Let's go inside and get you some water, or something. Cherry just talking like she always does."

FORTY-EIGHT

When Connie looked up from opening another beer, she was surprised to see Nolan. He'd come up from the basement and was passing her. Novella was exiting the bathroom. When the front of Novella came into Connie's view, she warned, "No more you two." Before she had gotten all of the words out, Nolan had already spit in Novella's face. She screamed as if he'd hit her. Nolan thought by backing up she was retreating to the bathroom to wash his saliva off her face. He got out about half of his victory laugh, before it became a pain-filled yelp. Novella kicked Nolan in the face, breaking his nose and sending him reeling across the room. Glass shattered as he crashed into a coffee table Connie was allowing Cherry to keep until she had more room for it.

"Gotdamn!" Connie shot up from the table. "Shit! Oh, shit!" Her beer can fell over as her thighs hit the table, moving it forward a few inches.

Normally, wasted drink would be a major issue. Normally, Novella didn't fight. Normally, Connie only witnessed sorry jab matches or slap and scratch tussles. Having seen what she believed to be a bad-ass karate or kung fu move, Connie wasn't mad about her wasted beer or her broken table. *My niece!* she inwardly exclaimed. *The girl is a ninja! Noey, gotdamn! Wooo, a ninja!*

Connie wanted the others to see the show, but she was too excited to do more than knock on the window to get the attention of the people outside. She then rushed over to the threshold between the kitchen and living room and waited for the next round.

Nolan rolled up carefully from the shards of glass, trying not to get cut. "Stupid, dumb, ugly bitch! I was trying to take it easy on you because you're my sister, but it's time for me to fuck up you for real." Blood ran from his crooked nose. Back on his feet, he rushed at her. Novella had slightly bent her legs and was in a defensive stance from which she kicked him again, this time hitting him in his chest. He fell to the ground near a statue of two pigs cuddling, with the words "Bacon in the Makin" inscribed on a plaque attached to it. Nolan picked it up, aimed for Novella's calm face, and threw. She easily dodged it. The piggies broke into three pieces as the impact created a hole in the wall.

Isaac came up next to Connie. "Don't mess up my mama's house!"

The fight between Novella and Nolan had again become the focus of the party. Cherry and Gent, however, were nowhere to be found. They were working out their difference of opinion on Novella, everyone would learn later, over a blunt in the garage.

Nolan thought throwing the statue was a good enough diversion for him to be able to rush Novella. *She won't have time to again kick me again*, he thought. Novella did not kick him again. She blocked his predictable punch by raising her arm to a 90° angle. Nolan was a pitiful opponent, easily handled with the most basic Krav Maga moves BETY Junior had taught her. In a maneuver similar to her earlier one, but harder and faster, she fired in more knee jabs. "Yah! Yah! Yah! Yah! Yah!" The family hollered in excitement. Also excited was Novella's Honest Demon. The knee jabs were more than enough to subdue him. But when she stopped kneeing him and the pitiful Nolan met her eyes, she became furious, her self-defense becoming retaliation. Krav Maga took a backseat to her "sorting him out."

She then did something she knew that would express her feelings better than the technical moves of a martial art: she slapped the shit out of him. She slapped him so many times and so hard that her hands felt like they were bleeding fire. The clap of her hand against Nolan's face and her own panting were all Novella heard until she fell atop him on the couch.

In a sober voice, she heard Connie say, "Noey, girl, you need to stop now."

Novella's Honest Demon thought otherwise. She rose from the sofa dragging Nolan with her, and then slung him across the living room. She threw herself against him, shoving him against the wall, busted from where the piggy statute had broken. There she mugged him, pushing the back of his head into the hole in the wall. She then began punching him in the stomach. Novella's Honest Demon didn't care that Nolan was no longer trying to fight back.

Novella eventually let Nolan drop to the floor near the biggest of the broken pieces of the piggy statue. When she left Cherry's house, he'd still be there flinching and moaning. Novella, with the back of her pretty dress bunched up above her butt, went out the rarely used front door.

Isaac yelled after her, "Fuck shit up then leave, huh? Why don't you take your damn brother with you? Both of y'all sadity asses got a gotdamn problem and need to be sorted the hell out! Tearing up my mama's house with y'all damn family issues."

Novella drove a little over three miles, before her vision became too impaired by tears. She pulled into the parking lot of the Cleveland Heights Public Library. There, she sat in her car crying uncontrollably amongst the patrons. Reaching over to the glove compartment, she was startled by a pair of hazel eyes. A little chubby-faced girl was peering into her passenger side window. The girl laughed as Novella drew back in surprise. Novella, after rolling her eyes at the girl, retrieved a few napkins from her glove compartment. Afterwards, as she wiped the tears from her face, the little girl, still staring at her, pouted her lips in empathy. She ran off, just as Novella's cell phone began to ring and ring and ring. Connie, Cherry, and even Nolan were trying to reach her. BETY Junior, though completely unaware of what had happened, was also trying to reach her. At that moment, she really wanted to be with him, to cry on his shoulder, to get a little praise from him for applying her Krav Maga training so well. Yet, at the same time, she didn't want him to know about this. She was embarrassed to have a brother who would call her a bitch and assault her. She wouldn't tell BETY Junior, or anyone else.

FORTY-NINE

June 2013

Chrystan was surprised that no one met them at the airport. "How are we getting to Grandma's house?"

Denise gave him one of her soft smiles. "The van."

Chrystan had never experienced public transportation until riding in the airport shuttle bus. He didn't like it. So, arriving at what used to be his grandmother's home, he climbed out too quickly to notice the house was completely dark and that some of the windows were boarded.

Denise and Chrystan had landed at Cleveland's Hopkins International airport at six thirty-seven that evening, and then waited about an hour-and-a-half for the departure of the next shuttle. Denise and Chrystan were the third to last of the passengers to be dropped off.

It was about thirty minutes after dark when the shuttle left them and their bags on the sidewalk in front of the locked and vacant home. Luckily, the enclosed porch was unlocked and furnished, so they had a comfortable place to wait for Grandma to return. After waiting for an hour, they called Chrystan's mom. She didn't answer. As worried as Chrystan was, he was even more tired. Denise had awoken him that morning at five. They'd shopped and packed. Then shopped and packed some more. He'd wanted a nap, but his mother had told him to wait to sleep until he was on the plane. He ended up watching a movie on his portable DVD player during the flight rather than napping. So, on that dark porch, he began to nod off. Denise, sensing his fatigue, pulled him to lay across her lap. Within a few minutes, he was in a deep sleep. Under normal circumstances, Chyrstan was undesirous of this type of coddling. He'd been a "good little man" long enough. He hadn't whined or pouted, about not wanting to come to Cleveland to be with a grandmother he didn't know. He hadn't whined or pouted, about the prospect of having only Denise and this grandmother he didn't know to rely on. He'd kept his composure even when he had to travel without his phone and later when he was packed in a van with strangers. The "little man," however, was tired. He was a child, and he truly needed to rest.

It had been two weeks since Chrystan had awakened to find that he and Denise were still on the porch. They'd called his mother all that day. She never answered, and she didn't have voicemail. Fear kept them from going to the authorities or to a hotel. The fear of Chrystan being put in a foster home and being separated from Denise stopped them from going to the police. The fear of running out of money stopped them from checking in to a hotel.

He and Denise were living off food from corner stores, a gas station, McDonald's, and Popeye's Chicken. Denise held guard over their cash, though it was Chrystan who spent it. He had decent money management skills. To keep him busy, his mother had often given him Visa debit cards that he mostly spent online buying comics, video games, t-shirts, and food. He learned how to get the most for his money. His mother was never bothered by what he bought. She only was bothered when he placed to-go orders that she had to pick up from the Olive Garden and Applebee's. "Boy, you need to ask me first. Who said I felt like going anywhere? I don't know why you can't stick to pizza and Chinse food delivery." His debit card experience had given Chrystan the smarts to shop for Denise and himself. He also possessed the know-how, more than she did, not to get distracted by strangers. However, just as Denise's slightness attracted the wrong people, so did Chrystan's age. The majority of the neighborhood's working-class homeowners had reached retirement age about twenty-five years ago. Generational wealth was as frail as those of them still around and living in their homes. Most of the neighborhood's residents were renters who lived below the poverty line. Their lawns grew tall, wild, and weedy. Not a safe place for an eight-year-old Chyrstan shopping with twenty- and fifty-dollar bills. To throw off the hard-lived folks who watched him intensely, he'd had to learn multiple routes to and from the stores.

"We can't stay here," Chrystan told Denise. "We gotta get in touch with Mama and tell her we need help."

Denise, living up to the nickname "Dumbnise," whined, "My phone is off." Turned away from the porch door, she lay on the sofa. Her back was to Chrystan, and he knew she no longer had service. Chrystan had known before she did, because when her battery died, he'd charged her phone at Popeye's Chicken. When it powered on, the "No service" message was the first thing he noticed. Desperate, he had attempted to call his mother, but not only was there no service, the phone's data was gone. No contacts, no messages—nothing. Everything had been deleted. After he'd returned to the porch, both he and Denise had cried. Neither of them had bothered to memorize his mother's number, as it changed every year when she upgraded her phone.

Chrystan and Denise were confused. Nothing had happened to Denise's phone; no water damage, no cracked screen. She took care of things. Her phone was always in its case, and she had never misplaced or dropped it. So, they wondered what had wiped out her data. It didn't cross their minds that the data wipe could have been intentional. They didn't know about the Find My iPhone app, specifically, the app's feature that allowed a phone owner to delete all data as a safeguard when a device has been lost or stolen. Even if they had known about it, neither would have thought Chrystan's mother would've reported Denise's phone as lost or stolen.

Chrystan's phone was "accidentally" left in Georgia. The night before he left, his mother had insisted he charge it in her room. She told him she'd give it back to him before he and Denise boarded the plane the next morning. She did not, and Chrystan hadn't remembered it, until he thought about which playlist he'd listen to first during the flight. But by then he and Denise were already through security and sitting by the gate. "I'll mail it to you," his mother had promised when he'd called her from Denise's phone. It was Chrystan's mother who'd bought and paid for the services for both his and Denise's phones. Of course, neither of the two had ever seen their respective bills, so they didn't know which mobile provider they had or how much it cost. Yet, Chrystan was aware cell phones weren't hard to come by.

"Let's buy new phones. They got some at the store we get the corned beef sandwiches from."

Denise turned her head toward him. "How much?"

Each would have to pay $79.99 for an off-brand, well below what they were accustomed to. Second-rate yet unlimited service would cost $40 a month. Adding in the activation and service fees, the cost of each device would be the better part of $200. Since they still didn't have Chrystan's mother's number, even buying one to share wouldn't be worth it. Instead, Chrystan spent about $10 on a pack of ink pens, notebook paper, a box of envelopes, and postage stamps. With them, he wrote a letter to his mom.

"Hello mama,

It's your son Chrystan. Please help me and Denise. We are homeless and scared. Come get us. Hurry. People are trying to hurt me.

I love you."

As the days went on, Chrystan continued to plead with his cousin, "Denise, we have to do something!" He didn't mean to yell, but he needed her to be an adult. "Denise, we need someone to help us. You have to do something. Right now!"

She began to cry. "I'm scared."

Chrystan huffed. "I know that . . . but men have been chasing *me*. They want to beat and rob *me*, and they know I don't have a home. And if they find me here, they're going to hurt us both!"

Every day, Chrystan was growing smarter and taller and would soon surpass the petite Denise in both categories. Right now, the top of his head reached her collar bone. Gently, he grabbed her arms as she stood in front of him on the porch. "Denise, get us a hotel. Something cheap. Real cheap. We don't need a swimming pool or room service. We just need a room that we can lock, and a phone. I'll leave a note for Mama, just in case she comes here looking for us. And I'll write her again from the hotel. Come on, Denise, let's look for a hotel. Maybe go downtown. All cities have hotels downtown."

Denise shrugged. "We don't have enough money, and I need to save money for Pampers for my baby."

Chrystan's handsome face balled up. "*What baby?*"

Denise shook her arms free from him and pointed at the locked front door of the house. "Cousin said Auntie would help me. But Auntie has moved or something."

Chrystan was confused. "My mama said . . . Grandma was going to help you get a baby?"

Denise gave him a terribly mean look for a few moments. She hadn't ever done that before, and it scared Chrystan. When she grabbed his hand, he pulled away.

"Wait," she told him. "I'm going to show you." Chrystan relaxed, allowing her to place his hand on her stomach. "Understand?" she asked.

He felt what seemed to be a small melon under her shirt. She then pushed his hand away, as if she hadn't placed it on her. Going to lie down on the sofa, she left him standing in the middle of the porch.

Chrystan had so many questions. "So, we're here because of you? But, why did I have to come?"

Denise, positioning a makeshift pillow formed from some of her clothing stacked and rolled together, yawned, "Chrystan . . . I don't know why you're here."

FIFTY

June 30, 2004
The Mercedes Night Club
Cleveland, Ohio

"Why are you even here?" Novella asked Dell, an odd question to someone who was supposed to be family. The thing was, they weren't really friends anymore. The same went for Novella and Yadara. Life's adversities were challenging the relevance of their childhood bonds, and they were finding it harder to relate to each other as adults. With every passing day, they were becoming people only connected by the length of time they'd known each other.

Novella was now thirty and having her very first birthday party. A big bash, with an all-white theme. The Mercedes Night Club wasn't a private hall, yet was hosting Novella's party almost as if she'd rented out the place. BETY Junior knew the owner, and the club was reopening after being closed for months due to a fire. Novella's upscale party, coinciding with the grand reopening, would help recapture some of the club's old patrons as well as attract new ones. It worked. By ten that night, the Mercedes was so white it was like a snowstorm had hit. The club was packed with patrons dressed elegantly in accordance with Novella's theme, though the queen herself was dressed in silver in a floor-length custom-made iridescent gown.

"Why did you keep your outfit a secret?" Dell asked, barely able to mask her scowl. "I mean from us, anyway, because I know you told *Bariah*." She liked saying his birth name rather than his nickname. Doing so made Dell feel like she knew him as intimately as she presumed Novella did. Dell also hoped that it irked Novella to hear her butter his name. *Bariah*, saying it with familiarity and affection. Novella was aware of Dell's intentions, but she was hardly bothered. She felt sorry for Dell, to still be so hot about someone who'd obviously rejected her.

"*Bariah*, he knew right?"

"Ardellya, it was to be a surprise," Novella told her. "An unveiling."

Yadara chimed in, "I figure it's because you didn't want to let on how much this party cost. I know BETY Junior helped you pay for it."

He had helped with all of it, except Novella's attire. There was no charge for the club, but he'd covered the cost of the DJ, the decorations, and the menu.

"Unceremoniously!" he'd offered. "We're just going to throw a jam for your birthday. It doesn't take months and months of planning; we'll just set it up. And do it all the way up! So, Ella La Bella, just dress yourself and show up." In the end, she didn't have to get herself there. BETY Junior surprised her by personally escorting her.

Yadara and Dell had arrived at Novella's apartment building at the same time. Before they had even made it into the lobby, Novella sashayed out onto the sidewalk. Expecting her to be in a cocktail dress, both of their mouths dropped open when they saw her. The gown, perfectly fitted to Novella's curves, was beyond flattering.

"What the hell is this?" Yadara asked. "You didn't say you were doing all this."

Just as Novella reached where Yadara and Dell were standing in awe and anger, they noticed her new friends trailing behind her. While not in gowns, they were also extra fancy.

"Is that for you?" Kanya asked Novella, nodding toward a white limo that had just pulled up in front of the apartment building. Before Novella could answer, BETY Junior stepped out in a relaxed white suit. Purcell, in a white dashiki suit, stepped out after him.

Yadara and Dell, although still rivals, shared a look of irritation. Novella had gotten them both excited about her upcoming party, and had asked them both to dress like the queens they were. "To be yourself, but ultra-fabulous!" Both had figured that most of the fabulousness would be in the overly excited Noey's head, and they definitely hadn't expected a limo. So, in spite of her request, they'd dressed for themselves. Dell, in tight white capris and a matching halter, looked cute. She was, however, the most underdressed in what was to be the birthday queen's entourage. Yadara, in a white one-shoulder body dress, was gorgeous, yet seeing Novella's ultra-fabulousness as well as that of BETY Junior, Purcell, Kanya, and Haze, she regretted not taking it up a couple of notches. Yadara also felt upstaged by the limo. She'd borrowed her father's BMW to escort Novella in style. Yadara was used to being the money in Novella's life, the friend who was better off, yet still down to earth.

The limo escorted all of them to the Mercedes. Yadara's attitude about being excluded from the planning of the party and their arrival to it deflated enough for her to enjoy the lush ride. Before entering the limo, Dell had looked back at her old Ford Escort. Reliable and clean though it was, it was not the right ride for such an occasion of black ultra-fabulousness.

In the limo, Dell brewed in a stew of her own dark thoughts. *Noey, alright already. I'll be in white, but this isn't the Grammy's or your wedding. So, just relax.* Her minimal effort was obvious, as was her regret when they travelled to Lake Erie to take pictures. "Noey, I wish you'd given me a

heads-up . . . I didn't know everyone was going to be all showbiz tonight."
She didn't enjoy the ride and was reluctant to be in any of the pictures. After
they arrived at the Mercedes, she was no different. The most she interacted
with Novella was when Haze and Kanya were escorted by BETY Junior and
Purcell to the dance floor. It was then that Yadara had started on Novella
about why she hadn't told them all the details.

"What difference does it make about the cost of the party, and who
paid for it?" Novella told more than asked Yadara. "I'm finally having a big
birthday party."

"Noey, don't even with me," Yadara replied. "You live in Cleveland
Heights now, but I know where you came from, and I know you. So, be real
with me." She flipped her hands up to reference their glamorous surroundings. "This is money. This entire club is lit up for you."

Dell snapped her fingers at Novella. "And, girlie, you're not banked
up like that. But the secrecy . . . why?"

Novella looked at them both. She had no intention of telling them
she'd scored a much better job, a salaried position. Despite what they
thought, she could have saved and paid for the party on her own, and that
while BETY Junior was a well-off friend, she did have her own hustle muscle and knew how to flex it.

Instead, she told them, "You two can enjoy the party or not. *This* is
the VIP section."

Novella's guests were seated in the Mercedes Lounge, the best spot
in the club. Replica Mercedes Benz served as the bases for the lounge's
marble tables. BETY Junior's association with the club's owner afforded
Novella exclusive use of all four tables. She and her entourage had a table
to themselves, and the other three tables were reserved for her close work
associates and other friends.

Novella enjoyed her special night. Yadara and Dell allied in their unhappiness until Dell saw BETY Junior eyeing Yadara. Dell decided to snag BETY Junior's attention, better known as cockblocking, by asking him to take a picture with her. She was left with her mouth hanging open when Yadara, noticing BETY Junior's interest in her, quickly took his hand and led him away.

It was obvious since that day Novella first introduced BETY Junior to Yadara that something spicy was cooking between them. It was just as obvious that something bitter and green was cooking in Dell's mind as she watched the two on the dance floor. Her face was tight until she realized Novella, Haze, and Kanya were watching her. She quickly relaxed her scowl, though her nose flared a few times as she struggled to appear unbothered.

FIFTY-ONE

BETY Junior, a cut up on the dance floor, was reserved with Yadara. Usually conservatively chic, Yadara was provocative with BETY Junior. Either to excite Dell's jealousy or BETY Junior's libido, Yadara danced in a manner that was slightly out of character for her. Feeling her big girl power, she threw her curves about. Her gorgeous face said she was in her own world, just enjoying the night—yet the world around her knew better.

BETY Junior eyed Yadara as if ready to catch her should she fall. He was actually standing at the ready if she were to grab at something of his that she should not. *Get freaky*. People often let themselves go at parties. His caution didn't come from a dislike for her; he definitely wanted to invite her closer and press her against him. For the moment, he'd watch and *feel* her moves, slow jam with her despite the current song, a hard-core rap tune. Ignoring its rough tempo, he'd grind with her within its soulful, poetic pitch. In a crowd of other dancers, they were having their most intimate encounter. He was enjoying it as much as Yadara was, although she was a bit younger than he usually liked. He imagined teaching her how to sate his ravenous desires, as well as how to explore and sate her own. Occasionally, BETY Junior was inspired to teach, and this night with Yadara seemed like just the occasion. She seemed ready, even if she normally seemed pretty stuffy. *Big booty, bad attitude; bad boy, big dick*, growled the tiger renowned to loosen the tightest stuffing. Unfortunately, cat-daddy would have to tuck his tail, as he'd made it a rule not to fuck his sister's friends. And fucking was what he was mostly about these days. He wasn't anybody's boyfriend. Yadara wouldn't be an exception. He'd *fuck* her, maybe for as long as a few weeks, and then he'd fuck up. He didn't know how much of him she wanted. Under the circumstances, BETY Junior considered them both lucky that he wouldn't inquire. Having a link, things could get messy. While he wasn't anybody's boyfriend, neither was he an asshole. He knew his relationship with his Ella was golden. He wouldn't do anything to fuck that up. To help melt the sexual tension, he decided to clown. Exploding out of his two-step, he began dancing playfully. Yadara laughed. Jamming off his silliness, they enjoyed two songs before the DJ broke them up by playing a line dance. As the "Cleveland Shuffle" by the North Boyz bounced into the fading rap tune, the DJ shouted, "Where in da hell are we? Where are we?" The hyped club answered, "Cleve-land!" "C-Town!"

FIFTY-TWO

Noticing Dell was still aggravated, Novella asked her to go to the ladies' room with her to give her a breather to vent her steam.

"I don't have to go," Dell told her flatly.

Dell had been sour all night, and Novella wanted to sort her out. *Why are you even here? You didn't want to dress up for my first party. You weren't excited for me in any way. Now you're here being a drag—a jealous drag.* Novella knew Dell had a mouth on her, and could dirty up the all the white party, so she decided it was best to sort her out another day. Tonight was about fun. Novella pushed away from table to go relieve her bladder.

The restrooms were down a flight of thickly carpeted stairs. The edge of each step, rounded and padded by the carpet, was too smooth for any shoe without a ridged bottom. Descending quickly to go relieve herself, freshen up, and get back to her party, Novella didn't mind her steps. She was smiling as she quietly sung, "Happy birthday . . . to me. Happy birthday . . . to me. Happy birthday . . ." By the third step, she was sliding. Grabbing the banister saved her from tumbling forward, but her feet were still sliding forward. She then overcompensated by leaning backwards, which caused her toes to come up from the steps. Out of embarrassment she suppressed her scream as her legs went out from under her. Quickly, she dropped onto her butt. It wasn't over, yet. Gravity, combined with the smoothness of both the thick carpet and her dress, put her in motion. On her butt, she began bouncing down the steps.

"Damn, baby!" she heard a male voice say from behind her.

"Oh! Oh!" said another.

Holding the handrail kept her comical descent in a straight line, but didn't stop or slow it down. Her hand slid against the handrail; her butt slid against the carpet.

The first male voice was getting closer and again said, "Whoa, whoa! Damn, baby! Damn! Oh, shit! Oh, oh, shit! Damn!"

Finally, she stopped. Awkwardly, getting to her feet, she felt hands lightly support her. "You alright, baby?"

Embarrassed, she kept her back to him. *Jesus!* she thought. *I just fell on my ass down the steps, and on my best birthday! Damn and damn!* She went about reassembling the sophistication her fall down the stairs had taken from her. As she straightened herself, and righted her beautiful dress, she felt to be still on her scary carpet ride. Momentum was coursing through her body and there was thumping in her butt, as if it was still bouncing against the steps. She was slightly wobbly. Looking up slowly, she saw the white matching dashikis of the men who had called out after her before she saw their twin ebony faces, which were as handsome as they were sincere with empathy. "Yeah, thanks," she said to them.

The two held back their laughter until after she resumed her trip to the ladies' room. Hearing their whispers, Novella could tell they thought she was out of earshot.

"What was going on with your hands, man?" one asked the other. "What the hell was that?"

"Shit, I was trying to catch her. I was reaching," she heard him say. "Trying to grab one of her arms, or something. But, shit, man, it was like her booty was a basketball. Bounce, bounce, bounce!"

There was a small lounge before the short hall that held the restrooms. Novella got wide-eyed looks from the people sitting there before a few muttered, "Happy birthday!"

"Thanks." She made her way through them, wondering if alcohol and other stimulants had dulled their sense of humor. *Of course they saw me go down*, she thought. The staircase had a spiral design. Its banister made of thin metal rods, spaced fairly widely apart. Those in the lounge had a clear view of whoever descended the steps.

Entering the ladies' room, Novella whispered to herself, "Damn, if I was tipsy, it would have been game over."

On the way back up to the main floor, she stepped more carefully. She hoped to have made her last trip to the ladies' room. *I'm not trying to come back down here.*

BETY Junior's light-brown skin flushed red as he bent over laughing when Novella told him about her fall. Her body still hurt, so his level of amusement felt over-the-top to her. "I'm done talking to you." She left him on the dance floor to get empathy elsewhere. She had to wait about half an hour because her entire entourage was spread throughout the club, and she had no desire to share her experience with her extended party. She did mingle with them and enjoyed some appetizers.

Kanya was the first to return to Novella's table. With big, expressive eyes, she held in her laughter. "Girl!" was the only thing she could manage to say before the giggles overtook her. No one else was as thoughtful. Haze grabbed her hand in sympathy, but hollered as she listened to the story.

Novella's fall was Dell's only enjoyment of the evening. She happily retold the story to Yadara, Purcell, and BETY Junior, who had already heard the story from Novella.

Yadara sniffed Novella's ginger ale. "Is it spiked?"

Dell leaned over toward Novella. "Your damn shoes are spiked! High-ass heels! Face it, Noey, you're officially too old for fuck-me shoes."

"Haters!" Novella laughed. She looked up to Purcell. "What do you do with the haters in your life?"

He replied with a 1980s' dance move, robotically snaking and popping his arms, chest, and neck. He then smacked away imaginary haters on either side of him.

Impressive and entertaining, his moves elicited a challenge from another guest, Novella's neighbor. The young guy repeated Purcell's moves, and then popped out different ones that were even more complicated. Purcell went back and forth with him a few times before giving up. "Damn, young blood!" he praised him. "You got it! Man, you got it!"

A few minutes later, the twins who'd witnessed Novella's fall entered the VIP section. "Hey, beautiful, we forgot to wish you happy birthday," said the one who'd attempted to catch her.

Novella stood and thanked each one with a light hug. "Have a seat and join us. Have some food."

They accepted. It turned out they knew one of Novella's coworkers who was seated at one of the other VIP tables. After a few minutes of conversation, the one who'd tried to catch her asked Novella, "You wanna dance, gorgeous? I promise I can hold on to you." Winking he added, "You won't fall on my watch, baby."

BETY Junior laughed from his seat at the table. "I'm gonna hold you to that, brotha."

Purcell, sitting across from him, said, "Well, her dress looks slippery, so cut the man some slack, B. Brotha man might lose his grip. His hands will probably slide down her like she's a greasy pole. He'll hit the floor with her."

Novella playfully threw a napkin at him before accepting the twin's hand to let him escort her to the dance floor.

When the DJ allowed them to catch a breath with a slow song, Novella started to leave the floor, but BETY Junior took her hand. "Nope, none of that." He answered her questioning look. "I see your new boyfriend isn't here."

She shrugged.

"Come on." He pulled her into position to slow-dance with him. "You don't have to sit out any song tonight. Every song is for you. It's your birthday."

She kissed his cheek.

After he spun her around, he told her, "I was coming to get you anyway. No twins, Ella. Don't date either one of those twins. If they were fraternal, maybe. But they're identical, so they can run some games on a woman. You'd end up being with both of them and not even knowing it."

Novella met his eyes. "Sounds convenient. A two-for-one deal. Maybe I've been going about this love thing all wrong."

BETY Junior shook his head. "Stop it."

Novella went on, "Maybe instead of one man meeting my needs, which are many, I should have two. I'm a whole a lot of woman, maybe expecting one man to handle me all by himself is unrealistic."

"Ella . . ." BETY Junior stared down into her taunting eyes.

She continued, "And if they were to look alike . . . hmmm . . . maybe they'd do everything alike. So, wow, twice as much of everything."

BETY Junior dipped her. "I'm going to drop you on this floor if you don't stop that trash talk."

"You wouldn't dare," she laughed.

He brought her upright. "No, I wouldn't. But, Ella, I am serious. Don't date identical twins, especially those two. They're grown-ass men, but they're dressed alike. Look at them with the same haircut and beard. Trust me when I say they share their women—with or without permission."

Novella looked through the crowd at the good-looking twins still mingling in her VIP area. "Relax. I'm not interested."

"Good," BETY Junior said quickly, and then added, "But I'll tell you this, your party is live. Great everything, including women. A lot of fine ones in here. And that was to be expected. So, any dude on the up and up, coming to snag a lady, doesn't want to be mistaken for any other man. And that includes his own brother. So, don't let them tell you shit about why their grown-asses are dressed alike on a night like this. It'll just be the beginning of the bullshit."

Novella stared at BETY Junior.

"What?" he asked her.

With a straight face she told him, "You're presumptuous and sexist. If they were women, you'd welcome the twin action and wouldn't care if they took turns with you. And I if were a dude, you'd be encouraging me to double-dip on those fine honeys. So, Bariah Elijah Tomas Young Junior, are only men allowed a double scoop of sex? And us *good* women are to go to bed hungry?"

BETY Junior stood taller. "Goddammit, Ella! Are you serious?"

She laughed, pushing him away, only to grab and hug him. "Yes and no. But don't worry, I love you."

He waited. "Uh-huh."

She told him, "And I wouldn't date identical twins because I wouldn't want to get played."

He smiled. "Good."

About two hours later, the club lights were flicking to indicate the last call for alcohol.

Novella grabbed a boneless wing from BETY Junior's plate.

Around a mouthful he told her, "Don't lose a hand. Your birthday was over about three hours ago."

She popped the wing in her mouth, and then grabbed another.

BETY Junior told her, "You must have knocked something loose when you flipped down the steps. What happen to you not eating meat?"

Still chewing, she almost choked laughing about her fall and her failed attempt at being a vegan. "I've decided just no red meat or pork. Sister's Raffie's fish got me."

Haze, from across the table, grabbed a shrimp from BETY Junior's plate. "Ella, be for real; wasn't it a rotisserie chicken from Boston Market?"

Kanya, on the other side of BETY Junior, reached over with a toothpick and snagged a meatball. "I thought it was a box of Popeye's spicy chicken."

BETY Junior leaned back in his seat. "Did I make this plate for every damn body? It's not the party platter."

Yadara, seated next to Haze, also snagged a meatball. "Kim's wings," she said. "It was six wings with a side of their baked macaroni and cheese and a grape soda. Can't say I blame her."

Purcell, sitting down at the table with a stacked plate, had, unbeknownst to him, also fixed a party platter. Dell helped herself to a rib. "I think Noey was vegan, vegetarian, or whatever for maybe a month-and-half. I know for a fact she baked some turkey wings a few weeks ago."

BETY Junior turned toward her for a full confession. "Ella . . ."

Novella was waving a chicken wing as she announced, "I eat what I eat!"

BETY Junior shrugged, "Alright," before taking a slice of her birthday cake and smashing it on her face.

FIFTY-THREE

"I would have danced the both of you under the table," Coddy Lee had told a seventeen-year-old Janet and a fifteen-year-old Novella. "Was my favorite thing to do. Didn't need no liquor to feel good. Just good music."

Novella had tried to imagine her granny working the dance floor, but she couldn't. Coddy Lee had a beautiful laugh, so Novella knew she could be joyful, but she couldn't see any remnants of her youth. Coddy Lee didn't dance, clap her hands to music, hum anything besides slow gospel tunes, and her style of dress was floral polyester comfort. As far as Novella could see, Coddy Lee could have been born the way she'd always seen her: as a beautiful granny. That was until she had shown Novella a picture of herself from 1959 in private. What Novella saw was Coddy Lee Lofton looking stunning. "My favorite dress," she said to Novella as she sat the picture on her bedside table. It was a knee-length red sheath dress with white polka dots and a drape neck. It nicely showed off the curves she'd passed down to Novella. It was a home-sewn garment that Coddy Lee had accessorized to fit the occasion.

Novella felt a familial nostalgia as she stared at the picture, wanting it to come to life. It did, in her head, when Coddy Lee said, "'Keep On Churnin' Til The Butter Come,' by, uh . . . What was his name? . . . Wynonie Harris. The local bands played it, so for a long while I didn't know who it was by. But, anyway, that was the song of *that* night. The band played it I think maybe four or five times, because couples were competing. Wasn't a prize or anything, just folks having a good time, challenging one another. I had a whole lot of fun that night."

Novella believed her. And it was the first and only time she saw a lush and vivacious Coddy Lee instead of her pudgy granny, a juke joint woman, a dark sexiness in a bright dress, shimmying and dipping in the middle of a jumping joint. "Boobsie's Suga Shack" was written on the back of the picture.

It was the last joint Coddy Lee juked in, as 1959 didn't go as she planned. Twenty-seven years old, with six kids, Coddy Lee found that pushing her husband away wasn't as liberating as she had hoped it would be. The Black Power Movement was ascendant, but Coddy Lee was in what felt like a different world. She wasn't an activist, but she was a rebel against her own politics. Women were to be free economically and socially, but Coddy Lee didn't want to work or be responsible for the consequences of her behavior. Feeling she'd had no childhood, nor time to grow into herself, she was tired of responsibility. Being free, however, she learned quickly, cost money. She had no job, so could not afford a babysitter. Freedom also took time. Coddy Lee couldn't afford the time to make party dresses or to socialize beyond run-ins with people at the market, school, church, or family gatherings. Coddy Lee's children—Merv Junior, Memphis, Marshall, Charlee Lu'a, Cannella Lynn, and Caddie Lea—were between the ages of four and ten. There was no doing as she felt when she felt. No longer a wife, she still had to be a mama.

She told Novella, "I didn't want to get married, but no one would help me. I wanted to get divorced, but no one would help me."

Coddy Lee might not have been happily married, but her kids weren't made under duress. This Novella had overheard a few months later from her uncle Merv. "Coochie Coo," he'd tell Gent and Isaac. "Daddy calling for

Mama. Us kids supposed to be sleeping, but I was always the last one to fall asleep. I'd hear daddy, ass-naked, coming from the tub, 'Coochie Coo, Cat Daddy's calling.'"

This conversation had taken place outside on the back porch that was under one of Novella's bedroom windows. Sharing a joint with his nephews, Merv went on, "Shit, then their bed would go squeaking like it's coming apart, and Mama and Daddy would be hollering like they think we're dead instead of asleep."

Merv told them he didn't know why his parents had separated, and according to a conversation he'd overheard, neither did his father.

"Daddy was saying she wouldn't cook for him, although he paid the bills and fucked her right." Merv paused, before adding, "And that since there were was nothing there for him anymore, he couldn't stay."

Merv, reflecting on his father's words, told Gent and Isaac, "When he left, there wasn't nothing for us either. Mama wasn't a good mama, and we got real hungry and dirty."

He went on, "Noey's mama Crazy Cara seemed like she just crawled from under Mama's dress one night. Mama had gotten a little round and started wearing bigger clothes, but we didn't know she was pregnant. Didn't know she had a man. Then one morning, she was lying in bed with a baby beside her. Gave birth in the middle of the night."

Gent asked, "By herself?" His voice tight, holding in his last puff. "She gave birth by herself?"

"Yep." Merv laughed lightly. "She had me run for the midwife, but not right away. First thing she wanted was for the girls to clean up the mess. Then a few hours after we'd been up, she yelled for Charlee Lu'a to come get the baby. Said she needed to sleep. Then, a few hours after that, she yelled for me to go."

Between two long pulls on the blunt, Isaac said, "Damn, that's crazy as hell. No wonder Auntie Cara is crazy. Not right to bring a baby in the world like that. Crazy."

Novella cried as she listened. She'd wanted to turn off her radio so she wouldn't have to lay on the windowsill to hear them, though she didn't want to let on that she was in her room and listening. Not wanting them to hear a creak above their heads, she didn't dare stand to go wash her wet face. Instead, she stayed where she was and wiped her tears with her blouse.

Merv continued, "Isaac, your mama's daddy was the first man we really saw Mama with after our daddy left. He was kind of a drunk, but he was cool. Cherry's daddy was the same, but rumor has it Connie's daddy and him were friends. And either they stopped being friends before they both messed with Mama, or after. I don't know about all that, because I had stopped being around so much. But what I do know is that Crazy Cara Louise, Cherry Latoya, and Connie La'Shell all came after the best times, which were with our daddy. But also after the worst times, which was after our daddy left. Mama was still out there for a minute after Crazy Cara was born, but her Honest Demon was mellowing out for sure when Connie and Cherry was born. She was getting tired. And by the time Willie came along, she was almost completely out of the streets."

Gent said, "Willie was cool. Right, Unc?"

Merv gave a hard laugh. "Old-ass house boy, little more than a live-in handyman fixing shit. Sure, I guess he was cool. Wasn't too much a drunk, either." He then asked, "Either one of y'all heard him fucking her?"

In the quiet that followed, Novella felt her cousins' discomfort, and imagined the looks on their faces.

"I got a nickel bag of this good-ass weed, for whoever going be real and tell me the truth," Merv persisted.

Novella couldn't imagine why Merv would want to know such a thing, but she knew Isaac had a story he wasn't telling from their childhood.

Willie and Coddy Lee's playfulness had been witnessed by a twelve-year-old Janet. While out on the porch, she'd overheard Willie say, "I don't know big titties. You tell me." Intrigued by what she heard, Janet crept back in the house. Coddy Lee and Willie were standing in the kitchen. Janet, standing by the stairs that led to the second floor, peeked into the kitchen.

Willie, unaware that anyone was listening, continued, "Which hammer you want, woman?"

He grabbed one of Coddy Lee's hands and put it against the bulge in his pants. Pulling her hand away, she playfully hit his chest. He then grabbed one of her large breasts.

Coddy Lee smacked his hand, which he didn't move away. "Alright now, you better gone on."

Willie grabbed her other breast, and then with both of his large hands full of her breasts, he walked Coddy Lee backwards until she was against the refrigerator. He told her, "Take that pistol out your brassiere, so I can with play with these big titties until you decide which nail you want me to hit."

Just as Coddy Lee began telling him to get off of her, Willie grabbed her hips, lifted one of plump legs and began dry-humping her. Janet's eyes were as wide as her curiosity was big.

"Let's go on upstairs before one of the kids come home," Coddy Lee told him.

Janet jumped back to hide, but there was no need. Just then, she heard Connie and Cherry stepping up on the porch. There would be no old-people sex that day.

Janet, with an excited look on her face, repeated everything she saw and heard to Novella, who was ten, and Isaac, who was eleven. Janet had giggled through most of it. "Willie . . . Oh my God . . . Willie's a dirty old man. He's a dirty old man."

"They're too old!" Isaac had said. "They'll break a hip or have a heart attack."

Isaac would not be telling Merv that story. "I ain't never heard or saw . . . I mean they've been old my whole life, Unc. So, I figured they were done with all that. Too old."

"Shit!" Merv replied. "I'm gonna fuck until they bury me. And if I could rise up as a ghost, then I'd go around fucking every fine thing I wanted for eternity."

Novella wasn't ready to process everything she'd overheard that night.

Despite everything, Novella revered Coddy Lee as the head of the tribe. She was the oldest person Novella knew in their family, and Novella wanted to connect with her. While waiting on that connection, Novella got a call that Coddy Lee was dead.

FIFTY-FOUR

February 3, 2005

She fell down coming from the kitchen.

"Mama?" Cherry was just letting herself into the house. She didn't see what was going on with Coddy Lee until after she'd closed and locked the door. Coddy Lee, clinging to a dining chair, had managed to pull herself up from the floor. She fell again after placing her hands atop the dining table for more leverage. The adhesive tabs that secured the glass round to its metal posts had lost their stickiness years before. The tabletop tilted under Coddy Lee's weight. Losing her balance, Coddy Lee fell, bringing it down on top of her.

"Oh my God, Mama!" Cherry rushed over.

Cherry rolled the table off of her and tried to pull her up. Unable to lift her mother, she had a short screaming fit before dialing 911. "I don't know what's going with my mama! Her eyes are open and she's breathing, but I can't get her off the floor. We need an ambulance. Maybe it's her diabetes."

Coddy Lee had diabetes and high blood pressure, both of which made her susceptible to a blood clot that could lead either to a stroke or a heart attack. In the end, it was a heart attack that killed her.

With Cherry's help, Coddy Lee was able to get to her knees. However, she didn't have the strength to complete the short crawl to the living room. She wanted to climb into her favorite chair or up on the sofa. She had to settle for slumping against the wall. She had nothing left after that, so she waited there for the ambulance.

Cherry was back on the phone. Coddy Lee heard her yelling, "Connie! Connie, shut the hell up and listen! Listen to me! Mama fell . . ."

Then she heard no more.

FIFTY-FIVE

Novella's demeanor became very quiet after getting the news of her grand-mother's death. Her mourning was obvious to her friends. A few days before the funeral, Haze and Kanya showed up with fish dinners and a bean pie from Sister Raffies, as well as a sharp pin-striped two-piece for her to wear to the service.

"Is this okay?" Kanya had asked.

It was then that Novella really broke down and cried for the first time. "I almost don't want to go. It was like she loved me, but not really. I don't know . . . I don't know, how I'm supposed to feel."

Haze told her, "Baby girl, you're supposed to feel how you feel."

Novella, accompanied by Haze, Kanya, and BETY Junior, would have felt like an outsider at the simple service, if not for her aunt Charlee Lu'a. She and Merv were the only ones of Coddy Lee's first six children to attend. Marshall and Memphis, off living their lives, had written Coddy Lee off years ago. "My brothers both said no," Charlee Lu'a told Novella. "They've been angry a long time. And Mama never apologized to them for the stuff she did and didn't do."

Novella nodded her understanding.

Charlee Lu'a went on, "Ya know, my daddy did take care of Mama, and us. After they split, he still paid the bills. And no matter what happened in Mama's life, she did like him at some point. Merv Junior was in her belly when they got married. Now, she would have told you that our daddy went too far, when they were messing around. I guess to say, he wasn't supposed to pop her cherry. But . . . she was into him. Truth is, she's more like her son. Merv Junior and her shared a tendency to run with their Honest Demons. Be mean and selfish. Merv still is, and he's not to be trusted." Charlee Lu'a gave Novella a meaningful look. "You know that, right? To stay away from Merv Junior?"

Novella, a little surprised, managed to calmly answer, "Yes."

"Good," Charlee Lu'a told her.

Charlee Lu'a beautiful features reminded Novella of Merv, though she was a few inches taller than he was. Charlee Lu'a and Novella fit nicely together, looking like the best of Coddy Lee's tribe: polished, poised, yet despised.

Cara, upon arriving and seeing Novella seated with Charlee, said, "Oh, I see y'all two have teamed up. The two snooties." Cara took a seat far away from them. Cara and Novella hadn't seen one another for a year at this point. It was never a happy reunion when Novella and her mother ran into one another. However, Cara had never turned away from Novella. "I guess she's like her mama and brother," Novella said to Charlee, who shook her head in disagreement. "Naw, Cara's her own kind of crazy. I should know; I took care of her for years."

Charlee Lu'a, although respected, especially for taking care of the funeral expenses, wasn't earnestly well-received by the rest of the family. Even though Charlee and Merv Junior came from the same period of their mother's life, they were nothing alike. He smoked, drank, and got dirty with his half-siblings. Charlee, on the other hand, had an urbaneness that reminded Cara, Cherry, and Connie of the life they never had with their mother: a life of stability and legitimacy, Mama and Daddy in the same house, all the children full-blooded siblings. That privileged experience they perceived she had was what made Charlee such a snooty, prissy bitch in their eyes. She was *raised* in a family-owned home, whereas they *grew up* in government housing. Adding to their jealousy, the first five were the best looking of Coddy Lee's children. Merv had told Novella years ago, "My Cleveland sisters are some regular-looking broads. Neither fine nor ugly. You know, just regular. Janet and you are more like Mama's first kids."

Novella didn't stay long at the repass. Isaac seemed to be trying to get drunk enough to push up on Kanya or Haze, or both. Nolan seemed to be waiting for the right circumstances in which to approach the much larger BETY Junior. His jealousy was apparent. Cara, enjoying a loaded plate of food, stepped right up to him. "So, BETY Junior," Smacking her lips as she sized him up. "Funny name you got. Anyway, you saved my daughter. I should say thank you, by the way, but what I want to know is how is she thanking you? She all grown now."

BETY Junior looked at Novella, who shook her head. "Don't answer her."

Cara kept chewing on her food. "Novella. Novella Renee Lofton. I am your mother. You telling me I can't talk to this man . . . that you're so close to?"

Novella stood up from the table and got very close to Cara. "So, I heard you were living between places. A little down and out, right now." Cara's cinnamon complexion started to redden until she saw Novella open her purse. "Here." She handed her mother $250. Cara quickly took the cash and stuffed it in her bra. "Good looking out, No." It was what Novella had come to do. She had given her money before, though she usually only did so when her mother looked clean and sober. Cara never asked why, because she knew. Partly it was hush money. Novella, usually, as she did now, wanted to shut her mother up. Money always worked. She was also motivated to give to her mother out of a mix of pity, love, duty, pride, and guilt. While the first three gassed the money train, the last two drove it.

Cara didn't like Novella, and made no effort to hide it. "My daughter's a prissy-ass snob. One would think she'd given birth to herself." Novella, although mostly estranged from Cara by choice, was embarrassed that she had so little tolerance for her own mother. Embarrassed not because Cara was crazy, but that they were barely on speaking terms. Novella had first given Cara money to shut down the family gossip that Novella hated her. Now, several years later, she had given her mother roughly $1,000. Cara always took the money, this $250 being the largest single amount. Content with her payout, she walked away. She left Novella and company in a peace that was sure to be short-lived.

"Let's not keep Pop waiting," Novella told BETY Junior, Haze, and Kanya.

Pop had offered to cook a big soul-soothing meal, expecting Novella to prefer repass to dinner with him and BETY Junior. By this point, Novella was basically a part-time household member. She had her own room on Pop's side of the house. It was where she slept when she was over late or needed a quick nap. Today, grief had her ready to completely move in—mentally anyway. She was ready to talk, to dish the family business and be served some comforting advice and guidance. Novella hadn't been sure how to talk about what she considered raggedy family behavior with people from a more sophisticated family.

When Haze had told her, "Girl, everybody got family shit," Novella had replied with, "Yeah, but mine has a whole bunch of shit, and our shit never gets better. Everybody who's fucked up stays fucked up until they die."

Coddy Lee had died, and Novella concluded that all the fucked-up shit she'd done, contributed to, and ignored was still demoralizing her tribe. "I know a lot of everyone's problems are her fault," Novella had said to Haze and Kanya before the service. "But, well . . . I also figured she could fix a lot of it. I don't know how, but who else could? I mean, the people in this family either really love her, or they don't. There's no middle ground. They are on one side or the other, and that has to mean something profound. Good or bad, it has to mean something."

FIFTY-SIX

After BETY Junior, Haze, Kanya, and Novella arrived at Pop's and were seated around the dining table, the doorbell rang. Pop thought it might have been his girlfriend. She'd said she wanted to pass by to offer her condolences to Novella. However, BETY Junior returned from the front door with Yadara and Dell. Novella shook her head disapprovingly at the sight of them.

Coddy Lee's death had not only allowed Novella to release suppressed emotions, it had also given her clarity. While her conscious mind was unaware, her subconscious had known for some time that Yadara and Dell had run out of passes. Their history with Novella had allowed them too many occasions of inconsideration, snippiness, lack of enthusiasm, late arrivals, and cancellation of plans. Missing Coddy Lee's funeral, however, was a big no. A "hell naw!" according to Novella's Honest Demon.

Novella's subconscious asked, "Who are Yadara and Ardellya to miss her grandmother's funeral when Haze and Kanya showed up?" Novella's subconscious answered, "Yadara's and Ardellya's season in your life has passed." Novella had believed they'd always be around and always be close to her. They'd be aunties to her children, and she to theirs. Novella had believed they'd be silver vixens together. Beautiful old women, laughing as often and hard as they did in younger years. Novella's conscious mind held on to those dreams in spite of the truths it had been shown. However, today it asked aloud, "Really? Why did y'all even bother? It's over. Hard part is done."

Dell was the first to respond, "Yuck. Your attitude. Must be grief. Anyway, I had to work."

Yadara followed with, "Noey, girl, we can all do only what we can do. I can't do funerals. Not since going to my mother's when I was a little girl."

Novella's Honest Demon answered them both, with a quote from Coddy Lee's book of real talk, "Horseshit!" Cursing in front of Pop was a first for Novella, and the unexpectedness of it made everyone go quiet. She continued, "I'm not entertaining any half-ass condolences! Best believe I will be shutting them down. And I do mean to!" That last statement also was a direct quote from Coddy Lee's book of real talk. "I do mean to" had always been Coddy Lee's profound statement of finality.

Novella's Honest Demon was not completely in control of her, as what it wanted to say was, "Who the fuck are y'all to show up, after the motherfucking fact? Gotdamn funeral over, Miss Sorry Ass Friend Bitch One and Bitch Two?"

Novella maintained some restraint because of Pop's presence. She, however, ended her scolding of Yadara and Dell with, "So, let's sort this out. Could I have played y'all asses like this? Huh? Go ahead and try to tell me . . . Go ahead . . . Some horseshit-ass excuse of how I could've played y'all like this! And y'all would have went for it!"

As Novella stared, waiting for a response, she felt a napkin gently touch her face. Kanya, who sat to her right, was drying the tears Novella hadn't noticed she was crying. Her subconscious and conscious mind had finally synced. She was saying goodbye to her childhood and much of the misplaced sentiment that was attached to it. This moment had been com-ing, as per the memory she had of something said by one of her school teachers. "Sometimes we can't bloom where we're planted. Not when we're being impeded by weeds." Novella knew she had to move beyond things and people who were not helping her grow, or helping her cope.

Drying her tears for herself, Novella told Yadara and Dell, "From now on, y'all are to me what I am to you."

Just as they started to respond, Pop pointed toward the bathroom. "Ladies, y'all can wash your hands in there. We'll wait to say grace until y'all are at the table."

Out of respect for the old man, they two held their replies and went to go freshen up.

Yadara and Dell stayed beyond dinner, having dessert and conversating a bit about local happenings. Leaving, they each gave Novella a hug that she made quick and impersonal.

Later that evening, Novella began to open up and talk about her family issues. During this time, she apologized to Pop. "I didn't mean to curse in front of you. I'm sorry."

Pop laughed. "Shit, no double standard around here. Bariah says what the hell he wants. Why can't you?" He then told her, "Ella La Bella, you can be yourself here. We love you, and this is your home. We're your home, your people."

FIFTY-SEVEN

Thanksgiving 2007

Novella decided to move to Georgia with Pop and BETY Junior, further clarifying that they—rather than her family—were indeed her people. It was a decision she wasn't surprised to find herself defending.

Yadara had cried. The tears weren't all for Novella, but she cried enough to fill the gap that life had wedged between them. Novella, for the first time in years, felt Yadara's sincere love for her as well as her anger and pain that Novella's decision had been made without her input. Novella's news made for the second time that day that Yadara had been *told* of a loved one's life-changing decision.

Thanksgiving at Pop's had been mellow, with jazz on the stereo, card games, dominoes, and easy conversation with very little company. Pop and BETY Junior usually traveled for the holidays, so when they stayed in town, they preferred to keep things intimate.

Before arriving, Yadara had texted Novella several times over a few hours. It was not like her to send so many messages. She wasn't a text spammer, someone who will send message after message to someone. Rather, she liked to put everything in one message. Often, her texts were so long, they would have to be broken into two, or even three messages.

"Hey girl. Happy Turkey Day!"

"You with BJ?"

"Gonna be there all day?"

"Well, I'm pissed."

"Probably not going home after service."

"So, very, very pissed, cussing in church."

"Wait till I tell you this b.s."

Yadara's family tradition for Easter, Christmas, and Thanksgiving included attending a morning church service. Novella had occasionally accompanied Yadara and her sister to church. The services for the holidays were usually done by noon. It was now after three, so Novella wondered, if Yadara hadn't been home, where was she? Driving around on snowy roads on a holiday?

Just as Novella angled her fork to cut another bite off her slice of pie, Pop's doorbell rang. Novella was nestled in a corner on the large sectional in the den. To her right, in a recliner, BETY Junior lay overstuffed on shrimp dressing. He groaned lightly as he adjusted the handle to bring him to an upright position. The Wiz was playing on Pop's big screen television. Watching it on Thanksgiving was a tradition that Novella had started. She grabbed the remote off her arm rest and pressed pause. BETY Junior stood and gave his long body a quick stretch, and then went to answer the front door. Novella guessed he would return with Yadara, and she was correct.

FIFTY-EIGHT

Yadara just showing like that up was audacious. Novella knew better than to take such a liberty. Yadara still lived at home with her sister, who was older and ran the house. Yadara hadn't yet grown up, as she obviously still enjoyed the benefits of being the baby girl. She was a big baby, though, in age and size. Yadara's family ran on the bigger side. Yamila, her sister, was just over six feet tall. She was the first person a young Novella had met and found to be a true nose-in-the-air, ass-high-on-her-back snob.

"Yadara, your little friend is here," she'd announce whenever Novella came over.

Novella knew "little" wasn't a reference to her height, but to her family's financial status. Even when they were adults, Yamila would ask Yadara, "Do you have enough money for the both of you?" as Novella and Yadara left for the likes of the movies or a restaurant. Yadara had told Novella that Yamila wanted her to find friends with more money.

Yamila had helped their divorced-then-widowed father raise Yadara and had taken the mantle as the woman of the house, even after Yadara turned eighteen. In Novella's opinion, it was fair that Yamila remained in charge. Yadara paid for her own cell phone, car insurance, and gym membership. However, the only house bill she paid was for DirectTV. Novella found this strange as Yadara managed a bank and earned more than enough to pay every bill in their house. It was their house, signed over, lien free by their dad to both Yamila and Yadara.

After BETY Junior led Yadara to the den, Novella took her to the kitchen to offer her food. Whatever had brought her over, Novella didn't want to hear about it. She hoped the food and movie would deter the bitch session she felt Yadara came to have. Novella prepared two full plates for her.

Although the official dinner hour had passed, Pop's dining table was still full. Although it had seated everyone during the meal, it was now the *adult* table. BETY Junior and Novella, youth in this setting, after enjoying their first servings of dinner and desserts, had excused themselves, the two taking refuge in the den before the well-aged, educated, and experienced began their deep conversations. Right now, there was a discussion on the African-American experience versus the experiences of those in the new-age African diaspora. Novella, not wanting to be dragged into what she felt was becoming a debate, led Yadara to the breakfast nook.

Yadara finished both plates quickly, obviously having been hungry. This made Novella pretty sure she really had been driving around for hours. Yadara, when upset, could be stubborn and unreasonable.

Sated by the homemade food, she asked Novella, "Guess who's getting married? And guess how I found out?"

Novella knew two things. First, she knew to wait for Yadara to tell her the answer, and second, she would not be returning to the den to finish the movie.

Yadara began, "It was a surprise. That's what my witch of a sister tells me, after having our pastor announce to the entire congregation that she and that apple-headed asshole that's too short for her are getting married."

Novella didn't care, and her Honest Demon wanted to say so, but Novella maintained control. "Oh, wow, Yamila's getting married." Her voice was soft but without emotion. "She didn't tell you? What about your dad?"

Yadara just stared at first. She was holding her reply back to keep from crying. After she'd successfully held the tears back, she answered, "He knew, so he played me too."

Novella knew she had to ask the question that might unleash a storm of emotion. "Why keep it a secret from you?"

Yadara shrugged. "Why did you keep your all-white birthday party plans a secret from me?"

Novella's Honest Demon asked, "What the hell does my party have to do with your sister's wedding?"

Yadara tried to answer, but Novella's Honest Demon spoke again, "You need to keep on track with the Yamila-getting-married story if you want me to keep listening. I'm not taking any pop shots, especially about some old shit. You can keep knocking yourself over the head with it, but I was over it way back when. You're gonna have to sort yourself out on your own about that shit."

Yadara eyed her quietly before saying, "I'm going to go get some more lemonade, and let you simmer down for a minute." Yadara finished her drink in the kitchen and returned to the breakfast nook empty-handed. Once back, she continued, "Anyway, I'm sure Yamila told Daddy because he's giving her away, and paying for the whole damn wedding. Money always makes her act right."

Novella smiled. "Yadara, who are you to talk? You'd still be living out of your father's wallet if he hadn't let you know you'd outgrown it. Girl, you're just as spoiled as Yamila. Actually more."

Yadara's beautiful cinnamon-brown face tightened. "Noey, my friend, you don't understand money and family. Because, well, you know, you've always been low on both. How do you think BETY Junior is living so well? He might be his own man now, but you know he had to get a boost from his grandfather in there. And he definitely has an inheritance coming. And, by the way, just because this is a side-by-side duplex doesn't mean his ass don't still live at home."

Novella, not her Honest Demon, wanted to slap Yadara. Saying "You've always been low on both" hurt her deeply.

"That was nasty," Novella said evenly.

Yadara's eyes were full of regret, as well as defiance. She didn't apologize easily. More than she hated being wrong, she hated admitting she was wrong. The bigger the wrong, the more stubborn she got. Dell had often told Novella that Yadara was a spoiled, self-righteous, wannabe, know-it-all snob.

Novella asked, "Why would you want to discuss your family problems with me since I'm so lowly?" Before Yadara could answer, Novella told her, "Well, whatever. Whatever with all that. You're going to need a new therapist or dumping ground, or whatever it is I've been to you. I'm moving. Moving away with the little bit of money and the little bit of family that my poor little self has. BETY Junior and Pop asked me to move to Georgia with them, and I said yes. I'm done here."

Yadara's mouth dropped open, her eyes glossed over with tears. "*Why?* Why in the world would you go anywhere with them? They're not really anything to you. Did you tell Ardellya? Does she already know?"

FIFTY-NINE

Ardellya hadn't known before Yadara. She did, however, have the same response: anger. Just as Ardellya been right about Yadara being a spoiled, self-righteous, wannabe, know-it-all snob, Yadara was correct in saying, "Dell is raggedy and jealous with an impoverished way of thinking. She can't be trusted."

Dell didn't cry over Novella's move. What she did was rage. "Noey, that makes no fuckin sense!" Initially, after Novella had given her the news, she'd huffed, "Waste of time and money. People basically leave the same way all over the world. Here or there, chickadee, you're still going to put your panties on one leg at a time."

Being a brown liquor woman, Dell gave her a complete reply after downing three Jack and Cokes. She'd asked Novella over for dinner. Novella had used her key to let herself into the apartment where she found Dell waiting for her like an angry parent waiting for a past-curfew teenager. It wasn't long before she began to rant. Drunk, she masked her feelings of abandonment, jealousy, and sadness with her anger. "Tell me how the fuck it makes sense for you to move somewhere with those motherfucking men! Neither of which you are fucking! I mean they are not really anybody to you. I'm your girl, I've been with you since back in the day. You didn't even invite me! Just going leave my ass in the rearview. I don't get an invite; you just fucking tell me you're leaving! Like . . . like I'm your employer. You putting in notice. And those new bitches . . . Haze and Kanya? How is this rolling out to them?"

Novella knew better than to fully engage with a drunk. She decided just to listen.

When Dell, with her golden-yellow face flushed red and her whiskey-pungent breath, got in Novella's face with, "Noey! Noey, what? What? What the hell!" Novella's patience ran out.

"Ardellya, if you don't chill with this, I'm leaving," she warned. "Back up! And don't come up on me like this again."

Dell backed off and took a seat at her dining table. She looked up at Novella. "I didn't cook shit. I mean, I'm not finished. I'm not finished with everything." The food was still uncooked and defrosting in the sink.

Novella told her, "You invited me over to eat, but you didn't cook shit."

Dell pointed toward the kitchen. "Well, everything is spread out. If you want to take over and make everything how you want it."

Novella shook her head. "I'm not cooking or staying here with your drunk ass. I'm leaving. And you should go to bed and sleep it off. Getting this lit on a Tuesday? Seriously, Dell."

Before leaving, Novella hid Dell's car keys in the filter basket of the coffee pot. Dell could be extremely determined and single-minded when drunk. If she all of a sudden wanted chips, she'd just get in the car to go get them. Novella didn't want that, and neither did a sober Dell. So, Novella ensured neither of them would awake the next day with regret.

SIXTY

Dell's feelings about Novella leaving would reach their peak months later, providing a real-life example of why Yadara said she couldn't be trusted.

Novella was indeed leaving Cleveland, but that didn't stop her from dating. She'd met a guy at a coworker's wedding, and they were getting along well. Dell had attended the same wedding, but the only guy she'd exchanged numbers with had pretended to be single when he was actually married.

Novella's new interest, Trevonte, had recently purchased a bar, which he'd then renovated. The beautiful Novella and her beautiful friends were welcome to drink at Trevonte's bar free of charge. Like the art and marble tables, he felt they added to the classy ambiance. Ardellya, as Yadara had said, would not because, "she's raggedy."

Her behavior had been off. One time, she had disappeared at a party where she supposedly knew no one except Novella.

"What's going on, Dell? Are you snorting cocaine in the ladies' room? What's with ghosting out, leaving me alone?"

"Noey, really?" Dell rolled her eyes. "Cocaine?"

Novella shrugged. "Well, where did you go?"

Dell gave her a get-out-of-my-business look. "Where grown people go?"

A fed-up Novella told her, "Oh yeah, well, the next time you go, your grown ass can stay there. I can find something else to do, too. I can be here by myself and leave that way." Novella had driven them, and, while she was not one to leave anyone stranded, she would not abandon her desire to have fun.

Dell stared at her before saying, "You know what's up. You just want to catch me or hear me say it. You know where I am going."

Novella raised an eyebrow. "Ardellya, are you drunk? Have you moved on to the hard stuff? Maybe you are snorting coke in the ladies' room. What the hell are you talking about?"

Dell poked out her lips. "Get for real, Noey. You want to know so bad. Think about it. Why do I keep getting invited to these parties?"

Novella reminded her, "Because you know me, Dell. My new boo invited me, so I invited you. Ardellya, you're here with me?"

Dell threw up her hands. "Okay, Noey, keep playing dumb." She walked away.

"Hey, hey!" Novella heard from behind her as Trevonte approached. Gesturing behind him, he announced, "I ran into these beautiful ladies at the bar, they said they know you." Coming up behind him were Haze and Kanya.

Trevonte, always busy when hosting, couldn't stay long. He ensured Novella and her friends were good. He'd given Novella a VIP table, and so followed her back to it. He then had to excuse himself to make sure everything was well with the party. Novella was relieved her friends were able to make it, and began to truly enjoy herself.

Kanya had recently dyed her short hair red and put it in dreads, and it was fire. It highlighted her big, brown, innocent-looking eyes and her full lips, which were always shiny. She wasn't chatting with Haze and Novella for long, when she was escorted to the dance floor by a very handsome man with long dreadlocks. Haze was next to leave, though she was back at the table before the song was over. "Fool couldn't keep his hands off me." Haze had the boom body: boom shakalaka in the boobs, double boom shakalaka in booty. She was just five-foot-two and had a tiny waist and thick long hair. Dark, mysterious eyes that were soft but not shy were set in a round butterscotch face. A woman of curves, she had to do a lot of smacking away of hands, especially at clubs and parties.

Novella, about to eat another appetizer, felt eyes on her. When she looked up, she saw Dell standing in a corner, her back against the wall. A guy was standing in front of her and seemed to be groping her. Dell was staring at Novella. It was a few moments before Novella realized that Dell was showing off, that she was smirking as if getting away with something.

Kanya's return to the table broke Novella's concentration. "Girl, dude was wearing me out on the dance floor. Got his number, though."

Novella felt a solemnity that she couldn't hide.

"What's wrong?" Kanya asked.

Haze seemed to already know. Her calm demeanor was that of someone waiting for everyone else to acknowledge the elephant in the room. After taking a sip of her drink, she gave Novella an encouraging look.

Novella didn't want to talk about Dell behind her back, especially to people Dell didn't like. So, Novella felt awkward as she said, "I don't know what she's doing."

Kanya and Haze nodded, understanding Novella's concern. Novella went on, "She's . . . Well, it's like she's trying to stick it to me, but I don't know what she's trying to stick to me. She is acting strange. And whatever her problem is, she's pissing me the hell off."

"Ignore her," Kanya advised.

Haze told her, "Ask her. Ask her what the hell is up. Seems like she wants you to know, so she'll probably tell you."

SIXTY-ONE

Dell was happy to tell Novella exactly what was up, especially in front of Haze and Kanya. Novella didn't even have to ask.

"I didn't know you two were coming." Dell gave a glance to both Kanya and Haze, and then asked, "Noey, who else are you packing at this table?"

Before Novella could answer, their waiter dropped in. "Anything else, ladies?"

Dell was quick to reply, "Another Long Island iced tea for me."

Novella reminded her, "You'll have to pay for that one. Trevonte's house service for VIP is two drinks and that will be your third."

Dell stared at her.

Novella raised her hands in defense. "Just reminding you."

Dell's eyes swept over the table as she tried to count everyone else's drinks. The waiter had done a good job of keeping the table clean, so she couldn't get an accurate count.

"Have you had both of yours?" she asked Novella.

Novella raised her eyebrows. "You're out of freebies."

Dell again stared at her, before giving her a knowing smirk.

The waiter smiled. "So, everyone is good?"

Dell snapped, "I said another Long Island iced tea."

The young man nodded, and then turned to leave. Snapping his fingers as if just remembering something, he turned back to table and asked Dell, "Ma'am, should I start a tab for you?'

Embarrassed anger exuded from Dell like cheap perfume. Where before it had been obvious that she didn't want to pay, now it was now obvious she could not. Struggling to remain calm and composed, she turned to Novella, "Girl, let me get your card. I forgot mine."

Kanya and Haze looked out onto the dance floor in an attempt to give Dell and Novella some semblance of privacy without leaving the table.

Novella knew denying Dell would cause a scene. Not that Dell was one for public scenes, but she was fast becoming *that* friend. Novella's other friends had started to wonder what exactly Novella saw in her.

Novella turned to the waiter. "No tab, but I got this one."

As the waiter left, Dell said, "Thanks," though there was no gratitude in her eyes or in her voice.

Dell's last drink was one for courage. She gave Novella's crew skeptical looks as she drank and ate the appetizers. Afterwards, she stood and left without a word only to return with Trevonte's cousin Tremonte. She grinned smugly at Novella. Until that moment, ugly hadn't been a word Novella would have used to describe Dell. But now it fit. Her eyeliner had run a bit. Her lipstick was patchy, sticky, and thin from the food and drinks. Not to mention her flared nostrils and bugged-out eyes.

"What the hell is up with you?" Novella asked her.

Dell placed her hands upon Tremonte's shoulders, before wrapping her arms around his torso. "You know what's up. Now, here it is up in your face."

Novella stood up and walked over to where Dell and Tremonte were standing. "What is it that's in my face?" Before she could get an answer to her question, she a felt a pair of arms wrap around her waist. It was Trevonte. He told her, "I can chill with you now, for about a half hour. Everything is running as it should." Novella relaxed her arms and looked back at him. She was given a soft peck on the lips. She nodded toward Dell and Tremonte. "Are they a couple?"

Trevonte gave a short laugh in her ear. "Doubt that. My twin cousin there is a straight hoe. He might be sticking her, but he's on the move for sure."

They referred to themselves as twin cousins because they were first cousins born from sisters on the same day. Resembling their mothers, who also looked alike, Trevonte and Tremonte were often mistaken for one another. Tremonte took full advantage of the resemblance. Making his trickery that much easier were their joint business deals and the similarity of their haircuts, attire, and names.

Dell unwrapped herself from Tremonte, and moved to stand beside him. Then her eyes started moving back and forth between Trevonte and Tremonte.

Novella had met Tremonte, though she realized now that Dell had not. Obviously, having met him on her own, she had thought he was Trevonte. Hence, why she thought she was now seeing double. Adding to Dell's fury was the sight of Trevonte lovingly holding Novella. No one present aside from Tremonte, Dell, and Novella knew what was going on. Still, as Haze would later point out, Dell had made a hateful fool of herself to herself by being "a gotdamn fool, trying to stick it to her best girl with the wrong dick."

At the same time that Novella was getting a kiss on the cheek, Dell got a pinch on the butt. She turned so fast to check Tremonte that it looked like she might sprain a muscle or get dizzy. She poked a finger on his chest.

"Don't even!" She then asked, "So, what is your name? Do you even own this club?"

Amused, Tremonte chuckled. "Now you want to get all specific." He then reached for one of her hands. "Let's sit down and have a talky-talk."

Dell slapped his hand.

He smiled at her tightly. "Relax. We're all consenting adults. Just having fun."

When he grabbed for her hand again, she pushed him. "Motherfucker! Fuckin' lying-ass bastard!"

Tremonte rolled his eyes. "Ha! Oh right, I'm the bad guy. You were only boning your best friend's boyfriend. Well, you thought you were. Whatever. Wrong guy, but you still got off." Trevonte rushed over just in time to stop Dell from landing a punch on Tremonte's face. She tried to hit him again, but was restrained by Trevonte. Not relenting, she struggled against him. "No, no . . . uh-uh . . . Get off me, motherfucker . . . Get off me! Get the fuck off me!"

Just as Novella came over to intervene, Trevonte turned his head to her and said, "She gotta go—now! Get her out!"

Novella didn't appreciate his tone. "Ardellya!" she began. "Ardellya, we can leave now! Dell! We can leave. Come on, let's just be on our way. It's all done here . . . It's whatever. Let's bounce. It's done and over. Bump it, girl. Let it all go . . ." After Dell relaxed and the men released her, Novella then turned to the frozen and shocked Haze and Kanya. "I'm sorry. If you're not too embarrassed, please stay and enjoy the party, but as you see, I got a situation here, so I gotta go."

When she turned back to Dell, she was met with, "You don't have shit, and you not all that!"

SIXTY-TWO

Dell rushed out of the bar on her own. Novella, Kanya, and Haze, however, were escorted out by security, not that they weren't already in the process of leaving. Novella had a dry throat from yelling at Dell, so had just downed the last of her Sprite when she heard a voice telling her, "Owners want you all out, now." She turned and saw four of the bar's bouncers. She didn't bother to ask for Trevonte. Him suddenly disappearing and sending his muscle to clear her out meant it was over. There was nothing more to say.

Outside in the parking lot, Dell was sitting on the hood of Novella's car. "Get off!" Novella yelled. "You know I hate that! Off my car!" Dell complied. Novella looked up at Dell. "Why are you here?"

Dell drawled, "So, you're going to leave me stranded? You always play me, Noey. Always choosing somebody over me. Now this dude got you ready to leave me down here with no car and no money?"

Novella knew Dell was more tipsy than drunk, so she asked, "Which dude? The one you banged thinking he was my man? Or my actual man that you had intended to bang? The one who just threw me out of his bar."

Dell looked off in the distance.

Kanya said, "Just get her home, Ella. She did you dirty, but she's drunk and doesn't have a ride."

Novella had no intention of abandoning Dell, but wanted to get at her for the disloyalty, for the drama, for killing her new relationship, and for getting them all kicked out. Her Honest Demon was down for a sound ass-whooping, but Novella was exhausted and only had enough energy for a thorough cussing out.

"How do you," Novella got in Dell's face, "How do you bring yourself to do it, to fuck over someone who loves you? When you know that they do, and when they always come through for you? How do you intentionally hurt them? And take pleasure in it? Are you that bitch? That low-down, not-a-friend-to-anybody kind of bitch?"

Dell shook her head no, as if ready to dispute it. Though, her only words were, "You don't understand. You have no idea. You don't know. You just don't get it."

Novella told her, "I know this, whatever kind of bitch you are . . . you're dumb. Fucking over your friend, your only friend, is fucking over yourself."

Dell sighed. "Like I said, you don't get it."

Novella walked away, pressing her key fob to unlock her car door. She got in her car and started the engine. Dell tried to open the passenger side door, but Novella hadn't unlocked it. The women stared at one another.

"Ella!" Kanya yelled as she drove by in her car. "Ella, girl, open the door!"

Haze honked her horn a few times in agreement before yelling, "Don't be like her, Ella! Take her home, then leave her there!"

Novella didn't want to leave Dell stranded, but she didn't want to let her in either. Reluctantly, she unlocked the door.

Their drive was quiet until they got close to Dell's home. At a stop light, Novella looked over at Dell and said, "So you're swallowing your own shit today, huh? You're getting what you gave, baby. Every shovelful you threw at me is going down your throat right now."

Maybe the analogy was true, because Dell looked to be trying to keep from throwing up.

"I'd have to be Boo Boo the Fool to think you haven't done this before," Novella said. "You know, screwed my man. Or tried to. So, who else?"

Dell didn't respond.

Novella was still staring at Dell when the light turned green. The driver behind them gave a hard honk. Startled, Novella hit the gas harder than she'd intended.

When Novella pulled into the parking lot of Dell's apartment complex, she saw Dell turn toward the door and place a hand over the lock buttons. So, Novella was ready when she stopped the car. Waiting to hear the click of Dell pressing the unlock button, Novella didn't bother to shift into park. She didn't want the distraction. As soon as she heard the click, Novella pushed the lock button on her own door. Dell, irritated, sighed heavily. She then again pressed the unlock button, however, only to be further irritated. Novella again pressed the lock on her own door. As Dell sighed again, Novella shifted into park, and then began.

"Look, I know your life isn't what you thought it would—"

"Pssst, you don't know me or my life like you think you do," Dell spat, her head still facing the door.

"I know you hate me, but it's not because of anything that I've done," Novella said matter-of-factly.

Dell, shaking her head, turned to face Novella. "You, you, and you. It isn't always about you. I'm me, and I do what the fuck I want to do." She waved an open hand at Novella. "Really, Noey, it's so narcissistic of you, thinking you're a fucking idol or something, a goddess. You really do think that, don't you? That you're a goddess. Please. Under all your nice dresses and jewelry, you're just you. Raised on Rough Hough."

Novella gave a thoughtful smile. "In comparison to the broad screwing her best and only friend's boyfriends, I *am* an idol. And because I'm above and beyond the insecurity and smallness of where such behavior comes from, yet still able to forgive and take pity on those who are not, I *am* a goddess."

Dell gave a bitter laugh. "Ha. Yeah, okay."

Novella continued, "And I pity you . . . bitch."

It was the first time Novella had called her that. Dell's shock was obvious, her eyes wide, as she searched Novella's for confirmation that she'd said what she said.

Novella gave her the confirmation. "And bitch . . . I forgive you."

Novella was shocked at her own swell of emotion as she turned to face her windshield, "Well . . . I guess this is it. We're officially *not* friends anymore." She released the unlock button and waited for a stunned Dell to exit the car. It took almost a minute. Dell's lips moved multiple times as she tried to find something to say, but nothing came. Finally, in a huff, she got out and slammed the door behind her. After she entered the lobby, Novella drove off.

"The shit that happens."

SIXTY-THREE

May 3, 2008

Stomach cancer is notorious for mimicking indigestion or a developing ulcer, often not being discovered until it is nearly too late. It is usually diagnosed during an ER visit due to severe vomiting or a bloody stool.

It wasn't odd for Pop to call Novella, yet seeing his name on her caller ID was worrying, because it was during the middle of her workday. Novella was already full of anxiety that she'd been doing her best to suppress. She, Pop, BETY Junior, and Purcell were a year away from their relocation. They'd already come up with a name—Greener Pastures, after what it was to mean for all of them—for their homestead, which they were still searching for.

A few months ago, Novella began clearing out her apartment, throwing things in the trash or giving them away. Once her lease ended in a few months, she'd move into one of Pop's guest bedrooms. Then some months later, she'd be in Georgia living in her own house on their jointly owned land. Pop, BETY Junior, and Purcell would only be a golf cart ride away.

That had been the plan, anyway. When Novella answered Pop's call, the fragility she heard in his voice told her the plan had changed.

"Hey, princess. I know you're at work . . . but . . . can you come to the Cleveland Clinic as soon as you can?"

Novella was afraid to ask, but did, "Why?"

Pop didn't answer; he just said, "Bariah should have called you, but he isn't ready for any of it . . ."

Novella's free hand went to her chest. "Ready for any of what?"

Again, Pop didn't answer. "ICU Room 3104. Come when you can, but if it's not until later, I'll probably be asleep. I'm so tired."

Novella immediately went into mourning. *Why does shit always have to happen? Pop can't die now!* She began shutting down her computer. *He's the youngest old person I know. He still works out. He has a girlfriend. What in the hell is going on?*

Driving to the hospital, she didn't want to hear anything, no traffic noise, no music. Windows up, radio off, she soon realized silence had her too much in her own head. Running a red light, she almost t-boned an Omni Hotel van full of passengers. "Novella!" she yelled at herself. *You can't be dead on arrival...Got to pay attention.*

She pushed on the radio. The DJ's jovial voice was another reminder that the earth hadn't stopped rotating on its axis just because she was experiencing a family emergency. The radio had to stay on because an irritating distraction was better than no distraction. Novella had to focus on the drive, so she rolled down her window. It wasn't so bad until, while stopped at another red light, a car with blaring music pulled up beside her. Yelling at a stranger at a traffic light would be ridiculous and dangerous, but Novella's anxiety and irritation was growing and needed an outlet. Rolling her eyes, she cussed the driver in a mutter to herself, "Turn that shit down."

Novella rolled up the window of her Dodge Intrepid. She was still bothered by the sound of her own radio, so she put on one of her favorite CDs: Anita Baker's *Rapture*.

SIXTY-FOUR

Stepping into Room 3104, she was surprised by the setup. Pop was asleep, but in the recliner. BETY Junior, who was also asleep, was in the bed. She was slightly relieved by the sight and allowed herself to hope, *I guess it's better the younger of the two is sick.* She reasoned BETY Junior would heal faster than Pop if broken. However, looking at him from the doorway, BETY Junior didn't appear broken, though his long, chiseled body did appear slightly diminished.

Neither of her men moved. She wondered how long they'd suffered before calling her. *What in the hell?* Scared and little pissed, she stepped out of the room. In the hall she tried to self-soothe with deep breathing. She told herself, *Damn, Novella no one said that anyone is dying. Don't jump to conclusions; just wait to hear what is going on.*

Pop, emerging from the room, startled her out of her thoughts. His solemn eyes greeted her. *Yes, it's as bad as you're thinking.* Drops on her chest told Novella that she was crying. She had yet to learn the specifics, but she grieved with Pop. His despair seeped into her as his long arms folded her against his chest and his white beard pressed against the smooth skin of her forehead. The aroma of Pop's peppermint candy and his Hugo Boss cologne enveloped their warm exchange. It had always been Novella's opinion that Pop-Pop gave the best hugs. *Everything would be alright when*

Pop-Pop prayed for you, fed you something really good, and hugged you, she had always thought. This hug, though, felt like the worst of the best, like the first of the last ones she would receive. It made Novella hurt more. She had no more assurance now than she'd had on the drive over; though whatever this was, she and Pop were in it together.

Endings were hardest when they came too soon. Novella had an urge to rush back into the room and shake BETY Junior awake. "What's wrong with you?" she'd scream. "What the hell is it? And why am I only finding out now? You are not allowed to die. You are not allowed to die. You're too strong, too good! Why does shit always have to happen?"

Novella had it in her head that no one she loved deeply should die before she did. She'd sometimes wondered how couples that had been married for a long time could go on after one of them died, how anyone went on when part of their heart stopped beating. BETY Junior was definitely part of her heart. She knew it was selfish, but she wanted to die first. The first in her close circle of friends, the first between her and her future husband, the first sibling. Living beyond those that were beloved to her seemed unbearable.

Pop had the doctor explain BETY Junior's condition to Novella, who did her best to take it all in. As she looked into Dr. Adebayo's dark eyes, Novella could feel herself trembling and hear her heaving breath. Her eyes swelled with warm, salty droplets, blurring her vision. The doctor was relaying her beloved's condition, and she could see him taking on the pain she experienced hearing about it. Fleeting thoughts raced through her mind, *So, doctors really do see patients as people and not just as carriers of illness. This Dr. Adebayo is a feeling, flesh-and-blood human. And he gives a damn.*

After finishing his explanation, Dr. Adebayo left Pop and Novella to one another's care, assuring them in his accented English, "The staff and I will give him the best care we can."

Lab results were pending, but BETY Junior's symptoms were consistent with late stage three stomach cancer. Novella wondered if the treatment offered hope. She also wondered, *How in the hell had death come for him, stalked and fed on him, without her noticing?*

SIXTY-FIVE

"Ella, there aren't any answers," Pop ran it down in regular talk. "At least, the doctors don't have any on why Bariah has cancer. I don't know it to run in our family, and he's otherwise healthy. Anyway, chemo might help him live a bit longer, but he isn't going to grow old."

To ensure Novella understood, he added, "I'll probably outlive him." Bariah Elijah Tomas Young Junior, his first and only grandson, was dying. Pop, if he could, would gladly suffer and die in his place. As it was, Pop couldn't do anything to save him. So, he'd see him out, just as he'd welcomed him in when he was born. Pop wouldn't have much left after that. Even now, at the beginning, he felt aged and wearied by it.

"I wish . . ." he took Novella's hand. "Honest to god, I know you call him brother, and he calls you sister, and I respect that. But I wish Bariah had married you. I wish . . . he'd had a family with you. I've been hoping for that for a long time now. I had a feeling about you the first time I saw you. When you were sixteen years old, a little woman sitting next to your grandmother in court. I had a real good feeling about you. And I'm glad you're here with us now."

Pop went on, "You're best the woman Bariah knows. And you two love each other so much. It would have been so good. But neither of you

. . . I don't know, maybe neither of you were ready for the seriousness of it. But I'd hoped he'd stop seeing you as the little pompom girl. Even now, cause he's not gone yet . . . if there's a miracle and he's able to have a decent life, I think you two should marry. I want him to experience that with a quality woman. He's been talking about getting married and having kids. You know that. And you need it too, Ella. You need a husband to love and respect you as much as Bariah does. He's never loved any woman as deeply as he loves you."

Pop dabbed at his wet eyes, and then said, "You're my granddaughter either way, but think about it. I'm going to pray on it, because I believe . . . Well, I know you two are an answer for one another."

SIXTY-SIX

August 2013

"Why is this shit happening?" Chrystan cussed. He'd only cussed once before, in kindergarten. "Dumbass!" he ridiculed a school mate for spilling a container of sidewalk chalk. Chrystan had been emulating the guy who used to be his daddy. Today, Chrystan was emulating any and every one he'd ever heard cuss out of frustration. He sat on a cushioned lawn chair inside the porch filling his belly with a can of Hormel meat and saltine crackers. The corner store food was sufficient, as were the baby wipes they bought there. He and Denise weren't starving, nor were they completely dirty. The weatherproof panels and door of the porch gave them privacy and shielded them from the rain.

Denise was twenty-two, but she was nearly as vulnerable as eight-year-old Chrystan. Denise was good at following instructions, was efficient with domestic duties, was a capable driver, and had an aptitude for numbers. Nonetheless, she required routine check-ins to keep her on track. Denise was a small woman and had a mild mental disability. As long as life was simple, she was good. She was managing in the present situation, but she couldn't manage to get them out of it. She was programmed to do what

Chrystan's mother told her to do. She had been told to go to this house, so, even locked out of it, she stayed.

Chrystan gave himself credit for having knowledge of some basic things. According to the Fossil watch he'd had gotten for Christmas, they'd been in Cleveland for almost two months. In that short time, Denise's cantaloupe belly had transformed into a watermelon. Her sleep sounds were different, louder. Her walk was different, reminding Chrystan of a duck. Her attitude was different. Preoccupied with her condition, she'd become unapologetically short with him. She'd also started disappearing, leaving Chrystan alone for hours at a time. He'd awake and find her gone, as he had yesterday. Though this time she stayed away all day and night. Her excuse upon her late morning return was, "I needed to check on my baby."

Chrystan imagined she'd spent the night in a clinic. The thought of her in a real bed with clean white sheets made him angry. "I don't want to sleep on this fucken porch either!" His third time cussing. "Are you so dumb, Dumbnise, that you've forgotten you're so supposed to be taking care of me?" He hadn't wanted to call her that, but he'd never been so miserable. "We're not supposed to be living like this!"

Denise had teared up, as she often did when he pressed her.

"I'm tired you always crying, and shit." His fourth time cussing. It was becoming a habit. "You're the fucking grown-up!"

Denise's face dropped in shame. From across the porch, she tried to shout, but her voice grew weaker with each word, "This is not my fault."

Chrystan wasn't blaming her, but he was holding her accountable. "That's no excuse to let it stay this way." He pointed at her. "Do something!"

She whined, "You're not supposed to be yelling or telling me what to do." Until this argument, he hadn't ever yelled or cussed at her. Sure, he'd pouted at times, and dragged his feet when she'd given instructions he hadn't wanted to follow. Chrystan was a bit spoiled, but was, overall, a good and obedient boy. However, he was no longer his mama's baby. She wasn't here to twist the caps off his OJ or tell Denise exactly how to feed and entertain him. Chrystan was lost, and his mama was missing. Chrystan felt like he had become a resilient weed given just enough nutrients to live, though each day he was growing taller and harder. In a much deeper octave than his normal preadolescent voice, he commanded, "Then do what you're supposed to do. Help us get out of this! We can't keep living on this porch, shitting in the backyard."

Dumbnise rolled her neck as she responded, "We go to the gas station and the McDonald's sometimes. And, boy, don't you remember? I gave you the money!"

He leaned over and snatched up his half-full bottle of orange juice. As he chugged down the sweet, tangy coolness, he thought, *Instead of a mommy, I got a dummy*. He decided their best chance was to go to the police. He had a wad of cash, but he couldn't rent a hotel or an apartment if Dumbnise didn't know how to help him. Fear was giving him street smarts, but was also keeping him on the streets. Two drunks had tried to rob him on one of his return trips from the store. Not long after Denise handed him the money, he started shopping alone. He was the faster of the two of them at both walking and shopping. Also, unlike Denise, Chrystan only showed the amount of money needed to pay for their items. Still, he was a little dingy but a well-dressed boy making near-daily trips to the corner store, always alone. So, two drunks went for him. Chrystan didn't know the neighborhood well, so needed a strong lead to outrun them and not lead them to the porch he called home. He dropped the groceries—a box of fried chicken wings and fries, his orange juice and Denise's Sprite, a box of Lorna Doone shortbread cookies, and bag of salt and vinegar potato chips—and ran. Chrystan pumped his arms, and ran like the little league MVP he'd been in Georgia. He outran the drunks with ease, but he'd been having nightmares about them ever since. In his dream, he woke up to find them standing over him, the uglier of the two laughing, "Uh-huh, we found your little rich dirty ass."

Another time, he was jumped by a gang of kids around his age. Following him around in the store, they begged him to buy them candy. "I can't. I can't," he repeatedly told them. Fear of living worse than he currently was had erased the word "splurge" and all of its synonyms from his vocabulary. "I don't have that much money." The four-foot thugs, though cheaply dressed, all had homes, or so Chrystan imagined. One that wasn't on a porch. "Ask your mama or daddy to buy y'all some."

When Chrystan left the store, they followed him. "You could have bought us penny candy with your change," one said, and they all agreed.

Chrystan shook his head. "It's not my money and I'm only allowed to buy food." Suddenly, a burning sensation spread across his face. One of the punks had hit him with a stick. Grabbing at where he hurt, a line from his left eye to the right corner of his mouth, Chrystan dropped his groceries. Kicks and punches forced him to his knees. Innately, he curled into the fetal position. The jump wasn't especially traumatizing. He'd experienced his share of playground scrimmages, some of them being pretty rough. Being an only child with no close friends, he'd fought all of them alone. Though his upbringing had been gentlemanly and scholarly, he had a warrior's heart. Wiry Chrystan was a strong boy. He was also smart. Hurting someone, especially a child, would attract attention. He and Denise didn't agree on what their next move should be, so they had to stay low-key until they could figure it out. Busting up even one of the little bad-asses, Chrystan knew, could be cause for an angry mama or daddy to call the police.

"I got the bag! I got the bag!" he heard as little hands pushed his body sideways, to free the groceries he was unknowingly shielding. After the bag was snatched from under him, the blows stopped and the world quieted. Getting back to his feet, Chrystan mumbled, "I should have punched at least two of them."

Chrystan's trips to the store were now all business, no munching, no strolling. He rushed there back on high alert. If he saw anyone who looked remotely interested in him, he either took a detour or postponed the trip. Though he knew it just was a matter of time before he encountered someone he couldn't outrun. "We need the police," he'd tried to convince Denise, but she'd warned, "We should wait because cousin," referring to his mama, "cousin will get in trouble."

Chrystan threw up his hands. "We're in trouble, Denise! We're in trouble! What about us? Where's Mama? Where the hell is she? Why did she send us to this raggedy house that we can't even get into?"

Denise rubbed her belly, unable to answer the questions.

They had tried calling Chrystan's mom, even after Denise's cell service was disconnected the day after they arrived. Denise checked her phone multiple times a day for two weeks, expecting to hear a dial tone. Her cousin had always paid her cell phone bill, yet she had no service. So, $10 was spent on a phone card. They walked two miles to the nearest payphone to call Chrystan's mom. "The number you've dialed either has been changed or disconnected." *How was that possible?* they wondered.

SIXTY-SEVEN

The nights were getting colder. Their money, Chrystan knew, would eventually run out. He suspected Denise would as well. "My baby, my baby, my baby," was what Chrystan heard at the beginning and end of each of their days. "What you want, some crackers or cookies?" she'd sweetly ask her belly. "You want to go for a walk? Night, night, baby."

Chrystan spooned up the last of the meat from the small can with his broken cracker. He decided he was done waiting to be rescued. He'd devised his own plan which he called, "Fuck the police," as in "fuck being afraid of them reprimanding his mother and fuck living like this!" So, tomorrow instead of evading Cleveland's black and white Crown Victorias, he'd be flagging one down.

Day was just breaking when Chrystan crept from the porch the next morning. He hoped for the last time. He was looking forward to a bubble bath and a meal served on a plate, no more fast food. He hungered for slow-cooked meat with stovetop or oven-baked sides and a sop-up piece, a buttery biscuit, roll, or slice of cornbread used to soak up the savory juices of a good meal, the broth of a meat, or as Chrystan's mother called it "pot liquor."

In case things didn't work out, Chrystan hid their remaining money in his underwear and socks. He wasn't worried about Denise. Chrystan had realized weeks ago that she hadn't handed over all the cash his mama had given her. Some of Denise's coming and goings, he noticed, included shopping trips. One of her solo excursions had included the purchase of vitamins for them both. From a white bag she'd pulled out a clear bottle of Flintstone Chewables. "You know what to do," she said, handing them to Chrystan. "Eat one a day." Her own vitamins were in a reddish-brown, translucent bottle, stickered with a prescription label that read "PRENATAL TABLETS." This morning as she slept, Chrystan left her, without guilt, to her own devices. He figured a reunion was inevitable after each of them in their own way was settled.

Just when Chrystan reached the end of the overgrown front yard, a boy shorter than him came from the driveway. He was as dirty as Chrystan felt.

"Can I go in there?" he asked. Before Chrystan could answer, the boy pointed at the porch. "This is your spot, right?"

"Who are you?" Chrystan stared at him. "Where did you come from?"

Panic spread on the boy's face. Chrystan thought he might run off, but he didn't. "Um, I just need someplace to stay," he answered.

Chrystan raised his chin. "Go on in if you want. I'm going to the police."

"Forget it then!" The boy's brown face reddened. "I'll just go some-place else."

"Not for you," Chrystan assured. "I'm not going to the police for you. I'm turning myself in."

The boy looked around cautiously. "Well, I can't do that."

Chrystan told him, "I didn't ask you to, but you should. Look at how dirty you are." He then turned to be on his way.

The boy walked up to the door of porch, but hesitated. "Is that lady in there?"

Chrystan stopped and turned around. He gave the boy a once-over, before offering, "Just come with me. We'll ask the police to help us both. She's not going to help you."

They boy shrugged. "But she'll let me sleep in there, right?"

Chrystan didn't know. "Why? Are you homeless?"

The boy's lips parted, but then closed before any words came out of his mouth. Chrystan, seeing the boy's reluctance to speak, decided to share his story first. "My mama sent us here, but there was no one here when the van dropped us off. That's my grandma's house, but we can't get in because of the boards and locks."

The boy then admitted, "I ran away, so no police. I'll be beat up if they find me."

"Who's going to beat you?" Chrystan asked, but the boy was done confessing. So, Chrystan tried another approach, "What's your name?" But that question only added to the boy's discomfort. "I won't tell anyone," Chrystan assured him. "I'm not turning you in."

The boy answered, "Christan, the same as yours."

"Man, how do you know my name?"

"I heard the lady calling you that."

"And that's your name too?"

"Yes, and I'm not lying."

Chrystan studied his dirty namesake. "How old are you?"

"Nine."

"Me too," Chrystan told him, and then asked urgently, "Look, I gotta go. Are you coming with me or not?"

With a shake of his head, the boy declined.

"Why do you want to live on the street?" Chrystan persisted. "It snows here. In a few months there will be ice and snow. Lots of it. You'll need boots and gloves and a house with heat that you can get into."

In a desperate tone the boy explained, "I don't want to go back to my foster home." His fear spilled out of him. "I don't know where they're going to send you, but I know they're gonna put me back with that lady. She will beat me and her son will beat me. They both will beat me."

Chrystan was at a loss for words; he'd never been beaten by adults.

The boy stood taller. "When I get big, I'll get a job. Then I'll be okay. I won't have to live with nobody."

Quickly, Chrystan reminded him, "That's years away. We won't be grown until we're eighteen."

The boy was unfazed. "So what?"

"So, you're just going to live on porches?" Chrystan shook his head. "Bad things happen to kids on the street. I had to run for my life."

The boy told him, "Bad things happen to kids everywhere. My grandma has a house, too, and she used to make me lie on her bed so she could beat me. She was mad because my mommy and daddy got put in jail, so she had to take care of me. And she was sick and tired. And when I ran away, she called the police on me. She said it was so she wouldn't get in trouble if something happened to me. And she said, anymore of my bullshit and she'd let the police keep me."

Pity ballooned in Chrystan for the boy. Chrystan thought of the two drunks who'd tried to rob him. "Some grown-ups kill kids." Then raising his chin toward the porch, he told his namesake, "There's food in there. Come on, I'll feed you."

SIXTY-EIGHT

Little Christan, as he would come to be called, ate himself to sleep: half of a corned beef sandwich, three chicken wings and a handful of fries, two Chick-O-Sticks, and half a roll of Lorna Doone cookies. The food and drink were kept in a large cooler Chrystan had found in the backyard. He said nothing as his namesake feasted as if he meant to empty the cooler. When the little guy reached for the orange juice, Chrystan barked, "That's mine!" and directed the boy to a gallon of water underneath a loaf of bread. "Drink some of that until I go to the store." Ignoring the disappointment on his namesake's face, he further instructed, "And you can't eat like this every day. We'll go broke."

Denise, waking up to their new porch mate, snorted, "You didn't ask me."

"So?" Chrystan rested against the now closed cooler.

"Boy!" Denise croaked.

Chrystan told her, "Your boy or girl is in your stomach."

"That's right!" she snapped. "Who does he belong to? Little bummy, dirty boy."

Chrystan, defending his new friend, asked, "How much cleaner are you?"

"I showered at the clinic," Denise told him, immediately regretting the admission. She quickly explained, "They made me. I had to, so they could check my baby."

Chrystan's light skin flushed red. "Why didn't you take me with you? I want a shower! And did you get real food? I want real food, like the kind we ate in Georgia."

Chrystan figured Denise was at least one layer cleaner than he was. He'd observed that grown-ups always managed to stay cleaner than the kids. Although both he and Denise were now homeless, he still expected to be dirtier than she was. It was him who huffed through the crummy neighborhood for their necessities. Chrystan expected Denise's hygiene to be fresher than his own, but not shower fresh.

"Why did you leave me here?" he whined.

Denise grabbed hold of the windowsill for leverage to rise from the old sofa. She was done talking. She pulled herself upright, and then left the porch to go relieve herself in the backyard. The street they were on had come to ruin before Chrystan's grandmother died, so there weren't many residents. Those that hadn't left didn't bother with other people unless they needed to ask to borrow something they'd never return. Chrystan and Denise could relieve themselves, if not in total privacy, at least in peace.

Denise exited the porch mumbling to herself. "Why does it always gotta be me to do every damn thing . . ." were the only words Chrystan could make out, either because she was speaking too quietly or the inferno burning in his chest had reached his ears. His eyes stung as if blazes were burning on either side of his head, blanketing his face in ash and smoke. His tone, when he replied, was a hiss: "You're not right, Denise." He wagged a finger at her when she returned to the porch. "You know better. You know it was wrong to leave me here. You're not that dumb."

After a few gulps of Sprite, Denise, not one for direct eye contact, met him straight on. Staring into his baby browns, she declared, "I can't be everybody's mama. I gotta be my own baby's mama."

From the beginning, Denise had mothered Chrystan with surgical precision to keep him shiny and perfect, her narrow digits de-crusting his eyes, ears, and nose long after he was old enough to bathe and groom himself. Early on, Chrystan understood that his cousin was his nanny and that she received some sort of compensation for it. Still, he believed she loved him. When his mama or the guy who used to be his daddy reprimanded him, Chrystan could see how it bothered Denise. But soon, she'd have her own baby. *Maybe she is that stupid, that simple,* he reasoned. *She can't love more than one baby at a time. So, since I'm not her real baby, it's "go away, Chrystan."*

A velvety cool touch startled him from his thoughts. Denise was cleaning his face with a baby wipe. "Hush, hush, hush." He hadn't realized he was crying.

"Leave me alone." He waved her away. "I don't need you to do anything for me anymore! Forget you!"

"Yeah, okay." She dropped the wipe in his lap, and then retreated to her side of the porch to finish her breakfast.

"I was going to leave anyway," he told her, as she ate. "I was on my way." He pointed to the food-comatose Little Christan. "I had left you, until this little boy showed up."

Denise smirked, "Boy, you didn't know where to go."

"The police would have helped me. That's what they do."

Denise, washing down a mouthful of saltines with another swallow of Sprite, shook her head. After burping, she pointed at him, "The police . . . hmm . . . What they do is beat black ass. Your mama isn't nothing but a black bitch to them. They'll beat her ass and lock her up for making a mistake."

Chrystan blurted, "Fuck mistake!" Denise had essentially pissed on his hopes in addition to trashing his intelligence. "I'm not stupid like you. This isn't a fucking mistake! Sending us to this raggedy, shit house and not calling us. Not coming for us. I'm her son and I'm only nine years old. You're her slow, dumb cousin. She knows we need her! Are we on the news like other missing kids? There aren't any pictures of us hanging in this neighborhood. She did this shit on purpose! She got rid of us! And now I don't need her or your dumbass, Dumbnise!"

SIXTY-NINE

Little Christan was without a doubt a starved version of his former self. Although he wore a belt, his filthy blue school uniform pants were folded over to keep them around his tiny waist. His school shirt, initially solid white but now a tie-dye of stains, draped his poor torso like a curtain. He wasn't wearing any underwear. The reason for this could be seen in streaks across the crotch and back of his pants. Obviously, the missing briefs had taken the worst of a distressed or unexpected bowel movement.

So, he shit himself, the bigger Chrystan observed silently while looking through his suitcase for cleaner clothes for the little guy. Chrystan figured, *Maybe he crapped while hiding from a beating, or during one.* Only on television and in movies had he seen stress cause people to lose control of their bodily functions. He'd witnessed, firsthand, scared and overexcited dogs pee as they whined or wagged their tail. He'd seen them poop out of anxiety on floors and even on sofas. Big Chrystan also noticed faint lines on Little Christan's legs and back that looked like bruises caused by a switch or a whip. Big Christian now heard the boy's words again, *I don't want to go back to my foster home. They both will beat me.* He now had no doubt it was possible for a human to be "scared shitless."

Little Christan, even after using half a bag of baby wipes, was still filthy. He needed a real bath. The clothes Big Chrystan gave him, as much

304

of an improvement as they were over what he had been wearing, still told the world he was poor. The jeans had to be cuffed nearly as high as his knees, meeting the hem of the shirt that fit him like a night gown.

Little Christan hadn't asked for the clothes, or the dry bath.

"Can I have some money?" he'd asked after waking up.

"Dang, you haven't even said thank you for all the other stuff." Big Chrystan shook his head.

"Thank you. Can I have some money?"

Big Chrystan closed his suitcase after wiping down and changing clothes. "No. I don't have any money to give away."

Little Christan persisted, "But I don't have any, and I'm hungry."

"You were hungry; now you're not," the bigger Chrystan reminded him.

"But what about later?"

"Later, I'll buy more food."

"And if you go away?"

"You'll come with me."

"I'm not going to the police!"

Big Chrystan plopped down in the cushioned lawn chair. "We can't live like this forever. School is about to start, and the snow is coming. I'll figure something out for both of us."

Little Christan tried again, "If you give me some money, I'll leave and do my own thing."

Big Chrystan was firm with him. "There is nothing to do out there except be hungry and get beat up. You'll probably freeze to death when it snows."

Little Christan didn't back down. "But I know how to crawl into small places. I don't have to stay here. Not if you give me some money."

Big Chrystan, jumping up from the chair, got in his face. "You want to leave? After I let you eat all that food and gave you my clothes? Leave, but I'm not giving you any money!"

Little Christan wanted to secure money for food too badly to feel ashamed or let fear overwhelm him. He wasn't discouraged, but for the moment, he shut his mouth.

"Go!" Big Chrystan pointed to the porch door. "Leave and don't come back. I don't need you or anybody to be my friend."

Little Christan looked at the door, but didn't move.

"You think you can rob me?" Big Chrystan challenged him. "You're going stay here and try to rob me? Take my money?"

"No," the little guy quickly shook his head. "No, that's not what I do."

Big Chrystan backed off. "Well, I'm leaving. I already told you that."

Little Christan begged, "Can you buy me some food before you go? Just one bag of food."

"Nope. I'm just going to go."

"I don't want to be hungry again."

"I can't give you money," Big Chrystan told him.

Little Christan settled down onto the floor of the porch. He put his small head in the cup of his small hands. He peeked over at Big Chrystan, and then looked down at the floor. He was pouting.

SEVENTY

May 2008

For months, BETY Junior had ignored his abdominal pain. While it was very uncomfortable at times, he didn't think it was serious. He guessed, at worst, he had an ulcer. That he might have an aggressive disease that was actually killing him had never crossed his mind. BETY Junior saw himself in Pop, and so presumed Pop's vitality as his own. A classic 1927 model, at eighty-one, Pop was free of wrinkles and meds, stood upright, and still had his wits about him. BETY Junior thought they were both a long way from the grave.

"I don't want to die before you," he told Pop. "I'm not ready to die—period—but definitely not before you."

The two were lounging in Pop's den. BETY Junior sat on the sectional; Pop was stretched out comfortably in his recliner. "Should be I worried you'll suffocate me in my sleep or poison my food?"

BETY Junior gave him a look. "Listen, old man, I'm trying to have a moment with you. Tell you how I feel . . . that I'm sorry that I won't be here for you in your last days."

Pop sat himself up and grabbed his beautiful walking stick. He tossed it at BETY Junior, who barely caught it. "Don't worry about me. Guys twenty years younger need this more than I do."

"You don't need this at all. Never have. This stick is just to make you look honest and wise while macking on foxy old biddies. And you grip it more like it's your golden rod of pimp power than a crutch."

Pop huffed, "My friend wouldn't have given it to me if I didn't need it. He had it blessed by a Yoruba priestess."

Pop was BETY Junior's favorite person to tease, so BETY Junior kept on him. "Yeah, okay. Was the blessing to give you a second puberty? Because you've been a curse to grannies ever since. King Mack Granddaddy!"

Pop settling back in his recliner, and told him, "Shut up."

BETY Junior smiled. "If I won't keep it real with you, who will?" Then in earnest he said, "I'm sorry, though. I want to be around for you, you know, when you give up your macking ways. I want to be here to look after you. Don't want you in a nursing home. Hell, no. Those places are like staffed coffins, and so many of the people who work there are assholes. If one was to hurt you, the world would burn."

Pop sat back up. "Bariah, don't start with that 'I'm sorry' nonsense. I know how sorry you are. You're a sorry-ass cook. You can't even dress well. I know what you should be sorry for. As far as leaving me alone, well, raising you extended my life. Don't you worry about me."

BETY Junior leaned forward. "That's bullshit. First of all, I'm good at everything. And seriously, I've been living like we're both getting younger. Didn't even give you any great-grandchildren."

Pop winked. "Then get to it. Still time."

BETY Junior was amused. "Well, you're too old to beat the kid's ass like you beat mine. So, who's going to raise him or her? I don't have a lot of time to hunt, so the random I bless with my seed may not be of the best quality."

Pop winked again. "That's already been figured out."

"What's already figured out?"

"Been a long time coming for you two."

"You two who? Who are you talking about?"

"Who else? What other woman would I so graciously give my blessing to?"

"I have no idea."

"Damn, Bariah! You're going to die dumb, aren't you? Ella, son."

BETY Junior shook his head no. "I don't want her dealing with any baby mama drama."

Pop exhaled. "So dumb. Listen, there won't be any baby mama drama for her to deal with if she's the baby mama."

BETY Junior was dumbstruck. "What's this shit you're saying to me?"

Pop smiled. "Ella. There's no need to gamble with a random because you got Ella."

BETY Junior laughed. "Yeah, I need to stay alive to take care of you. You must have dementia or something. How does that make any sense? She's my sister."

Pop dropped his smile. "No, she isn't. And she isn't a child anymore."

BETY Junior stood up. "Pop, you've been calling her your granddaughter for years."

"Yes," Pop agreed, adding, "and you can make that legal by marrying her."

"Crazy!" BETY Junior sat back down.

Pop told him, "Maybe so, son, but crazy isn't necessarily wrong. Stupid is, though. It's absolutely stupid-wrong not to consider marrying the woman you've loved more than any other woman in your life."

"I love her like a sister."

"Pssst . . . all that means is she's not a blood relative yet closer than a friend—and you're not sleeping with her."

"So, you're good with me having sex with Ella? Ella La Bella?"

"Hell, no, you young, dumb boy; you're missing the point. This isn't about you getting laid. This is about family; it's about love. I want you to love her in the Biblical sense, 'my heart, my sister, my spouse.' Make it clean and marry her."

BETY Junior was quick to respond, "Hell, naw, no you didn't just Bible-thump me. Listen, Deacon Keenum Bariah Elijah Young of Union Grove Baptist Church baptized in a clear pond in the backwoods of North Carolina, I'm pretty sure you're preaching those words out of context. Check yourself, Deacon. Check . . . your . . . self."

"Ha," Pop coughed. "You slept through Sunday School."

BETY Junior raised his long arms as if to Heaven. "I got my Sunday School certificate of completion every year. You can't just throw verses at me like I don't know the Word."

Pop dismissed him with a wave. "You're a hoe."

BETY Junior shook his head. "Is that how a saved man should speak, Deacon?"

"Hand me my walking stick." Pop extended a large hand.

BETY Junior refused. "Why? So, you can beat my ass? Beat me into compliance? It's fine over here."

Pop smiled. "So, you're not so dumb after all?"

BETY Junior laid the stick across his lap. "Let's continue with this bullshit conversation. I understand what you are asking, Pop, but it won't work."

"Yes, it will," Pop explained. "And you know you're her problem with men. You claim to be her brother, but you protect her like she's your woman. Cockblocking all the damn time."

"Okay, now you're making stuff up. Cockblocking?" BETY Junior grinned. "Old man, what do you know about cockblocking?"

Pop explained, "Old man is right. The game existed long before your generation started chasing and sticking tail. What you think, cause y'all got all these new names and songs about sex, y'all invented it? Or that it wasn't any good until y'all started doing it? Now shut up and think about what I am saying to you."

BETY Junior exhaled. "Make a baby with Ella?" Shaking his head at the absurdity of it, he continued, "What is this about, Pop? Long live the empire? Preserve the bloodline."

Pop firmly replied, "This isn't about me. I could have had ten more children by now. What this is about is your life, which is ending too got-damn soon. And the quality of your life, again which is ending too got-damn soon."

BETY Junior placed the walking stick aside and leaned forward. "And what about Ella's life? She'll lose three times, Pop: her brother and friend, her husband, and the father of her child."

Pop was quick to reply, "Life isn't worth living unless we have things in it that we are afraid of losing."

BETY Junior nodded. "And she will lose. She . . . will . . . lose. Why do that to her? She's not the one dying; I am. So, why rush her into a shotgun wedding like it's her last chance?"

Pop answered, "Maybe it is her last chance to have a husband who loves her as much you do. Don't you want her to have a loving husband, Bariah?"

"What I want for her is to have a husband she can grow old with."

"Sure," Pop agreed. Tightly, he added, "I wanted to grow old with your grandma, to watch our children have children. I prayed for it, but we still buried our first child as an infant. Then we buried your father, our second and last child, when you were young. And then . . . I buried her."

BETY Junior warned quietly, "Take it easy."

"Don't tell me to take it easy!" Pop barked. "I've never been able to take it easy. Life hasn't been easy on me; it's been hard. And now it's being harder on you."

BETY Junior opened his arms. "Then why make it hard for Ella? I can't just take what I want from her, like she's been on standby all these years as my backup woman. You say marry her, but I'm already married to the notion of being her brother. Our relationship has purity, Pop. I'm her brother."

Pop raised his chin. "Purity? Okay, how pure would your feelings for her have been if you hadn't met her how and when you met her? If you met her, say, five years ago in a club or at a party? Saw her in a mall?" He didn't give BETY Junior time to answer. "'My heart, my sister, my spouse.' When you were born into my life, you were my Bariah's boy. Then one day my Bariah was gone. You then became more to me, and I to you. We evolved into what we both needed, father and son. Now that you're a man, in a way you're my little brother and my best friend. Yet you're not any less my son, not any less my grandson. Nonetheless, the dynamics of our relationship have changed. And you were counting on another change and becoming my caretaker, as I had been yours. Time does that. Life does that; it changes us and our needs . . . and sometimes even who we are to each other." Pop then asked, "What have I always told you, Bariah?" Then answered for him, "Be encouraged."

BETY Junior's eyes glossed over at the reminder of where his customary saying had come from.

Pop continued, "Be encouraged, son. Be encouraged to live until it's all done. Use up all your energy; empty the reserves. You've made your money and played the field. Now make a family life for yourself. Have that joy in your life."

BETY Junior exhaled. "And Ella, what do you want her to be encouraged to do? Give her heart and body to a man she's sure to lose before her child starts preschool."

Pop told him, "I would tell her to be encouraged to enjoy the best love she may ever have from a man."

BETY Junior found himself getting a little angry. "Pop, you don't know that . . . You have no way of knowing what her future holds."

Pop held his position. "I know more than you."

BETY Junior admitted, "Getting with Ella seems desperate. Oh I am dying, so let me grab a hold of whichever chic is closest and knock her up with my seed."

Pop, feeling he was winning, smiled. "No, son. It's been a long time coming. Should have happened way before now. It's just that now it's crucial. And in my vision, years from now, she'll look in that child's face and cry tears of happiness that he or she is there."

BETY Junior's mind easily opened at the idea of Novella raising his child, and so reluctantly opened up to the possibility of her being the mother. "Pop, I love you more than I'll ever be able to tell you. I love you, I love you, and I love you. I'll do whatever you want me to do. Whatever. But I don't know how to love Ella the way you're telling me to. It'd be a humongous change in what we've be doing, how we've been living. A big flip in the script."

Pop chuckled as he got to his feet. "For sure, boy. However, the script needs to flip."

SEVENTY-ONE

Since his diagnosis, BETY Junior didn't know what he needed, so he'd focused on those closest to him. Pop needed a caregiver; Novella needed financial security. A will and a trust would handle both concerns. BETY Junior had eventually wanted to marry and have children. Though, when being told his life would end sooner than later, he'd given up on that want. Now that Pop had argued for him starting his own family, BETY Junior again wanted one. Specifically, a child. He wanted his Ella to be a part of it. So, if her to part of it was to be his wife, then he wanted them to fall in love and make it right. He thought, *A woman like her should make love to make babies. The man making babies with her should be in with love her, and she with him.*

BETY Junior already regarded Novella as family; he already loved her and felt as if he needed her. She was his soulmate, his kindred spirit, someone he expected to have in his life until the end. Making her his wife would be as easy as promising to be good to her. *Of course, I'd be good to her.* It was that other part that was the issue. "My sister, my heart, my spouse," meant changing the nature of his love and need for her. Seeing her with the same eyes he viewed other women with, lusting after her.

It wasn't that he didn't see the woman in her. He'd made a decision to keep it pure between them, and it had felt right to do so. Her female

315

energy had been a missing link in his life, and not just in his, in Pop's as well. Once, though, BETY Junior thought Mother Nature had her way with Novella and him.

It was normal for them to fall asleep together, to keep talking until one of them started snoring, after watching a movie, partying, or on road trips. One morning, BETY Junior awakened in Novella's bed in just his boxers. It was odd because he always left his pants on when he slept with her. It was also somewhat alarming as King Vic was sore. BETY Junior's ego was yay tall and yay long, so he'd given his penis two names: The Victor and King Vic.

Oh shit! he thought. *What did we do, King Vic? What did we do? What did we do?*

BETY Junior called out, "Ella!"

She still lay next to him, asleep in her cocoon. Her apartment was quite warm, but she liked being covered. She hit BETY Junior with a pillow after he shook her and snatched the comforter off her face. "Leave me alone."

"Get up!" BETY Junior shook her. "Seriously! Ella, what the hell? My dick is sore! What the hell happened?"

Novella shouted. "Are you out of your mind? Your dick problems are your own problems, Mr. Hoe of Hoes!" She then tried to pull the comforter back over her head, but BETY Junior held it.

"Are you naked?" BETY Junior asked her.

Novella was irritated. "Listen, you're being stupid, and I'm sleepy."

BETY Junior asked again, "I can only see your t-shirt. Are you wearing bottoms?"

"Yes!" Novella yelled.

BETY Junior kept on, "Who else is here in this apartment?"

Novella pushed him. "Hey, crazy guy, stop being crazy!"

BETY Junior left the bed to sort out his near nakedness. Entering the empty living room, he yelled back, "Why is the heat on so high?" Speaking out loud to himself, he said, "Shit, I must have stripped in my sleep to survive. It's a damn sauna in here!"

Cupping King Vic, he still wondered why he was sore. BETY Junior strolled back to the bedroom. The bed was empty. He could hear the flow of Novella's urine from behind the door of her half bath. BETY Junior inspected the bed and found his cell phone. Judging by where he found it, he realized it must have been under his crotch the whole night. He vaguely remembered adjusting himself multiple times throughout the night but being too done over to get up and completely right himself. "Damn," He grumbled. "I must still be drunk. Waking up dumb on some bullshit, full of accusations."

That scare had happened years before, and neither of them felt awkward about it. They kept sleeping together. Today, thinking on Pop's words, BETY Junior wondered what would have happened if King Vic had broken the code. Would Ella have welcomed the change of conduct? Would she now be a regret, or would she be his wife?

BETY Junior went to his side of the house. He'd just laid back on his chaise when he heard the sound of his front door being unlocked. It was Novella using the key he'd given her. She came into the room, met his eyes with a smile, and sat beside him.

"I love you." She slipped one of her small hands into one of his. After they gave each other a gentle squeeze, he told her the same, "I love you."

SEVENTY-TWO

August 7, 2010

"Go home, Ella." Pop raised his chin, gesturing for her to turn around and leave. Pop had met her at the elevator and then walked her to the family lounge. They were in the United Sisters in Christ Hospice Medical Center. "Go home. Don't come back until you can tell him goodbye."

Novella was there so frequently that it was obvious to the staff and other regular visitors that her heart was in Room 2020.

"He's in so much pain," Pop told her, "so much pain that we're not in a hospital. You know that right, Ella? This is hospice. Not rehab or assisted living. This is where people are sent to die as peacefully as possible. He'll take his last breath here. I think our home would be best, but the pain is too much. He's going to die here, and because of the pain, it needs to be sooner rather than later."

Novella was silent as she searched Pop's eyes for why he was upset with her. A fleeting thought was that he was annoyed with her because his blessing wasn't heeded and there wasn't a Bariah III or a little Novella in her womb or on her hip. Novella couldn't think of any other explanation for his growing agitation with her, which had apparently reached a head.

"Bariah's holding on for you," Pop accused her. "He's afraid to leave you. You gotta tell him you're going to be alright. I can see your fear, and I'm pretty sure he can too."

Novella gave him a look that said, *Yeah, I'm scared. Of course, I'm scared.*

She was missing the point, so Pop explained, "You need to give him assurances. Show him your strength. He knows you can take care of yourself, Ella. He needs to know that you will. That while you'll mourn, you won't fall apart. That the Ella he knows won't die with him."

When Novella finally spoke, she didn't like that it sounded as if she was admonishing Pop, but she was too worked up to change her tone. "Maybe it's you he's afraid for . . ."

Pop shook his head. "Because I'm old? No, Ella Bella. He's not worried about the old man, because he knows the old man knows what's up. It's baby girl he's worried about. You're the baby. Our baby. And we love you dearly, but you need to grow up and accept that Bariah is dying. From the day he was diagnosed, there wasn't any hope for him to beat it. This has been a long goodbye. This time next year . . . he'll be gone."

Novella's emotional defenses were raised to red alert as she thought, *I don't want to hear any shit about next year. Fuck next year. It's now. Everything is now. Every day is for right now. All he has is now.* For the first time she was mad at Pop. Novella's chest felt to have cracked open, and with tough love, Pop widened the gap by asking, "How much morphine do you want them to pump in him? Because that's what it's taking for him to get through each day."

Pop gently grabbed both of her shoulders. "Hear me, Ella. Hear me. Instead of praying that God heals him like I know that you are, pray that God takes his pain away, that he stops his suffering." Then Pop being the deacon that he was, gave her the Word, "Timothy, verses six through seven:

'For I am now ready to be offered, and the time of my departure is at hand. I have fought a good fight, I have finished my course, I have kept the faith.' You see, Ella, we stand with him, but this isn't our fight. And we weren't ever going to get what we want. We're just here to be what he needs, at every step of the way . . . and we're at the final step. And Ella La Bella, you need to step up."

Novella believed that you don't bury someone until they're dead, so she wondered, *What's with this sappy premature bullshit about telling him goodbye, telling him that it's okay to die? He's alive, and I've to come to make him comfortable, to give him reason to live.*

Pop again told her, "Go home, Ella. Come back soon, real soon, but not until you're ready."

Novella left sad and mad. She was so sad that she felt nauseous. She was so mad she became irritated by her own jewelry, dangle earrings, and three gold bangles. After removing them and placing them in her car's center console, she got on her way. *How could he put me out? Is something wrong with him? Maybe he needs to go home and rest. Maybe he's the one who needs to get sorted out.* Upset as she was, still she was amazed by Pop. Novella was convinced Pop was a superhero—if not an angel. How else could he be so solid on the eve of the end of his lineage? Novella was a wreck—and a disaster *waiting* to happen. She was a little less than four miles from home when she rolled her car. She was unconscious for about five minutes.

Confused about how she'd gotten upside down, Novella stared in shock at the large scissors cutting through her seatbelt. "Come on! You made it," she heard someone say when the pressure on her chest and thighs was released. Small yet strong hands grabbed hold of her. The rescuer, a stout, darkly-skinned woman, had been traveling on the same road as Novella but in the opposite direction. "Not today," the woman assured her. "You won't be dying today, baby girl." Being called baby girl caused Novella to reflect on Pop's words, *It's baby girl he's worried about.* Instantly, she felt guilty for almost dying. Soon the woman had Novella sitting on the median, and was asking her where she felt pain. Novella, however, wasn't answering. She was looking at her 1995 Dodge Intrepid, nicknamed Electra, now dead on her back. Pop's words hit hard. She realized that, by this time next year, she will have put at least ten thousand miles on Electra's replacement. Even worse, it was the truth that, by this time next year, BETY Junior would be months gone. As Pop had firmly yet heartfully pointed out, from the day he was diagnosed there hadn't been any hope he would be cured. Novella now accepted that switching them to organic everything, getting into juicing, and making BETY Junior drink herbal concoctions had only delayed the inevitable.

In junior high school, Novella had asked a teacher the difference between crying and weeping. The teacher had answered, "It's just a play of words until you've done both."

At the time, Novella had smiled and said, "I don't get it."

The teacher smiled back at her before explaining in a serious tone, "When someone cries, you feel sad for them. When they weep, you worry about them. Because weeping happens when loss is profound. When it's big, very big. And a heart has lost all hope of getting back what or who was lost. And a heart feels hopeless in being able to recover from that loss."

Nearly twenty years later, sitting on the concrete median in the arms of a stranger, Novella was in the misery of that distinction. For the first time in her life, she wept.

SEVENTY-THREE

October 2012

The Georgia homestead plan had died with BETY Junior. Purcell would stay in North Carolina, and Pop would move back there soon. Novella, also needing to leave Cleveland, chose Austin. She decided that if she was going to leave all people and things that were familiar to her, then she should at least have warm weather. Well, more like hot weather, as in over 100°. And that wasn't just in the summer. Austin's spring could also bring dollar and change temperatures.

The fastest growing city in the United States easily made Novella's short list. The steady economy and comfortable balance of green and asphalt appealed to her. Not too country, not too big city. So, after a five-day girls' trip there, Novella confirmed it as her next home.

Moving to Austin wasn't an upgrade from Cleveland. Renovation was upon the historically industrial city. Much of it looked as it did sixty years ago, including the neighborhood demographics—whites mostly on the westside and blacks mostly on the eastside—but change had been underway for the last ten years.

Lake Erie had become a backyard for hundreds. Factories had been torn down or remodeled into loft apartments and coworking spaces. Even parts of "Rough" Hough, Novella's childhood neighborhood, had gotten a makeover.

Novella didn't feel to be missing out by leaving during this renaissance. She did, however, have one doubt about her move—Pop. Novella had been helping look out for him, since even before BETY Junior's diagnosis. She accompanied him to doctor appointments, church functions, and even to visit family in North Carolina. BETY Junior hadn't liked him travelling on his own, and neither did Novella. Pop wouldn't be alone now. He had family in North Carolina, though Novella had vowed to be his family, too. *So, how can I be moving to Austin?* she often wondered. It had been Pop's idea to put distance between them, at least temporarily. He felt she was trapped in the trauma of BETY Junior's death, that when she said goodbye to him, what she was actually saying goodbye to was seeing him and being able to touch him. While she wasn't waiting for a resurrection, neither had she moved beyond his death. Pop knew this of her, even though she had been stoic in her mourning, hiding her pain by keeping busy.

He told her, "Ella, you're still a young woman. Don't give up on happiness. On having a joyful life, and . . . don't feel guilty for moving on. Go and *live* just for you. Someplace that doesn't remind you of Bariah. Make decisions which are just for your life. Meet new people. You hear me? Meet new people . . . and that includes men."

Novella would leave after liquidating BETY Junior's estate. Pop and Purcell were financially set, so BETY Junior had willed everything he had to Novella, securing her financial future. Novella, coming into wealth, was so grateful she'd safeguarded her credit. She'd been a victim of identity theft multiple times. Her mother, Cara Lee, was the culprit for each hit. Refusing to send her own mother to jail, Novella had paid $3,000 for a furniture set, $400 for two roundtrip tickets to Alabama, and several expensive shopping sprees. Now worth more, Novella knew her mother's thievery, if not blocked, would be even more extravagant, especially since Novella knew her brother Nolan was likely to be involved. Credit accounts at men's clothing stores had also been opened and charged to her.

SEVENTY-FOUR

Novella received an interesting inquiry about her most expensive property from Yamil Yadar Ross, Yadara's father.

Novella had seen him as something of a shadow. A car pulling up, a phone call, or text—always in the distance, even after they were adults. Novella had never met him. Not even at church. He'd never been there when she'd accompanied Yadara and her sister.

Yadara had told Novella that her father was spiritual, not religious. He didn't believe that there was one religion or belief that would fit everyone. "God, the creator, he or she, can't talk to all of us in the exact same way," he'd told her. He'd sent Yamila and her sister to a Baptist church, because they were without a mother and aunties. He wanted them to have an extended family of good women, have a home away from home. And because people who believed what he believed didn't gather in communities, they didn't meet up like Baptists did. So, while encouraging his daughters to be faithful to their own curiosities, he asked them to embrace the familyhood of the church he'd chosen for them.

Yadara had also told Novella that he'd had entrusted almost everything female to her sister Yamila. Though when it came to men—from boyfriends to male teachers, church officials, and neighbors—he was very involved. Novella figured she'd probably never meet him, though she'd formed an opinion of him on the basis of the comfortable life he'd arranged for his daughters. Novella assumed that he was hardworking with a no-nonsense attitude, and she was right. However, Yadar, as he'd introduced himself, was also kind, humble, charismatic, and very handsome.

Yadara, when telling Novella she'd passed her number to him, had giggled, "Try not to fall in love, girl."

Sixty-five years-old, Yadar was six-feet-three-and-a-half-inches of lean and ripped experience, set in glowing, tight cinnamon skin. Hearing his smooth deep voice and crisp diction over the phone made Novella expect no less. Speaking with him enticed her to heed to Pop's advice and meet new people. When she saw Yadar up close, however, Novella was enticed to *meet him, greet him, eat him.* Fortunately—or unfortunately— the charged attraction was mutual.

SEVENTY-FIVE

Yadar's bid was on the largest of the apartment buildings in her portfolio. Modern, with amenities that included a fitness center and clubhouse, it was a choice property. The building residents only moved out to buy a home or relocate. So, despite its four-digit monthly rent, potential tenants gladly waited an average of two years for a vacancy. Novella was strongly advised that she might be better off keeping the property despite the fact that she was relocating. Yadar was hungry for it, yet he seemed in no rush to finalize anything with Novella.

"So, does it bother you at all that I'm so much younger than you?"

"You're not nineteen. You're thirty-eighty years old."

"I'm younger than your oldest daughter, and the same age as your youngest."

"You're no daughter of mine; I didn't watch you grow up. You're a beautiful, sexy woman who I was introduced to by way of business. A beautiful, sexy woman, who happens to be younger than me."

Novella, after her casting her vote at Shaker Heights Public Library for Barack Obama, had headed for her first meeting with Yadar. The two met at Zanzibar Soul Fusion. He and Novella had quickly gone from meeting in restaurants to rendezvous in his brownstone off Lake Erie. Yamila and Yadara, who both worked and lived uptown, rarely dropped in there. For casual visits, they usually went to one of his businesses, or he met them at their respective offices or homes. Novella had no intention of taking Yadar to the home she'd shared with BETY Junior and still shared with Pop. So, Yadar's place was their cozy, private "no judge zone."

From the moment they shook hands, they were comfortable being close and couldn't stop touching one another. Everything from admiring jewelry to saying hello or goodbye required some type of touch. Novella was glad to be out in the world when with him, especially since there was no plan; Yadar was just happening.

They were cuddled up on his sofa one night with Novella's legs across his lap, her hands making repeat roundtrips from his thick impressive beard to his hard chest.

"It's really bothering you?" he asked. "Our difference in age."

"Not really." She shook her head. "It has more to do with the fact that I grew up with your daughter. I mean we're not the friends we once were, not really friends at all, actually. No bad blood or anything, we just grew apart. But it's still weird. It's like, when I'm with you, I . . . am . . . with . . . you. You know how to treat a lady, and I enjoy being with you. But when I'm not with you, and I'm thinking about you, I feel . . . like I'm having an affair with my friend's father. And I don't want to be that woman. I am not that woman."

Yadar took her chin in one of his large hands. "And I am not the man who messes with— or ever messed with—underage girls. Neither am I now chasing women half my age in order to make myself feel young."

Novella believed him. Yadar looked at most fifty, and his presentation of vitality was no illusion. He was sharp and moved with fluid agility. In his clear, bright eyes, black pupils sparkled like the indicator lights of an energy stronghold. His Afrocentric style of dress, while high-end and sophisticated, was relaxed and timeless. He was neither old-fashioned nor trendy. From the faint hair pattern on his shiny head, Novella surmised that being cleanshaven wasn't a forced decision. There was no evidence of balding. And while the salt and pepper mix in his mustache and beard showed he was a man of somewhat advanced age, it only added to his appeal. No, Yadar didn't need women half his age to make him feel young. He was young in every way that he and a lucky lady needed him to be.

He asked, "So, if not for your history with Yadara, you wouldn't be embarrassed to introduce my old self to your friends, introduce me as your man?"

Novella shook her head. "Nope."

"Well, then you're caught up in the past," he told her, "and you'll have to decide how much weight it carries in the here and now. I just want you to be comfortable. I don't want anything from you that you don't want to give me. I don't want anything from you that you'll regret giving me."

Novella smiled. "Hmm, give you, huh? What do you think I want to give you?"

Suggestively, Yadar's eyes playfully scanned her upon his lap, where she had positioned herself. Afterwards, he placed a soft yet passionate kiss on her forehead and stared deeply into her eyes.

Novella indulged in his heated gaze for a few moments before asking, "Have you told Yadara?"

With her in his long arms, he leaned them toward his coffee table. Novella understood what he was trying to do, so she passed him his wine glass.

"Thanks," he said, as he took his wine-filled goblet from her. "Well . . . no. But I don't normally discuss my personal affairs with her."

Novella asked, "And you don't think this warrants an exception to that rule?"

Yadar, after a few sips, chuckled. "I'm not worried about her. Anyway, she probably already suspects that we're attracted to each other and, at the very least, flirting. She'll probably warn you not to fall for me. Now, if she finds out that we're doing more than flirting, Yadara is more likely to be an annoyance than be against us. She's always gotten a kick out of women being interested in me, and the more offbeat the situation, the more she's entertained. Yamila, on the other hand, would react in the complete opposite manner. She knows better to come at me sideways, but you . . . she'll try to give you hell. I know you can hold your own, but I'd prefer to keep her off you." He handed his glass to Novella. "Please and thank you." He then leaned them to allow her to place it back on the table.

Back upright, she said, "You're welcome. So, tell me why I shouldn't fall for you."

Yadar gave her a seductive smile. "That's Yadara's opinion. Woman, I invite to do whatever you want. I'm open."

SEVENTY-SIX

So, old friend, did you do my daddy? Novella imagined Yadara asking her. For the moment, she was spared the discomfort of trying to tell her old friend a half truth. She was in a safe place: she was at Haze's place for brunch.

Returning from the stove with the teapot, Haze asked, "Okay, girl, what's up? And keep it real with your girl. Don't make me find out by watching you walk. You've been uptight and on lockdown for a long while. So, anybody who knows you will know if Yadar has gotten to *know* you."

Amused, Novella rolled her eyes.

After filling their cups, Haze placed the teapot on a serving grate in the middle of the table. Before sitting down, she placed her small hands on her big, round hips. "You may speak, Novella Ella La Bella."

Novella leaned back from Haze's well-set table. "I have not . . . gone all the way with Yadar."

Quickly, Haze asked, "Why not?"

Novella stared at her.

Haze feigned surprise. "*Really?* Okay, okay, okay . . . if it truly feels wrong, then don't. My advice is to base what you will and will not do on how *you* feel, not how you think someone else is going to feel. I mean, at the end of the day, whose damn business is it anyway? And you only live once. So, all I'm saying, girl, is don't miss out because of misplaced loyalty. And if it's going to be just sex since you're leaving, then you don't have to tell anyone about the relationship. Except for me. Girl, you better tell me. Now if it's more than sex, and it's something that goes on and on, then middle finger to anyone who has a problem with it. Girl, you gotta get you some joy. He's not married, and neither are you. And Yadara, girl, please . . . ask yourself what if it was her and your daddy. How much of a factor would you be in her decision-making process if she'd enjoy herself?"

Novella shrugged. "And if it was me and your daddy?"

Haze had just picked up a slice of bacon. She dropped it back onto her plate. "I'd be uncomfortable with it if I thought it would affect our friendship. And affecting our friendship includes me becoming the go-between for y'all hooking up and any subsequent issues. And honestly, if it was just sex, I wouldn't want to know about it. Grown folks do what grown folks do. Besides, if my dad looked like that with you looking like that, I wouldn't be surprised. And like I said, if it didn't affect our friendship, it wouldn't bother me. We all gotta live and be happy. And too many rules of engagement just oppress people and keep them lonely. And horny." Haze then gave Novella a wink as she smiled. "And speaking of horny, lover girl, you said you didn't go *all the way*. So, how far did you go? Or let him go? Or how far did y'all go together? You and that old-ass man."

SEVENTY-SEVEN

Austin, Texas
September 13, 2013

Novella found Austin and its suburbs cult-like when it came to running. If you ran, or even walk-ran, you had a dedicated crew. Novella found the links to hers at Lady Bird Lake. Stretching after a run, she had one of her heels on the trunk of her car when she heard, "Sasa, dada mrembo?" She turned to see a tall woman with a beautiful smile. Novella hadn't understood what she'd said and had actually thought she'd heard the woman say, "Salsa da-da flamingo." She was in the city of Tex-Mex, after all.

Novella lowered her leg and waited for the brown-skinned woman who was still approaching to reach her. When she did, Novella saw that she wore a thin beaded bracelet. It was red, black, green, and white, with the word "Kenya" on it. Before Novella could ask her to repeat what she'd said, another woman stepped from behind her. Shorter and darker than the first woman, she was just as beautiful.

"Karibu!"

With kindness, both women stared at Novella as if they knew her.

Novella gave a short laugh. "I don't understand."

They'd mistaken her for a Kenyan and had been speaking to her in Swahili. The women were of the Kikuyu tribe from Nairobi. They figured Novella was also Kikuyu, or Luo.

"What's up, beautiful sister?" was what Na'kessa, the first of the two women, had asked her. "Welcome," was what Shoni, the other, had said. They'd seen her on the Lady Bird Lake trail a few times and had been waiting for an opportunity to meet her. Early-morning runners like herself, the two nurses invited Novella to join them.

"Us sistas must take care of each other," Na'kessa had said as they exchanged numbers. "We must be family, even if we aren't the best of friends—though I think we will be."

Starting out under a midnight-blue sky, Novella met with her new sistas on many days. Seeing the morning sun rise through a pink blaze before being welcomed by its bright yellow rays was both calming and energizing. Their runs ended just as the moon disappeared behind a baby-blue cloud cover. Moonlight Runners was what they eventually named their WhatsApp chat group. Aside from Na'kessa and Shoni, there were three more Kenyans, two Ghanaians, two Nigerians, one Trinidadian, and one Tanzanian. Novella ran with these women at Lady Bird Lake, the Brushy Creek Trail, parts of the Greenbelt at Walnut Creek, and in each other's neighborhoods. It was fun, and it was training. The Moonlight Runners aimed to participate in all of the Austin great races: the 3M Half Marathon, the Capitol 10K, the Capitol to Coast Relay, the Run for The Water, and the Turkey Trot. At times, Novella couldn't tell if her sistas were running life into her, or out of her.

Novella enjoyed her group runs. However, she also enjoyed running by herself—her music, her thoughts, her pace. She'd just run up her driveway after finishing an eight-mile solo run, when the volume in her headphones went down. She knew that meant an incoming call. Although her phone was set to "Do not disturb," her headphones still recognized calls.

She hated that. She was glad that, when a call stopped, her music returned to her set volume.

Removing a bottle from her running belt, she ignored whoever was calling. Since starting off a little over an hour ago, the temperature had risen ten degrees. It was now eighty-nine. Novella, although never setting off on a run without water, hardly ever stopped to drink any of it. Fingers swollen from her body trying to retain water, she was quite thirsty. She quickly guzzled down the six ounces. Seeing her neighbor leave for work, she was reminded just how early it was. Novella knew a call around this time usually only came from one person.

Walking into her new house, she slid her headphones from her ears to her shoulders, and then removed her cell phone from its pouch. She saw what she expected: a missed call from Pop. Instead of calling him back on her phone, she decided to call from her laptop. They both preferred video calls. Before ringing him back, she needed to feed her hungry body.

After putting away her running gear, she grabbed her laptop and placed it on her kitchen counter. She then began blending a green smoothie. Once finished, she opened the laptop and selected the icon for Yahoo Messenger to call Pop. Right after taking a seat at her dining table with the laptop and smoothie, she looked up and saw his face.

"Ella La Bella, I've been busy."

"Hey, Pop-Pop! And that's what I want to hear. Busy means you're doing good."

"Yeh, I'm alright."

"Soooo, what's this busy business? What are you up to? And will you need bail money?"

Pop shrugged. "Well, it's a bit of a story."

Novella, after downing some of the blended goodness, gestured for him to share his story. "Come on out with it, Pop." Novella drank a bit more of her green smoothie. Just when she had returned the cup to the table, Pop began talking.

"This is going to hurt as much as it's going to feel good. It's going to blow you away."

Novella raised her eyebrows.

Pop tried to prepare her further. "I pulled rank on this one, Ella. I had to be sure for myself first. Had to hold it in, until it was confirmed." His large hands moved toward the screen as he told her, "You have a son. We have a son." Then he said, "Now, check your email."

Novella could only stare.

"Check your email, Ella La Bella. Check it right now."

Still too confused to speak, Novella minimized the window of their video call. Bringing up her email, she began shaking her head in wonder. *What in the world is going on? Pop did not just go and adopt a kid*, she thought. She hoped.

After scrolling a few moments, she huffed, "I don't see a new email from you."

"Not from me." He waved a hand. "I had you copied."

Her eyes going from her inbox to his face, she asked, "Copied on what?"

Just as he said, "DNA test," she noticed an email from True Results Lab. She looked over at Pop. "Who took a DNA test?"

"Read it, Ella."

She scrolled down to the paragraph entitled "Conclusion." "This result determines Keenum Bariah Thomas to be a close biological relative . . ."

Novella didn't realize she'd risen from her seat until her thigh bumped the table. "How is this possible? Where did he come from?"

Pop leaned forward, coming very close to his camera. "Bariah. He came from Bariah, his father."

Novella wanted to ask how old the boy was but couldn't get the words out. Pop's image filling her screen made her feel he was capable of stepping out of it. Novella wished he would.

Novella's Honest Demon looked at her smoothie. As if irritably whacking at a pestering fly, it reached out and hit it. A green mess flew out as it first hit the edge of the counter and then dropped to the floor. Green goodness was splattered on the counter, the cabinet doors, the wall, and all over the floor.

Pop sighed, "Ella. I told you this would—"

"Blow me away," Novella finished for him. What he didn't know was that, besides being shocked, she was also jealous. Very jealous. "How is this possible? Who is this *woman*? The mother." *Some random*, she thought.

Pop began, "He's nine years old, Ella. He was born before it all. And I don't who his mother is."

Hope, of having an important place in the child's life, dulled her jealousy. Still overwhelmed, she began to cry. "What? Was he just dropped off, on your doorstep or . . .?"

Pop laughed. "Ella La Bella, get yourself to Cleveland. I'm already here."

SEVENTY-EIGHT

Cleveland Hopkins International Airport
Later That Day

Novella was on her way to catch a shuttle to go get her rental, when a large hand gently grabbed one of her arms. She turned and was surprised to see Yadar.

"Oh my God!" She smiled. "You scared me!"

It had been months since they'd parted ways. Still, they easily wrapped around one another into a long, tight hug. She inhaled him deeply. As always, he smelled fresh, robustly delicious, and inviting.

He felt good pressed against her. Novella, as she had before, wondered if his spirituality was of the juju variety. The large wooden beads of his necklace, sandwiched between them, reminded her of his affinity for ethnic jewelry. He always wore at least one piece: a ring, a necklace, or a bracelet, even earrings. Elegant and stylish, obviously not mass-produced. Afrocentric pieces of wood, metal, leather, and gemstones that looked meaningful—enchanted.

"Damn, woman." He leaned back. "You're glowing even brighter than you were the last time I saw you. And you feel even better, although you've lost a few of those hug-me-squeeze-me pounds that I enjoyed hugging and squeezing."

Novella looked at him, wondering what was the meaning of this encounter: touching down in Cleveland and immediately seeing this man she'd barely been able to resist. Barely as in she could still remember how his beard felt between her breasts.

She took a deep breath before asking, "How have you been?"

He answered after raising her chin and giving her lips a soft kiss, "I'm alright."

Touched, but not taken, she smiled. "I could be married or deeply involved."

He gave her a knowing smile, one that she hadn't seen before. It added to her idea of him having some special juju.

"If either was the case, I would able to see it on you. And if somehow, in my eagerness, I missed seeing it, with you in my arms, I'd be feeling it."

He kissed her again, and this time she kissed him back.

Yadar had just dropped off Yamila and his son-in-law for a flight to Zanzibar. Now, he offered to help Novella with her bags and take her to pick up her rental. After they had gotten her rental squared away, they found a place to park where they could sit in his Infiniti SUV and talk. After hearing Novella's reason for returning, Yadar asked, "How can I help?"

They were holding hands. Novella gave their relaxed clasp a gentle squeeze. "I think we are good. We have a good lawyer. That's what I'm told anyway."

Playfully, Yadar gave Novella a scrutinizing look. "So, why did I see you again?"

Novella pretended as if she hadn't been wondering the same thing. "Because I'm still alive and live on this earth."

Yadar kissed the back of her hand and then asked, "Remember what I told you before you left?"

Novella smiled. "Of course."

He told her anyway, "That I'll always come if you call. But make me the last call—"

Novella finished for him, "Because it'll be hard to get rid of you."

Yadar laughed. "Hell, yeah. I don't want to let you go right now. I want to help you, baby. And help you and help you. And keep helping you, baby."

Before they parted, they made out. Initially, Novella, just as in the airport lobby, gave off an air of "as if," though it wasn't long before she was returning his affection and enjoying their unexpected reunion.

SEVENTY-NINE

Cuyahoga County Juvenile Detention Center

Novella was dressed as if going on interview, because in a way it would be. She wanted to appear friendly and motherly to the boy. Child Services had to be impressed by her. She hadn't known what to wear, so she dressed as she normally did, only a bit more conservatively.

Pop, as a biological relative, was a more ideal candidate for custody, though he could be denied because of his advanced age. There was also Purcell, but his petition for custody would be very risky.

"His brain shuts down under emotional stress," Pop explained. "He just goes stupid, and not just for a few moments. It'll be an episode. The court would open a custody case for him."

He'd be a last resort. They'd only turn to him if their joint effort failed.

Novella, wanting her first glimpse of the boy to be in person, declined looking at any pictures of him. Besides, the only available pictures were those from the county's files, and they were more likely to look like mugshots than snapshots of a cute kid. BETY Junior, as she'd seen from Pop's photo albums, had looked like his grown self as a kid. So, since this long-lost son was said to be his twin, Novella believed she'd recognize him on her own. She was going in all heart.

The boy, initially, had been in a group home on Euclid Avenue. It was there he'd been spotted by a woman who'd known BETY Junior since he was six and she was sixteen. She'd been his babysitter. Seeing his likeness in the boy, she'd told Pop, was initially disturbing, especially since he wouldn't talk for days; he'd just look at her and the staff as if waiting for them to explain themselves to him. The story he told, when he finally spoke, gave the woman hope. It took her about a week to mull over the possibility that he was BETY Junior's son, which included placing the time of this child's birth on the timeline of BETY Junior's life.

When she called Pop, anxiousness pressed her mouth close to the phone and made her breathing shallow. "I wouldn't want to do anything to hurt you, Deacon Young. I just don't . . . I don't want to have not said anything. If this is real—and praise the Lord, I think it's real."

By the time the DNA test results were in, the boy had been moved to a detention center for fighting. Novella and Pop hoped it would be his last county home.

Novella left the main office of the small administrative building. After a quick right, she would reach the recess yard after about thirty steps. Novella's eagerness propelled her ahead of Pop and Purcell, but they didn't mind. They smiled at her excitement.

When she got to the door leading to the recess yard, Novella stood on her toes and peered through the window. She saw a boy with his head down sitting on a concrete stool. She was about to look toward the rambunctious sounds of the other boys playing, when the boy looked up at her.

"Oh my God!" She gushed. Their eye contact didn't last long. Another boy suddenly appeared and jumped him. Novella ran outside.

EIGHTY

Chrystan was shoved off the stool, and then further attacked with a round of punches.

"Fight! Fight! Fight! Fight!" yelled the other boys.

Chrystan was quick to roll the boy and get on top of him. Using his knees, he immobilized the boy's arms. His payback was merciless.

A man in a cheap security uniform crossed in front of Novella just as she entered the yard.

Chrystan was snatched off the boy. "Motherfucker!" he shouted as the guard dragged him away. "Yeah, I know how to fight, motherfucker, and now you know! You thought because I didn't come from the projects like you, I couldn't fight. Well, now you know, bitch! Tell your friends! All them motherfuckers!"

Novella, with her mouth open, looked back at Pop who'd just stepped out into the recess yard with Purcell. Pop shrugged. "He got it honest. Bariah didn't take no shit either. And was the same way after his own mama abandoned him."

Novella turned back. She didn't like seeing the guard drag Chrystan. The man was being way too rough. Novella rushed over. "We're here for him."

343

The guard was awkwardly built with skinny legs, a potbelly, wide but round shoulders, and a head that reminded Novella of a melon. Maybe the man had fruit for brains, because it was as if he didn't hear or see Novella.

"We're here for him, for Chrystan!" she said louder. "You can let him go. Now, please! Ms. Daniels will tell you that we are here for him."

The guard's annoyance with her became obvious. "Well, Ms. Daniels isn't here; you are. And you're not in charge out here; I am."

Novella felt her heels sinking into the mulch, so she shifted a bit of weight to her toes. Her Honest Demon liked this taller stance. "In charge of what? Throwing little boys around? Where were you when he was getting punched? And why is he the only one being hauled away? He didn't start the fight!"

The guard, still holding Chrystan, told her, "You don't know any-thing about this place."

Novella's Honest Demon got the lead. "Sure, I do. Pays you, what, ten an hour? It's not a prison, but you still get to flex a little. So, since you think a playground rumble is a reason to drag kids around, then how about trying to lock my arms up over my head like that? I'm smaller than you, too." Ready to fight this man, her Honest Demon had her on standby for the signal to remove her shoes and earrings. "Come on, Rent-A-Cop, try to do me like you're doing that child. Who, by the way, has busted a lip."

Purcell stepped up. "Look, my man, we need you to unhand the boy. He's our family. I'm sure you got family, too, and they wouldn't want you to lose your job."

The guard released Chrystan, who immediately turned as if ready to throw down. The guard, however, had set his sights on the other boy. Walking toward him, he pointed, "Come here! Your yard time is over!"

Righting his clothes, Chrystan gave Novella a curious look. His face still full of anger, he walked over to Pop, who'd claimed a seat on the bench by the door. Chrystan sat next to him.

"Hi, great-grandpop."

He'd taken to Pop easily, maybe because he could see their resemblance. Novella would have to work harder as she already had a strike against her.

"Pretty women are usually liars," Chrystan would later tell her.

EIGHTY-ONE

In order to prove her trustworthiness to Chrystan, Novella was asked to rescue and adopt another kid.

"I promised to find him a home, that he'd go where I go," Chrystan pleaded in his first full conversation with her.

Novella's heart went out to the other kid. She just wasn't keen on adopting a stranger. For all she knew, Chrystan, the miracle discovery he was, could still be a hellion. Two of them could have her gray by Christmas.

"I promised," Chrystan went on. "He's living on that porch just like I did. But he's alone, and he's not smart like me. He's not going to make it. He thinks he can live on the street in the cold. Just be out there for years until he's grown. And he doesn't even know how to keep himself clean. And he eats too much, so he's going to run out of food. He has no money."

Novella and Purcell found the boy, just as Chrystan had described him, but worse. They discovered he'd found a hundred dollars in between the sofa cushions. He had overspent on food and was nearly out of money. Worse than that, he was sick from the overindulgence. The porch smelled of farts, urine, mildew, and something sour they couldn't name.

Little Christan had barricaded the door as Big Chrystan had taught him to do, so Purcell, who met him first, had to convince him they were there to rescue him, not to rob or hurt him. "Chrystan didn't mean to leave you, little man. He got picked up by Child Protective Services. He thinks maybe his cousin sent them for him. And now he's sent us here for you, so you can stop being alone and living like this. Both of you are getting a new start. You're going to be safe."

They could hear Little Christan struggling to move things so that he could open the door. He was crying.

"You want me to break it down?" the more-than-capable Purcell asked. "Don't stress. I can bust in if you need me to."

Little Christan got the door open. When he finally came into view, Purcell stepped back in shock. Novella gasped. The boy was dirty. *Enough to plant a bed of flowers on him*, Pop would have said.

Purcell finally spoke, "We have to do this by the books."

Child Protection Services was parked behind Novella and Purcell. The assigned social worker, a tall brown-skinned woman, stood behind Novella, who was at the end of the walk. The woman, Novella thought, looked too young for a such serious job, though she had Novella's respect as she was all business.

"I'm calling for an ambulance," she told Novella. "That boy looks in need of more than a bath."

So, to the Cleveland Clinic they all went, where Little Christan cried for hours. After being scrubbed down and shaved, he was thoroughly examined by a doctor. He was then given an enema. Dehydrated, an IV was inserted into his arm. Blood was drawn for testing. His ears and mouth were also swabbed for testing. Since he had a fever, and lots of bruising, he needed to be checked in.

"So, this boy was about to die?" asked Novella.

"Sooner rather than later," the doctor said as he raised his glasses from his nose to his short afro. "It's why he had trouble walking, and why he was in so much pain. He didn't have enough water in him to flush his system. He obviously hasn't had any fruit or vegetables or water in a long time. Just lots of junk food. The waste in his system would have poisoned him."

The social worker told Novella, "Charges are most likely going to be filed. His foster mother didn't even report him as missing. So, it's going to take us a while to sort this case out. Right now, he'll stay here to ensure he doesn't get worse. Also, to confirm he doesn't have any diseases, including STDs."

Novella felt her skin crawl. The social worker saw her disgust.

"It happens, unfortunately. He was obviously put in a bad home and then lived on the streets for months, even before he was found by the other boy. So we have to be sure on everything we can get assurance on, at least as far as his physical health."

Purcell, standing nearby, shook his head.

The social worker went on, "So, you probably won't hear anything for a while. No one is going to call you and keep you updated because we're too busy for courtesy calls. When everything is clear, provided there is no biological parent or other relative petitioning for custody, the county will be ringing your phone for you to come and get him, ma'am. To free up a bed and save a plate of food for the next case. It's sad, but it's the truth. Now, it could be quick, though it could also take weeks, maybe even a few months. But when you get that call, be ready to receive him within a few days, if not the same day if the call is in the morning."

The social worker told no lies. Three weeks later, Novella got the call from a different social worker just after seven in the morning.

"I hope I didn't disturb your sleep. I usually start early, for the sake of the children. Christan is healthy and ready. I can process him out today. How soon can you get here?"

EIGHTY-TWO

Pop hadn't cleared out or sold his home in Shaker Heights, so that's where they lived: Novella and Little Christan on what had been BETY Junior's side, and Pop and Big Chrystan on Pop's side. Novella had actually gotten Little Christan a week before Big Chrystan was released to Pop and her.

The boys were surprisingly quiet. Big Chrystan was the reason for it.

"And don't forget to clean up behind yourself," he could be heard parenting Little Christan. "You took a bath today? Brushed your teeth?"

Novella wanted them both to be little boys. "I'm happy you're being a big brother, but you're not anybody's daddy. And right now, that's a good a thing. A very, very good thing. So, enjoy your childhood. Try to relax."

Big Chrystan shrugged. "Okay, but he doesn't know how to act. He's not used to anything nice."

Novella gently squeezed his shoulders. "Thanks for telling me, and helping out. We'll . . . We will work on him together. I will do most of the work for now, because you still have to be kid yourself. Agreed?"

He warmed Novella's heart with a half-smile, the most he'd ever given her. "Agreed."

Novella did wish that Big Chrystan had some influence with his brother when it came to hair. Big Chrystan was calm in the barber's chair.

Little Christan squirmed like a toddler getting his first haircut. The sound of the clippers made him anxious. Novella had to stand next to him, coaxing him to be still, until the barber was finished.

"Can I have dreads, or at least braids?" Little Christan begged until Novella relented. C-town was full of talented hair braiders, so she easily found one.

School was another issue. Big Chrystan was happy to go, but kept getting into fights, epic fights: him against two or three kids, him against a kid twice his size. He wasn't ever the aggressor, but he didn't back down, nor did he easily back off. He fought to win, and usually did.

Little Christan had a bellyache, a headache, or some other kind of ache every school day. He practically had to be marched through the front doors of school. Homework time was the easiest part of the school day for Novella. While Little Christan was slightly behind, neither boy was problematic when it came to completing their assignments.

Throughout it all, Novella was trying to convince Pop to move to Texas.

"I'm over this snow," she pleaded. "Aren't you?"

Pop had smiled. "What happened to you being sentimental and sappy? You don't want to raise our boy in his father's home?"

He had her there. Novella was trying, but hadn't come up with a good rebuttal.

EIGHTY-THREE

June 2014

Little Christan's adoption had been finalized in November. He'd been in the system for years and had been expected to age out. So, there was no waiting period for him, just paperwork.

Big Chrystan was a different type of case. Generally, parental rights were terminated by the Department of Human Services after fifteen months of foster care. His case was created ten months ago. Because he had been abandoned, the termination of rights could come after six months of no contact. Big Chrystan, however, had been left in the care of an adult with "reasonable" mental capacity. Denise, since she was sixteen years old, had been a licensed driver, and having been employed a number of times, was considered competent. Human Services made an exception in favor of Big Chrystan's biological mother because states are required to be "family-friendly." Instead of terminating her parental rights after six months, which would have been in February, she was given one year.

Pop had decided that Novella alone should file to adopt Big Chrystan in August, though he would, of course, maintain grandparent's rights. Novella wasn't hearing that. She felt the boy was more his than hers. So, whereas Little Christan would have one adoptive parent, Big Chrystan would be adopted by two parents: Pop and Novella would share the responsibility of raising him equally.

Now that school was out, the intermixed tribe went to North Carolina as they waited for that happy day in August to arrive. Novella, with Little Christan in tow, had been back and forth to her house in Texas throughout the year. Neither Pop nor Novella had been allowed to past the state line with Big Chrystan. Novella could tell Big Chrystan, although understanding the restriction, felt some kind of way about it.

Little Christan, having spent time with Novella's Austin family, always returned sharing new Swahili words he had learned.

"Habara gani?" he asked Big Chrystan and then told him to say, "Nzuri" if he was good, or "Si nzuri," if he wasn't good.

They were now near the end of the waiting period and the travel restriction had been lifted. Novella could take both boys with her to Texas, though Pop wanted Big Chrystan's first trip to be to see his heritage in North Carolina. It was there, on his ancestral acres in Charlotte, that he and his brother completely came out of their shells. They were loud. It was the sound of joy for Novella, who for the most part loved it. They all wanted it to last the full summer, though after a month-and-a-half, the tribe was back in Ohio.

Human Services had obtained Pop's North Carolina address to keep tabs on Big Chrystan and in case they needed to be in touch with Pop or Novella. Dated July 12, certified letters addressed to Pop and Novella arrived on July 15 to inform them that Chrystal Simmons was claiming her parental rights. The court date was set for August 11, coincidently, the four-year anniversary of BETY Junior's death, as well as a week before what would have been the termination of Chrystal's parental rights.

EIGHTY-FOUR

When first seeking guardianship of Big Chrystan, Pop had bid Novella to seek guidance from the highest authority: their Lord and Savior. "Ella, ask the man upstairs to bless us with this miracle child." It was to be a joint effort, and so with Pop leading, Novella bowed her head. She was ashamed for deceiving the old man by pretending to pray with him and cry as he sang. Not only did Novella feel ashamed, but she felt unworthy of her Pop-Pop's grace. And he was so very graceful. Pop, aka Deacon Keenum Bariah Thomas Young, had a tenor that defied age. Listening to him sing was both an aural and a visual experience, soothing a listener into a hopeful daydream. It was akin to seeing a heap of fallen leaves blow away to someplace where they might again become green, where they might become their own tree. Novella had always found Pop's gospel singing inspiring. Since BETY Junior's death, however, it had only given her the blues.

Novella hadn't considered herself a devout Christian. In more hopefilled times, if asked whether she had turned her life over to God, the twice-baptized Novella would have answered some of it. She had sex outside of marriage and was highly likely to again do so again. She cursed, and while not exactly foul-mouthed, she did so unapologetically. Her biggest failing, she felt, was not having completed her walkthrough of the Bible. Still, she had been a believer. Since BETY Junior's diagnosis and death, she had come to be at odds with God, and those odds kept stacking up, to the point that even hearing Scripture and hymns from her favorite person no longer moved her.

Pop and Novella took in the disappointment of their letters, which included a summons to appear in court. Novella's Honest Demon cut off Pop's attempt at encouragement.

"Have faith, Ella. God has not—"

Novella's Honest Demon was creating some colorful mental imagery of what would happen in court. Her Honest Demon was ready to fly back to Cleveland to get to smacking around Chrystan's raggedy estranged mama.

Novella and Pop were in the great room. Pop sat in his recliner. Novella stood in the middle of the room, staring at the fireplace. Fuming, she kept her voice low so as to not be overheard by the boys. They were somewhere in the large house, and the great room had three ways in which they could enter.

"Who in the hell does she think she is, leaving this boy to fend for himself for months? And then just . . . 'Oh, yeah, uh, Your Honor, that's my kid. I'll take him back him now.' That bitch! How could she possibly explain this shit?" Novella was as scared as she was angry. It hurt her that Big Chrystan had suffered, but she didn't want his mother to be able to explain it all away. Visitation wouldn't be enough for Novella—she wanted to raise him as her own. A growl rolled from within her along with a mess of tears. In seconds, her face, neck, and chest were wet.

When she felt two slender arms wrap around her waist, she gasped, "Oh!"

Big Chrystan had entered from the breakfast nook. He came around to face her and grabbed her arms. "What's wrong? What's wrong?"

Novella had tossed her letter on the coffee table, and now regretted it doing so. It didn't take Big Chrystan long to see it and figure it was the reason for her tears. He grabbed it before Novella could tell him not to read it.

After seeing his biological mother's name, his eyes turned angry. He screamed, "No! I'm not going back to her. She dumped us and turned off our phones so we couldn't call her!" Novella was shaking her head, to tell him not to worry when he screamed, "And why are you crying? You're just going to give me up? Just let her take me?"

Pop slapped a hand on the end table. "You lower your voice, boy! You best not ever talk to her like that again! *She* is your mama, and *she* won't *let* anyone do anything to you!"

Big Chrystan exhaled and took a few moments to settle himself. Then he threw his arms around Novella. "I'm sorry . . . I just want to stay with you. You're so good, and you're always here. So nice . . . not like her at all."

It was the first big hug he'd given her, and the first time he'd shared his feelings for her. Gratefully, she wrapped her arms around him. If he wasn't nearly as tall as her, she would have picked him up.

"I want you forever," she told him. "I'm crying because . . . because I was counting on that. Us having you forever."

Holding her son, words from Scripture suddenly popped into her mind: psalm Sixty-eight, verses five and six, "God sets the lonely in families."

"So it's written," Novella whispered to herself. "But it is also written that, so shall God giveth, shall God taketh away."

EIGHTY-FIVE

It would indeed take more than finding Big Chrystan and receiving his fearful outpouring of love to redirect Novella back to God. She'd have to win! Losing custody would feel like another death—and the last one had nearly drowned her. Before moving to Texas, she hadn't realized that she'd worn two faces. There was the one she wore to convince everyone she was getting along just fine; then there was the one that she allowed to surface only when she thought herself alone. Pop, however, could see the second face no matter what she was doing or saying. And in his encouragement for her to go live for herself, he'd let her know.

"Ella, you need to go and be something other than a widow."

"It's what I signed up for," she'd lied. In truth, she'd signed up to help BETY Junior beat the cancer. Novella had *really* believed BETY Junior would be a man who'd beat the odds, that all she had to do was consistently nourish him with an organic love—and pray. And she had done both until she ran out of faith.

It was storming the night that BETY Junior's cardiac monitor sounded the slowing unsteady rhythm of what would be his last heartbeats. He was leaving behind his grandpop, who was actually his poppa; his wife, who would be more appropriately termed his heart, his sister, his spouse; his cousin, who was actually his brother.

Pop and Novella sat against one another. Purcell, unable to handle witnessing his best friend's exit, was downstairs in the hospice's chapel. The rain poured as if Cleveland's wash cycle had been set to heavy duty. The belief that, if it is raining when someone is dying, it means heaven is opening up to reclaim one of its angels, was lost on Novella. For her, it felt like her faith was being swept away and drowned by the downpour. *My God, my God, why hast thou forsaken us?*

As the Bible says in 1 Peter 5:7, "Cast all your anxiety on him, because he cares for you." After BETY Junior's passing, Novella had tried to pray for consolation, for understanding, but she couldn't even imagine that her prayers would be heard. She felt that her prayers for him to be cured or to live a bit longer hadn't been heard. She still believed God existed, but the anger that had taken hold where her faith used to reside gave her the mindset that He didn't care that *she* existed, that BETY Junior had existed. And as far as the forever-faithful Pop, Novella had dared to ask God, "How many sons is one man to bury?" And after BETY Junior's death, she'd accepted God's answer to be all of them.

There weren't any Biblical verses or analogies that could inspire Novella. Her hope and faith in keeping her son was a belief in own her strength and ability to endure; she was a determined lioness baring claws and teeth for the fight of her life. She met with their lawyer two hours after they landed at Cleveland Hopkins Airport.

EIGHTY-SIX

August 11, 2014
Cuyahoga County Family Court

Chrystal Simmons, in a button-up emerald green knee-length dress, fashioned into the courtroom as no surprise, as she was very much the late BETY Junior's type. She was nearly six feet tall, with radiant black skin that covered a fit body. The blossomed flower that was her round hips and behind made her look like a real-world supermodel. So, while her voluptuousness wasn't usually to be seen on high-fashion catwalks, any path she took became her runaway.

"Life can be cruel for a man," Pop whispered to their lawyer Ken Aku. "Isn't fair when a bad woman looks that good. Her name should be 'Damn.'"

Novella, sitting on the other side of Pop at their table, gave him a look that he returned with a shrug. The courtroom was empty expect for them, Chrystal and her lawyer, and the stenographer. Big Chrystan was in the next room with Purcell and a social worker. The judge had not yet arrived.

Chrystal had been given an opportunity to meet with Pop and Novella before their court date, but had declined.

"She's asking only to see her son," her lawyer had told them.

Pop had immediately refused, "Hell no! If she doesn't have enough respect to at least meet me, the boy's great-grandfather, then every damn thing must go through the court. It'll take a court order for me to allow her time with him."

Now in court, Chrystal eyed Pop and Novella. She obviously had issue with both of them: Pop because Big Chrystan favored him, and Novella because BETY Junior had favored her. Women tend to give other women a hard time. Simple women, anyway. Novella had learned that at a young age. She stared back at Chrystal with a calm confidence that said, "I'm here to win."

After the judge entered the room and court got underway, Novella's posture and mindset changed from client to paralegal. She began conferring with Pop and Ken, reconfirming the important points in their case. Chrystal, however, kept throwing glances their way. As Novella had hoped, it was nervousness, as she wasn't able to give good reason for her absence.

Going through a divorce, she'd sent her son, in the care of his slightly mentally challenged cousin Denise, to go live with his estranged grandmother, whom he didn't remember and with whom Chrystal hadn't spoken for nearly a year. Well aware that her mother wouldn't have agreed to take the boy, Chrystal didn't call to inform her that he was coming. Neither did Chrystal follow up to confirm her mother would keep him. Chrystal, instead, sent the boy with $3,000 that the cousin was instructed to distribute to Chrystal's mother in increments. The money was to pacify her as she lived off Social Security and Food Stamps.

Chrystal's case was strengthened by the boy himself. Big Chrystan entered the courtroom with an angry face that softened at the sight his biological mother. Large tears gushed from him. Although he didn't run into her open arms, he did go stand in front of her. It was obvious he wanted to hug and forgive her.

"Where were you?"

"I thought Grandma and Denise were taking care of you."

"Why didn't you check on me?"

"I thought . . . I thought . . . they had you and that you were good."

"You didn't miss me? You didn't even want to talk to me, or come see me? What if had I died? I could have . . . because I got jumped . . . and old men were chasing me."

"Chrystan . . . listen . . . I didn't know any of that. Like I said, I thought Grandma and Denise had you and you were good."

"That neighborhood was bad. And I know you knew that 'cause it's where you came from. And you took my phone, and disconnected Denise's phone, and you changed your number."

Chrystal looked to her lawyer, who said, "Your Honor, I think the mother and her son should be allowed to spend some time alone."

The Honorable Judge Springs, with her short afro, serious round eyes, and proud nose, looked more like a tribal guru than a judge. She disagreed with the lawyer's request. "No, things are going as they should, right here in this courtroom." She looked to Chrystal. "Ms. Simmons?"

Ken stood up. "I beg your pardon, Your Honor."

Judge Springs obviously didn't like being interrupted and raised a perfectly arched eyebrow, "Yes, Mr. Aku?"

What he told her, raised both her eyebrows, "Mrs. Matthews, Your Honor. Her name is Mrs. Matthews. Simmons was the surname of her former husband, the man she pretended was Chrystan's father. As of March 15 of this year, her last name is now Matthews. That is, according to her marriage certificate which is on file with the Miami-Dade County Clerk of Courts. She married again, in Florida, to a Clyde Matthews, her attorney's brother."

Chrystal's attorney and brother-in-law quickly said, "Your Honor, the technicality of a name change has no bearing on her petition for custody of her son."

The judge leaned back in her chair. "Oh, but it does. And it is anything but a technicality."

Big Chrystan turned to Purcell and the social worker. "I don't want to be in here anymore."

Novella's heart broke seeing his pain.

Judge Springs denied Big Chrystan's request to leave the room. "Sit the boy down. Now, I believe in reuniting families, yet only if there is potential for them to stay together. For that, transparency is needed." She then scolded Chrystal and her lawyer, "How dare you two attempt to deceive my court? Falsifying her name, and thereby omitting facts. For that, you are both held in contempt, and hereby charged to pay restitution to Cuyahoga County for the care and processing costs for the child Chrystan Simmons. The clerk will tally and forward those costs to both of you."

Chrystal gasped, and the judge warned her, "No dramatics in my court room, *Mrs. Matthews.*"

"Now," the judge continued, "transparency. Mr. Aku, you have the floor."

Ken stood. "I call Mrs. Chrystal Matthews to the stand."

Chrystal had not only traveled to Miami and gotten married in the months that Chrystan was out of her care, she had traveled to Montego Bay, Jamaica; Maui, Hawaii; San Francisco, California; Manhattan, New York; and Las Vegas, Nevada. She no longer lived in an apartment, but a brand-new three-thousand-square-foot house with her husband. She'd started new—and private—social media accounts to secretly show off her new life. Her most shallow exploit, Mr. Aku argued, was the reason she was there for Big Chrystan.

Chrystal and her new husband had visited fertility clinics. Medical records were privileged information, but acquiring travel records and credit card statements was easy for a good lawyer. Getting Chrystal to confess to her husband's issue was also easy after the information was presented to the court.

Her lawyer objected, "You Honor, there's no proof my client wouldn't have returned for her son regardless of the reproductive issues she is having with her spouse."

Pop and Novella's lawyer interjected, "Your Honor, the fact that Mr. and Mrs. Matthews were family-planning when she hadn't checked on a child she'd already given to birth to, suggests her petition for him now is to keep secure the significant upgrade in her lifestyle. To appeal to her new *childless* husband."

EIGHTY-SEVEN

Later that Day

Big Chrystan was mentally exhausted by the happenings of the day, but not so much that he could not enjoy the welcome he received when he returned home.

His brother rushed him with a big hug. "Y'all won! Thank goodness! Y'all won! Y'all won!" Little Christan had been kept home, and watched over by Kanya and Haze.

"It's not final, lil cuz," Purcell said, taking a seat on the sofa.

During dinner, Big Chrystan was grateful that was there was no talk of his biological mother or the case. He was in his own head and didn't want to hear what was inside anyone else's head. Anger and sadness flashed in his dark brown eyes like an impending thunderstorm. Everyone saw it, and so they left him to his food and his thoughts. He normally enjoyed the conversations at his great-grandpop's table. He hadn't experienced that with his biological mom. She and Denise had fed him, but usually hadn't sat with him at the table unless they were at a restaurant.

After dinner, it was obvious that Big Chrystan only wanted the company of his brother.

"Goodnight, everyone," he said weakly, before he turned to go shower and then rest in his room. Little Christan followed him, and could be heard talking until his words were stretched into incoherence by his yawning.

"He can stay," Big Chrystan told Novella, when she came to send Little Christan to his own room. Hearing that, Little Christan, curled up at the foot of the queen size bed, crawled to the top. He slipped under the covers, and, minutes after dropping his head onto the pillow, was asleep.

Big Chrystan fell asleep about an hour later, but woke up around midnight. Sitting up, he wasn't surprised to see Novella. She was asleep in a chair by the door. Her in his room in the middle of the night was a new sight to him. Still, he'd expected her to do some type of contemplation over him. He knew that he was very much on her mind. The light of his nightlight reflected off of something metal cupped in her hand. Big Chrystan could tell that it was his great-grandpop's locket. She usually wore the antique on a long silver necklace that she'd told him had belonged to his father.

Big Chrystan eased out of bed, careful not to rouse his brother or his mama. Then, even more carefully, he crossed his room and gently took the locket. Opening it, his jaws tightened to keep his crying silent. Staring at the picture of his father, his anger and sadness returned. When he looked back up at his sleeping mama, he found that his emotions went beyond his concern for how the custody decision would affect him. He felt sorry for her. No longer worried about waking her up, he placed a kiss on her forehead. She stirred, but didn't wake. After placing the locket around his neck, Big Chrystan headed to the kitchen for a snack.

EIGHTY-EIGHT

Novella had been so sure that she was doing the right thing. She had been forewarned that trying to hold on to Big Chrystan would be war, and that she would be entering the war at a disadvantage. Her petition for him was weak. Pop had a stronger case as he was the boy's great-grandfather, but he was too old to be a serious threat for full custody. Pop needed Novella, yet she needed a miracle. She could be a formidable opponent, she was told, but only if she was willing to go all the way.

After court, Mr. Aku had explained the situation in an astute analogy: "I'm a general, your general. And you see, you're a queen mother here, trying to protect your prince son, who's all you have left of your deceased king husband. Chrystal is a warlord threatening your prince. Chrystal has all the right weaponry, and her blood ties to the prince is an army four times larger than your own. You have to understand that saving your prince isn't about defeating her, because you can't fight her and win. To have a chance is to forge one, to create opportunity where there is none. And that would be in destroying Chrystal. Burning her country and all her places of refuge to the ground. Are you able to give that order?"

Seeing Big Chrystan's hope-filled reaction to Chrystal had caused Novella to question herself. *Am I doing what's right for him, or just being a desperate widow? I wasn't able to make a baby with my husband, so now I'm trying to take this child from his mother. What type of person does that make me? She didn't mean for him to live the way he did; she was just trying to get away with dumping him on her mother so she could land a rich man. None of us is perfect, and who am I to judge her? Who am I to decide that she isn't worthy of her own flesh and blood?*

Novella needed counsel and knew it needed to be as virtuous as what she was seeking. She'd gone to bed that night scared that, whether she did the wrong or the right thing, she'd still lose. It had been four years since she'd been scared of losing someone. In the aftermath of that loss, she had been contending with immense grief that often spoke of its cause. *I miss you and don't want you to be gone. It's so unfair. It hurts so much being without you. I still love you.* Novella's fear now spoke—and begged for a reply. *Help me. Tell me what to do. Please don't let me mess this up. Whisper in my ear. Write it on the bathroom mirror. In whatever way you need to communicate, just tell me. I'm still your wife, Bariah, and I need you. Pop needs you, and Chrystan needs you. He . . . needs . . . you. Help us.*

Novella fell asleep wearing the locket that she usually removed and left on her nightstand before going to bed. A few hours later, when she felt a body behind her, she couldn't tell if she was awake or dreaming. She'd never forget any part of BETY Junior, nor how any of his parts had felt against her. The weight of one of his long, chiseled arms was around her waist. The thick soft hairs of his goatee and gentle snoring were at her ear. His ghost, she thought. She wanted him too badly to be afraid. So, quickly she turned to face him expecting him to disappear. He didn't. Instead, he opened his eyes. Then she heard a baby cooing, before BETY Junior leaned over and gave her a big kiss that she could feel the warmth of and taste its hint of mint. He told her, "It's your turn, wife. I can't. I'm too tired. You go get him."

Novella didn't know all of what happened next. She remembered climbing atop of BETY Junior and him telling her to stop playing around and go get the baby. She played for a while, though, having enticed him to play with her. Then, somehow, she woke up in Big Chrystan's room. He was asleep and, to her surprise, wearing the locket.

EIGHTY-NINE

Ken Aku's second cross-examination exposed Chrystal's shallow soul. The queen mother had given the burn order, and her general had complied. Still, Novella and Pop lost their petition to adopt BETY Junior's son. The case, however, had dragged on for several months. Chrystal was granted visitation rights in order to re-establish Chrystan and the court's trust.

On April 23, 2015, the prince himself brought the war for custody to an end. His request to speak on his own behalf was a surprise to both parties.

"If I stay with my great-grandpop and stepmom, I get to see everyone and they get to see me. Because my great-grandpop and my stepmom are nice people, they won't keep me away from my birth mom. But if have to go . . . if I'm to go back with my birth mom, I'll lose everyone else. My birth mom, she isn't nice like that. She only cares about what she wants. So, she isn't going let me see everyone else. I'd lose my brother, and I don't want to lose my brother. And it would be hard on him to lose me. And by staying with my dad's family, I'm learning who he was by being with them. My birth mom doesn't care anything about that, but it's very important to me. And like I said before, staying with my great-grandpop and stepmom, I could still visit my birth mom."

Judge Springs agreed with him, and so made Novella and Pop his legal guardians while granting Chrystal visitation and certain parental rights. Her signature would be required for international travel, any name change, and major surgery. The first two items ended up becoming an issue for the two mothers.

Novella married Ken, whose full name was Kentori-Abasi Aku. He was a forty-three-year-old Nigerian from Akwa Ibom. Their wedding, set in his home city of Uyo, was held up by Chrystal refusing to sign for Chrystan's passport. "How do I know y'all will bring him back?"

Novella had tried to keep Big Chrystan unaware of Chrystal's refusal, hoping she'd eventually agree to sign for this passport. However, the boy could always tell when his biological mom was causing problems.

"You know after I turn eighteen, it will be my decision to visit you . . . or not," he told Chrystal on a WhatsApp video call. "Mom, why do always have to make everything about what you want? This is what I want. I want to go to Africa and everywhere else, to travel. You just went to Costa Rica."

Chrystal relented.

His request to change his name gave Novella mixed emotions.

"Wait, son, now wait. That's your biological mother's mark. You change it and you're going to break her heart."

"And what did keeping my biological father from me do to my heart? Mama, I want his name. I thought you'd be happy."

"I am . . . I am happy. It's just . . . well . . . Can you wait until you're eighteen? How about twenty-one?"

"Mama . . . I've waited long enough. I just want to do it. Now."

She reached up and took his head in her hands, and he leaned forward so she could kiss his forehead. "Alright, Bariah, be your father's son."

Chrystal refused and kept refusing even after he told her that, in four years, he could do it without her consent. "Do what you want then, but now you can't. I'm not signing. Those people have taken enough of you from me."

Novella believed Chrystan was where he belonged, though she respected where Chrystal's refusal came from. She had given birth to him, after all.

NINETY

Novella Aku soon found out that Chrystan wasn't the only one in her household who had concerns on where they fit in their family.

Just waking from a nap, she found her husband in bed with her. Lying on his side, he was leaning on one of his large arms and facing her. He'd been waiting for her to wake up.

"Sometimes I feel like Big Chrystan is more my son than you're my wife. Because you're still Bariah's wife," he told her. "That's what I wanted to say to you . . . sometimes," he went on, "that was my problem."

Novella told him flatly, "I don't know what I'm supposed to say to that."

He leaned and kissed her forehead. "Nothing. Like I said, that *was* my problem."

Novella asked, "Alright, so now what? I appreciate your honesty, but why are you telling me this?"

"So that you'll understand."

"Understand what? You still haven't told me anything, besides that you are jealous."

Ken smiled. "I have something that belongs to you that I've made better." Before he gave it to her, he completed his confession. "I was jealous because I know you still miss Bariah, still love him."

Novella didn't want to say anything to that, so she said nothing.

Ken went on, "Yeah, well, you should still miss him and still love him. He was very good to you, and you sacrificed for him. And I should be grateful to him, because your life with him led you to me. It's not easy for me, but I'm working on it . . . because I know that you truly love me."

Ken reached in his pocket and brought out two small velvet pouches. He handed one to her.

She quickly opened it, and then gasped, "Ken! Oh my . . . Ken! Kentori-Abasi!"

Pop's locket with BETY Junior's picture still inside it had been restrung on a strand of polished malachite beads. Novella hadn't worn it in years, yet she remained its keeper.

Ken opened the second pouch and brought out the link chain the locket used to hang from. "I know this belonged to Bariah, but it doesn't do justice to Pop-Pop's antique locket, especially given its sentimental value."

He was right. The malachite glamourized the locket. Novella was grateful.

"Husband, thank you. They're going to love it. And I do love *you*. I really, really do."

"I know." He patted her round belly before bending his large frame over to kiss it.

"Good." She eyed him. "Because as you know, this is my second *geriatric* pregnancy because of your doings."

"You love my doings, and I'm pretty sure all of Shaker Heights can hear that you do. Ahdi and Bara were made with fire, and so was this one."

Their toddler twins were somewhere in the house being spoiled by their big brothers. Their unborn was beginning his or her afternoon dance inside her: kicking, kicking, and then kicking some more.

Novella didn't begin seeing Kentori-Abasi Aku until after the custody battle was settled.

During a handshake, which lasted the length of their conversation, she'd smiled. "Thank you for fighting for our family. For your diligence, your patience, and for being honest when it didn't look good. Thank you."

Staring up into the dark and inviting warmth of his eyes, saying goodbye didn't feel right. So, she didn't.

"Join us for dinner?"

Novella and Ken's home was a manor that was just over fifty-three hundred square feet in size. Novella had begged the now ninety-three-year-old Pop to move in, and, after a year of her begging, he'd agreed. The manor on McCauley Road was less than three miles from his old house, which he had kept in the family. Cousins from North Carolina were now its residents.

That next morning, Pop and Novella took their usual walk, a half-mile stroll down the path behind the manor and back.

Novella, reflecting on her husband's words, turned to Pop. "What do you think it all means? Of course, I want Bariah back amongst the living. For his son, for you, and for his own self." She paused and closed her eyes, as she said, "And . . . for some part of me." She opened her eyes and continued, "I don't know which part, but I do want him here. Sometimes, I look up wanting to see him. It's the same with my granny. I sometimes want to her to appear and say something . . . explain why . . . why our family was such a mess. And why things were never sorted out and made right. But Bariah—I don't know what I want him to say to me."

She continued her confession, "You know, my friends told me that I had sacrificed for Bariah in marrying him after he was diagnosed with cancer. And Ken believes that as well. But, Pop, I realized back then that I wasn't sacrificing at all. You see, when you sacrifice for someone, it means you love them more than you love yourself. Maybe not your whole self, but at least a significant part of yourself, a part of yourself that you love, a part that has needs and wants. And you give up those needs and wants. Well, I didn't give up anything. I was just pressed really hard into collecting all the love I had for Bariah and giving it to him all at once. Pop-Pop, I married your grandson because I loved him enough to love him whatever way he needed me to. And we joked around . . . We'd discussed if it was a mistake— the diagnosis—would we stay married? And he said to me, and I agreed, 'We were meant to love each other this much. And being married is just one of the ways we're loving each other. There's no wrong or right way for us. I belong to you, and you belong to me.'"

Novella exhaled, "And cuddled with Bariah, that felt good. It felt forever, as in eternity. Now I'm married to Ken, and I love him. Am in love with him, but . . . all of that with Bariah . . . well, it's haunting me. There's a lingering . . . something."

Pop took her hand. "Ella, I know you struggled with your faith in God; you're still struggling, but I have to tell you that Bariah's in a place we all hope to be when our time here is up. So, he's not missing anything, or anyone. We're missing him. And what it all means for you and for the rest of us is that we'll continue to miss him until we join him. There's nothing in life that can happen that will ever change that. So, just continue to live in the present *with your husband*, but let your feelings be what they are and what they're gonna be. These types of thoughts will come and go, so don't dwell on them." Pop then laughed. "You're a lucky woman to have had two great loves."

When they reached the wooden bench, their rest stop and turn-around point, they sat down. Novella raised a second concern, "And another thing—it's like I have no past, Pop-Pop. No childhood. There's no one around that knows me as Noey. I love everyone that's here in my life right now, and I understand why other people aren't here. But sometimes I regret that my children can't see any part of me that existed before their fathers. Only pictures in photo albums of aunties and cousins . . . who they will never meet. There's no one around to tell them what I was like as a little girl, when I was their age. Whereas, Ken has family flying over from Nigeria left and right. And most of them can tell the kids an Aku family story about something that happened a hundred years or more before they were born. So can you, Pop-Pop. But for me . . . well it's just me. You know what I mean, Pop?"

He gave her a warm smile. "The roots of a tree don't need to be visible in order for the fruit to grow. Your kids don't really need yesterday, but they absolutely need today and tomorrow and the day after. You as you are now is more than enough. Now listen, there are two things to remember when it comes to life's haves and have nots, 'because of' and 'in spite of.' So, *because* you came from a broken home, you found a different family. And, *in spite of* coming from a broken home, you ended up with a great family. Do you get it, Ella?"

She rested her head on his shoulder. "Yes. Yes, I do."

"Good," Pop told her. "Because real soon, you'll probably have to explain that to Bariah III and Christan. Especially Christan. You know, Ella, you talk about pictures, but you don't have any baby pictures of them. When you not only have baby pictures and videos of the girls, but even ultrasounds from before they were even born. As a matter of fact, all of us in the house have our baby pictures—except the boys. You're sitting here whining about feeling like an orphan of sorts, when that's exactly what your sons were. You weren't around to hear their first word, or see their first steps, yet you are still their mama."

Novella raised her head. "Oh my God, I didn't even think of any that."

Pop patted her arm gently. "You know my tribe was missing a daughter, and then you came."

She smiled. "And you can't get rid of me."

After a few moments of gazing at the ducks in the small pond in front of them, Pop said, "Be encouraged, Ella La Bella. Be encouraged. You know nature will uproot a tree, and then reuse it to grow another one."

Novella sighed. "Yep."

Pop went on, "And so he says, in John 14:27, 'I do not give to you as the world gives. Do not let your hearts be troubled and do not be afraid.' And Ella what I say to you is this: in every story I've ever read or been told about a black warrior queen, tells that as she rises to her glory, her name changes with her. But not without battle scars outside and within. Not without losing people. Because there are no wars without casualties. Noey was a girl who became a queen, and that might be the best story your kids will ever hear. Especially, if the queen herself tells it to them. So, be encouraged, honey."

Novella laughed lightly as appreciative tears fell. "Pop-Pop, I love you so, so so much."

He kissed her forehead. "Well, yeah. Of course you do. What's not to love?"

EPILOGUE

June 26, 2019
Shaker Heights Farmer's Market

The perv often saw the woman at the market shopping. Rarely alone, the sexy-ass broad was usually smiling at something one of her brats or her husband said to her. Occasionally, she shopped with other women, who, although they didn't look like her, seemed like sisters. Pregnant had been the woman's condition for what seemed years. The glow that came from carrying life had added to the perv's lust for her. Working at a vegetable stand with his uncle, the perv had been itching for a chance to talk to her—actually, to touch her. She looked magazine-beauty soft, and as if she smelled of a sweet flower, something rare and expensive. He noticed that, even when she came to the market alone, other customers and vendors made conversation with her. Her Bluetooth stayed in her ear, and the watch on her wrist was always lighting up. Her family no doubt checking in on her. *This beautiful bitch is obviously a precious somebody, to a bunch of overprivileged motherfuckers.* The perv decided no one else could afford to live in this neighborhood. No one else could afford such a fresh, elegant-looking woman. The perv wouldn't dare attempt to follow her home. Besides her call-every-fucking-five-minutes family, her Bougie-Boss-Bitch

SUV warned him of what to expect should he try to: nosey-ass neighbors, home security, and big-ass dogs.

One day, the perv was loading a large order of tomatoes into his uncle's truck. Reaching for another crate, he noticed the woman walking from the restroom. Here behind the carts, stands, and tents of the out-door market, *she* was alone. Finally. Overwhelmed by what he saw as an opportunity, the perv rushed over. "Hey . . . see you here a lot. What's your name?"

Gruff in manner and grungy in appearance, he knew he wasn't any-one she'd welcome into her personal space. Her problem, not his. Whether she liked it or not, that's where he was aiming to go. He looked to his right to ensure her entourage wasn't nearby. He then looked to his left, where he saw the tallest and most serious-looking of her brats. Somehow the boy had come up on him.

"Why are you talking to her? Her name isn't your business!"

The perv backed up. *This young-ass motherfucker must hit the gym hard.*

The boy was lean, with long arms and large hands. The chisel in his young body seemed beyond the training of high school sports. The boy and the perv were the same height, yet the perv's stocky body was no match for the iron suit of this brave mama's boy.

Fucking with this bitch ain't no good for me. If the fucking brat is this damn bold . . . shit, then that big-ass husband is probably five times worse.

As the boy took his mother's hand, and the two headed back to the market, the perv went back to his tomatoes. He hoped the family didn't report him to his uncle. He hoped he wouldn't find himself facing her hus-band. He was done fantasizing about how the woman might become will-ing with him, as well as how he might still have her if she wasn't willing. Having it confirmed the woman wasn't a "free catch," his lust dwindled, an acceptance that she was as out of bounds for him as the brand-new Ford Mustang he'd dreamed of owning. He didn't have what it took to have acquire either one of them.

Though the woman continued to frequent the market as usual, she no longer shopped at his uncle's stand, making it that much easier for the perv to ignore her. *Obviously, she's a precious somebody.*

THANK YOU

T. J. Sykes for your realism, friendship, enduring support and being my family. Creshanda Rollison for being a blessing of a sister; always giving me the "real talk" and hours of laughter. Tara Jones for helping to keep our friendship as you put it, like the good stuff that holds baked macaroni and cheese together. Uncle Raymond for always checking in on me, and making me laugh. Lily Leo for being my dada nzuri, my horror movie and laugh all night partner and for feeding me into food comas. Jackie Everett for being my birthday sis; going along with my celebratory antics. Uwakima Udom for welcoming me into your community; I am Idorenyin because of you. Maggie King, my dada mkubwa, for being a remarkable friend and making me your dada mdogo before you departed from this world. Sista Circle for joining me in the support of black women, and for us always being that group that's having the most fun. To every kind and supportive person who I was blessed to cross to paths with, and to the readers of this book.

Lang